The Acheron Deception

Patrick F. Rooney

SAVOIR PRESS

Copyright © 2014 by Patrick F. Rooney

All rights reserved.

Cover Design: Tom Rodriguez and Shelley Schadowsky

This is a work of fiction. All the characters in this book are fictitious and the creation of the author's imagination. Any resemblance to other characters or to persons living or dead is purely coincidental.

No part of this publication may be reproduced or transmitted in any form or by any means, electronic or mechanical, including photocopy, recording, or any information storage retrieval system, without permission in writing from the copyright owner.

Published in the United States by Savoir Press

ISBN: 0-9907436-0-8
ISBN-13: 978-0-9907436-0-6

DEDICATION

For Michelle, Patrick, and Arika.

ACKNOWLEDGMENTS

I'd like to thank Edward Hamlin, Susan Szollosi, Jean Marie Boyer, Melissa Lowe, Andrew Spiegel, Marian Brown, Linda Gilk, Glenda Diggins, Elizabeth Reisinger, Tammy Salyer, Marc Sobel, Christian Thiede, Patty Childers, Mike Fitzgerald, and Suzanne Holmes for their honest feedback and encouragement.

To Scott Patterson, whose book entitled *The Quants: How a New Breed of Math Whizzes Conquered Wall Street and Nearly Destroyed It*, provided valuable insight into the world of derivative traders on Wall Street.

To Sandra Loflin, for weapons and martial arts advice, and for sharing anecdotes from her ten-year career in the United States Marine Corps.

To Annys Shin, whose October 2001 Washington City Paper article entitled *The Terrorists Next Door*, described the actions of the 9/11 Pentagon terrorists prior to the hijacking of American Airlines Flight 77.

And to Jeremi Suri, whose Wired Magazine article entitled *The Nukes of October: Richard Nixon's Secret Plan to Bring Peace to Vietnam*, described the Giant Lance military operation.

Do not be afraid; our fate
Cannot be taken from us; it is a gift.
- Dante Alighieri, *Inferno*

1. Games

Albuquerque, New Mexico—March 1987

The boys fidgeted with bowed heads as Father Aloysius prayed. They looked up when Coach Goldsmith stepped in front of them.

"St. Michael's has never made it to the state basketball finals," the Coach said. "This will put our school on the map. Channel 7 is broadcasting the game across the state."

Sean McGowan's teammates nodded at each other.

This is my chance, the 6'foot tall, seventeen-year-old junior told himself. *The television announcers will probably mention that I'm the highest-scoring point guard in the state, but that will be meaningless if we don't win.*

"I know Highland has taller players," the coach continued, "but we're quicker and smarter, and we're in better shape. We'll wear them down with our running game. Just trust your instincts and leave nothing on the floor. Now let's go have some fun!"

Willie Goldsmith, their big-hearted-but-stern African American coach took Sean aside as they left the locker room. "There'll be some recruiters here today," he said. "We'll need to win if you want to stand out. No one ever remembers second place."

Sean nodded. "I'll do my best, Coach. You know I won't leave anything on the floor."

Goldsmith chuckled. "I'm sure you won't. Just don't foul out."

The Santa Fe fans cheered when they ran out onto the court. The Pit—the nickname for the University of New Mexico's 15,000-seat underground basketball arena where the tournament was being held—had a reputation for being loud.

Sean waved at his sixteen-year-old sister, Carolyn, and his mother, who were sitting in the tenth row.

Both teams fought hard. The lead passed back and forth several times. St. Michael's was down by two points with sixteen seconds on the clock. Sean had twenty-eight points and four fouls.

Coach Goldsmith called a time-out and they hustled to the bench. The building began to rumble as the end drew near.

Be careful! Sean told himself. *Another foul and I'll be out.*

Sister Margaret checked the gauze crammed up his nose—the product of a Highland elbow just before half time. *I know it's probably broken, but I can't stop playing now.*

"Okay men, this is it," coach Goldsmith said. "Are you ready to win?"

"Yes, sir!" they shouted.

"Do you have another three-pointer in you, Sean?"

"Yes sir."

"Good. Now here's what we'll do."

They listened to Goldsmith's plan.

The buzzer sounded, and they hustled onto the court.

That's when Sean saw them: The gray men—sitting in the stands staring at him... always staring. Sean and his friends called them "gray men" because of their serious expressions. They'd been spying on him and his sister with binoculars for years in a black car parked down the street from their trailer park.

When he'd asked his mother why the men spied on them she'd said, "They're from the government—probably something to do with the Pandora's Fire project your father worked on at Los Alamos before they sent him to 'Nam."

"What's Pandora's Fire?" he'd asked.

"That's the name of the top-secret project he was working on, developing war games for nuclear attacks. The gray men bother me, too," she'd continued. "When I told the Santa Fe police, they said they couldn't do anything because the men are with the federal government."

The referee handed Sean the ball.

Highland launched a full-court press at the whistle.

Jose swung around fast and Sean rifled it in.

The ball bounced back to him as he crossed the half-court line.

Two Highland players surrounded him hands darting out trying to steal the ball.

He heaved it to Arturo who was open at the three-point line and broke to the basket for the rebound.

Arturo passed it back.

He had no choice. Time was running out. He had to shoot.

He leapt high and shot. Swish.

He didn't see it because a Highland player took out his legs.

Cheers erupted as his backside slammed the wooden court.

The scoreboard added two points. Tie game.

The referee called a foul.

Sean jumped up ready to fight but Jose held him back.

"Don't get thrown out," Jose warned. "That's what they want."

Sean glared at his opponent. *I could take him out with one tae kwon do punch to the throat*, he considered, *but then I'd get tossed.*

He averted his gaze. "You're right. Let's win this."

Highland called a time-out and both teams hurried to their benches.

The marching bands from both schools went crazy then, bellowing out fight songs trying to outdo each other. The tubas, trumpets, trombones, saxophones, clarinets and flutes blew as loudly as they could while the drummers pounded furiously inciting the spectators to hysteria. The Pit rumbled and shook when the crowd joined in cheering and stomping their feet.

"Good job, Sean." Coach Goldsmith yelled above the din.

"Sorry about the three-pointer, Coach. I didn't have a shot."

"You did great. Just take your time and make the net yours. Everyone ready?"

The entire team—players, coaches, priests, and Sister Margaret—put their hands together in a circle and yelled out the school cheer, "Go St. Mikes!"

Sean hustled to the free-throw line and the ref bounced him the ball.

The Highland crowd shouted and waved trying to distract him.

St. Michael's fans responded with a chant: "McGowan! McGowan! McGowan!"

Sean took a deep breath and blocked it all out: the score, the fans, the blood seeping from his nose—even the gray men.

It's time to win this, he told himself.

He aimed the ball and let it fly.

It bounced off the backboard and landed on the front of the rim, teetering there for a second that seemed like a minute before careening backwards rolling around the inside of the hoop and dropping in.

The crowd roared.

Highland inbounded the ball and hurled a desperate shot.

It fell short at the buzzer.

Game over. St. Michael's wins by one point—their first state championship.

Sean's teammates lifted him onto their shoulders and paraded him around the gym while St. Michael's marching band boomed out the school song. A newspaper photographer snapped the shot that would appear on the front page of the Albuquerque Journal the next morning.

A tall man approached Sean as the arena emptied. "May I speak with you for a moment, Mister McGowan? My name is Joel Davis. I'm the assistant basketball coach at New Mexico State University, in Las Cruces."

"Sure," he said, returning the man's handshake. "Can you walk with us to our car? My mom's taking me to the hospital to get my nose checked. She thinks it's broken."

"Does it hurt?" Davis asked.

Sean wiped blood from his lip with a tissue. "Not at all."

Davis flirted with his mother as they walked. She was attractive—at least that's what people always said.

Davis has no chance, Sean observed. *Even though the government sent her a Missing in Action notice for Dad in 1972, she's still waiting for him to come home. She thinks the government is hiding him somewhere.*

Davis turned to Sean. "We'd like to offer you a full scholarship if you agree to an early commit. This assumes you keep your grades up. That shouldn't be too hard. Coach Goldsmith said you have straight A's."

"Will I be able to play saxophone in the jazz band?"

"Sure, as long as it doesn't interfere with basketball. What do you want to major in?"

"Computer engineering. I want to design computer games."

"I hear computers are a good field these days."

Sean studied Mr. Davis. "Can I start in the fall? I can finish high school a year early if I load up on classes this summer."

"Are you sure? Senior year can be a lot of fun."

"I'm tired of sharing a bedroom in our trailer with my sister. I want to be rich… like Bill Gates."

His sister shrugged. "That would be fine with me."

His mother chuckled. "My son has big plans, Mr. Davis. His father was always that way too."

Davis smiled. "He'd better get started then. We'd be glad to have him. I'll send you the paperwork next week."

Bagram Air Base, Afghanistan

A fierce snowstorm had brought Soviet battle operations in Afghanistan to a halt earlier that day. Five officers at Bagram Air Base twenty-five miles north of Kabul were taking advantage of the break with a late-night poker game.

Major Nikolai Petrovna called his bet. "This is the last hand for me."

None of the other officers folded.

Nikolai placed his full house on the table.

Colonel Baranov smirked. "I can't believe your luck, Major Petrovna. You've taken half my paycheck tonight."

Nikolai gulped the rest of his vodka and stood up. "That's why I'm leaving now… so you'll have something to send home to your wife."

Nikolai gathered up his rubles, sucked in his gut and zippered his jacket.

Yvonna's cooking is starting to show, he realized. *I need more exercise.*

"I heard a joke the other day I think you'll appreciate, Major Petrovna," Colonel Baranov said.

"What's that?"

"What two sizes does a quartermaster carry?"

Nikolai laughed. "I've heard that one before—too large, and too small."

Everyone chuckled.

"Are you sure you don't want a ride?" the colonel said. "That's quite a squall out there."

"No thanks. I'll be fine."

A harsh gale smacked Nikolai's face when he confronted the storm. The wind howled beneath the dark, portentous sky, pummeling machine-gun-pellet ice crystals that bit like razor wire into his skin.

Good, he told himself. *It'll help me sober up. Yvonna has an insatiable appetite. I can't be too drunk to perform.*

He stooped lower, shielding his face with his arm. A Mussorgsky ballad called "Trepak" played in his head, about a Russian peasant who freezes to death in a blizzard while dreaming of summer.

Remnants of the evening's conversation returned as he plodded past carefully ordered rows of corrugated barracks, helicopter gunships, and tanks. Their unspoken disillusionment with the eight-year war pervaded the dialogue. Stories about women filled in the rest of the blanks.

I'm glad I have Yvonna, he reflected.

The other officers always invited him to their poker games. As their quartermaster, he was a good connection to have when they needed supplies.

I know it's my vodka—the good stuff, smuggled in all the way from Moscow—that really garners my invitations. Otherwise, they'd be drinking that obnoxious potato swill cooked up by the conscripted in the barracks.

He hobbled up the icy steps to the front porch of his three-room officer's shack thirty minutes later. Sparks exploded in his brain when he slipped and smacked the concrete.

"God damn it!" he bellowed.

He struggled to his hands and knees. An acidic burp escaped his throat as his world began to spin—slowly at first, then faster, reversing direction and accelerating, swimming around him in circles in a blurry, merry-go-round waltz.

The blast through his throat came without warning: Red wine, half-digested sausage, potatoes, cabbage, carrots, and beet-red borscht, all marinated in vodka. The explosive waves continued long after his stomach was empty.

It's God, punishing me for my hedonism, he decided. *I'll never drink again if you end this Oh Lord.*

But beyond his hazy stupor he knew it was a lie. He'd launched the same prayer many times. Nothing ever changed.

He pulled himself up against the doorframe and knocked on the door. "Yvonna," he called out. *The light is on. I know she's awake.*

He knocked louder. "Yvonna! God damn it Yvonna, let me in!"

No response.

"Shit!"

She's only eighteen. Why's she acting like some disillusioned housewife three times her age?

He examined his keys, selected one, and shoved it in the keyhole.

The handle turned, and he rushed in and slammed the door.

That's when he saw the gun: a Makarov—standard Soviet issue, like the one by his side—but this one was pointing at his face.

The intruder pulled Nikolai's pistol from its holster. "I'll take that."

"Who the hell are you?" Nikolai demanded.

The intruder wrenched Nikolai's arm behind his back and shoved him facedown to the floor. "Put your hands behind your back," he ordered.

The man lashed ropes around Nikolai's wrists and ankles. He then heaved him into a heavy armchair near the door and tied him to the chair with a black nylon rope.

Nikolai studied his assailant: About thirty-five, very tall, lean and broad shouldered, with steel-blue eyes and short, military-cropped blond hair, wearing a black suit and tie with military boots.

"You're a stinking mess, Major Petrovna," the intruder said. "What a poor excuse for an officer you are. No wonder we're losing the war."

Nikolai lurched when he saw Yvonna tied spread-eagle to a chair, her pubic hair clearly visible beneath her white silk negligee.

"What are you doing to her?" Nikolai yelled.

He thrust upwards in the bulky armchair with all his strength. The chair rose an inch and plunged to the floor.

Yvonna's eyes reached out to him fearfully. Her moans, barely audible beneath the gray duct tape shackling her mouth, eked out like the whines of a hurt dog.

"I'm not doing anything to her yet, Major Petrovna. What happens, will depend on you"

Nikolai thrust upwards. "Let her go!"

The armchair barely moved before it crashed to the floor.

The intruder cast a lascivious grin at Yvonna. "She's a real beauty. Those beautiful brown eyes of hers could steal a man's soul."

He turned back to Nikolai. "But you've always had good taste in women, haven't you, Major Petrovna? Like the girls at your brothel in Kazakh. I never saw Yvonna there though. I certainly would've remembered her if I had."

Nikolai rose and crashed several times, struggling like a ship on a heavy sea. "Untie her!"

The intruder removed his identification card from his wallet and pointed it at Nikolai's face. "To answer your first question, my name is Mikhail Volkov. I'm with the Committee for State Security."

Nikolai stopped struggling. He was panting heavily. Fog billowed from his mouth in the freezing room.

"Are you here to arrest me?" Nikolai asked.

Mikhail returned his identification card to his wallet. "What I want is more complicated than that, Major Petrovna,"

He kneeled down beside Yvonna and shoved his hand beneath her negligee.

Nikolai lurched. "Don't touch her!"

Yvonna's eyes widened as she squirmed and rocked in her chair trying to evade Mikhail's groping hand.

Nikolai rose and crashed. "I'll kill you if you don't leave her alone!"

Mikhail grabbed Yvonna behind the neck with one hand. Holding her firmly, he resumed his exploration.

"I think Yvonna will be a nice addition to my stable," Mikhail said, smiling at Nikolai.

"Leave her alone!"

Mikhail stood up. "I'm going to leave her out of this for the moment? That's not what I came here for. I'll have plenty of time with her later, if that's what you decide."

He lifted Yvonna in the chair, carried her into the bedroom, and placed her sideways on the bed. He pulled a blanket over her shoulders, closed the door, and returned to face Nikolai.

"You know it's illegal to bring a woman into a war zone, Major Petrovna. I could have you court-martialed for this."

Nikolai spit at Mikhail. The phlegm, lacking propulsion, only made it as far as his chin where it remained, dangling like a stranded acrobat.

"You really should watch your manners, Major Petrovna, especially if we're going to be working together."

Nikolai sneered. "What the hell are you talking about?"

Mikhail sat down on the couch, pulled a folder from his briefcase, opened it, and began to read. "Yvonna was only fourteen when her mother brought her to your modeling agency."

His gaze floated up from the page. "That was just a front to recruit prostitutes—one of your side projects at the Semipalatinsk Nuclear Test Station."

Nikolai was shivering nonstop. He didn't answer.

"I looked the other way when I discovered your brothel," Mikhail continued. "I actually thought it was quite comical that you—the officer in charge of procurement at our country's main nuclear test facility—had set up a whorehouse. You've always had a good head for businesses though, haven't you, Major Petrovna. You're an expert in supply and demand, just like Adam Smith and the other predatory capitalists. I've added ten more girls since I took over. It's making me a fortune now."

"You son of a bitch!" Nikolai yelled. "That was my business."

"*Da*. Now we're finally getting somewhere. You should be grateful, Major Petrovna. I could've had you arrested last year, but instead, I had you transferred here. Besides, haven't you heard? Our American handlers convinced the Kremlin to decommission the nuclear test site. It's a shame… all our girls will be out of work soon." He laughed loudly. "At least they'll be trained for husbands."

Nikolai didn't respond to the joke.

Mikhail pulled another folder from his briefcase and began to read. "I see you've been quite busy here in Kabul, too." He looked up. "For a young man of thirty you're quite an entrepreneur, Major Petrovna. You're the same age as my younger brother—Vladimir—who lives in New York."

Mikhail placed three large photographs on the coffee table. The pictures showed Nikolai handing weapons to men dressed in Arab clothing.

"We've been monitoring your money transfers to Switzerland," Mikhail said. "We know you've made millions selling weapons to the Mujahideen—purchased with money they receive from the American CIA to fight our troops." He raised his voice. "That's treason, Major Petrovna! Politicians all over Washington are laughing at us. You'll be dead by firing squad before dawn if I show these to Colonel Baranov."

Nikolai's Adam's apple contracted.

"And Abdul, that Egyptian who works for you who told the Mujahideen he's a Muslim freedom fighter? Our mole at the Egyptian embassy told me he's a freelance spy."

Mikhail gaged Nikolai's reaction before he continued. "You know, it's smart to shield yourself using people like Abdul to do your dirty work, but that's not enough. You need many layers of protection, and you must conceal your money transfers. Never use electronics if you want to avoid detection. You have much to learn, Major Petrovna."

Nikolai creased his forehead. "What do you want from me?"

"I want the nuclear weapons you stole from Semipalatinsk." Mikhail paused. "And I want Yvonna, for my New York brothel. There's a huge market for exotic young women there."

A carnal vision of disease-ridden men devouring Yvonna's body assaulted Nikolai's synapses. Focusing his brain, he worked furiously through all his options. He always arrived at the same conclusion.

Yvonna is pregnant he agonized. *I need to protect her.*

A shudder rolled down his spine. He looked at the propane heater in the center of the room. "Why is the heater turned off?"

Mikhail smirked. "I turned it off. I like the cold. It reminds me of the Moscow subways where I grew up."

Nikolai was shivering nonstop in the armchair. "I don't know anything about nuclear weapons."

Mikhail pulled his Makarov from its holster and pressed the muzzle into Nikolai's forehead. "Don't lie to me, Major Petrovna."

Fog from their breathing mingled between their faces.

Mikhail squeezed the trigger, slowly, millimeter by millimeter, pointing it at the ceiling just before the bullet exploded.

Nikolai screamed when the gunpowder cauterized his forehead.

Echoes from the blast temporarily cloaked the storm, but soon, the furious gale returned, accompanied by the mournful wail of a whistle through the hole in the ceiling left by the bullet.

"I conducted a forensic audit of your paperwork, Major Petrovna," Mikhail yelled. "So I know you stole four, W54R portable nuclear weapons from Semipalatinsk. Now where are they?"

Mikhail stared sideways at the bedroom door. "Or shall I entertain myself with Yvonna while you think about it?"

Mikhail holstered his gun, walked to the propane heater and turned on the heat.

He filled a glass with water at the kitchen sink and returned to face Nikolai. "Drink this. You need to sober up, Major Petrovna."

He placed the glass to Nikolai's lips and waited while he drank.

"Isn't that better," Mikhail said when the glass was empty. "When we work together as partners?"

"What do you mean partners?"

"I want you to work for us, in America. We need men like you."

"What does America have to do with anything?"

"Haven't you heard? Our country is beginning a grand experiment. The old Communist state is dissolving. The next period of our history will be the era of entrepreneurs."

Nikolai scoffed. "That has nothing to do with me."

"Look around, Nikolai. My KGB colleagues are taking ownership of Russia's oil, mining, farming, utility, and telecommunications industries. I'm keeping our operational assets in America and the bank the Romanovs concealed in Switzerland."

"What do you mean by operational assets?"

"Businesses we established during the Cold War: drug trafficking networks, security and surveillance companies, and gentlemen's clubs to name a few. Not only are they very profitable, they're a great way to gather information. My brother, Vladimir, is using our Swiss bank as a holding company to take over the biggest casino in the world."

Nikolai's eyebrows narrowed. "What's that?"

"The international stock markets."

The propane heater popped and sputtered as its sheet metal casing expanded.

"How much will you pay me for the weapons?" Nikolai asked.

Mikhail chuckled. "Now we're getting somewhere. So what do you think they're worth?"

"Abdul has a buyer—an Arab from the Middle East—willing to pay ten million dollars."

"Ten million, for four bombs?" Mikhail retorted. "We'll make ten times that with the right buyer."

Nikolai studied Mikhail for a moment before he continued. "How much will you pay me to work for you?"

"How does a million dollars a year plus profit-sharing sound?"

Nikolai's head snapped back with surprise.

Mikhail nodded. "That's right, Nikolai. You could become a very rich man. Of course, your earnings will vary based on what you produce. That's how it's done in America."

"I'll think about it... if you untie Yvonna"

Mikhail smirked. "Why are you so worried about *her*? I have plenty of girls in my brothels. You can have as many as you want."

"I won't tell you anything if you hurt my wife!"

Mikhail's mouth hollowed. He made a note in his folder.

"You're not married." Mikhail pointed at a light bulb hanging from the hallway ceiling. "I've been observing the two of you for weeks through a camera and microphone hidden in that light socket. I never heard you say anything about marriage."

Nikolai recoiled, looking at the floor. *How many voyeuristic journeys has this pervert witnessed at our expense?*

Mikhail's depraved grin confirmed his worst fears.

"Our engagement is a secret." Nikolai said in a monotone. "We're getting married next month, at my parents' farm in Baku."

Mikhail's lips bent sideways into a smile. "What if I let you bring Yvonna to America?"

"Won't the Americans kick us out if they find us?"

"I'll get you green cards. Vladimir was eighteen and I was twenty-three when we got ours, in 1975. The Americans were handing out *détente* scholarships to Russians in those days. I worked undercover for the KGB while Vlad went to college. He made a fortune trading bonds at Drexel Burnham after he graduated from Wharton. Now we need people like you to help us expand our operations."

Nikolai listened attentively without responding.

"This is a great opportunity, Major Petrovna. The old American mafias are soft. We're taking over. We'll be invincible with our army of lawyers. You'll see. Lawyers wielding pens are much more powerful than guns in America."

"I don't know anything about finance, or lawyers."

"I've been observing you for a while, Major Petrovna. I'm sure you'll learn what you need to know. You're a quick study. I'm actually quite impressed. The way you falsified test records at the Semipalatinsk nuclear site so you could steal the bombs was really quite ingenious. Modifying the train manifests when you transferred the nukes to your parents' farm in Baku was also smart thinking."

Nikolai's head snapped back.

"*Da*, Major Petrovna. My agents are there now interrogating them. We'll dig up every centimeter of their farm to find the weapons if we have to, but don't you think it would be better to work together as partners?"

Mikhail shoved the barrel of his Makarov into Nikolai's eye. "I'm done with talk. Where'd you hide the bombs?"

Nikolai reeled backwards. "My parents have nothing to do with this. Why not just split the profits and go our separate ways?"

Mikhail shook his head. "You and Abdul will need to work for us once you know we have the bombs. We can't risk letting you tell someone about them. Otherwise, I'll have to kill you."

Mikhail shoved the barrel into the seared skin on Nikolai's forehead. "This is it. Decide! Or say goodbye to your life."

Nikolai grimaced. "The bombs are buried beneath a pile of pig manure."

Mikhail pressed the gun harder into the wound. "Where?"

"They're buried in titanium, radiation-proof suitcases at the north end of my parents' farm, with some launching bazookas and tripods."

Mikhail pulled the gun away and sat down on the couch.

"I'm glad you made the logical choice, Major Petrovna. The next thing we need to talk about is the money you wired to Zurich. We know you've made twenty million dollars selling weapons to the Mujahideen. You need to transfer half of that to me."

"I earned that money," he yelled. "Why should I give it to you?"

"This is a gift," Mikhail intoned impatiently. "I'd originally intended to take all of it in exchange for your life. You can consider this a wedding present. We'll fly to Switzerland in the morning to make the transfer, and from there we'll go to America."

A smile creased Mikhail's lips. "I have an even better idea. I purchased a farm with a huge fallout shelter near DC to store the weapons. I'll transfer the title to you for three million. That way you can keep an eye on the bombs yourself, and you'll have a nice home for Yvonna."

Nikolai shook his head side to side. "Three million is too much."

Mikhail laughed. ". No, it's not. It's a beautiful horse farm on two hundred and forty acres next to a river. I'll even throw in the yacht I bought to haul the weapons up from Cuba. My agents will transport the bombs to Havana after they dig them up."

"Where's the farm?"

"It's located next to the South River a few miles west of Annapolis, Maryland. I know the area well. I made many trips there when I was a handler for a captain we were running at the naval academy."

Mikhail chortled. "It's ironic when you think about it. The fallout shelter was built in the early sixties by an American admiral afraid of a Russian nuclear attack."

Mikhail walked to the kitchen, dialed the rotary phone on the wall, and relayed the bomb location to his agent in Baku.

He then returned to the living room, sat down on the couch, and removed his boots and tie.

"Now we wait," he said. "By the way, your military career is over. I'll call Colonel Baranov in the morning to tell him the KGB needs you for a top-secret project. I have a transport with two pilots waiting at the airfield. They'll fly us to Zurich when the storm lets up. Here's an important lesson, Major Petrovna: Always transfer your money in person, to avoid electronic eavesdropping."

Mikhail loosened the top button of his shirt. "We should get some sleep. We have a long day tomorrow. Would you like some water? You'll feel much better in the morning if you do."

Nikolai nodded.

Mikhail dropped a white, tasteless powder into the water as he filled a glass at the sink.

He returned and held it to Nikolai's lips while he drank.

"Thanks," Nikolai said.

"You're welcome. I think we'll be good partners one day."

He reclined on the couch letting his long legs dangle over the end.

* * *

Mikhail moved his feet to the floor when he heard Nikolai snoring. *The sedative did its job*, he mused.

The wind was beginning to die down; indicating a retreat of the storm was imminent.

He tiptoed to the bedroom, entered, and shut the door.

Yvonna's cinnamon-brown eyes fumed with anger as he sat her chair upright on the floor.

He smoothed her long, auburn hair out of her face. "I'm sorry I had to tie you up but as I promised earlier, we'll be on our way to America soon. It was necessary while I made arrangements. Will you keep quiet if I remove the tape?"

She nodded.

He carefully dislodged one end and yanked.

"Ahhhh!" she cried out.

He untied the ropes unshackling her from the chair.

"Is Nikolai okay?" she asked, rubbing her wrists and ankles to restore the circulation.

"*Da*. He's fine."

She stood up. "Why was there a gunshot?"

"I was trying to scare him. Don't worry. He's asleep now. I gave him a strong sedative."

Her slap jerked his head sideways.

He caught her next blow and the next, and clasped both of her wrists together above her head in one large hand.

Her face reddened as she squirmed. "Let me go!"

I'm glad she's spunky, he observed. *I like a bit of a wildcat.*

He stared into her eyes. "I won't hurt you, Yvonna."

She gradually gave up.

He wrapped her in his arms when she began to cry, hugging her to his chest.

He brushed away her tears with his thumb after a moment. "It's okay," he said, trying to sooth her. "I'll take care of you."

Her woman scent is intoxicating, he realized *...and her voice.*

He moved his hand beneath her negligee. Caressing her with his fingertips, he explored the small of her back, tenderly, up to her shoulder blades. She trembled when his hand shifted to her belly.

She's six feet tall—a perfect vessel for my six-foot, five-inch frame.

He leaned to her lips.

Her head twisted sideways, evading his assault.

He pulled her into him, pressed the fullness of his arousal against her belly, and kissed her neck tenderly, below the ear.

"Don't worry," he whispered. "Nikolai will never know. You can scream as loud as you want and he won't wake up."

He leaned back. "You're Ukrainian, aren't you?"

"How did you know?"

"Your country has the most beautiful women in the world."

Her bold stare quickened his heart. He leaned to her lips.

This time they parted, tentatively at first, before accepting him.

Her hands moved to his back and she kissed him hungrily, melting into him, and the tip of her tongue found his.

He pushed her backwards onto the bed. *I knew I would have her.*

2. Joshua Tree

Twentynine Palms, California—November 1999

Major Robert O'Connor picked up speed as the Marine base disappeared in his rear view mirror. His two-year-old daughter, Malia, is asleep in the car seat behind him.

He is heading west to pick up his wife, Captain Beate Nicholson—who's also in the Marines—from the Los Angeles International airport. She'd flown to Washington earlier in the week for a job interview.

He was twenty-six when they'd first met five years earlier. Beate was a twenty-one-year-old recently commissioned second lieutenant then, with a computer science degree from the University of Colorado. Her Military Occupational Specialty—network and information system design—had brought her to the Marine base at Twentynine Palms for advanced training.

I fell beneath her spell instantly when I saw her, he mused, reminiscing about their early days together. *Her presentation to the Logistic Command's information technology council proposing that we modernize the Corps' outdated analog networks with state-of-the-art digital routers was especially prescient for someone so young.*

I knew she had something special when she convinced my sharp-eyed accounting colleagues and the risk-averse general to fund her project. She had a way of connecting with people on an emotional level that was beguiling.

He smiled to himself. *And she enchanted me, too.*

She secured several quick promotions afterwards to ensure she had the authority she needed to drive the massive project to completion. *Some astute political maneuvering on my part had kept me with her at the base.*

That's over now, Robert realized.

"Your next assignment will be in Bahrain—for a year," his battalion commander had told him earlier that day. "You'll have a good shot at a promotion if we go to war with Iraq."

Although her tight, athletic body, sparkling-green eyes and the persuasive sway of her hips had gotten my attention—the timbre of her voice sunk the hook deep. It was like an aphrodisiac; resonating inside me whenever she spoke... especially when she laughed.

Robert stared at the moon shining down on the odd-shaped Joshua tree cacti as he accelerated.

I'll never forget that night we made love in the desert.

It took a lot of persistence to get her to go out with him. First, he'd had to convince her there weren't any military fraternization issues. They had different chains of command, so that wasn't a problem. Then he'd had to promise to keep their meeting discreet. She didn't want stray gossip to jeopardize her project deadlines.

They met for coffee at a bookstore in Palm Springs for their first date. She liked to read and so did he, so they already had something important in common. Things progressed quickly from there.

He picked her up the next morning for a hike in Joshua Tree National Park. They pushed each other hard along the trails before they stopped to make breakfast, on a tall cliff overlooking a broad valley.

"I'm impressed," she'd said. "I can't believe you brought plates, silverware, and napkins—even a tablecloth."

"It isn't often that I get to have breakfast with this kind of view... or company," he'd explained.

"You even brought green chili for the omelets? I love that."

"You mentioned that your parents own a chili farm in Colorado so I presumed you might want some. I like it too."

She'd reached over and squeezed his hand. "That was very thoughtful."

The jagged, Medusa-stricken rock formations gave them plenty of discussion topics while they ate. They then began the next leg of their adventure: rappelling 120 feet down the side of the mountain.

Working together during the dangerous climb brought us close in a hurry.

"I'm impressed," he'd said when they reached the bottom. "I know you've won several Marine sharpshooting contests at the base, and now I see that you're an expert with ropes, carabiners, and belays. Is there anything you can't do?"

She'd laughed. "Thanks for the compliment but there are lots of things I can't do. For instance, I love music, but I can't play a note. I guess I've never had the patience to practice."

They stopped for a water break beneath a large Joshua tree cactus after hiking another eight miles.

"The Mormons named the cactus Joshua Trees in the 1850s," he'd informed her, "while they were travelling across the scorching Mojave Desert. They thought the branches looked like fingers reaching for the sky. It brought them visions of the prophet Joshua beckoning them to the Promised Land."

"I can see that," she'd replied. "Their journey must've been arduous in this heat."

"I'm sure it was."

"Speaking of heat, I'd like to get a run in before we finish. I know you won't be able to run with that heavy backpack you're carrying. Is it okay if I meet you at the top of the next hill?"

"Sure. Have fun."

He caught up with her a few minutes later.

She looked majestic, standing on the summit, he recalled.

"This is wonderful," she'd said smiling down at him. "I've had a great time with you today."

Robert smiled as the lights of LA appeared in the distance. *She looked like a goddess then,* he reminisced, *gleaming with sweat, the sun illuminating her strawberry-blonde curls, crowning her with a halo.*

She dumped water on her head to cool off. Most of it dripped down her neck, soaking her tank top, revealing the prominent swell of her breasts as her nipples sprang to attention.

You… are… so… delicious, he'd fantasized.

I wanted to say it then, but I held back. It was only our second date after all. I didn't want to scare her off.

"Do you want to keep going?" she'd asked.

"Maybe next time. Let's head back, before you have to carry me."

Her fleeting kiss before she bounded down the hill took me by surprise. I found out later it surprised her, too.

Their third date began with two rounds of margaritas at her favorite Palm Springs Mexican food restaurant.

The tequila loosened my tongue as well as my inhibitions.

"I fell for you the instant you walked into the room," he'd confessed. "I would've approved anything you wanted that day."

She chuckled. "Really? I guess I should've asked for more funding."

"Would you like a suggestion?"

"Sure. I'm always open to advice… as long as it's good."

He'd laughed. "Accountants always feel it's their sacred duty to make budget cuts somewhere as a project progresses, so it's good to have some padding. That's how the game is played."

She'd reached across the table and taken his hand. "Thanks. I'll keep that in mind."

"That's enough about work," he'd continued. "What I really wanted to say is… I think you're gorgeous."

He'd looked away for a second, embarrassed by his forwardness. "I love your accent, too, and your name. It's quite unusual. Where'd you grow up?"

"I was born at Ramstein Air Base in Germany. My dad was a colonel when he met my mother. She was a math professor at Heidelberg University. We moved to Colorado Springs when I was fourteen."

"Why'd you move?"

"Dad took a post at the Air Force Academy. He'd grown up on a farm in Colorado, so he thought it'd be a good place to retire after his twenty."

"How about your name?"

She was caressing the inside of my palm with her fingertips while she spoke.

"The English version is Beatrice"—she'd chuckled—"like the woman that shows Dante around Paradise, but always from a distance. They had an unrequited love, I guess."

They'd decided on a whim—while driving back to the base—to make a detour to Joshua Tree National Park. He grabbed a sleeping bag and a flashlight from his trunk and they headed up the trail. A crescent moon painted exotic shadows around them as they walked.

He spread the sleeping bag on the ground on a high plateau, and they lay down next to each other.

The pungent, prickly pear wildflowers filled our senses as the Milky Way leapt into view, painting the sky with billions of stars.

Folded, naked, entwined in each other's arms, their ardent song rang out across the canyons. The coyotes and birds joined in, filling the night with passionate refrains.

They got married at her parents' farm in Brighton, Colorado, six months later.

LA's downtown skyscrapers glowed yellow-orange beneath the smog. He merged west onto the 105 and looked in the mirror.

Malia was still asleep with her Mickey Mouse doll in her arms. *Even at two-years-old, she looks a lot like her mother.*

He turned north onto Highway 1 at the sign for LAX.

Beate's commander had asked her to fly to Washington to interview with an undisclosed government agency earlier that week. *The timing is good. Both our service obligations are about to end. We need to decide soon if we'll re-up, or join the private sector.*

I'm glad I took the rest of the week off to spend time with Malia. Having time away from work made me realize how bored I've become pushing paper through the machine.

The traffic slowed as he entered the airport arrivals area. Beate was waiting for him at the curb.

She crawled into the back seat next to Malia while he placed her luggage in the trunk.

Beate stroked Malia's cheek. "Hi, baby. Mama's home."

Malia awakened and stretched her arms to her mother. "Mama."

Malia fell asleep by the time they reached Interstate 105, so Beate moved up front.

He spoke quietly. "So how did it go?"

"Very well," she said.

She seems pensive, so I'll wait. She'll speak when she's ready.

"The interview was with *the Agency*."

"You mean the CIA?" he asked.

"Yeah. They want me to manage their data analytics department."

"That sounds interesting. What do you think?"

"I liked the job, but we'd have to move to DC. I don't want to do anything that will affect your career so I'm not sure what to do."

Robert accelerated past the speed limit. It was 11 p.m., so traffic was light.

"I think you should take it," he said.

"But what would you do?"

"I've had a wonderful week with Malia. She's quite precocious, you know—like a miniature version of you. I could take care of her while we get settled in DC."

"But what about your career?"

"I found out today that my next assignment will be in Bahrain. I don't want to spend a year in the Middle East away from you and Malia."

Beate's mouth slackened. "Being away from each other would be difficult, but we could do it, if that's what you want. Maybe I could negotiate another assignment here at the base. There's still a lot of work to do, and it's nice to have your parents close by in Malibu."

She knows what it takes to serve, but that isn't the issue.

"I'm ready for something new," he said. "I'm sure my parents will come visit us in DC. It sounds like your job is important—for the country."

"I can't talk about the details, but I know they need my help." Her gaze found the skyscrapers. "It's a great opportunity."

"I could work part-time from a home office once Malia starts school," he suggested. "I'm a Certified Public Accountant after all. I'm sure there are lots of jobs for accountants in DC."

"That's true, and we'd save on day care costs. It would be great for Malia. I've always been close to my dad, so I understand how important that is for a girl."

"Are you sure you want to work with spies?"

"Yeah, I think so," she said with a wry smile. "We'll have to tell everyone—including our parents—that I'm a computer industry lobbyist. That would be my cover. We can't tell anyone where I really work. Are you okay with that?"

"Wow. It's already starting… the secret stuff, I mean. I'm okay with it. Are you?"

"Yes." She chuckled. "I think it's perfect for me."

She does have her mysterious side, he observed. "You won't mind if I'm a stay-at-home-dad—a kept man, so to speak?"

Beate's fingertip glanced over his cheek. "I'd love to have a man like you waiting to massage my feet when I come home every night."

She giggled, removed her seatbelt, and sidled up next to him. She loosened his belt and slipped her hand inside his pants.

He chuckled. "I guess I made the right decision."

She giggled. "You did… but I would have done this anyway."

3. Boot Camp

Geneva, Switzerland—December 1999

Rahim Delacroix was pleased when the United Nations offered him a job as a language translator after he graduated from the University of Geneva. Although he'd majored in mathematics, his proficiency in six foreign languages was what interested the UN.

Having a job in Geneva also meant he'd remain close to Sister Anne, the Catholic nun who'd raised him at the orphanage outside Montreux. She was the only family he had, other than his spiritual brothers at the Geneva mosque.

Rahim had often heard rumors about their Imam's generous benefactor, Abdul, but he'd never the man until he showed up for salah one evening. Abdul asked Rahim to have tea with him afterwards.

"I hear from your friends that you'd like to join our *jihad*," Abdul said, after the waiter delivered their refreshments. "They said your family was killed by the Israelis."

Rahim displayed the hand he'd been concealing beneath the table. "I would like to join, but I'm not sure what I can do," he replied. "My mangled hand will make it difficult to shoot a gun."

Abdul's dark black eyes bore into him. "Don't worry. I'll train you for your role when you come to Hamburg, after you complete the first phase of boot camp in Pakistan."

Rahim arranged a two-month leave of absence from the UN and flew to Pakistan the following week. *Hiking the mountainous frontier of northwest Peshawar and living in caves was arduous, but I loved the camaraderie. I never had many friends at the orphanage.*

He arrived in Hamburg a month later, where Abdul trained him and the other three members of his cell in options trading, international banking, and message-encryption techniques.

Trading structured securities is much more enjoyable than hauling weapons through the mountains, Rahim decided. *I especially love the elegant simplicity of the one-time cryptography we'll use to exchange messages. The algorithms are mathematically unbreakable when used correctly.*

Rahim was disappointed when he learned he'd be working alone after boot camp. *I envy my al-Qaeda brothers in Pakistan, who'll maintain loose affiliations with each other while they establish residency as sleeper agents in foreign countries.*

"Never contact anyone," Abdul had reiterated many times. "You must always work alone to maintain compartmentalization. It's essential to your mission, and your safety."

The men talked excitedly as they approached the Hamburg Fischmarkt warehouse. It was 10:00 p.m., and tonight was their final. Tomorrow they'd return to their former lives and wait for Abdul to activate them—for him, Geneva, for the other three members of his cell: Singapore, Dubai, and New York. Abdul would be their case officer.

"Perhaps it's a graduation party," Rahim said as they approached the door.

"You can never tell with Abdul," Mohammed from Dubai replied. "He could just as well take us out drinking, or to a strip club."

Mohammed was always joking. "Debauchery is part of your training," he said, mimicking Abdul's stern voice. "You need to understand decadence to fit in with the infidels."

The men laughed.

Abdul met them at the entrance door. "I have a special treat for you tonight."

He slid the door shut and bolted it when they were inside.

The pitch-black warehouse instantly accosted them with the choking stench of rotting fish.

"What's that awful smell?" Mohammed said.

Abdul walked towards a lighted inner room without responding.

The four men followed.

Light spilling from the doorway revealed a warehouse filled with barrels of bloated fish guts lined up in rows, covered with armies of quivering, rice-shaped maggots. Rahim doubled over and puked.

Abdul stopped to watch, and then he laughed. "There's plenty of food in those barrels if you get hungry later."

Abdul continued into the room.

Rahim wiped the vomit from his face with his sleeve and hustled after them. He stopped when he entered.

A sandy-haired young woman was lying motionless, prostrate on a brass bed, with her wrists and ankles shackled to bedposts by yellow nylon ropes. She wore a short, black dress and black stiletto heels. A white scarf gagged her mouth. Two tall, incandescent medical lamps—the kind used by surgeons in an operating room—looked down on her from each side of the bed.

She looks close to my age, probably twenty-one, Rahim guessed. "What's going on here?" he said.

"Sit down," Abdul ordered.

Rahim sat in the remaining chair near the foot of the bed next to a movie camera perched atop a tripod.

His gaze strayed over her body. He tried to look away, but couldn't. *She's too beautiful. Please, Allah: Forgive me for my sin.*

Abdul bisected and quartered the girl's short black dress with shears, cutting from the knees to the neck and across each shoulder. He pulled the clothing scraps away, revealing a red silk thong and matching bra that barely contained her breasts. The girl—obviously drugged—remained as motionless as a corpse.

Abdul smiled pruriently as he presented her with an open hand, the way an art curator exhibits a painting. "Does anyone want to have a go with my girlfriend?"

Rahim looked around at his friends. They'd already given Abdul—whom they guessed to be about forty—the nickname "crazy eyes" behind his back.

They're as shocked as I am, Rahim observed. *This sacrilege against Islam is far beyond anything we've witnessed so far. Shouldn't we help her?*

Rahim shook with fear. *Although Abdul's dark-black eyes and large build are intimidating, the man's vitriolic rage scares me the most.*

Then something odd happened. *I feel a stirring—down there… a feeling I've only experienced vaguely… in dreams. I'm becoming aroused. Impossible!*

Two doctors had used compassionate words, but their message was the same: "Your burn-scarred, marble-sized testicles are as useless as shriveled-up berries on a tree."

The Israeli bomb that killed my family took my manhood too, he reminded himself.

Abdul pulled five goblets and a bottle of single malt Scotch from a satchel. He filled each glass halfway and handed them to the men.

"It's time to celebrate," he said. "It's your final, after all."

The men drank as ordered. Rahim only pretended.

"Ahhh… delicious," Abdul said. "As I've told you before, you should have fun during your missions when you can."

Abdul drained his glass and poured himself another.

"Drinking will help you fit in with the infidels," he continued. "They won't suspect you're a Muslim if you drink. It's a part of your cover, so take advantage of it."

Each man took another sip. This time so did Rahim. *I don't want to appear weak.*

The liquor burned as it dribbled down his throat.

Abdul picked up the shears and sliced the girl's bra and panties. The men gasped at her nakedness when he pulled away her lingerie.

Abdul frowned. "This is the whore that reported me to the police last year."

He pulled a syringe filled with a yellow liquid from his satchel.

"I had to disguise my appearance for weeks every time I went out," Abdul continued. "She was working the same corner when I found her tonight. I gave her a shot of etorphine in the car. This is the antidote." He chuckled. "I want to make sure she doesn't miss anything, especially since she's the main attraction."

He jabbed the syringe into the girl's shoulder and pushed the naloxone through the plunger.

The girl slowly stirred. Her eyelids fluttered.

She jerked when her mind registered the restraints. She fought the ropes furiously thrashing side to side, as muffled screams droned out mournfully beneath the white scarf covering her mouth.

Abdul leaned over her and looked into her eyes. She stopped.

"Remember me, Kristen? I told you not to go to the police."

She lurched and fought with renewed vigor. The slipknots gnawed into her wrists and ankles leaching blood into the yellow nylon ropes turning them tangerine orange.

Abdul sipped his Scotch, relaxed and insouciant, as if he already knew how things would play out.

Rahim shuddered, no longer aroused. *This is awful. Why doesn't somebody do something?*

Wheezing gasps seethed through her nostrils like a steam engine. Flies, drawn by the scent of fresh blood, swarmed through the doorway diving like kamikaze pilots to her oozing sores.

Kristen tried to shake them away. They clung on undeterred, feeding in a gluttonous frenzy.

I have to do something, Rahim decided, *but Abdul is our mentor, and our duty is to obey. Murder is no stranger to him, but I didn't agree to torture women. We have to help her. She needs us.*

Her frantic stare darted around the room desperate for an ally. Each man looked away, until her beckoning gaze fell upon Rahim.

He stood up. "Stop torturing her!"

Abdul glared at him.

He kneeled on the bed next to Kristen. "Stop looking at my men!"

He pummeled her furiously with his fists producing dark red lesions beneath each pulverizing blow.

He stepped back, panting heavily.

Rahim slowly sat down.

Kristen's lungs, desperate for oxygen, forced a sickening wail through her shattered nostrils.

A distant foghorn cloaked the drone of thousands of flies swarming into the room.

Abdul grabbed a garrote from his satchel and stretched the thin wire between the wooden handles. "This weapon is quick… and quiet."

He looped the wire over her head, pulled it down to her throat, and tightened the noose.

Her nostrils ceased their screeching yowl as her back arched and her eyes bulged out.

Abdul relaxed the wires, and her lungs resumed their struggle. "Some people find it difficult to kill like this."

He tightened the grips. Her breathing stopped again.

"The most important thing is confidence." Abdul relaxed his grip. "That's why Kristen is here—so you can practice. You'll need to do this without hesitation when the time comes. Tighten the handles until you hear the thorax bones crack. Who wants to go first?"

The men stared at the floor.

Abdul moved to the foot of the bed, turned on the video camera, and tossed the garrote to Mohammed, who was sitting across from Rahim.

Each man took his turn. Abdul stood behind the camera, sipping Scotch, making them repeat the lesson until they'd perfected their technique. Rahim was last.

At some point, she died. It was hard to say when. Her mouth was propped open, ghostlike, in a silent scream declaiming the horror, when her gag fell off.

Abdul turned off the camera, ejected the tape, and stuck it in his pocket.

He cut her shackles with a hook knife, and tossed a rubber body bag to Rahim.

"Pack her corpse into the bag and break down the bed," Abdul ordered. "Take everything in the room out to my yacht. It's moored to the pier."

The men worked in a leaden trance as they loaded everything into the stern of the boat. Abdul then wrapped the body bag with iron chains attached to a large concrete block.

"You've passed your final," Abdul announced as he stood up. "Congratulations. Remember—never contact each other again. I'll kill you if you do. Is that clear?"

The men nodded, remaining glum.

"I'm heading out to the ocean to dump everything," Abdul said. "The sharks will take care of her. I'll contact you when I have a mission. You're dismissed."

The men didn't speak as they walked across the gangplank to the pier.

Abdul climbed a ladder to the helm and punched the ignition button. He maneuvered the yacht slightly astern and pulled the videotape from his pocket. "This recording is insurance," he bellowed, "in case anyone talks to the authorities."

He laughed as he gunned the throttle, steering west towards the North Sea.

His acolytes stared at the yacht as it sped away, watching the triangular swells from the boat's wake slap the dock until it disappeared.

Chesapeake Bay, Maryland

Nikolai was at the wheel of his own yacht heading north on Chesapeake Bay in Maryland when Abdul's call came in. He'd spent the day with his family casting for bluefish off the eastern shore.

Gregor, age twelve, and Stefan, age nine, were playing video games below deck. Tatiana, their inquisitive, blonde-haired three-and-a-half-year-old daughter sat on Yvonna's lap next to Nikolai.

"We're ready," Abdul bellowed through his phone above the engine noise. "Have you heard any good operas lately?"

"I hear the new rendition of *Salome* in Vienna is worth seeing," Nikolai replied.

"Excellent. I always enjoy the scene where she strips naked in the 'Dance of the Seven Veils'—a fair bargain for John the Baptist's severed head, don't you think?"

"I'm not so sure about that."

Nikolai ended the call.

He hurled the burner phone from his captain's perch into the bay.

"Mommy?" Tatiana said to her mother.

"Yes, honey."

"Why did Daddy throw his phone in the water?"

Yvonna stared at Nikolai. "Why don't you ask him, dear?"

Nikolai shrugged his shoulders. "The phone was broken."

"Is that littering, Daddy?"

The couple laughed.

Nikolai tickled her affectionately and lifted her onto his lap. "You're right, honey. I won't do that anymore. Do you want to be ship captain?"

"Yes, Daddy."

Nikolai placed her tiny hands on the wheel between his, and steered between the lighted buoys, letting her believe she was piloting their sixty-five-foot luxury yacht up the Chesapeake.

* * *

The CIA spy satellite orbiting the Atlantic transmitted the men's conversation to NSA headquarters at Fort Meade, Maryland, as it does with all international calls.

When the seditious word detection and person-of-interest voice-recognition software programs failed to register a match, the application spooled the recording to its archives.

4. Crescendo

Vienna, Virginia—September 10, 2001

Beate picked up her secure CIA cell phone. The call was from Director Matthews, the head of the CIA's Directorate of Science and Technology. "Hello, sir."

"Hello, Beate. I'd like you to present at the DS & T planning meeting tomorrow morning. I know this is short notice but we've had a cancellation."

"Yes, sir," she said without hesitation. "I'd love to."

Using "sir" when talking with superiors was something she'd learned as a child from her father, Colonel Anthony Nicholson. The habit was instinctual by the time she finished boot camp at Parris Island and Marine Corps Officer Candidate School at Quantico.

"You'll be first on the agenda at eight a.m., for thirty minutes," Matthews told her.

"Thank you, sir."

"I'm looking forward to seeing your presentation," he continued. "Everyone knows we need to upgrade our data analysis capabilities, but as you know, IT budgets are slim these days. You'll need a compelling business case before I can take it up the hill to secure funding."

"I think you'll be impressed with the architecture, sir," she assured him.

"Be prepared for a grilling by the accountants," he warned. "They can be brutal."

"Yes, sir."

"Make sure you emphasize that detection and prevention are key components of our anti-terrorism strategy. Eliminating even one attack will pay for itself many times over. I'm in your corner, but I need your help getting past the number-crunchers."

A surge of adrenaline gushed through her body as she envisioned herself tangling with the tough-nailed bureaucrats.

"I'll make it happen, sir."

"This is going to get very political," he said. "The Senate Intelligence Committee will need to approve information sharing between agencies. We have strict covenants that prevent us from exchanging data. This has never been done before—at least not officially."

"We'll have better luck finding the enemy if we coordinate our intelligence resources," she said.

"I agree. At least we'll have a chance now. The previous FBI director had no interest in computers. He wouldn't even use e-mail. The new director is much more enlightened. Getting information from the NSA will still be problematic, though. Perhaps we can make some unofficial arrangements. Of course, it's hard to work with an agency that doesn't really exist."

They chuckled.

"I imagine you've heard the term *No Such Agency* before?" he joked.

"I have, sir," she replied. "I've also heard it called *Never Say Anything*."

He laughed. "Yes... that too. See you in the morning."

"Good night, sir."

The director's support means a lot, she realized.

DS & T accountants had postponed her presentation three times the past six months. *I can't let this opportunity pass by*, she told herself.

Robert wasn't happy. She expected that. They had tickets to fly to Los Angeles for their vacation the next morning. They decided he and Malia would fly to LA the next day as they'd planned, and Beate would join them later in the week.

She rehearsed her presentation in front of the bathroom mirror until midnight. She began again at 5:00 a.m.

Robert watched her through the doorway. *I want him to. He always gives me good feedback.*

She described how the Agency was drowning in trainloads of data while numerous requests for actionable intelligence by operatives in the field went unanswered. There simply weren't enough resources. Her new information analytics architecture was the answer. It would allow them to store, classify, search, cross-reference, catalog, retrieve, analyze, and develop useful leads from data feeds across the globe.

She left out all the top-secret details, since Robert no longer had a security clearance.

She faced him through the doorway when she finished. "What do you think?"

"My only suggestion is to be careful with technical jargon," he replied. "Do they really need to know the difference between transactional and dimensional databases? You don't want to lose them."

"Thanks for reminding me. I'll put that in the backup material, in case I get a question."

"Your thesis is very compelling. I wish I could be there to watch you skewer anyone that tries to shoot you down, although I know you'd do it gracefully."

"I'm not so sure." She turned to the mirror. "I might be cranky. I didn't get much sleep."

"I think you'll do great. They'll love you."

"Thanks honey. It's always nice to have a fan."

"The fifty people working for you are fans, aren't they?"

"That's true, although they may not like me as much if this gets approved. We'll be working a lot of overtime to build the system. I'll need to double the size of my team."

"Just like you did back at Twentynine Palms?"

"Yes… just like that."

She watched him pack through the steam-fogged mirror after her shower. *He's disappointed*, she realized. *Late nights and weekends have become standard fare since I took the job, but this is the worst interruption yet.*

"I'm really sorry I can't go with you today," she said.

He continued packing without looking up. "So am I."

The move from California was good for us she ruminated. *Things will change when we get back. Malia starts pre-school, and Robert will start working part-time as an accountant. We need this vacation. The timing couldn't be worse.*

"I'm going to the kitchen to make some coffee," he said.

"Thanks, dear."

She was dressed in a white silk blouse and dark blue skirt when he returned. He handed her a cup of coffee spiked with cream, just the way she liked it.

"Is it time to wake Malia?" she asked.

He resumed his packing. "Let's let her sleep. We have plenty of time."

She brushed her hair in front of the bathroom mirror, twirled it into a braid, and pinned it at the back into a bun. She applied lipstick and rolled her lips together, ensuring the translucent pink glowed evenly.

"How do I look?" she said, facing him with her hands on her hips.

He grinned. "Delicious… and very professional."

"Thanks for listening this morning."

He returned to his packing. "Maybe I should apply for a job at the Agency. At least then we'd get to see each other once in a while."

She let his cynical comment slide as she assessed her face in the mirror. *No wrinkles yet. They'll come soon enough.*

She hadn't told Robert that her boss had placed her on the executive fast track. That conversation would come later, perhaps during a walk along the beach in Malibu. *Unfortunately, a promotion will mean even more time away from home.*

"It isn't just to meet some minority quota," her manager had told her. "The director wants you to work for him. We'll be peers, if you take the job."

She glanced at Robert's broad shoulders and V-shaped physique in the mirror. He was wearing pajama bottoms. His muscular chest and six-pack abs were still as tight as when he was a Marine.

Her body tingled as she applied her eyeliner.

It won't be the end of the world if they reject my proposal, she decided. *Politicians far beyond Langley control the Agency. My department will still have plenty to do. After all, no other spy agency in the world—except perhaps the Mossad in Israel—can tap computers and communication networks the way we can.*

Does my data warehouse proposal really have a chance? The DS & T Covert Operations team harvests most of the money for new technology. Spy satellites are expensive after all. Regardless, we still have many successes—described in slides I couldn't share with Robert.

Just last month, tapping a Malaysian travel agency database, they'd identified and taken out a contract assassin stalking CO agents in Asia.

Her affinity correlation application had also proven to be quite useful. Using dimensional analysis with data retrieved from airlines, credit card companies, phone logs, e-mails, web surfing logs, and closed-circuit TV cameras, they'd located several Middle East sleeper agents living illegally in the United States. After thorough, advanced–interrogation-technique interviews, they'd passed the spies along to the FBI for deportation.

Satisfied with her makeup, she entered the bedroom. "It looks like you're ready," she observed.

Robert moved his suitcase off the bed. "So what do you think?" he asked. "Should I apply at the Agency?"

They hugged, and their hips found each other.

"I don't know." She feigned concern. "They have cameras everywhere. What if they catch us? You know how wild I get around you."

She found his mouth.

His strength grew instantly against her belly.

"Besides..." She kissed his neck. "I'd never get any work done. I'd constantly be thinking about places we could hide."

"That's it, then. I'm applying as soon as we get back."

Her hand moved beneath his pajama bottoms.

His pulsed reaction was immediate.

"Mmmm..." he sighed. "This is a nice surprise."

His fingertips tested the front of her silk shirt. She pushed him backwards onto the bed and pulled off his pajama bottoms.

She smiled. *I know he likes it when I dress up nice.*

Eying him steadily, taking her time, she released the buttons of her blouse one by one. Gauging his pleasure, she dropped her blouse to the floor and then slowly removed her skirt, slip, stockings, and panties, until she wore nothing but her white bra.

Crawling forward concentrating on his eyes, she touched him softly with her fingers, and kissed him gently. Bracing herself with her hands on his chest, she slid onto him until he filled her.

He released her bra strap and cupped her breasts in his hands.

She glanced sideways at the dresser mirror as the rosy glow emerged like sunburn on her chest. He held her firmly—strong—the way she liked so she couldn't stray.

She grabbed his breasts as her song soared to a higher pitch, and the crescendo of their quaking bodies shook the bed.

Falling forward breathing heavily she caught her breath. "I love you," she murmured softly.

"I love you, too."

She rolled onto her side and turned out the lamp.

He pulled her close, and she nestled her back into him, matching the cadence of his breathing. Dawn crept through the curtains, bathing the room in a diaphanous glow.

She was almost asleep when he slipped out of bed.

Malia arrived a moment later dragging the well-worn blanket she wasn't quite ready to give up.

"Mommy," she said rubbing her eyes.

Beate pulled up the sheet. "Hi, baby."

Malia crawled beneath the covers and nuzzled her face into her mother's chest. They drifted off to sleep.

Robert entered the room. "Where's my pumpkin?"

Malia poked her head out.

"There you are," he said. "I thought you'd gone to see Mickey without me."

She stood up reaching for him. "Not without you, Daddy."

Beate looked at the clock as they left the room: 6:00 a.m.

A smile touched her lips when she saw her clothes strewn about the floor. *Now I'm ready.*

5. Quants

Luxembourg City—September 11, 2001. 12:00 p.m. CET

After six months of development by four programmers a database architect and two testers, the new derivatives trading platform was finally ready. Sean McGowan, the chief architect of the software application, and Pankaj Mehta, his Goldberg Cohen colleague from New York, exited the Banque Lux elevator with large cups of coffee. They pulled their badges through the security reader and entered the trading floor. There were no windows seven stories below street level.

The avaricious traders crowded into the large room barely acknowledged Sean and Pankaj as they deftly navigated islands of tables filled with computer displays to the corner desk of Jonas Kramer, the floor manager.

Jonas sat behind a large walnut desk housing two telephones, three keyboards, and six LED computer displays stacked two high, arrayed in a semicircle in front of him. A six-foot display screen on a stand next to his desk faced the trading floor.

"Any luck tracking down the volume spike anomaly you saw on Friday?" Jonas said as he stood to shake the men's hands.

Sean gulped his coffee. "Nope. We just tested everything again. It must've been a fluke. I think we're ready for your traders to switch to the new trading platform now—if you are."

"Everyone's a bit nervous about the change," Jonas said.

"Their fears will evaporate once they start making more money, at least that's what happened when we rolled it out in New York."

"I hope so."

Sean McGowan, thirty-one-years-old, had designed several important software applications for Goldberg Cohen, but none had the visibility of this one.

He turned to Pankaj. "Do you think you're ready to manage our deployments in Hong Kong and Dubai on your own next month? Rachel's gonna kill me if I don't get off the road soon."

"Sure," Pankaj said.

"Good. I'll let you do part of the demonstration today to get more practice."

"Thanks. I do enjoy learning about the trading side of our business. Perhaps I can make the leap from information technology to the trading floor the way you did someday. I hear you guys make tons of money."

Sean chuckled. "We do... when things are going well, right, Jonas?"

"That's right... those of us that survive."

"You're not paid all that badly are you, Pankaj?" Sean joked. "I know what you make. I used to have your job."

Pankaj grinned. "I'm not complaining."

Sean had hired Pankaj—a graduate of the University of Texas who'd immigrated to America from India—a few months after he joined Goldberg Cohen.

Jonas glanced up at a large digital clock hanging on the wall. "One thing you may not realize about the trading floor is the pressure," he said. "A few bad trades... and you're out."

Sean nodded. "Making money gives you instant credibility, though. It would've been impossible for an engineer to become a trader a few years ago. The gut-feel guys used to laugh at me when I told them quantitative models would reduce their risk. They had no idea what I was talking about, and no interest in learning. Most of those guys are gone now—the ones that couldn't adapt anyhow."

"I remember," Pankaj said. "You did make some enemies."

Sean sipped his coffee. "Now everyone at Goldberg Cohen uses statistical arbitrage. Of course, developing programs using statistical inferencing, differential calculus, and quantum physics was second nature to me. I developed mathematical weather models using supercomputers at NCAR, before I moved to New York from Colorado to join GC."

Jonas peered at the clock. "What's NCAR?"

"NCAR is the National Center for Atmospheric Research, in Boulder. I was working there when I met Angela Cohen at a supercomputing conference. That's where she recruited me. We develop our trading models together now. Her behavioral finance expertise is a big reason for our success. It's not just about the math."

Jonas smiled. "I enjoyed my time with Angela and your team when I was in New York last month. Is it hard to work around someone so... beautiful?"

Sean laughed. "No, not really. I *am married* after all."

"I'm glad I had a chance to hear your band play," Jonas said. "How do you have time for everything?"

"Music and exercise are stress relief for me. I couldn't keep up this pace without them."

"When's your band playing again?" Pankaj asked.

"Next Saturday night. You and Celina should join us. Rachel and Angela will be there, too."

"We will."

Jonas chuckled. "I love the name of your band: *The Quantaholics*. Are all the musicians in the band quantitative analysts?"

"Yeah, except our female singer. She's married to the guitar player."

Sean gulped the rest of his coffee. "I'm looking forward to getting home tonight," he said, stifling a yawn, "assuming everything goes well. Rachel hates being alone in the city."

Jonas looked at the clock. "Shall we get started?"

"No time like the present."

Jonas pulled his floor microphone to his face. He spoke in English instead of Luxembourgish, in deference to his American guests. "Good morning ladies and gentlemen. Could you please join me at my desk?"

Sean studied Banque Lux's twenty-two traders as they trickled forward. Although they were similar in age to his colleagues in New York, their clothing was different. Here, the men wore pastel-colored shirts and artistic ties, whereas white, button-down shirts and conservative ties were the norm back home.

Jonas stood up to address the assembly. "First of all, on behalf of Banque Lux, I'd like to thank Goldberg Cohen for letting us be their guinea pig."

A muted chuckle flowed through the room.

"As some of you may already know, Goldberg Cohen has been partners with Banque Lux since the end of World War II. This is another major milestone in our relationship." He turned to Sean. "Would you like to say a few words before we begin, Mister McGowan?"

Sean scanned his audience. "As I mentioned during our training sessions last week, the GC trading platform will increase your profits and lower your risks, *if* you use it correctly. I know you've all heard this before, but please remember: Trading is all about risk management. Once you begin making more money you may be tempted to 'amp up' your capital to juice your profits. That's dangerous, especially when the markets turn. Do this a few times, and you'll be looking for a new job."

The assembly chuckled, but not too loudly. They knew. Disregarding risk was the quickest route to the unemployment line. Most traders never imagined it would happen to them but often it did, as the eighty-five percent who eventually changed careers knew all too well.

"Preservation of capital is everything," Sean continued. "No one hates losing money—or paying taxes—more than the rich."

Everyone laughed at the truism. It didn't matter what a client's ethnicity, skin color, or religion was—they all hated losing money. The only time they did take risks was when they had inside information, which was why they were so wealthy.

Sean turned to Jonas. "Let's use one hundred thousand euros for our first trade."

The six-foot screen facing the traders displayed everything Jonas typed.

"After analyzing current conditions, the program is suggesting a butterfly spread," Jonas said as he entered the order. "The market is stuck in neutral, with slightly rising volatility, so the tight butterfly spread seems reasonable. I'll set a stop loss at one-tenth of a percent, and the profit target at two-tenths of a percent. Here we go."

Jonas pushed the *Submit* button.

Sean could barely conceal his excitement. *This is momentous—not only for Banque Lux, but also for Goldberg Cohen.*

Redesigning and porting the program Goldberg Cohen used on their own New York trading floor for partner banks had taken months. Everything was on the line now. The program's profit-sharing licensing agreement would be a gold mine for GC if it worked… and a costly embarrassment if it didn't.

The past few days had been nerve-wracking after an elusive volume spike had appeared on Friday. They'd spent the past three days chasing it without success.

A failure would be especially embarrassing for Angela Cohen. It was her idea to use the program to expand her father's investment banking empire. She'd lose a lot of credibility if it didn't work.

Several phones beckoned for attention as the profit-and-loss graph danced on the screen.

The trade terminated thirty seconds later, and a point-two-percent profit—two hundred euros—appeared in Jonas's account.

A subdued cheer erupted from the traders.

Emma, the sole female in the room, stepped forward. "I assume you'll use the repeat-execution function next, right? If we can make that much profit every thirty seconds we'll be in pretty good shape by the end of the day."

Everyone smiled at her astute observation. Harvesting small gains repeatedly throughout the day with minimal losses was their *modus operandi*.

Sean smiled. "That's right. The repeat execution function lets the algorithm continue without human intervention until market conditions change. Shall we demonstrate that next, Jonas?"

"Sure," Jonas agreed. "The program is still recommending the butterfly spread, so we'll stay with that."

Jonas selected the repeat-execution function and resubmitted his trade.

The program shoveled profits into his account for four minutes. He'd accumulated 1,400 euros when the trade terminated.

"Market conditions just changed," Sean said. "The program has already deduced a new trade recommendation. Our high-frequency trading mode will let you switch to the new algorithm without human intervention."

"How does it calculate everything so quickly?" Emma asked.

"The application matches market conditions with seventy-five years' worth of historical trading data," he explained. "It's like using seasonal weather temperatures, wind, and barometric pressure to develop a forecast. We use thirty-five statistical factors, along with behavioral finance algorithms and artificial-intelligence heuristics. Would you like to demonstrate the high-frequency trading mode, Pankaj?"

"I'd be happy to."

Jonas rose, and Pankaj took his seat.

Pankaj pointed at the six-foot screen next to Jonas's desk. "Let's examine the current situation. The markets are beginning to rise. The program is suggesting a bull-put-spread algorithm. Does that seem reasonable to everyone?"

Heads nodded up and down.

"We'll bump up the trade capital to one million euros, and keep the profit-and-loss target percentages the same. Is that okay, Jonas?"

"That sounds fine."

Pankaj entered the parameters and pushed the *Submit* button.

A 2,000-euro profit hit the account twenty seconds later. The algorithm continued for several minutes until market conditions changed, and then a new algorithm began to execute.

"The profitability of this trade is now twenty-two thousand euros," Pankaj said. "There's no way a human could assess the markets and react that quickly."

"When can we begin?" Emma said. "I don't want Jonas to have all the fun."

Sean chuckled, along with everyone else.

I know what Jonas meant now when he talked about Emma during his visit to New York last month, he observed. *She's witty, smart, and strikingly gorgeous.*

"She's a Belgian beauty," Jonas had said during his visit, "just like my wife, and she's already my top trader, even though she's only twenty-six. Her only liability—through no fault of her own—is the difficulty some men have concentrating when she looks at them. Her hourglass curves, auburn-red hair, and almond-brown eyes are impossible to ignore."

Sean's gaze returned to the traders. *They seem anxious to get started.*

"I think we're ready," Jonas said to the assembly. "Just click on the GC icon on your trading screen and log in to start the program. Let us know if you have any questions."

The traders clapped as they hurried back to their desks.

"That went well," Jonas said, taking his seat when Pankaj stood up. "There's something I've been wondering about though."

"What's that?" Sean said.

"What happens during a steep market reversal?"

"The trade governor helps," Sean said. "If the program comes across something it doesn't understand, it closes out the position and runs back to its cave, so to speak. Steep reversals are a good time to make a killing, though."

"How so?" Jonas said.

"Our quantitative models kick into high gear when the markets reverse direction. Greed and fear run rampant when that happens. Angela incorporated behavioral finance algorithms into the program to take advantage of market psychology."

"Having fast computers is also important," Pankaj added. "Our code has been optimized for speed, to run close to the silicon. We created a high-performance operating system shell specifically for trading. No one has our capabilities."

The Luxembourg traders talked excitedly as they became comfortable with the program. Sean had seen the same thing happen at Goldberg Cohen in New York.

The genie is out of bottle now, he reflected. *They'll never be able to go back to their old ways.*

"I'm going to grab a quick power nap," Sean told Jonas. "I didn't get much sleep last night. Call me if you need me."

He took the elevator to the eighth floor below street level, entered his temporary office, turned out the lights, and stretched out on the couch. Within seconds, his comatose musings soon merged with the darkness lulling him to sleep.

6. Ascension

Washington, DC, September 11, 7:00 a.m. EST

The skies are clear and bright—perfect flying weather. Beate hugged Robert and Malia while the Dulles Airport skycap loaded their luggage onto a cart. "Call me as soon as you arrive, okay?" she said.

"You'd better join us soon," Robert said. "You don't want to miss Mickey."

"Why can't you come with us, Mommy?" Malia said.

"I'll be there as soon as I can, honey. I want to see Mickey, too."

Beate stood beside her car as they strolled up the sidewalk to the gracefully curved entrance façade of Dulles International Airport. They waved goodbye at the door and disappeared inside.

She wiped a tear from her cheek as she drove east towards DC.

Her mind was consumed by her impending presentation when she merged north onto the crowded Washington beltway. She entered the DS & T conference room a few minutes later.

Luxembourg City

Sean dropped into the chair next to Jonas. The clock said 2:20 p.m.

"How's it going?" he asked.

Jonas motioned with his eyes to the screen. "I've made more than two hundred thousand euros with the new GC trading platform. The markets are up though, but you said that doesn't matter—right?"

"That's right. The program has algorithms for rising, falling, and sideways markets."

"How'd you come up with the idea to share your trading platform with partner banks? Aren't you worried about someone stealing your code?"

"No," he replied. "We have safeguards. Besides, Goldberg Cohen is a Banque Lux stockholder."

"That makes sense."

"Angela and I came up with the idea during a happy hour one day," he elaborated. "I guess we were feeling creative."

Jonas chuckled. "I imagine she has a pretty bright future, being David Cohen's only child, especially since he owns most of Goldberg Cohen's stock."

"I'm sure she does. That reminds me—I should call her to let her know how things are going."

Jonas handed him a printout. "Here's a report."

Sean scanned the graphs. "It looks like your team's trading profits are six million, two hundred thousand euros. Is that higher than normal?"

"Absolutely... thirty percent higher!" Jonas said.

"That's good news. Have you told your director yet?"

Jonas smiled mischievously. "Actually, I told the president of the bank. He'll be down here in a minute to congratulate you."

Sean pulled his comb from his pocket. "Perhaps I should spruce up a bit. I'm sure I look pretty ragged after not shaving for two days."

Jonas laughed. "You do, but I wouldn't worry about it. The suits upstairs have no idea what we do down here even though we make most of the bank's profits."

"Have you seen any weird volume or volatility spikes?"

"No. Everything's been fine. When can we use the platform to trade commodities?"

"I've developed some initial models, but they need some work. Commodities behave a bit differently than stocks. I'll let you know when I have something we can share."

"Perhaps we can help. Emma's our top energy trader. Her dad is a petroleum engineer on a North Sea oil rig, so she follows energy commodities pretty closely."

"That's good to know," Sean said. "We could use her expertise."

They stared at Jonas's computer screen, chugging along, expropriating euros from the unsuspecting and depositing them into his account.

"This is a great step forward in our partnership," Jonas said. "I've heard that Arthur Goldberg, your former chairman, helped us reconstruct Banque Lux after World War II."

"Europe was in pretty bad shape after the war," Sean remarked. "I imagine your relatives had a rough time."

"They did. Unfortunately, the Flemish plains have been a ripe battleground over the centuries. I guess it comes with the territory when you're located between two antagonistic behemoths like France and Germany. The armies of Julius Caesar invaded two thousand years ago. After that it was Attila the Hun, Charlemagne, Napoleon, and two World Wars in the twentieth century."

"Let's hope that was the end of it," Sean said.

"We can always hope."

Sean rose from his chair. "I'm going to see how everyone's doing before I call Angela. It looks like we'll be heading home later tonight."

"Are you sure you don't want to go out and celebrate?"

"Thanks for the offer, but I need to get back to New York."

Everyone sat up straight when the president of Banque Lux arrived. He left after ten minutes.

"Pankaj and I are going to the conference room to finalize our travel arrangements," Sean said.

"Okay," Jonas replied. "I'll call you if we need you."

Pankaj called the pilots from their conference room. He finished the call and hung up the phone. "The pilots said we can leave at six p.m."

"That's perfect," Sean said. "Following the sun, we'll be back in New York later tonight."

Pankaj yawned. "I'll probably sleep the entire way."

"Me, too. I'm exhausted."

The conference room telephone rang. Sean picked it up. "Hello."

"You'd better get up here," Jonas said. "The program is going crazy."

"Be right there."

Sean dropped the phone into its cradle and jumped up. "Let's go," he said as he ran out the door. "We have a problem."

Jonas was pointing at his screen when they arrived. "I just made one hundred thousand euros trading U.S. pre-market derivatives. This can't be right."

Pankaj typed some commands into the keyboard. "That's interesting." He typed some more. "Everything looks fine."

Sean peered at the BBC news display on the wall. "There's nothing unusual on the newswires."

"It looks like the US markets will plunge at the open," Pankaj said. "The European markets were up one percent a few minutes ago. They're dropping now."

"Look at that," Sean said, pointing at the SPY option tables displayed on the screen. "There's a huge Put option position in the queue. Someone thinks the markets are going to crash."

"Is there a problem with the program?" Jonas said. "We can't be making that much money, can we?"

"The application is working fine," Sean said. "It looks like you'll get to see how the program handles a steep market reversal when the US markets open in a few minutes."

"I'm sorry I alarmed you," Jonas said.

Sean studied the display screens arrayed on Jonas's desk. "It looks like Wall Street will have a rough start today. It doesn't matter. The program handles all kinds of conditions, including a crash."

CIA Headquarters. Langley, Virginia

"Your presentation was excellent," Director Matthews said as Beate packed up her laptop computer.

"Thank you, sir. We'll get started right away."

"Good. My contact on the Senate Intelligence Committee tells me our funding request will probably be approved, so full steam ahead okay?"

"Yes, sir."

She floated out of the conference room and hurried down the hallway towards her building.

It had gone much better than expected, she concluded, *but now we have a ton of work to do.*

She called her secretary using her CIA-issued secure cell phone. "Please assemble my managers and our IT consultants in the conference room. I'll be there in three minutes."

"Yes, ma'am."

Our IT consultants deserve to hear the good news too, she decided.

She'd spent months with the country's leading data warehouse and computer analytics experts developing the best-of-breed architecture. Even with the hefty discounts given to the government by the vendors, it would still be the most expensive computer system ever built by the Agency.

Beate dialed her personal cell phone to access her voice mail.

Busy.

The Director had been very helpful when one of the accountants had said, "You can develop this for twenty percent less. Just squeeze the computer companies."

I wanted to scream. He has no idea what it takes to build a system with these capabilities at such a low cost.

The vendors—all of whom had Top Secret Sensitive Compartmented Information (TS/SCI) security clearances—had worked diligently to develop the least costly solution.

The Director spoke up before she displayed her irritation. "The architecture looks good to me," he'd said, "and the cost projections seem reasonable. Your team did an excellent job, Beate. I'm authorizing you to begin the next phase immediately. Does anyone disagree?"

Silence filled the room. The accountant who'd confronted Beate had stared at his hands, knowing it would have been a career-limiting move to argue with the director after he'd made his decision.

"We need to get moving on this," Matthews had continued. "I know our primary mission is to conduct operations outside the United States, but our FBI colleagues have seriously under-invested in technology for years. Their new director agrees with me. Coordinating intelligence leads will help us combat terrorism. We're working this issue together with the Senate Intelligence Committee. They're beginning to understand the importance of cross-agency coordination. The examples Ms. Nicholson provided, describing how data analytics are being used to save agents' lives in the field, will give us good traction with the Senate."

Then he'd dropped the bombshell: "I'd like to see a complete project and staffing plan by the end of the week. My secretary will schedule a meeting with you on Friday, Ms. Nicholson."

Crap, Beate had cursed inwardly. *That means California's out.*

Her team was waiting when she entered the conference room.

"Our proposal was approved," she announced.

Everyone clapped.

Michael Chen, one of her managers—a naturalized citizen whose parents had fled China when he was five—raised his hand. "What's the next step?" he asked.

"The director has given us the go-ahead to proceed. He wants a detailed project and staffing plan by Friday."

The euphoria kindled by their victory quickly drained away.

I know they're exhausted, she observed. *That doesn't matter. Our country is at war—a silent, undeclared war. They'll make it happen.*

Her managers disbursed to inform their teams.

Beate dialed her cell phone message number. The carrier answered with beeps, signaling the network wasn't available.

I can never tell what kind of reception I'll get in the building.

"I'm going to the cafeteria for some coffee," she said as she walked by her secretary.

Jubilation washed over her. *Back-office technology projects like ours rarely received this much funding. Satellites, miniature cameras, and the latest technology—surveillance drones—usually gobble up most of the DS & T budget.*

She dialed her cell phone. *Still busy.*

She ordered coffee.

Her mind strayed to Malia. *They're on their way to LA now.* Regret stained her face. *I hope she won't be too disappointed.*

Beate smiled to herself when she remembered her early-morning lovemaking interlude with Robert.

I'm so lucky… the way he loves us, she mused. *He could've made a lot of money as a Certified Public Accountant, but our parenting priorities are more important to him. He's a proud father too, always bragging to our friends about being a stay-at-home dad.*

She headed towards the entrance courtyard to find a better signal.

She toggled her cell phone off and then on as she passed the security guards. She saw that Robert had called—twice—when her phone powered up. *They must have had a flight delay.*

She fantasized about racing to the airport. Then her mind spun. *I'll have to tell him I'm not coming,* she realized.

She dialed her phone messages. *Busy.*

She walked farther away, chuckling to herself as her mind strayed to the meeting. One of the accountants had actually fallen asleep while she described how her star-and-snowflake schema would allow the Agency to do time and location-based surveillance.

More significant were the director's words: "I see what you're saying," he'd said, "and the metadata will allow us to identify threats in real-time. This is excellent."

She stopped near the fence and dialed. This time she got through.

"Hi, darling," Robert said in his message. "Our flight is just about to take off. Talk with you tonight."

"Bye, Mommy," Malia said.

An ear-splitting alarm rang out across the CIA campus. Beate cupped her hand over her ear as she forwarded to his next message.

His tone was frightening. "Some hijackers took over the plane!"

Her heart stopped. She looked around.

"… I think we're heading back to Washington. Yes… we are. I see the White House… and the Washington Monument… to the left."

People were screaming. Malia was crying.

"Oh God." His voice was trembling. "We just took a sharp turn. We're flying very low. People are bleeding. The flight attendants said the pilots are dead. I don't know if the hijackers know how to fly…"

His call ended in static.

The Langley public address system blared out a message: "Please proceed immediately to your designated security area! Please proceed immediately to your designated security area!"

Her phone rang. It was Robert. Her breathing stopped.

"Where are you?" she yelled.

"We've been hijacked! Can you do something?"

She heard Malia crying.

Her gaze circled the skies.

More screams.

"I don't know what's happening," Robert yelled. Tears stained his words. "Can you do something? Oh my God… "

Screams and shrieks.

"The pilot is landing… but there's no… "

Static…

Silence.

*　*　*

She'd remember that moment later, forever… spinning dizzily in circles searching the sky. The explosion pointed her south towards the Pentagon.

She screamed and dropped to her knees. Bowing up and down holding her stomach, she shrieked and howled at the ash-gray cloud ascending into the heavens above Arlington.

The security guards called an ambulance when she refused to move. She was still screaming when the medical technicians shot her up with a sedative and carted her away.

7. Stranded

Luxembourg City

The screeching alarm startled everyone. An announcer boomed out instructions in Luxembourgish over the loudspeakers above the nerve-grating whine, and the Banque Lux traders jumped up from their seats and dashed to the elevators.

Jonas motioned from across the room for Sean and Pankaj to join him.

"There's an emergency," Jonas said when they reached his desk. "We need to go down to the security floor in our operations center."

"What's wrong?" Pankaj said.

"I don't know, but this isn't an exercise—it's real."

Jonas executed an emergency shutdown procedure from his master administrator console to terminate everyone's trades, and they hustled to the elevator.

The floor numbers ticking away slowly on the digital LED display above the doors seemed abnormally lethargic; the way a watched clock slows to hinder time.

"I'll find out what's happening when we get down there," Jonas said.

The elevator doors opened and the crowd squeezed in, and twenty seconds later, they were dropping to the subterranean bowels of the building. The pungent odor of someone who didn't believe in deodorant made the short journey memorable.

The elevator disgorged its inhabitant's twelve floors below street level into a tall-ceilinged room populated with a labyrinthine maze of desks and computer terminals. The room looked like a NASA mission control center.

Several huge displays mounted high on the walls provided status for the bank's computers and networks. Four presented news and weather broadcasts. The 200 refugees already crammed into the room focused on a CNN news broadcast.

Sean gasped when he saw a large passenger plane crash into a skyscraper.

"That's the World Trade Center," Pankaj said.

"I think so," Sean said. "How could a plane get that far off course?"

CNN flashed a video of a second plane plowing into the adjacent tower.

"Oh my God," Sean said.

Jonas consulted a nearby security guard and returned.

"There's been a terrorist attack in New York," he announced. "The security manager asked us to come down here as a precaution. It's unclear whether attacks are being launched against other financial centers around the world."

The animated throng spoke a cacophonic mélange of languages. Although Sean could pick out some Flemish, French, and German, most of them spoke Luxembourgish, which he didn't understand at all.

He tried his cell phone. "I can't get a signal."

"Sorry," Jonas said. "There's no service down here."

Someone in the room turned up the English version of CNN. The newscasters seemed amazingly calm as they spoke about the unfolding tragedy.

"Both buildings were targeted," Pankaj said. "This was obviously no accident."

"It couldn't have been," Sean said. "This is awful."

A noticeable hush cloaked the room. The camera zoomed in on someone breaking out a window near the top floor of one of the burning buildings. A woman appeared on a ledge with her clothes on fire, hesitated a moment, and jumped.

Shrieks erupted as she fell. Pankaj, Sean, and Jonas looked at each other, too shocked to say anything.

An emergency banner appeared on the bottom of the screen: *A third plane has crashed into the Pentagon in Washington.* News reporters from DC appeared with the Pentagon burning in the background.

Jonas looked at Sean. "How could your Pentagon, the headquarters of the most powerful military in the world, be so vulnerable to an attack?"

Sean shook his head. "I need to call Rachel," he said. "She goes to school at NYU—a couple of miles from the World Trade Center. Can I get a line out of here?"

"No. I'm sorry. The phone lines are reserved for official bank business during emergencies."

"Why can't my cell phone signals get through?" Sean complained.

"Luxembourg banks, like those in Switzerland, have been built to withstand bomb blasts. The concrete and steel that shields us from radiation also prevents cell phone signals from getting through."

"This is like a modern-day Pearl Harbor," Pankaj said, "but this time it's New York and Washington, and it's being broadcast around the world. Someone must have planned it this way."

"Attacking our Pentagon was very bold," Sean said. "I'm sure we'll retaliate."

The 110-story South Tower of the World Trade Center began to crumble, and then it collapsed, melting from the sky. The crowd in the operations center shuddered with expletives as the building disintegrated into a huge cloud of dust.

"My God," Pankaj said. "I'll bet hundreds of lives were just lost."

Sean wasn't usually religious. He bowed his head anyway. His thoughts strayed to Charon, the ferryman rowing the departed to the underworld as he prayed for their souls.

Holy Mary, Mother of God, pray for us sinners, now and at the hour of our death, Amen, he said to himself.

The North Tower collapsed thirty minutes later.

Everyone was in a daze from the mind-numbing images searing their brains when CNN announced that another hijacked plane had crashed in Pennsylvania.

The Banque Lux security manager broadcast an announcement saying they could leave three hours later.

Emma accompanied Jonas, Sean, and Pankaj to the lobby.

She hugged Pankaj and shook his hand. "I hope your family is okay."

"Thanks, Emma."

Then she hugged Sean. "Please call me if you need anything."

The tenderness in her voice fell upon him like a blanket. He held her longer than he probably should have, squashing emotions he'd kept bottled up all day.

"Thanks," he replied. He pulled away and looked at her. "Perhaps you can help me develop some commodity trading models… in a couple of weeks."

"I'd be glad to help."

Jonas shook Sean's hand. "I know this probably isn't the best time, but I just checked today's trading report. We had our most profitable day ever, by thirty percent."

"Thanks for letting me know," Sean said solemnly. "I'll talk with you soon."

Pankaj flagged down a taxi while Sean checked his messages.

His first call was from Rachel. Her voice was hysterical. "Please call me! The World Trade Center is on fire. I'm going down to help."

Damn, he thought. *I feel like someone just punched me in the gut.*

Her next message was frantic. "Where are you? A plane just crashed into the other tower!" Her voice was barely audible above the sirens.

Sean slid into the back seat of a white Mercedes taxi and dialed her number. She didn't answer.

He left a message. "Rachel, this is Sean. We just got out of a security lockdown at the bank. I hope you're all right. Please call me."

Pankaj finished his call with his wife. "Everyone's fine at home. How's Rachel?"

"I don't know. She left me two messages. She's pretty scared."

Sean looked out his side window at a copper-stained cloud shimmering over the horizon. The streets were eerily deserted.

"She saw one of the planes crash into the World Trade Center," he said.

"That's awful," Pankaj said. "Where is she now?"

"I don't know."

They paid the driver and sprinted into the hotel. The Goldberg Cohen pilots were watching television at the bar.

Sean slid into a seat next to Mark Sebastian. "When can we get home?"

"Not tonight," Mark said. "All the airports in the US are closed. The FAA is forcing international flights over the Atlantic to land in Canada and Iceland. It's a real mess."

"Can we leave tomorrow?"

"I doubt it," he replied. "I'm not sure when we'll get permission to land. The military is forcing all flights in the US to the ground. Airports are running out of space. You'd better check back into your rooms. We may be here for a while. People are stranded everywhere."

Sean and Pankaj hustled to the line in front of the hotel clerk.

Sean's phone beeped. The call was from Angela.

He moved away so he could talk in private.

"Hi, Angie. Are you okay? How's your family? Have you heard from Rachel?"

"Hi, Sean," she said. "My family is fine. Rachel called me a while ago. She said she couldn't get through to you. She's making her way north on foot to White Plains. Most of the streets in Manhattan are jammed. My driver will pick her up as soon as he can reach her."

"That's good. Thank you."

"I hope you're okay," she said. "I know you didn't get much sleep last night."

"I'm fine. I gotta run. I need to check back into the hotel. Talk with you soon."

As usual, Angela is looking after Rachel while I'm away.

He'd barely been home the past month, between his business trips to Dubai, Hong Kong, London, and Dublin.

He dialed Rachel again. This time she answered.

"Hi, Rachel. Where are you?"

"I'm in… the Bronx, I think," she told him. "Why didn't you call me?"

Sean stepped onto the sidewalk in front of the hotel. "We were in a lockdown at the bank all afternoon. We couldn't leave. I'm sorry. Are you all right?"

"No! I've been running for hours. I went down to help. A huge dust cloud covered us… I couldn't breathe."

"We saw the attack on the news. It's terrible."

She began to cry. "A jet crashed… into the World Trade Center. All those people… dead. In the building… on the plane… dead. I saw people on fire… jumping out of windows."

Sean walked to a small park down the street from the hotel and sat down on a bench. The streets of Luxembourg were unusually quiet.

Everyone must be home watching the news, he assumed.

"That's awful," he said. "I just spoke with Angela. Her driver will pick you up as soon as he can reach you."

"Do they think bombs… will start falling?" she asked.

"CNN said the Air Force has fighter planes around the city. I think you're safe. Just keep going north. I'm sure you can stay with Angela until I get back."

"When will you be home?"

"US airspace is closed. Our pilots aren't sure when we'll be able to return."

"Why can't you be here when I need you?" she wailed. "This is why I didn't want to move here."

He took a deep breath. *Had it really been a good idea to move to New York from Colorado? Yes, it had been… at least for me. Pushing my brain full-throttle with millions of dollars on the line—I can't imagine anything more exciting—but Rachel has never been thrilled with the fast-paced city.*

"I was running... toward the World Trade Center," she panted. "I heard a roar... a jet passed by over the Hudson... before it flew into the building. They're all dead!"

She wailed despondently.

I feel helpless to comfort her, as if I'm swimming with stones tied to my legs.

"I got lost in the dust," she said between whimpers. "I started to run east, then north. I helped an old woman struggling with a walker. A man picked her up. He ran with her... cradling her like a baby."

"People in New York have hearts of gold beneath their hard shells," Sean said.

"How would you know?" she yelled. "You're never here! Are we at war? Who are we fighting?"

"CNN said it was terrorists."

"Why did you insist we move here? I can't do this anymore."

She hung up.

He dialed her again. She didn't answer.

He called her every few minutes for the next six hours. She never answered.

He was watching the news in his hotel room when Angela called him at 2:00 a.m. "Hi, Sean. I hope I didn't wake you."

"You didn't," he replied. "I can't sleep. Did Rachel call you? She won't answer my calls."

"Harold picked her up in my limousine and took her to a friend's house a while ago."

"Where is she? Is her phone broken? Why won't she return my calls?"

"Did you guys have a fight? She said she doesn't want to talk with you."

"I wish she'd call me," he said. "Thanks for picking her up. Where is she?"

Angela paused. "I'll call you after I have a chance to talk with her. I've got to run now."

"Okay," he said after a moment. "Thanks for keeping her safe."

8. Waterzooi

Luxembourg City—Friday, September 14

Rachel didn't return any of Sean's phone calls the rest of the week. He was about to leave his hotel room to join his colleagues in the lobby when Angela called.

"Hi Sean," she said. "Sorry it took me so long to get back to you. I had a hard time reaching Rachel."

"She hasn't returned any of my calls," he said, exasperated. "Where is she?"

"When are you coming home?"

"Mark Sebastian told me we've been given permission to fly into Westchester Airport tomorrow evening."

"Do you want me to pick you up?"

"Thanks," he said. "That would be nice. So what's up with Rachel?"

Angela hesitated. "She told me she needs some space from you. I think she's in shock... or having some kind of nervous breakdown— I don't know—like half the city, I guess."

"Space?"

"That's what she said. I'm sorry to have to tell you this over the phone."

"Can you bring me to her after you pick me up tomorrow?"

"Sure... if that's what you want."

"I do. So how are you doing?"

"I'm okay. I've been watching the news all week. Thousands are still missing, including more than three hundred forty firefighters and sixty policemen."

"That's terrible."

"What are you doing tonight?"

"Emma—one of the traders here at Banque Lux—is preparing a Belgian meal for us. Veronica, Jonas's wife, is helping her. Jonas says they love to cook, so it should be quite a treat."

"I'm sure it will. I love Belgian food. Are you going to tell him tonight?"

"Yes."

"Good."

Angela paused long enough for Sean to hear the static from their cross-Atlantic connection. "Rachel wanted me to tell you she doesn't want to see you when you come home. I don't know what she's thinking."

"Where is she?"

"Outside the city," she answered vaguely. "She doesn't want me to tell you. The important thing is… she's safe."

"I'll call you when we're ready to leave," he said. "We'll arrive late in the evening, New York time. I've gotta run."

"Okay, Sean. Take care of yourself."

"Thanks, Angie, for everything. You're a good friend." He hung up.

The sting of Rachel's rejection scalded him like a cauldron of molten steel. He let go of his emotions and allowed himself to cry. He doused his face with cold water to extinguish the tears, and drifted down the stairs to the lobby.

Emma greeted Sean and Pankaj in her lobby with air kisses since she knew them, and shook hands with the two pilots. The men followed her into a large living room furnished with Scandinavian couches stuffed with pillows on a Brazilian cherry wood floor. An eclectic mix of contemporary art adorned her walls.

"It smells wonderful in here," Pankaj said.

Emma smiled. "How about a quick culinary tour while I get you a drink?"

They greeted Jonas and Veronica in the kitchen. After selecting one of Emma's Belgian beer offerings—De Koninck from Antwerp, Chimay from Chimay, or Stella Artois from Leuven—she gave them an epicurean tour of the pending gastronomic feast.

The women laughed when Sean asked if he could help.

"We'll be fine," Emma said.

Jonas guided them through the living room and out a sliding door to a large outdoor deck. They sat down at a table on the fourth-floor balcony.

"Emma and Veronica grew up in Belgium," Jonas said. "Preparing cuisine is an art form for them. I'm very lucky that way."

"That sounds nice," Mark Sebastian said. "Perhaps I should find myself a Belgian wife. The women here sure are beautiful."

Sean faked a smile. "You say that in every city we go to, Mark."

The men chuckled.

Emma and Veronica giggled in the kitchen, laughing about Sean's offer to help.

"They're good friends," Jonas said, "and they love to cook together. We would've just been in the way."

"Thanks for having us," Sean said. "It's been a rough week."

"It's our pleasure," Jonas replied. "I hope you have a safe journey back to America tomorrow."

Sean raised his eyebrows to the pilots. "I'm sure we will."

Mark lifted his Chimay. "You're in good hands. I won't be hung-over—I promise."

The women arrived with platters filled with an assortment of rustic breads, paté, dried fruits, and soft cheeses. They placed the food on the table and returned to the kitchen, giggling about something unbeknownst to the men.

Jonas grinned. "Don't worry. They're having fun. They started into the wine an hour before you arrived."

The men laughed, feeling less guilty about not helping.

Emma came to the screen door a few minutes later. "It's time for dinner."

They followed her into the dining room.

Jonas described the Wallonia region of southern Belgium as he filled their wine glasses with chardonnay.

The women entered carrying the first course.

"This is a starter," Emma said, "called *tomate-crevette*. We blended small grey shrimp harvested from the North Sea with mayonnaise, and stuffed it into hollowed-out tomatoes."

Everyone savored the succulent offering, and the first course became history. Jonas refilled their wine glasses.

Emma brought in the second course—a large serving bowl filled with a soupy mixture of carrots, onions, potatoes, celeriac, leeks, herbs, chicken, cream, and eggs. She placed it in the center of the table and handed Sean a ladle.

"This is called *waterzooi*. Help yourself."

The men clapped when Veronica and Emma marched in with the next chapter of the feast: Large plates piled high with steaming mussels, and chips that looked a lot like American-style French fries, only larger.

The third course disappeared more gradually. Everyone took their time, cracking the black clamshells to reach the hidden delicacy, which they then dunked in garlic butter.

The last course was *Salade Liégeoise*, a salad composed of green beans, bits of bacon, onions, and vinegar.

"This dish is from Liege, an area in Belgium with wonderful cuisine," Veronica said. "Unfortunately, the city has been a battlefield in many wars. We're lucky our recipes survived."

Everyone became silent... remembering the week's tragedies.

Sean proposed a toast. "To the end of war," he declared.

"Hear, hear!" Jonas echoed lifting his glass, and soon everyone was laughing.

After lavish praises to the chefs, the meal concluded.

Sean asked Jonas to join him on the patio.

He closed the sliding door to ensure privacy. He looked down at the street from the fourth floor balcony, and turned to face Jonas.

"Goldberg Cohen has just purchased your bank," Sean announced. "That's why we chose Banque Lux for our first partner deployment."

Jonas's eyebrows rose. "Really? I didn't know we were for sale."

"We were already part owners. I guess David Cohen came up with an offer your private shareholders couldn't refuse. David wanted you to hear this from me. He's hoping you'll stay on after the acquisition. You'll have a much larger role if you do."

"What do you have in mind?" Jonas asked.

"We're purchasing Banque Lux to expand our derivatives trading team. Angela and I presented the idea to her father a couple of months ago. We need your expertise in Euro bond, commodity, and currency-based statistical arbitrage. I've been evaluating your team. Some of your employees, like Emma, have a good grasp of our concepts. She's a quick learner, which makes you both a good fit."

"I'm glad to hear we'll have jobs," Jonas remarked.

"Here's the bad news. About a third of your trading team will probably be gone within six months—at least that's what happened in New York. Traders who use outmoded, traditional techniques like value analysis or gut intuition won't be able to adapt to our system. We've seen this before. You'll need to keep an eye out to determine whom you want to keep."

"Wow—that's a shock," Jonas said. "Bank employees in Europe expect lifetime job security. That's especially true for the bankers upstairs in the three-piece suits. Actually, they're usually out on the golf course… or playing polo when the weather is nice."

The men laughed loudly.

"Your team will earn a lot more money now—even more than the suits," Sean told him. "Goldberg Cohen uses a merit pay system."

Jonas's face broadened into a smile. "I like that idea. When is the announcement?"

"I'm not sure. We were going to announce it this week but now, it may be a week or two. I'll let you know, assuming you want to stay on."

Jonas laughed. "Of course I do." He raised his glass. "*A votre santé, mon ami.*"

"*À la votre,*" Sean said, reciprocating his friend's wish for good health.

They returned to the living room. Plates filled with dark Belgian chocolates and miniature waffles lined the coffee table.

Emma handed Sean and Jonas tulip-shaped brandy glasses filled halfway with Remy Martin Louis XIII cognac.

She raised her glass. "I'd like to make a toast."

Everyone quieted.

"To you, Sean, for all you've done. Your trading program is brilliant."

A round of "tchin tchin's" and clinking glasses circled the room. Everyone sipped.

Sean blushed. "Thanks, Emma, but if I could cook like you, I'd probably change careers. The dinner you and Veronica prepared was fabulous. Thanks for having us."

Sean remained quiet, concentrating on the sweet brandy appeasing his tongue. *Where is Rachel? What is she doing?*

He stared into the tulip for an hour before he announced he was tired.

The Americans then thanked Emma, Veronica, and Jonas, and boarded a taxi back to their hotel.

9. Cleopatra

Zurich—Saturday, September 15

Rahim knocked on Abdul's penthouse door at the Widder Hotel. Abdul motioned him in and directed him to a red leather couch. The elegant suite—furnished French provincial—had several nineteenth century Impressionist prints hanging on the walls.

Abdul moved to the bar. "Would you like some wine?"

"No thanks."

Abdul stared at the offerings in the wine rack. He pulled out a vintage German Riesling, removed the cork, tasted it, and smiled.

"You should have some. It's very good."

"You know I don't drink," Rahim retorted.

Abdul smirked. "Things went well this week. We should celebrate."

"I wish I could've been more involved."

"Oh, but you were," Abdul said. "Your role was very important. I checked the accounts this afternoon. Your trades made over sixty billion euros. That money will fund many important projects in our *jihad*."

"What I did was not so hard, compared to our brothers."

"You have different skills. That doesn't mean what you did was less important. By the way, I deposited two million Swiss francs into your bank account this morning."

"Thank you."

Abdul drained his glass and poured another. "Are you sure you don't want some?"

"We should celebrate through prayer, not drinking."

Rahim regretted his words as soon as they floated from his mouth. *I shouldn't provoke him.*

Abdul's eyebrows furrowed into a menacing stare. "Watch your tongue, or I'll cut it out."

Rahim trembled. "You're right. I'm sorry I said that."

"We should go to dinner. Wait here while I change."

Abdul walked into his bedroom and turned at the door. "I almost forgot—some women are meeting us at the restaurant tonight. I hope you brought plenty of condoms. It's time to lose your virginity don't you think?"

Abdul cackled with laughter as he shut his door.

Rahim grimaced. *I wish I hadn't told him about my impotence*, he chided himself. *I thought I could trust him at the time. Now it's just a running joke that comes up every time we meet.*

Abdul returned to the living room ten minutes later wearing gold chains around his neck and a red silk shirt that made his watermelon gut spill over his belt. He'd greased his thin black hair back over his scalp to cover a bald spot on his crown.

Rahim forced his teeth together so he wouldn't laugh. "Where are we going to eat? I'm catching a train back to Geneva tonight."

"We're meeting the girls at the Veltliner Keller. You can pick the one you want. It'll be fun."

Abdul lifted the Riesling bottle to his lips and drank.

A shiver rolled down Rahim's spine when he remembered Kristen... and Abdul's idea of fun. He shoved the brutal images aside.

"I'd like a bigger role in our *jihad* next time," Rahim said. "Can you tell me more about our operations?"

Abdul frowned. "Remember what I told you during boot camp? Don't ask too many questions. Information is compartmentalized, for your own safety."

"But our brothers in America did so much. Can't I do more to help?"

"We accomplished most of our goals. One plane never got off the ground, one crashed, and three reached their targets. Everyone knows we're more than just chattering teeth in the desert now."

"What I did was insignificant in comparison," Rahim lamented.

"That's not true," Abdul assured him. "The money you made buys weapons and food for our people—your people, in Lebanon and Palestine. So how did everything go at the banks?"

"Fine. I executed the trades as I normally do. I was in and out in ten minutes."

"Good. Remember, Rahim—Allah has a plan for each of us. This is yours. Let's pray together before we go to dinner."

Rahim caught Abdul's arm when he staggered, and steadied him to his knees on the carpet. They bowed their heads to Mecca.

Rahim had difficulty concentrating while he prayed. *Perhaps I do have an important role*, he considered. *The messages I decrypt are complex… and travelling to eight banks on the same day is exhausting. Still, martyrdom to meet seventy virgins in heaven with a penis that functions sounds much better.*

He sighed silently to himself. *I'm exhausted. I wish I could make my trades remotely, but I know Abdul would never allow that.*

Abdul had drilled it into them during boot camp: "Governments monitor everything going across the Internet. International laws crafted by the infidels require messages to use encryption ciphers they can decode. Never use the Internet to make trades. Always make them in person."

The maître d' at the restaurant ushered two gorgeous brunettes to their table as they finished dinner. The women wore sleek, black, body-hugging couture, diamond necklaces with matching earrings, and black high heels—attire befitting the vocational expectations of their high-class clientele.

Abdul greeted them with air kisses on each cheek and they sat down.

"As I promised, you can pick the woman you want," Abdul said.

Rahim blushed as the women eyed him salaciously, exchanging inquisitive glances that spoke a thousand words.

He stood up. "I'm sorry. I need to catch a train this evening."

Abdul showed no disappointment. "Have a good trip."

Rahim squeezed the outstretched fingers of each woman, picked up the briefcase he'd kept beside his leg at the table, and hustled to the lobby. The sommelier was opening another bottle of wine when he glanced back at Abdul.

* * *

Nikolai, who'd been observing the dinner scene from the other side of the restaurant, signaled Abdul with a nod after Rahim left. He retreated to the bathroom and checked the toilet stalls to make sure they'd be alone.

Abdul made a beeline for the urinals when he entered.

Nikolai bolted the door so they'd be alone.

"So that's Rahim?" Nikolai asked.

"Yes. He did well this week."

"I agree. He executed every trade exactly as New York instructed. Sixty billion is our biggest haul ever. His other two colleagues each made forty. New York should make close to sixty when the Stock Exchanges reopen next week. You'll have to thank your friend in Yemen for giving us the heads-up about the attack. I transferred a billion into his Zurich account today."

"I'm sure he'll appreciate that."

Abdul flushed the urinal. He combed a stringy hair back into place in front of the mirror.

"Does Rahim suspect anything?" Nikolai said.

"Don't worry," Abdul scoffed. "He's a true believer."

"How do you know?"

"He has lots of reasons to be angry," Abdul explained. "The UN drove his grandparents from their land in Palestine when they created Israel in 1948. Rahim was the second generation born at the refugee camp. The Israelis killed his family with a bomb attack when he was four years old. He barely survived his burns, and his injuries made him impotent."

"Perhaps we should consider him for covert operations," Nikolai mused. "Orphans make the best spies."

"That's true, and he's convinced he's working for the *jihad*. We can use that."

"I deposited a bonus into your Lichtenstein account this morning."

"Excellent! Do you want one of the girls before you go? You can have either one."

"No thanks. I'm returning to DC tonight. Yvonna and the kids are anxious for me to get home. Our youngest, Tatiana, has a soccer game tomorrow afternoon. I'm catching a red-eye now that the FAA has lifted flight restrictions around DC."

Abdul gloated. "You should see the villa I just purchased on the Italian Riviera. The view is spectacular."

"That sounds nice. I've always loved that area. Perhaps I'll buy a flat near Monaco one of these days. I like the Monte Carlo casino."

Abdul unlocked the door. "Good luck." He chuckled. "Be careful. I hear air travel isn't as safe as it used to be."

"I guess not."

Nikolai relocked the door and dialed Yvonna. She didn't answer.

She must be busy with the kids, he assumed.

* * *

A blustery breeze blew through the corridors of Zurich's perfectly ordered streets and concrete banking fortresses as Rahim hustled to the *Hauptbahnhof*. He wrapped his scarf around his neck and picked up his pace.

He welcomed the warmth of the first-class cabin when he boarded the train. He located his window seat, sat down, and anchored his briefcase to his ankle with a lightweight ceramic cable.

When someone saw him doing this and got curious he'd just say, "I don't want to lose my students' papers."

He peered out his window at the clock on the wall.

I like the 8:32 p.m. departure, he decided, *a time when most industrious Swiss are at home with their families. It's less likely I'll have to talk with anyone.*

Swiss trains run like clocks, so I'll arrive in Geneva in precisely two hours and fifty-two minutes. After a quick jaunt along the waterfront promenade, I'll be home by midnight.

The train pulled away from the station.

His window darkened as the station lights receded, revealing the reflection of a young man dressed in a suit, tie, hat, wool coat, and scarf. The agnostic cabin lights ignored his olive-colored skin.

He placed his hat, scarf, and coat on the empty seat across from him and settled in for his journey.

The briefcase did contain student papers—part of his cover, in case someone started snooping. The papers were indistinguishable from the instructions he'd picked up at the bank that afternoon.

He'd learn the details of his next mission when he decoded the instructions using a one-time code cipher he'd pick up from a drop site in Geneva. That would come later.

The train was soon hurtling down the tracks at 250 kilometers per hour. He smiled when he recalled how excited he used to get in the early days, less than two years ago. Now he couldn't wait to get home.

He pulled his ticket from his pocket so he'd be ready when the conductor came. The appellation said Rahim Delacroix.

That wasn't his real name. Sister Anne had given him the Delacroix surname when he'd arrived at the orphanage. He'd been barely four years old then, recovering from severe burns.

"I love the paintings of the French artist Eugene Delacroix," she'd told him when he was older. "So I figured it would be good name for you. We didn't know your real last name."

She was right. Art lovers throughout Europe always recognized his name, and having a respectable French bourgeois moniker in class-conscious Switzerland helped him fit in. He needed all the help he could get. People often had a strong reaction to his burn-scarred neck and missing finger.

A dense forest wrapped the train in darkness. The resentment he'd stuffed during his meeting with Abdul returned. *The jokes about my impotence are more than annoying. The bastard tried to drown me when I told him I wanted to use my real surname.*

He'd begun his investigation into his past a few weeks earlier, with a visit to Sister Anne. They met in the meager lobby of the nunnery she called home outside Montreux. She wore her nun's habit. In her late sixties now, she was still as energetic as a fiddle, with the same smiling eyes that had often comforted him as a child.

"I'd be happy to buy you a home, Sister Anne," he'd told her as they sipped peppermint tea. "I can also provide you with a monthly income."

"That's nice, Rahim," she'd replied. "You're such a considerate young man, but I have no interest in possessions. My life's work is here, taking care of orphans. This is my mission."

He'd listened patiently as she described her latest batch—civil war refugees from Uganda. He'd almost told her that he *also* had a mission—supporting Muslims in refugee camps—but he'd sworn to Abdul on his life that he'd keep their work a secret.

He'd bent the conversation to his past by the time his teacup was empty.

"Here are your records," she'd said, handing him a file folder she'd retrieved from the office. "I figured you'd want these someday."

"Bless you, Sister Anne."

The folder had the word "*Rahim*" scribbled at the top, next to surname "*Delacroix*," carefully penned in Anne's handwriting.

The first document was a letter written to Father Francois—the orphanage administrator at the time—from a hospital clerk in Parga, Greece.

Dear Father Francois—

With your permission, as we spoke about on the phone, we'll be transferring a four-year-old boy recovering from burns to your orphanage. His name is Rahim.

The rest of the letter significantly downplayed the extent of his injuries.

His gaze pulled up when he'd finished reading. "I was in Greece?"

"Yes, at a hospital for burn victims."

The next document contained his academic records.

She'd smiled proudly. "I've never met anyone who could learn languages and mathematics as quickly as you."

Rahim stood up. "Thank you, Sister Anne. I need to leave now. I'll be back to see you next month."

He took a flight to Parga the next day.

Apprehension filled his heart as the taxi careened around potholes on the pockmarked dirt road paralleling the river to the hospital. The taxi driver's colorful commentary only increased his trepidation.

"The Acheron River there is known as the pathway to hell," the driver said, looking at Rahim through the rear view mirror. "Virgil wrote about it and so did Dante, in his book *The Inferno*, and that hospital you're visiting is rumored to be Charon's departure point."

"Why is that?"

The driver chuckled. "Because so many people die there."

They approached a chalk-colored, three-story building stranded on a cliff, surrounded by a chain-link fence topped with barbed wire. The taxi wound its way through the unkempt grounds to the entrance.

An ominous pall settled over Rahim as he surveyed the mottled steps leading up to the faded wooden entry doors.

"Are you visiting someone here?" the driver inquired.

Rahim stepped out of the taxi. "No." He passed a hundred-euro note through the window.

The driver pocketed the money for the thirty-euro fare and sped away without offering change.

A rough-shaven hospital administrator ignored Rahim's request to see his records until he placed fifty euros on the man's desk.

The civil servant pointed his fat finger at the end of the hall. "The records are down there. The door is unlocked. I'm not paid to help you, so you're on your own."

The storage room greeted him with the musty odor of decomposing bureaucracy. He toggled an ancient switch, and a light bulb dangling from the end of a frayed ceiling wire sprang to life.

He rifled through dozens of unlabeled boxes. A dusty, yellow haze cloaked the room when he finally located his records just before dawn.

A triage nurse prioritizing the injured must have authored the first scribble, Rahim guessed.

Rahim, four-year-old boy, arrived from the UN refugee camp hospital in Rashidieh, Lebanon. Severe burns. Faint heartbeat. Continue morphine for pain. Prepare for surgery and burn unit.

A second note in a different-colored pen said: Father Kritikos baptized him and gave him last rites.

A shiver rolled down his spine when he saw his nametag—the kind tied to the toe of a corpse. It had the word Rahim on one side, and his full name—*Rahim bin Tariq bin Khalid al-Hadaad*—on the other.

Several documents described his injuries and medical procedures.

He stuck the folder in his briefcase. *No one will care.*

The train braked through a curve, rousing him from his reverie.

He closed his eyes and resumed his musings.

An excursion to Lebanon the next day brought him to the archives of the Beirut library. A female librarian showed him documents describing how the United Nations constructed Rashidieh as a temporary refuge camp for Palestinians displaced by the formation of Israel, in 1947.

"The UN built many *temporary* refugee camps in Lebanon and Gaza when they created Israel," she said. "Most of them have grown into ramshackle towns filled with tents, shacks, metal barracks, and wooden outhouses over the subsequent decades."

Digging deeper, he found evidence that the UN army—primarily American and British soldiers—had removed his grandparents at gunpoint from their 400-acre citrus grove in northern Palestine. His grandmother was pregnant with his father at the time.

How ironic, he realized, *that I now work for the same people that dispossessed my family.*

Rahim told his friends at the mosque about his findings when he returned to Geneva: "Israeli bombs launched by American cannons killed my family," he exclaimed angrily.

Abdul invited him for an evening boat ride on Lake Geneva the following week.

"I discovered my real name," he'd told Abdul as they pulled away from the dock. "*Rahim bin Tariq bin Khalid al-Hadaad.* I'm using it from now on, instead of *Delacroix.*"

"You stupid fool! You're not changing your name."

"But I want to use my Muslim name."

"*Delacroix* is a great cover name for a Swiss businessman. You're not changing it!"

"You can't tell me what name to use."

Abdul didn't speak again until they reached the center of the lake. He stopped the boat and without warning, tossed Rahim overboard.

"You're not just some angry Arab martyr!" Abdul had yelled from the deck. "Don't you realize the importance of what we're doing?"

Abdul looked like a fat devil there, standing in the moonlight.

Abdul kept shoving him beneath the water with an oar every time he swam close. He almost drowned. Abdul finally pulled him back on board when Rahim agreed he wouldn't use his real name.

He was depressed for a few days afterwards, until he realized he'd actually become quite attached to the Delacroix name.

"*Billet, s'il vous plait?*"

The conductor stared warily at the briefcase tied to Rahim's ankle as Rahim handed him his ticket. The conductor made a note, handed his ticket back, and moved forward to the next passenger.

The train swayed gently, maintaining full speed through a carefully engineered curve.

Rahim looked out his window at the dark forest, trying to feel good about their victory. *I hardly slept all week*, he pondered.

Reminders of the attacks were everywhere. Images of the destruction crawled into his dreams every time he came close to sleep. The front page of the *Neue Zürcher Zeitung* newspaper displayed pictures of the World Trade Towers in flames just before he boarded.

A jangling food cart jolted him alert.

"*Bonsoir?*"

"*Bonsoir. Un café'crème, s'il vous plait.*"

The server prepared a cup of coffee with cream.

Rahim handed him several Swiss francs and signaled keep the change.

"*Merci beaucoup.*"

Steam wafted above the cup in spirals, like a genie escaping a bottle. Lights from an unknown town flickered past and with a swoosh they entered a tunnel.

The murmuring purr of the engine was mesmerizing. He closed his eyes, and the harmonious, low-pitched hum lulled him to sleep.

His dream brought him to his top-floor condominium, where he's peering out at the snow-capped Alps on the other side of Lake Geneva.

A turbulent storm swirls over the water forming a huge whirlpool reaching for the sky.

A huge monster, a Cyclops appears, as the water drops away. Its slithery tail reaches out and coils itself around him, squeezing him until he suffocates.

Spiraling dizzily downward through a cone-shaped cave, he reaches Rashidieh and his three-year-old sister is sleeping next to him.

A tremendous explosion jars the earth. Their tent disintegrates in flames.

He is looking up at stars in a black sky as fire engulfs them.

Another bomb explodes. The ground shudders as molten steel rains over them.

His sister screams a blood-curdling wail.

His hands find the flames on her chest but it is too hot.

Her piercing cries fade to gurgles as her tiny body convulses.

A light flashes in her eyes when she finds Allah, and she is still, smoldering amidst the orange flames.

Two charred slabs of meat sputter and pop next to him where their parents' tent once stood. Rivers of blood ooze through cracks in their black skin. An acrid stench—worse than burning tires on the beach—floods the air.

His lungs fill with smoke. It is too painful to scream but he does anyway.

The white devils come. Their bodies are white. Their hats are white. Their faces have white masks.

The rancid smell of burning flesh—his own flesh—makes him vomit but the tube choking his throat stuffs it down.

The white devils stab him with needles and more needles, and the light bulb above their shrouded faces goes black.

They stare at him when he awakes. Some eyes are blue above the masks. They speak words he doesn't recognize.

The naked light bulb watches everything. The pain is excruciating. He screams through the tube as the white devils tear away his flesh. No one cares in hell: His penance for not saving her.

"Please forgive me, Allah," he begs.

But there is no forgiveness in hell—only pain.

The white devils rip away his skin. The throat tube stifles his protests. He can only scream inside his head.

Train brakes squeal, stirring Rahim awake.

The railcar veers sideways through a sharp curve.

Rahim checks his hand. *My finger is still missing; my fingertips are still numb—no feelings, no nerve endings. My difficulty grasping small objects—buttons, string, needles—are other reminders: It wasn't just a dream.*

I'm very lucky to have Sister Anne in my life, he reminds himself.

She'd given him the Qur'an on the night of his Catholic confirmation—his most cherished gift.

"You must keep this a secret," she'd said. "Your people say it's a holy book from God, like the Bible. I'm sure your father would've given you a similar gift if he could be here."

He wasn't sure what to do with it at first, but once he started reading—he knew. The revelations were deep, yet familiar.

Fragments of light reflecting off the lake greet his window.

The train pulls into Geneva's *Gare de Cornivan* station a moment later.

He walks several blocks north on *Rue de Lausanne*, enters his building, and ascends the elevator to his twelfth-floor apartment.

America has tasted the sword now, he tells himself, as he looks at the mountains across the lake from his balcony.

Images of the dead and injured he'd seen on TV assault his mind.

There is no pleasure in my revenge, he realizes, *and what about Muhammad's message of love?*

He concentrates on the stars. *Please give me guidance,* he pleads.

As usual, he receives no answers, or if there are any, he can't hear them.

Baltimore, Maryland

Mikhail adjusted his tie in the hallway mirror.

Yvonna rose from the bed and followed him to the door. "Can't you stay a little longer?"

"No," he replied hurriedly. "I'm already late."

"When will I see you again?"

"Check the wall safe every day. I'll send you a message when I'm ready."

The door clunked shut.

She drifted past the bed, opened the curtains, and looked down from the thirty-second floor of Baltimore's Harborplace Hotel. Life is business as usual in the harbor: ships cruising in and out of the docks conducting commerce for the masses.

Not knowing how long Mikhail would want her, she'd hired a babysitter until 8:00 p.m. *I have an hour to kill before driving back to Annapolis.*

She dropped her white cotton bathrobe and twisted side to side in front of the bathroom mirror. *The red spank marks are already fading,* she noticed. *None of them will cause a bruise this time.*

A smile touched her lips as she eyed her figure. *I'm glad I can still turn every man's head when I walk into a room,* she tells herself. *I don't care about other men, though, only Nikolai… and Mikhail.*

Her cinnamon-brown eyes blink back. *Nikolai would never understand my need for Mikhail. How could he? Even I can't understand it.*

A shiver jerks her shoulders. *He'd murder us both if he found out. Nikolai has despised Mikhail from the moment they met. So why doesn't he quit?*

I'd tell him… if he'd understand.

She recites her excuse to herself in front of the mirror: "Our two hundred forty-acre horse farm is lonely when you're out of town."

He'd never buy that.

Nikolai never discusses what he's been doing while he's gone. *I know it's illegal,* she reasoned. *How else could we have so much money?*

Everything about her men is a mystery. They'd both told her repeatedly: "Never ask questions, for your own protection."

She strolls naked around the room. *The Francesca suite next door is nice, but this one, the Cleopatra, is my favorite. I especially like the large, jetted hot tub next to the bed.*

She adjusts the water faucets to almost scalding and pours bath oil beads into the tub. The strawberry scent fills her nostrils when she turns off the faucets at three-quarters full.

Submerging herself inch by inch into the foamy cauldron, she comes to rest with her face just above the bubbles.

She turns on the jets and looks at the dark-red welts on her wrists—a consequence of Mikhail tying her to the bedposts with her stockings.

The mark on my right wrist will fade in a day or two, but the sore on my left is raw. Nikolai will be home soon. I'll have to wear long sleeves and meet his needs somewhere dark—perhaps in the forest next to the river. He likes it there.

She remembers Mikhail's other women, and scrubs herself vigorously between her legs. *I've never confronted him. How can I?*

She just laughs—cringing inside—whenever Nikolai jokes about Mikhail's latest sexual escapades. The most onerous occur when he purchases a new strip club or casino.

"Mikhail insists that intimate knowledge of the women he employs makes them more loyal," Nikolai had told her recently. "They certainly didn't teach me that in the MBA classes I took at the University of Maryland."

She'd chuckled, pretending it didn't matter. "Perhaps that was an advanced course," she suggested.

Yvonna stepped out of the tub, and grabbed her cell phone from her purse to check her messages. She didn't answer when Nikolai called her two hours earlier while she was driving to Baltimore. *The last thing I needed before my illicit liaison with Mikhail was to talk to Nikolai.*

He'd called her again just before Mikhail left.

She smiles and closes her eyes. *Mikhail was behind me then, with my face pressed down hard into the pillow so my screams wouldn't alarm anyone. Knowing both men wanted me at the same time: The pulsing, seismic contractions almost devoured me.*

She looks at her wrists. *I'll use my adult co-ed soccer league for an injury excuse.* She chuckles. *Maybe I won't have to make love with Nikolai out in the woods after all.*

Should I have told Mikhail that Tatiana is actually his daughter? I can't tell Nikolai. He's a good father. Mikhail would be a terrible father.

She'd explained away Tatiana's silver-blue eyes as "a recessive gene from the father I never knew." *It could've been true. Mother always had men at the house.*

Nikolai had doted on Tatiana from the moment she was born. He'd never said anything about her tall stature, thin physique, or straight blonde hair—so different from the dark curls and sturdy builds of their two brown-eyed sons.

10. Robber Barons

Luxembourg City—Sunday, September 16

The Goldberg Cohen team boarded the corporate Gulfstream at Luxembourg's Findel Airport. Sean called Angela as Mark Sebastian powered up the jet.

"We're on our way, Angie. I'm sorry about our change of plans yesterday. The FAA finally gave us permission to fly home this morning. Have you heard from Rachel?"

Her voice was tense when she responded. "I'll take you to see her after I pick you up at the airport if you'd like."

"Thanks. We should be home in about eight hours."

"There's something I need to talk with you about," Angela began.

"What's wrong?"

She hesitated. "Never mind... I'll tell you tonight."

"Okay. See you soon."

That's disturbing, he thought. *It's not like her to prevaricate.*

The wait for permission to enter New York airspace had been agonizing. Sean had learned just that morning that two of his Texas Hold 'Em poker buddies who worked at the World Trade Center were missing.

The voyage across the Atlantic seemed to take longer than usual, probably because everyone was anxious to get home. Mark Sebastian approached Westchester Airport from the southeast, which allowed them to see the huge fissure in the lower Manhattan skyline.

The Gulfstream touched down on a runway flanked with planes a couple of minutes later. They taxied to Goldberg Cohen's hangar and disembarked for the terminal.

Angela embraced Sean when he entered. "It's good to have you back," she said.

"Thanks for picking me up, Angie."

Several people stared at her as they hugged. Her statuesque figure and perfectly sculpted Scandinavian cheekbones always got people's attention. At twenty-seven-years-old and the sole heir to the Cohen dynasty, she was already a fixture in New York's fashion magazines.

Sean and Angela said goodbye to Pankaj and the pilots, and she whisked him outside to her limousine.

Harold, her chauffer, placed Sean's luggage in the trunk while they slid into the back seat.

"I was hoping Rachel would join us," he said.

"I'll take you to her now, unless you want to go home first."

"I'd like to see her now, if that's OK."

Angela flipped on the microphone switch for the driver's compartment. "Please take us to Rachel."

"Yes, ma'am," Harold replied.

She flipped the switch off.

The car exited the airport and headed east toward Connecticut.

"What do you think about the Banque Lux traders?" she said.

"Jonas has a good team." Sean summarized his trip.

"I guess our human factor user interface redesign paid off," Angela said after he'd finished.

"It did. The intuitive layout made the application easy to use. Our developers did a great job. It's important we keep them together. The synergies we're getting are outstanding."

She nodded. "I'm glad we didn't follow our accountant's advice to outsource code development."

"Thanks for keeping those guys out of my hair. They don't understand that creativity and experience can't be outsourced. I'd like to give Pankaj a bonus. He's been invaluable."

"Let's talk about bonuses next week," she suggested. "I think the entire team deserves a vacation on a beach somewhere."

"I'm sure they'd appreciate it."

They looked out their windows in silence for several minutes as they passed through Greenwich, Connecticut. Normally they'd be elated after such an important achievement. Things were different now.

A gray veneer dropped across the sky as dusk approached. The streams lacing the rolling farms and meadows turned into silver ribbons. White-rail fences flying past their windows merged into a blur.

The acreages here, carefully segregated by fences and clumps of forest, grew larger, the further into Connecticut they drove.

"I felt helpless." Angela's voice cracked. "Thousands of people are still missing."

Sean put his hand over her shoulder. "It must've been awful."

Her face found his chest and she cried. "Juliette, a friend I went to school with at NYU, is still missing."

Her grief poured into him. He let go too, and they cried together.

Harold cast a concerned gaze through his mirror as he slowed the limousine and turned onto a narrow, two-lane road.

Angela blew her nose and wiped her face with some tissues. They both chuckled when she handed him the box. He did the same.

"Where are we going, Angie?"

She stared out the window. "We're almost there."

"Do you think she had a nervous breakdown? It must've been horrifying to see a plane crash into the World Trade Center."

"I don't know, Sean. She is a psychotherapist. I don't know if that makes a difference or not. Perhaps she'd recognize the symptoms if she was losing it."

They laughed, which broke the tension of their mutual meltdown.

"Maybe living outside the city is what she needs," Angela continued. She blew her nose and wiped her eyes again. "Perhaps we all need to."

The lengthening distance between the farmhouse lights revealed much larger acreages here. These were old-money estates, procured by monopoly industrial robber barons during the unregulated decades before the Great Depression.

Harold turned into a driveway flanked by brick pillars anchoring white rail fences that headed in opposite directions as far the eye could see.

Angela tapped the microphone switch. "Can you stop for a moment?"

"Yes, ma'am."

She turned off the speaker as the limo pulled to a halt. Lights gleamed through the forest fifty yards down the road.

"Why are we stopping?" Sean asked. "Is Rachel here?"

Angela took his hand. "I need to talk with you before we see her."

"What's going on?"

"Rachel didn't want me to bring you here, but as your friend, I think you need to see how things are with her. I feel conflicted, being in the middle of this, but mostly, I feel it would be awful for you to go home without knowing. I think this is the right thing to do, but I'm not sure."

Her nervousness is making my stomach churn. "Where are we?"

"This is Marshall Silverman's house. He's one of Rachel's friends, someone she met through me. She's staying with him."

"Couldn't she find someone else to stay with?"

"I asked her to stay with me, Sean, but she decided to stay here."

His mouth dropped open. "How long has this been going on?"

"I'm not sure. I introduced her to Marshall about six months ago. He meets us at nightclubs when I go out dancing with my girlfriends. He's a film student at NYU. He's forty-three. Rachel is twenty-eight, right?"

Sean's voice was shaky. "Yes… three years younger than me."

"Marshall's been in school for years, but he's never finished a degree," she said, revealing a hint of sarcasm. "He's a trust-funder who likes to have fun. School gives him an excuse to get into the city. He stays at his parents' penthouse on the Upper West Side when he takes a class."

"Are they just friends, or is she staying with him?"

Angela paused. "She's *staying* with him. He owns this estate. His great-grandfather was in the steel business in the early twentieth century."

Sean's hand found his chest. "I can't believe it."

"Do you still want to see her? We can come back later if you're not ready."

"Does she know we're here?"

"No."

The fury inside him ignited by her infidelity suddenly fanned into flames. "I need to see her now!"

Angela pressed the intercom switch. "Please proceed to the house, Harold."

"Yes, ma'am."

The limousine pulled to a stop in front of a wide staircase with brick stairs leading up to a wrap-around porch lined with twenty-foot columns. The manor looked like the regal antebellum residence of a Confederate slave-owner before the Civil War. A gibbous moon illuminated white-roofed horse stables, barns, and outbuildings behind the mansion.

Harold opened the back door and Angela stepped out. "You should wait here," she advised. "I'll convince her to come outside. It'll be impossible for her to avoid you now that we're here."

"Okay. I'll wait."

Two security guards appeared as Angela approached the stairs. They greeted her with recognition, and she proceeded to the porch.

A butler ushered her into the house.

Sean took a deep breath as he stood outside the limousine. *Remember your marital arts training,* he told himself. *You can kill him in seconds with your hands unless he has a gun… or is smart enough to stay a safe distance away.*

Then he reconsidered. *No, killing him wouldn't be right. If Silverman is her choice—I don't want her anyway… but maybe she'll return with us. Maybe Angela doesn't know the truth.*

Angela walked back down the stairs ten minutes later followed by Rachel and a longhaired man with a beard. The porch lights revealed tears on Rachel's cheeks.

"Sean, this is Marshall," Angela said.

Marshall didn't move. Neither did Sean.

The security guards, sensing danger, stepped closer.

Rachel took a hesitant step and stopped. "I'm sorry, Sean."

"Are you okay, Rachel?"

"Yes," she said. "I'm fine."

Sean stepped towards her. "Don't you want to come home?"

"No," she sniffled. "I'm staying here."

He stiffened, speechless.

"I'm sorry we interrupted you," Angela said to Rachel, "but I think Sean needed to see this for himself. I think it's only fair, don't you?"

Angela waited for an answer. None came.

Sean slid into the back seat behind Angela and closed the door.

Rachel was crying in Marshall's arms as the limousine pulled away.

Sean barely spoke during the drive to his home in Greenwich Village. He gasped when he saw the enormous gap in the skyline.

"I can't believe the World Trade Towers are gone," he lamented.

Harold pulled to a stop in front of his townhome.

"Do you want me to come in?" Angela said.

"Not tonight. Thanks, Angie… you're a great friend."

He grabbed his luggage and bounded up the narrow steps to his three-bedroom brownstone.

11. Evolution

Vienna, Virginia—December 2001

Beate had always been strong—mentally as well as physically. That changed after her family was murdered.

To prevent a complete nervous breakdown she consciously deadened her mind. She adopted the demeanor of her German grandparents, who'd acquired their dispositions as children—always taciturn, regardless of the occasion—after surviving more than thirty Allied bombing raids while living in Cologne, Germany, during World War II. Her grandfather told Beate once, after he'd drunk too much wine, that they had to search through the rubble and cart the dead to the street as the smoke cleared, and match blown-off arms and legs with bodies.

Beate kept her emotions in check—before and after Robert and Malia's funerals—by focusing on the details of death: the mortuary, the Defense Department, insurance companies, the Arlington Police and Fire Departments, the FBI, cemetery plots, casket selection, wording for the gravestones, flowers, what to wear, food catering.

She went through the motions mechanically, without anger, without grieving. She wore her mask well. She shed no tears, even when everyone around her cried their hearts out, including her elderly German grandparents, who'd flown over for the funerals.

She dug deep into her fortitude reserves to anesthetize her mind. *I have to* she kept telling herself. *I'll fall apart if I allow myself to feel my pain.*

The nightmare continued for weeks. It took over a month for the FBI and Arlington County Fire Department to release Robert and Malia's bodies. The coroner had to use dental records to identify them. The fireball inferno inside the plane had burned their bodies beyond recognition.

The news media swarmed her neighborhood looking for a story. The journalists appeared less often when the police began issuing tickets for loitering.

She finally did allow herself to grieve after the burials. She'd take a taxi to the cemetery each day and kneel at their gravesites. *I'd be next to them except for the chance fate of circumstance*, she realized as she cried.

Her parents stayed with her during those difficult days. They pleaded with Beate to come back to Colorado with them after the New Year.

"You should come home with us," her father kept repeating. "Working the land will do you good."

"*I can't,* she insisted. *I need to be with them.*"

Her neighbors, who'd kept mostly to themselves before the attack, reached out to her after her parents returned to Colorado. Some brought casseroles to her porch each day.

Most of the food remained untouched. She weighed 120 pounds before her family died. She was down to 100 by January.

I'm glad I'm finally alone she told herself after her parents left. *I can cry whenever I want to, as long as I want to, without anyone interfering.*

Her tears poured out for hours once the dam burst. No longer able to sleep in the bed she'd shared with Robert, she'd sometimes wake up in the middle of the night curled up in a fetal position on the living room floor. She'd sleep on the couch or in Malia's bed with her nose nuzzled into the pillow, grasping for a scent of her daughter.

Director Matthews gave her a leave of absence from the CIA immediately after the attack. Many of her coworkers and people she'd never met at the Agency sent her condolence letters. Sometimes they'd add a note saying they were doing everything they could to track down the terrorists behind the attacks.

I know they will, she thought indifferently, *but the idea of revenge seems empty. Retribution will never bring my family back.*

She kept her curtains drawn, remaining isolated from the world, except for her daily sojourn to the cemetery. The weeks crept by. The only time she'd answer her door was when the police came to check on her.

Parishioners from the local Catholic, Methodist and Lutheran churches and the Hebrew synagogue took turns coordinating food deliveries, bringing casseroles, milk and other necessities to her porch each day. Men and boys in the neighborhood cleared her driveway and sidewalks when the snows came. The mail carrier bundled her mail and left it inside her screen door. The Vienna police department patrolled constantly, pressuring the occasional reporter or photographer to move along or face arrest for loitering.

She began leaving her neighbor's washed casserole dishes on the porch with a note taped inside when spring arrived:

I deeply appreciate the kindness you've shown me during this difficult time. I know Robert and Malia would thank you too, if they could be here.

Sincerely,

Beate Nicholson

Sometimes she'd listen to music she and Robert had shared. She'd play Sade's *"No Ordinary Love,"* and Sting's *"Fragile,"* crying and hugging his pillow.

She gained a deep appreciation for Beethoven's *"Late Quartets"*—Robert's favorites, written when the composer was almost deaf—and Mozart's *"Requiem."*

She was still wearing her flannel pajamas, her usual apparel when not visiting the cemetery, when Director Mathews called her one afternoon in late March.

"Hello," she answered plaintively.

"Hello, Beate. I wanted to give you a project update. The work on your new data analytics warehouse is going very well. We're working around the clock. It's full steam ahead."

"I'm glad, sir," she responded flatly.

"The possibilities, now that we understand the breadth of your vision, will greatly enhance our intelligence-analysis capabilities," he told her. "We'll be able to identify even more threats once we pull in data from Europe, Asia, and the Middle East. Congress is talking about making the Office of Homeland Security a permanent Cabinet post."

"Great," she responded sarcastically. "Just what we need… another government bureaucracy."

He ignored her cynicism. "We could really use your help."

"I'm glad you called, sir," she replied. "I've been meaning to send you my resignation letter. I know the Agency can't afford to have an absentee manager."

He paused. "Take more time, Beate. There's no need for you to resign."

"I'll mail you my letter tomorrow, sir."

"You can send it if you'd like, but I'll just keep it in my drawer. Everyone realizes the value of your architecture now. You're the best person to lead the project."

"Talk to Michael Chen," she advised. "He'll know what to do."

"Are you sure?"

"Yes, I'm sure," she answered irritably. "His team develops the search algorithms."

I need to end the call before I lose it, she told herself.

"We're all really sorry about what happened to your family," he said sympathetically.

"Yeah... me too." She hung up.

* * *

Director Matthews called Colonel Nicholson after his conversation with Beate. Matthews had known her father since he'd flown missions for him at Ramstein Air Base in Germany, before he joined the CIA.

"Beate told me she's planning to resign, sir," Matthews said. "I hope she changes her mind."

Colonel Nicholson paused. "I'm surprised. I know she loves her job."

"She seems angry, and depressed," Matthews continued. "Do you think she's suicidal?"

"Maybe anger is a good sign," the colonel said. "Perhaps she's entering the next stage of the grieving process. What do you think?"

"That sounds reasonable, sir."

"I'll fly out to Virginia tomorrow to check on her. Thanks for letting me know."

Colonel Nicholson called Beate after he made his travel arrangements. "I'm coming to see you tomorrow."

He gave her the details for his flight into Dulles.

"No, Dad. I can't go there again." she protested.

I know she'll pick me up, he contemplated, *if I don't give her a choice. It's time for her to face her demons.*

A tempestuous blizzard a few days after he arrived broke Beate's pattern of daily visits to the cemetery. They watched the storm throttling the streets through her living room window.

"Daisy is much happier when someone rides her," he said. "Don't you miss her?"

"Yes," she acknowledged. "I do."

"A hundred and twenty acres is a lot of chili to plant. We could really use your help."

Denver, Colorado

Beate gripped her armrests during the turbulent white-knuckled descent into Denver International Airport two days later. Eight inches of snow had fallen earlier that day. The pilot landed the vacillating plane on the de-iced runway without a hitch.

The next day she rode her horse, Daisy, to some hills near her parents farm in Brighton; a ritual she continued every evening.

She spotted a disturbing article in the newspaper a week later:

American Airlines Flight 77, flying out of Washington Dulles to Los Angeles, was the third aircraft hijacked on September 11, 2001. The flight crashed into the western façade of the Pentagon at 9:37 a.m., Eastern Time. Investigators have determined that five hijackers broke into the cockpit that day. After killing the pilots, they herded the passengers to the rear of the aircraft. Several passengers were able to use the airline's on-board GTE air phones to make calls to family members and the police. However, no one could react quickly enough to stop the crash.

She tossed the newspaper into the fireplace and watched it burn.

They'd tilled the land and sowed a new chili crop by the end of April. They celebrated the night they finished with green chili-chicken enchiladas and margaritas.

Beate was in a talkative mood after the libations.

"I'm glad you dragged me back here, Dad. Working the soil has been good therapy. Driving tractors with cultivators, chisel ploughs and a seed drill has been fun. I've even garnered a taste for some of your country music."

Her parents laughed.

"Your mother got me into that," he said.

Her mother, Alice, rose from her chair and hugged Beate from behind. "It's so nice to have you home, dear."

Beate stared at the logs burning in the fireplace that night. *I think I'll stay for a while*, she decided. *There's nothing left for me in DC.*

A vision of Robert and Malia lying cold decomposing in their graves choked her heart. She excused herself and went to her room to cry.

She trained hard with her father during May for the Bolder Boulder—an annual Memorial Day 10k race they'd run in several times when she attended the University of Colorado. She passed him near the finish line beating him by four seconds.

"That won't happen next year," he said afterward, as they sipped beers at the Boulder Brewery.

Beate laughed. "You're right—next year I'll beat you by at least a minute."

"In your dreams," he chortled. "There's no way that's going to happen."

The stress-relieving endorphins from exercise helped her sleep. She continued her rigorous training regimen the rest of the summer.

She rode Daisy with the family dog—a gray Weimaraner named Penelope—to a nearby canyon at dusk every evening. Sometimes she'd walk beside her horse holding the reins, drinking in the sunset.

The clouds over the horizon presented a different show each evening: odd-shaped thespians garbed in white, adorning themselves with orange-and-red cloaks below a pale blue sky.

Her tears flowed when they needed to. They came less often as the summer progressed.

Physical labor restored her spirit, and her mother's cooking restored her body. By the end of August, she'd regained most of the weight she'd lost during the miserable winter.

She'd stare at the logs in the fireplace every night, watching the yellow flames burn down to ash. Time passed quickly as she meditated on the bloodshot embers—the logs popping and spitting as they dissolved into ribbons of gray smoke.

They harvested a bountiful chili crop in September. She continued to ride Daisy to the canyon each evening as the cooler weather set in.

I'm not sure I'll ever return to DC, she told herself in early October. *I should resign, and put the house on the market.*

Penelope liked to run ahead of her to the nearby canyon when she was out riding.

Beate spurred Daisy to a gallop when she heard the distinct yelping of coyotes.

Five bushy-tail predators were attacking Penelope when she entered the canyon. Penelope howled as the beasts tore away her fur. One coyote had its teeth firmly affixed to her throat.

Beate jumped down from the saddle and yelled. A coyote lunged at her snarling with bared teeth, as the other predators continued their attack. They'd tasted blood, and weren't about to retreat from their meal.

Beate pulled her father's revolver from its holster. She always carried the gun when she rode in case she came across rattlesnakes.

She took aim with both hands and squeezed the trigger. The snarling beast at her feet blew backward in a puff of fur.

Her next shot launched the coyote gnawing Penelope's neck five feet in the air. She downed two more in quick succession.

The last varmint disappeared into a fissure in the karstic walls.

Beate holstered the gun and ran to Penelope.

She tried to comfort her as she placed her bleeding body across the saddle and secured her with a rope so she wouldn't fall.

Her parents pulled up in their red pickup truck as she guided Daisy by the reigns out of the canyon.

"Are you all right?" Anthony yelled.

"Look what the coyotes did!" she exclaimed.

"She doesn't look good," he said.

He removed the ropes, carried Penelope to the back of the truck, and placed her on a sleeping bag.

Her mother opened a first aid kit and cleaned her bleeding neck wound. Most of the fur was completely missing from one of her rear legs. A front leg was broken. The others had teeth marks. Penelope whined and licked Beate's hand as Alice bandaged the lacerations.

"It's my fault," Beate said. "I wasn't watching her closely enough."

"I heard shots," Anthony said. "Was that you?"

"I got four of them," she responded, "but one got away."

"Those coyotes are good hunters," Anthony said. "Penelope is slowing down a bit in her old age. They probably thought she'd be an easy meal. I'm glad you were here to save her."

"This wouldn't have happened if I'd been more attentive," Beate lamented, anger seeping through her voice.

"I'll stay in the back while you drive to the vet in Brighton," Alice said. "We'd better hurry. I don't think she has much time."

Tears flowed from Beate's eyes. They came much easier these days. "I'm sorry."

"Don't be so hard on yourself," Anthony said. "It wasn't your fault." He started the truck. "We'll see you at home in a while."

They returned several hours later. Penelope was bandaged, and heavily sedated. She hardly moved when Anthony placed her on a sleeping bag in front of the fireplace.

"The vet told us she'll survive," he said. "Unfortunately, he had to amputate one of her legs."

Beate stayed with Penelope's the rest of the night, nursing her with pain medication mixed in a water bottle whenever she moaned.

Her father entered the living room at 5:30 a.m. "You should get some sleep," he said. "I'll take over now. She made it through the night, which means she'll probably live."

Beate churned her jaw. "I need to go out."

"Where are you going?"

"Out," she replied irritably.

A light snow had begun during the night. She dressed in long underwear, waterproof fleece, hiking boots and a ski jacket with a hood, and slung her father's M1 Garand semi-automatic rifle over her shoulder. Anthony acknowledged her with a nod as she exited the farmhouse.

Light snowflakes drifted around her as she walked to the canyon.

I haven't fired a weapon in years, she realized, *except the revolver last night. Can I still shoot? The last Marine marksmanship tournament I won at Twentynine Palms was several years… and another lifetime ago.*

I like the Garand. Weighing just ten pounds and accurate to within four inches at four hundred meters, the magazine holds eight, 30.06 cartridges—perfect for hunting. I won several marksmanship tournaments with it as a teenager. Dad was very proud of me when I beat the boys.

She crouched down when she arrived at the mouth of the canyon. Remaining downwind, she watched the grass sway. Gossamer flakes spun slow circles as she reconnoitered.

Compensate the telescopic sight when you reach that perch in the canyon wall, she told herself.

She progressed stealthily to the scene of the attack. The coyote carcasses were now the domain of a large murder of black crows. They offered unwelcome cries as she approached. Several circled overhead while the intrepid feasted, watching her warily with a cocked eye.

Beate saw fresh coyote paw marks in the snow. *Good.*

She climbed a rock-strewn ravine high enough to observe the entire canyon floor, and positioned herself cross-legged in an improvised hunting blind between two large rocks. She placed the barrel of her rifle on a makeshift tripod and sighted her scope, compensating for the effects of gravity, altitude, and wind.

The snow ended.

Dawn broke above the plains, painting the clouds silver-gray.

The crows gnawed on the coyote carcasses, oblivious to her presence.

She stilled her breath and centered her scope when the coyote appeared.

The coyote paced and circled, annoying the squawking crows. It ripped a chunk of meat from one of the carcasses and sat down to eat, lying cross-legged in the snow.

Keep your breath smooth when you pull the trigger, she coached herself. *Just as Dad taught you. The shot should always come as a surprise.*

The slug punched the coyote into a pile of fur.

Echoes from the blast boomed through the canyon.

The murder of crows took flight soaring as one to the sky as the reverberations rolled away.

I can still shoot.

She cleaned and packed the Garand in its case, and scurried down the ravine.

Breakfast was waiting when she returned home. She said nothing as she devoured her food.

She lay down next to Penelope that night, studying the burning logs: yellow flames raging to orange-and-red cinders, melting to white-gray piles of ash. Her focus cleared as the smoke faded away. *Ashes to ashes, dust to dust.*

Yes, I'll return to Washington, she decided. *Yes, I'll remain with the CIA… but no, I won't be an IT geek slaving away in front of a computer. Clandestine operations will be my future. I'm going to do the hunting from now on.*

New York City

Sean McGowan and his attorney, Andrew Greenstein, were taking advantage of the pleasant fall weather with a Sunday afternoon game of chess at one of the stationary marble tables in Washington Square Park. Their eyes strayed to three scantily clad NYU college coeds playing Frisbee.

Sean chuckled. "I bet they have no idea they're running around on top of dead bodies. The city buried twenty thousand vagrants and criminals here in the 1800s when this was a potter's grave."

Andrew laughed. "Shall I tell them?"

"Only if you want to scare them away."

Sean perused the divorce decree Andrew had given him earlier. "At least Rachel doesn't want me to pay her for the privilege of shacking up with someone."

Andrew moved his black bishop diagonally across the table. "You're lucky," he said. "She might get alimony if you went to trial. Some judges believe wealth redistribution is their sacred mission, regardless of the reason for the divorce."

"So if I sign this—it's over?" Sean asked.

"That's right," Andrew affirmed. "She doesn't want anything."

Sean signed his name below Rachel's on the last page.

He moved a white knight, forking Andrew's black king and rook. "Check."

Andrew stroked his chin. "Hmmm… I didn't see that coming."

"At least she has some integrity," Sean said. "Tell her attorney I wish her all the best."

"It's too bad she doesn't want to say goodbye to you herself. Perhaps she feels guilty."

Sean handed Andrew the document. "This is a hell of a way to end a four-year marriage. Let's get out of here. I think a good Scotch is in order."

Andrew stood up. "I think you're right."

Sean was nursing a hangover when he arrived at Goldberg Cohen's trading floor at 7:30 a.m. the next morning—late for him. Everyone was standing around a large table.

He noticed the words "Congratulations, Sean" on the top of a cake as he approached. A chef next to the table was doling out scrambled eggs, bagels, and green chili—his favorite breakfast.

Forty people turned to watch his reaction.

Angela smiled. "You're running a bit late this morning."

Sean furrowed his forehead. *Divorce isn't something to celebrate.* "What's going on?"

"Andrew told me you're a single man again—or at least you will be after he files the paperwork this morning."

Sean nodded without smiling.

"But today's celebration isn't about that; it's about your promotion to partner."

Everyone applauded. Angela planted two euro-style air kisses on his cheeks.

David Cohen shook his hand. "Congratulations, Sean."

"Thank you, sir."

David looked around the room with his arms raised. The room quieted.

He addressed his employees. "Sean's quantitative trading models have catapulted us into the twenty-first century."

He turned to Sean. "You're also the first engineer to become a partner. You're blazing trails in many directions."

"I wouldn't have been able to do this without everyone's support," Sean said. "Angela deserves most of the credit though. I was her Pygmalion project when I came here from Colorado... just a nerdy engineer with a pocket protector."

Everyone laughed.

David raised his hands again to quiet the crowd. "I'd like to take a moment to make an announcement while we're here together, before rumors start flying around—rumors that aren't true."

Everyone became attentive.

"As you already know, we're now the most profitable private banking firm in the world. That, plus our international branches in Luxembourg, Dubai, London, Dublin, Hong Kong, and Singapore, has made us a desirable acquisition target. I'm bringing this up because a Swiss banking conglomerate is taking a run at us. I want you all to know that we aren't for sale. I'd know it if we were."

A murmur ebbed through the room.

"I also want to reiterate that we're not going to trade securities tied to collateralized debt obligations. I know many of our competitors are slicing and dicing all kinds of CDO's into securities to create derivatives. CDO's are time bombs destined to collapse. The ripple effects across the financial markets will be impossible to predict. We're not touching them."

Some of the traders whispered to each other. CDO's were becoming the most lucrative game on Wall Street now that the politicians had gutted the rating agencies. Many banks were feeding at the trough, but David Cohen wouldn't let them participate.

"So again, we're not for sale. Please tell your manager if anyone approaches you seeking information. Our Swiss suitor is known to get pretty nasty when someone spurns their marriage proposals."

Angela stepped forward. "Thanks, Dad. Now let's get back to the real reason for today's celebration."

She turned to Sean. "I don't recall you ever wearing a pocket protector."

The room erupted with laughter.

Sean smiled. "Believe it or not, I did have one of those in college. It was a fashion statement for engineers. Perhaps you should wear one during your next magazine interview."

She chuckled. "Perhaps I will. Seriously, though, we're pleased and grateful for all you've done. We've been planning to make you a partner for over a year, but with everything else going on, we decided to wait."

He smiled at Angela. *Thank you my dear*, he commended silently. *You probably saved me millions in alimony and months of brain damage by waiting. Rachel's pit-bull attorney would've chewed my arm off to gnaw into the firm's tax records if I'd been a partner.*

"I hope you still like the green chili," she said as he ladled it on his eggs.

He took a bite. "I love it. Where'd you get this? It's delicious."

"I had it flown in from Hatch, New Mexico. That's your favorite, right?"

He nodded. "That's very special, Angela."

Sean looked around at his co-workers. "Hatch is north of Las Cruces, where I went to college at New Mexico State. Green chili is the best cure I know of for a hangover."

Everyone filled their plates and hustled back to their desks.

"I have something to show you," Angela told him when he'd finished eating.

Sean followed her to her corner office, which was now empty.

"This is your new office," she said. "I moved upstairs, next to Father."

Sean looked out across the skyscrapers to the Statue of Liberty reflecting red-gold in morning light. "Wow," he said. "Thank you. I've always loved the view from here."

She moved next to him at the window. The skyline to their left still brandished the wound where the twin towers had once stood like sentinels, guarding the epicenter of world capitalism.

"I bought you some new furniture," she said. "I know you like to sleep here when you have a project, so I ordered a couch with a comfortable fold-out bed. Amy, your new office administrator, will coordinate the movers when you're ready."

"That was nice of you. I'm sure it'll be perfect. Thanks."

"There's a partner meeting this evening to discuss the hostile takeover. Our Swiss suitor won't take 'No' for an answer."

"I'm sure your father told them we aren't for sale. What else do they need to know?"

"It's complicated," she said. "Our suitor has politicians in his pocket down in DC. They're putting pressure on us from all sides."

"That sounds illegal."

"It is, but people with friends in high places often get away with things."

"I have a fourth-degree black belt in tae kwon do if you need my help," he offered.

She laughed. "I'll let you know."

Sean's gaze fell to a commuter ferry heading south on the Hudson.

"There's something I need you to take care of," she said.

"What's that?"

"Two of our traders—your traders, now that you're their manager—have been synthesizing CDO swaps. Have you ever fired anyone?"

She passed him a report with the transactions and names of the culprits underlined in red.

"I'll take care of it," he said.

"Our benefits specialist, Sally Matheson, will attend the dismissal meetings with you. I want them out of here this morning."

"No problem."

Angela stepped to the doorway and turned. "By the way, we set aside your portion of last year's partnership payout. It's earning interest in an escrow account."

Sean's eyebrows rose. "Really… you're making this retroactive? That's very kind of you. How much is it?"

Her eyes flashed affectionately. "Father insisted. You're a five-percent owner now. Your portion is sixteen point two million. We had a good year… a lot of which had to do with you."

Angela winked as she turned and walked away.

He stared out at Lady Liberty as he dialed Emma in Luxembourg. *We'll celebrate in style when she flies over for the weekend.*

12. Moonbeam

Zurich, Switzerland—November 2005

Rahim's train pulled into the Zurich *Hauptbahnhof*—two hours late due to snow delays. He surveyed the ashen sky as he exited the station. Large bulbous flakes swirled around him like angry wasps disturbed from their nest. A phalanx of taxis lining the street spewed white exhaust clouds that floated ten feet before vaporizing.

He stopped to observe the drivers huddled comfortably inside. *No*, he decided, *the walk will do me good.*

He plodded through the heavy snow to the Bahnhoquai and continued to his hotel near the Paradeplatz.

The blizzard worsened after he checked in, with whiteout conditions engulfing the street. *It's not worth the hassle to go out for a meal*, he told himself as he looked out his hotel room window.

He locked the student papers he'd brought with him in the room safe, said his prayers, and burrowed himself beneath the blankets.

The phone whined two double beeps at 4:30 a.m.

He jolted upright. The phone droned again.

He turned on the lamp next to his bed, navigated to the stopwatch application on his cell phone, and started the timer at the next double beeps. He remembered he was in the German-speaking region of Switzerland as he picked up the receiver.

"*Gutenmorgen.*"

The line was silent. The call ended precisely forty seconds later.

He put the phone back in its cradle.

Measuring the length of a call was a way to convey information with silence, in case someone was eavesdropping. *Abdul taught us that in Hamburg. Dividing by ten, I now know that I'll find the one-time pad, the OTP, at the number-four drop site.*

He walked his mind through the steps of his mission: *Retrieve the one-time pad with the cryptography cypher, decipher the coded messages embedded in the student papers, and spend the rest of the day travelling to eight different banks executing the trades.*

He smiled to himself. *I'm proud to be a soldier, using the same tools as the enemy.*

Abdul always spoke fondly about the training he'd received from his CIA case officer. "The CIA recruited me to fight with the Mujahideen against the Russians in Afghanistan," he'd told Rahim's cell in Hamburg. "I know their tricks. Know thine enemy by keeping them close, and then turn their weapons upon them."

Rahim gulped his coffee down as he looked out the window. *I wonder what calamity will befall the financial markets this time. Will it be an unexpected change in the price of oil, or something more sinister?*

This mission is probably about oil, he guessed, *since there's an OPEC meeting under way in Vienna.*

Rahim inserted a small hair above the upper hinge on the outside of his hotel room door and placed a *Do Not Disturb* sign on the handle. *I'll know someone was in my room if the hair is missing when I return.*

He trotted down the rear stairs and exited to the street at 5:30 a.m.

The snowstorm had ended, leaving the pristine air still and clear. Streetlights illuminated snow-laden sidewalks unadulterated by footsteps.

It'll be easy to spot someone following me when I backtrack.

His boot crunches echoed between the buildings. The city seemed deserted, except for a shopkeeper unloading a vegetable truck and a baker placing strudel in a pastry shop window.

The number-four drop site—the Zurich Weinplatz Tub Man Fountain—is vintage Abdul, he contemplated. *Awaken me at 4:30 a.m. after he'd partied all night at some plush Viennese wine bar to send me to a fountain the Swiss used centuries ago as a wine press. He's teasing me because I don't drink.*

Rahim stopped abruptly every hundred feet to listen and look around, making sure the only footsteps echoing off the buildings were his own.

Dawn had colored the sky gray by the time he approached the Weinplatz. He scanned the plaza with binoculars searching for the telltale sign designating the drop site: A chalk mark on the side of a bench.

There it is.

He circled the wine tub, brushed snow from the designated park bench, and sat down. A lack of boot prints in the snow confirmed: *The cutout agent must have delivered the one-time pad the previous day.*

His gloved hand found the small plastic bag beneath the seat. He pulled the package from the tape, stuffed it inside his coat, and erased the chalk mark with his glove—a signal to the cutout that he'd picked up the delivery.

Stepping in his own boot imprints, he backtracked to his hotel keeping a sharp eye on the streets to make sure no one was following him.

He locked his hotel room door and removed the student papers from the safe.

He'd asked Abdul once, "Who sends the messages?"

"It's not me," Abdul had responded angrily. "The instructions come from above. Don't ask me again. Compartmentalization is essential. The less you know, the more likely you'll live. Assiduous interrogators use many methods to extract the truth—torture, coercion, and drugs are but a few. Once they get what they want, your life will be worthless."

Rahim arranged the numbers in the first student math paper into a five-digit grouping.

MSG: 26978 45682 70408 44893 34444 44444

He then copied the one-time pad deciphering code beneath the numbers:

MSG: 26978 45682 70408 44893 34444 44444
OTP: 24765 93659 55146 03380 18202 02020

After subtracting the OTP numbers from the message using non-carrying math rules, he derived the Result (RES):

MSG: 26978 45682 70408 44893 34444 44444
OTP: 24765 93659 55146 03380 18202 02020

RES: 02212 52023 15262 41513 16242 42424

The last step in the decoding process was to split these numbers into pairs, and map them to letters of the English alphabet. This operation yielded the Instructions (INS):

RES: 02 21 25 20 23 15 26 24 15 13 16 24 24 24 24
INS: B U Y   T W O   Z X O M   P X X X X

The Z was shorthand for zero, and XOM was the stock symbol for Exxon Oil. Orders were always in thousands, so the resulting instruction was thus: Buy twenty thousand Exxon Mobil Oil puts.

The next instruction in the student paper specified the strike price, expiration date and sell stop. *The trade will produce a hefty profit if the value of Exxon Mobil stock drops sometime during the next few days.*

He decoded and documented similar orders for several other energy companies on a small piece of saliva-dissolvable paper, and flushed the one-time pad down the toilet when he finished.

The price of energy stocks will need to drop for the trades to succeed. I don't know how that would happen. That's someone else's business, he reminded himself.

He pulled the longhaired wig disguise he used during his missions over his hair, glued a mustache above his lip, and checked out of his hotel.

His first two banks were near the train station. He entered just after they opened, made his trades, and hustled to the *Hauptbahnhof.* He spent the rest of the day travelling to banks in Liechtenstein, Basel, Bern, and Luxembourg to execute the same trades.

He was exhausted when he arrived for his final trades of the day at Banque Lux.

Rahim placed his palm on the computer screen to verify his identity. The guard nodded his approval, and Rahim entered the private trading floor.

* * *

Emma Dumont, now thirty-years-old, and Sean, now thirty-five, became very close when they developed GC's commodity-trading models together. It paid off. Their algorithms, fed by years of historical trading statistics and real-time oil and gas reserve data, produced extremely accurate forecasting models.

Her achievements brought her a promotion to floor manager when Jonas moved upstairs to become the vice-president of the bank.

She'd been following the business channels closely that afternoon. OPEC was meeting in Vienna. *A change in production quotas always affects oil prices. A politically motivated oil embargo is also a possibility.*

I need to be ready for anything, she told herself.

Leaning back in her chair, she decided on a whim to create a report showing their clients' current backlog of energy-related orders. Nothing looked out of the ordinary during her first couple of queries. Then something caught her eye.

She sat up straight. A client had just placed several huge option orders. *They'll pay off handsomely if the price of oil drops.* The client, Michel Bowen, was placing his orders from a terminal *inside* the bank.

That's weird, she realized. *Most clients managing their own accounts use our secure Internet trading application. I'd like to meet this Mr. Bowen. Anyone putting hundreds of millions on the line based on a hunch must be an interesting person.*

She took the elevator to the private client lobby, badged in through security, and sat down on a leather couch on the trading floor.

A short man with light olive skin, long dark hair and a mustache emerged from a trading room a moment later. He didn't notice Emma as he walked to the elevators.

"Mr. Bowen?" she called out.

He pushed the up arrow.

She rose from the couch and moved next to him. "Mr. Michel Bowen?"

He looked at her with a blank stare. A cloak of surprise covered his face. "*Bonjour, mademoiselle.* How may I help you?"

"Do you have some time to talk, *Monsieur* Bowen?"

His mouth hollowed. "I don't have time today."

The elevator doors slid open and they entered. Bowen stared at his reflection in the stainless steel doors as they vaulted to the street-level lobby.

She extended her hand as they passed the security guards. "Thank you for doing business with us, *Monsieur* Bowen."

He returned her handshake.

She ignored his disfigured hand when she handed him her business card: *Emma Dumont, Director of Commodity Trading.* "Please call me the next time you're here, *Monsieur* Bowen. We have many services you may be interested in."

His stare swerved to her face. "Thank you, *Mademoiselle* Dumont. I will."

An awkward feeling grabbed her as he darted through the exit. *He seemed reticent. Maybe his missing finger and the scars on his hand and neck embarrass him.*

She returned to her desk and configured an alert that would pop up on her screen the next time Bowen logged in. Then she scribbled a note to herself in her notebook: *Michel Bowen—OPEC connection? Whale trader follow-up next week.*

The clock indicated the markets had just closed.

It's time to close up shop and go home, she decided. *I can't wait for Sean's call. We're making our honeymoon vacation plans tonight.*

* * *

Rahim's heart pounded beneath his chest as he scurried around the streets outside the bank. *How did I screw up* he asked himself? *I can't tell Abdul. It isn't worth the beating, drowning, or other humiliation I'll have to endure.*

He wracked his brain for a plan. *She's beautiful… those enchanting, almond-brown eyes, and luscious curves of hers. Perhaps she likes me.*

No. Women like her are never interested in someone like me, and even if she was—I'm impotent!

He entered a restaurant near the bank and sat down next to the window.

Emma emerged an hour later and hailed a taxi.

He left money on the table and sprinted outside.

"Please follow that car," he said to his taxi driver.

The man looked at him suspiciously. "Why?"

"I want to see where my girlfriend's going. She hasn't been returning my calls."

Emma's taxi stopped in front of a high-end residential condominium. Rahim passed the driver his fare plus a twenty-euro tip.

"Thank you," he said, trying to sound relieved. "I live here. She must be coming to see me."

Rahim crossed the street to observe. He spotted a security guard at a desk and two cameras monitoring the entrance lobby.

A light appeared behind a curtained window on the fourth floor. Emma emerged on the balcony with her phone at her ear.

That's when he formulated his plan.

* * *

Emma was sitting at her desk a week later when Michel Bowen's alert popped up on her screen. She examined his trades.

He made a fortune when OPEC announced they'd be increasing oil production to "help" the world economy, she observed.

The anticipated oil glut caused energy prices to plummet, which made his put options skyrocket.

He has inside information! Now he's wiring his gains to an offsite account at another bank.

Her inquisitiveness propelled her to the elevators.

Bowen was sitting on the couch when she arrived.

She extended her hand. "*Bonjour, Monsieur* Bowen."

He stood up. "*Bonjour,* Emma—that's right, isn't it? How are you today?"

"I'm fine. How are you?"

"I'm well," he replied. "How may I help you?"

I didn't think about what I would say before I got here, she realized.

"Would you like some tea?" She drew her best smile. "You can't turn a girl down twice, can you?"

"I'm afraid I'm in a rush today. Shall I call you before my next visit? That way, we'll have plenty of time to talk."

"That would be nice."

He bowed as he grasped her fingers. "Until next time."

"I'm looking forward to it."

She called Sean when she returned to her desk. *I want to tell him about the whale I found and wish him luck before his monthly quantitative analyst charity poker tournament.*

Amy, his assistant, said he'd already left for the day.

Emma didn't leave a message.

* * *

Rahim brooded as the waiter removed his dishes from the table. She blew it, he concluded. I gave her a chance. She's watching me. I have no choice. I have to take her out.

He pulled a small backpack he'd brought with him over his shoulders and left the restaurant.

He walked around the streets for several hours trying to calm his nerves before he arrived at her building.

A misty rain had fallen earlier in the evening. Most of the clouds had retreated now, leaving the moon bright and full.

He pulled on mountain-climbing shoes and gloves, and began his ascent to her fourth-floor balcony, by shinnying up a six-inch wide metal gutter spout that descended vertically from the roof.

A glob of ice broke off in his hand thirty feet up and crashed to the sidewalk. He hugged the gutter waiting to see if anyone would come. No one did.

He stretched his foot to the top of her balcony when he reached the fourth floor and pushed himself over.

Crouching down so passers-by couldn't see him; he inserted a six-inch stiletto knife into a sheath on his belt and stuck a wire garrote in his back pocket.

Her sliding door was unlocked. *Good. I won't have to use the glasscutters.*

He stepped inside and slid the door closed. A kitchen appeared to his left as his eyesight adjusted. A hallway to his right led to bedrooms.

Moonlight creeping through her clerestory windows guided his steps. He passed a bathroom and an office. The next door was slightly ajar.

He placed his ear to the opening and strained for a sound. *Nothing.*

Adrenaline gushing through his veins pulsed like tympani drums in his ears. He tried to slow his breathing but couldn't.

He pushed the door an inch. *Nothing.* He pushed it again.

His heart stopped. An errant ray of moonlight, a moonbeam, streaming through a crack above her curtains was illuminating her large, round breasts.

She's a goddess—like Rodin's statue of Adele, he marveled.

His hand found the US Marine standard-issue stiletto. He pulled it from its sheath and took a step, and then another, moving hypnotically to the side of her bed.

Seconds became minutes. He watched the moonbeam creep from her breasts to her perfectly chiseled shoulder. *Adele Abruzzezzi, Auguste Rodin's lover, the rapturous model he uses in his sculptures, couldn't compare to Emma,* he decreed.

Her breasts heaved gently, rising and falling with each breath.

The tingle shocked him. *It's getting hard—down there!*

This is a mistake. How can I kill her? Maybe she does like me. Perhaps she doesn't know about my business with Abdul. Maybe I can have her.

He watched himself as if from above: The blade of his stiletto pointing down at the cleft between her breasts. A shudder passed over him.

He stepped back. The floor popped.

She stirred, and rolled over sideways, her breasts no longer visible.

He almost peed. His panicked gasps came in stumbles. He imagined himself a statue—her lover—protecting her.

The sigh of her slumber returned.

He expelled a breath. Stepping carefully, he reached the door.

He turned for one more gaze. *Goodbye, my angel. You will live. There must be another way. Perhaps I can hide from Abdul… run away.*

The side of her face radiated blue-gray in the moonlight. He turned to the hallway.

The tip of his knife caught the doorframe knocking it from his hand. The clanging blade bouncing across the wooden floor jolted the silence.

Rahim dropped to his knees searching frantically with his hands.

"Who's there?"

She turned on the lamp next to her bed.

Rahim grabbed the knife and lunged at her pointing the tip at her eye.

"Eek!" she screamed.

His gloved hand covered her mouth. "Keep quiet!"

The knife found her throat. "I'll kill you if you scream."

Her face paled. She pulled the sheet up over her breasts.

"Will you stay quiet if I remove my hand?" he whispered. "I'll kill you if you don't."

She nodded.

He released his grip.

Her body began to tremble.

"Lie down... on your back."

She slithered lower.

What do I do now he asked himself?

He yanked the sheet away.

Her left arm darted across her breasts as her right hand shielded her auburn-red crotch.

She's more beautiful than Adele is. The stir erupted again. *I'm alive... down there*!

"Mr. Bowen? Is that you?"

He wasn't wearing his longhaired wig and mustache disguise.

"Yes, it's me."

She crouched forward still hiding herself. "Why are you here?"

"Lie down."

She reclined backwards. Her trembling body made the bed quiver.

Rahim sliced two long strips from the sheet with his blade. "Turn over, onto your stomach."

She shielded her butt with her hands as she rolled over.

Cries erupted into her pillow as he bound her wrists behind her back.

Her gaze followed him in U-shaped circles as he paced around the bed.

He removed a glove.

Her cries grew louder when he traced her backbone with his fingertips.

"Don't do this... please... Mr. Bowen."

"Be quiet."

Her chattering teeth and fearful cries crushed his arousal. *There's nothing down there now, even with a beautiful woman like this.*

He pulled his glove back on and tied a blindfold across her eyes.

"Get up... on your knees."

She shivered with fear as she scooted backwards into a kneeling position.

"Please don't hurt me," she petitioned between whimpers. "I won't tell anyone if you leave now."

He studied the pallor of her skin, her rounded curves, every inch of her—every crevice, every muscle. *Nothing. Dead. Flaccid.*

His knife found the sheath. He pulled the garrote from his back pocket.

She shouldn't have stalked me, he reasoned with himself. *She's lucky. Her journey will be over soon.*

He looped the wire around her throat and yanked.

She lurched sideways, ramming at him with her shoulder.

He held on tightly as she fell to the floor.

He rammed his knee into the small of her back and wrenched the handles tighter. Blood spewed from her mouth spraying the floor and walls.

Her fight grew weak after two minutes, and she went limp.

A groan escaped her throat when Rahim released his grip. He wrenched the bloody wire from the fissure in her throat and pulled off her blindfold.

Her body was grotesquely misaligned. A gruesome death grip consumed her face as her eyes stared out trancelike, barren, like a vacuous desert devoid of sustenance.

He washed the garrote in her bathroom sink and shoved it into his backpack. The stench of death clung to the air when he turned out the light. The moonbeam was gone.

He stepped carefully through the living room, exited onto the patio deck, and slid down the slick drainpipe to the sidewalk.

Walking in shadows, he threaded his way through the city to the railway station. He boarded the first departure for Paris a few hours later.

His journey to the *Gare de l' Est* took two hours. He rode a taxi to the *Avenue des Champs-Élysées* Marriott and checked into a penthouse suite using the name Rahim Delacroix.

His top-floor window looked out at the *Arc de Triomphe*. The majestic war monument commissioned by Napoleon shimmered with a golden hue in the morning sun.

The left window of his penthouse suite looked down upon the *Boulevard Champs-Élysées*. A brochure in the room said the street was named for the

Elysian Fields in Greek mythology—an abode for the blessed in the afterlife, reserved for righteous and heroic mortals chosen by the gods.

Please Allah; forgive me my sins on Judgment Day.

Unable to sleep, he exited the hotel and hailed a taxi to the *Musée Rodin*.

He strolled around listlessly for hours in the garden museum, bouncing between Auguste Rodin's six-meter high Gates of Hell door sculpture and the Eternal Spring, the statue of his imaginary lover: Adele—procreated for eternity in all her magnificence… in an erotic kiss with her lover.

New York City

Sean ignored the first two calls. He'd gotten to bed at 6:00 a.m. after making the final table at the Texas Hold 'Em poker tournament. He'd eventually placed third—very respectable, considering he was playing against one hundred of the top quants in the country.

The caller is annoyingly persistent,' he told himself when his cell phone rang for a third time.

"Hello," he said sleepily.

"Sean, this is Jonas."

He moved to his elbow. "Hi, Jonas. What's up?"

Jonas's voice was breaking up when he spoke. "I have some bad news."

Sean swung his legs to the floor. "What's going on?"

He pushed aside the curtains and squinted at the sunlight.

"Something awful has happened."

Is Jonas holding back tears? "What is it, Jonas?"

"Emma is dead."

Sean looked at the clock: 11:00 a.m. "What?"

"Yes, Sean—she's dead. I can't believe it."

His mind reeled. "Are you sure?"

"Yes. Veronica was supposed to pick her up this afternoon to go shopping for wedding dresses. I came over when Emma didn't answer her door. The security guard let us in. That's when we found her, Sean—murdered… next to her bed!"

The words skewered him like a sword. "What?"

"I'm sorry."

Jonas broke down in tears. "She was such a sweet, beautiful girl. I can't believe someone would kill her."

Sean heard Veronica wailing in the background.

"Sean... Are you there?"

"Yes," he murmured. "I... I can't believe it."

"Neither can I, but I saw her."

"What... happened?" Sean asked.

"Someone strangled her, beside her bed. When can you come?"

Strangled, he repeated to himself. "Uh... I don't know... soon."

Hazy images reached out to him from Emma: Her sparkling brown eyes and disarming smile, her witty, self-deprecating humor, and contagious laugh. *Our twice-a-month cross-Atlantic liaisons had evolved to an engagement in September for a wedding next June. Not this!*

It's a hoax! It can't be true. "I'll be there soon." He hung up.

He dialed Emma's cell phone. *No answer.* He called her home phone. *No answer.* He dialed her work phone. *No answer.*

He threw clothes into a bag, took a quick shower to wipe the sleep from his brain, and dialed Angela as he rode in a taxi to Westchester airport.

"Hi, Sean," she said. "How'd your tournament go last night?"

"I just got a call from Jonas," he replied grimly. "He told me Emma was murdered."

"Oh my God," she gasped. "Are you sure?"

Angela and Emma had become quite close. She was going to be one of Emma's bridesmaids.

"Jonas is sure," he said. "Can I take the jet?"

"Of course. I'll tell Mark Sebastian to meet you at the airport."

"Thanks, Angie."

"My God, Sean." Her voice faltered. "How did it happen?"

I need to end this call before I lose it, he told himself. "Jonas said she was strangled. I can't believe it."

Angela's voice was shallow. "Let me know if there's anything I can do."

Sean called Pankaj, who'd be his best man at the wedding, and Andrew, who'd been looking forward to having Angela on his arm as her groomsman.

He called Jonas as the Gulfstream was taxiing down the runway. "I'm on my way," he said.

"Good. I'll pick you up at the airport. We'd like you to stay with us."

Sean paused. "Thanks, Jonas. I'll call you when we land."

He occupied his brain with logistics to calm himself as the jet punched through the turbulence. *I can't bear to think of her being gone.*

He'd packed a black suit, just in case.

The first thing I'll do is go to her apartment to dismantle the hoax.

He looked down at the olive-green whitecaps on the ocean seven miles below. His thoughts strayed to the hundreds of submarines beneath the surface filled with nuclear bombs, ready to strike. Jonas's words crept like shadows through the haze.

Could our calls filled with laughter really be gone—and our passionate, erotic lovemaking, and our dreams of raising children together?

He checked his watch. They'd only been up fifteen minutes.

Flailing like a desperate man filling sandbags below a collapsing dam he crammed his brain with mathematical conundrums to push away the pain. *I can't grieve now. It will devour me.*

He dialed Jonas when the Gulfstream touched the tarmac at 3:00 a.m. "I'm here."

"I'll be there soon," Jonas said. "The police want to meet us at her apartment at nine a.m. They want you to look around to see if anything is missing."

"Okay," Sean said.

He hung up and dialed Emma. She didn't answer.

The police were waiting when they arrived at her apartment. They'd stripped Emma's bed to gather forensic evidence. The blood-splattered floor and wall laid Sean's hoax theory to rest.

The police asked him to look around to see if anything looked out of place.

"Other than the blood on the walls and the missing sheets, the apartment looks the same as when I visited two weeks ago," he told them.

"Emma's engagement ring was missing from her finger when I found her," Veronica said.

The fifty thousand euros Sean had spent for the diamond in Antwerp gave the police a motive.

Sean, Veronica, and Jonas spent the rest of the morning at the police station providing fingerprint, hair, blood, and DNA saliva samples. The police needed these to screen them out from other evidence collected at the scene.

Emma's parents gave Sean permission to view her body in the morgue.

He wasn't able to control himself when he saw her lying there, cold and pale in a body bag. He huddled and cried with Jonas and Veronica in the lobby when he exited.

Paris, France

Rahim was halfway to the railway station in a taxi that afternoon when he diverted the driver to the *Musée du Louvre*.

He wasn't sure what commanded him to the painting by his namesake, Eugene Delacroix: *Dante and Virgil in Hell*. He meditated on the tormented sinners drowning in the River Styx for an hour. *Perhaps that will be me someday*, he speculated.

Rahim arrived in Geneva a few hours later. The newspaper stands shrieked headlines about Emma's slaying calling it a rape-robbery-murder. One of her neighbors had a vague recollection of a scream. No one else had heard anything.

They have no clue, he speculated.

Emma's photo, effervescent and smiling, appeared below the headlines next to a statement released by Banque Lux:

We are deeply saddened by Emma Dumont's passing. She was a dedicated, creative, and hard-working employee. Our grief is beyond words. Anyone wishing to make a donation in her honor should contact her favorite charity, The African Women Out of Poverty Education Fund.

Rahim extracted the newspaper articles with scissors when he returned home. He placed them with the ring he'd pulled from her finger in a large manila envelope. He locked the envelope in a safe behind the rollout dishwasher in his kitchen.

He crawled into bed and pulled blankets over his head. *Allah, please forgive me for killing one of your beautiful angels.*

Bruges, Belgium

The police held Emma's body for three days before they released it to her parents. Pankaj, Angela, David Cohen, Andrew, and Sean's mother and sister arrived four days later for the funeral.

Her parents held the service at the Catholic Church she'd attended while growing up, next to a canal encircling Bruges, Belgium.

David Cohen closed the Banque Lux trading floor so her colleagues could attend. Several hundred people from town who knew and loved her also came. The high school choir she'd sung in was the highlight, especially the melancholy, Gregorian chants—her favorites.

Sean travelled to Luxembourg with her parents a few days later to pack up her belongings. He visited the police several times pressing them for updates. They had no leads.

Sean and Jonas arrived at Banque Lux late one evening to clear out her desk. Sean placed her pictures into a box for her parents. He kept a large one for himself—the two of them smiling, holding hands in front of the Eiffel Tower.

He stared at it numbly, holding the frame with both hands. "That was a good trip," he said, his voice barely audible.

"She told us she fell madly in love with you in Paris."

Sean brushed away a tear. "Do you mind if I go through her files on my own? You should go home to Veronica. She needs you. I'll catch a cab back to your house later tonight."

"Sure," he said. "I understand. Call me if you need anything."

Sitting alone on the trading floor, at the desk where she'd spent her days, where they'd first met, he let himself cry.

I had no idea a man could produce so many tears, he told himself afterwards.

He logged on to her computer using the password Jonas had given him. He found formulas in spreadsheets, ideas for new trading models, and queries to generate reports. He copied everything to a flash drive and moved on to her notebooks.

His tears fell again when he came across the notes she'd scribbled after their cross-Atlantic telephone calls.

God, how I miss you.

You said you'd swim to me in my dreams tonight. I'll meet you there, my love...

And her last note, written the afternoon before she died:

I hope you win. I know the poker game is important to you, but I wish you'd asked me to fly over for the weekend. My craving is out of control. God be with you, my love.

13. Heaven

Tel Aviv, Israel. December 2005

Roaming the deserts of North Africa and the Middle East with her Bedouin Jew parents gave Judith an invaluable education. Their nomadic lifestyle propelled them from Morocco to the Greek Isles. She absorbed it all: languages, culture, religions, and century-old tribal conflicts—everything.

Her family settled in the Negev desert in southern Israel when she was twelve, after border security became onerous, they could no longer sell their wares.

Judith had a lot of catching up to do at the kibbutz but her brain was like a sponge. She graduated at the top of her class, entered college at the age of eighteen, and joined Israel's Mossad security service after a stint in the army.

Her extensive language skills, Islamic, Hebrew, and Christian tribal knowledge, and dark-green eyes made her a natural for the risky undercover assignment: Posing as a sheik's wife in Sana'a, Yemen.

The Mossad knew they needed to get close to the sheik after MI6—Britain's foreign secret intelligence service—passed them recordings of known terrorists asking him for money. A cousin of one of the Kuwaiti royals, he was already on Mossad's radar, but only categorized as a sympathizer. The MI6 intelligence proved he had a much larger role.

Although Judith was reluctant to take on the honeypot assignment—using sex as a lure to trap a man—she agreed when her katsa, her field officer, pointed out the importance of her mission. "The director isn't exactly sure when it will happen," he said. "But we know the sheik's deep pockets will eventually lead to another request for funds. We need you there when that happens."

Judith had no problem getting the sheik's attention. Her dark-green eyes captivated him instantly at the bazaar where he bought silk for his wives. They married a few weeks later.

At thirty-five years old, she was the eldest of the sheik's four wives. Although she'd impressed him with her intelligence at first, it was her erotic lovemaking—things she did that he'd never imagined—that really blew his mind.

Being strong-willed and the most attractive of his four wives, she soon convinced him to give her domestic control of the household. Before long, she was dictating everything from what they'd eat for dinner to which wife he'd sleep with each night.

She became a skilled business manager for his affairs. She accompanied him to meetings—always sitting behind him remaining silent, since she was a woman. The sheik would take her aside and ask for her advice when the other men weren't looking.

The proposal to purchase a backpack-sized nuclear bomb from the Russian mob came from Rashid, a Pakistani with deep al-Qaeda connections.

"So what do you think?" the sheik asked her after the meeting. "One hundred million dollars is a lot of money."

"Can you trust him?" she asked with concern. "What if this is a ruse, to steal your money?"

He stroked his long gray beard. "So, what should we do?"

"We need to meet the sellers and verify the authenticity of the bomb," she said. "They'll probably want a down payment before they'll show it to us. Ten million dollars should get their attention. I'll accompany Rashid to the inspection."

The sheik nodded appreciatively. "Are you sure?"

"Yes," she insisted. "I'll be fine."

Rashid arranged a meeting with the Russians. They'd meet at a hotel in Munich the following week.

"I'll travel separately and wear Western clothes so I won't look suspicious in Germany," she told the sheik as she prepared to leave.

He nodded. "I guess we all need to make sacrifices."

Washington, DC

Nikolai always disguised his appearance before his meetings with Mikhail at the *Taste of Heaven*. The strip joint, located on Wisconsin Boulevard in northwest DC, was near an intersection with traffic-control cameras. As Mikhail's security chief—one of several operations he managed for the Volkov brothers' empire—he didn't want to end up in some FBI database classified as a voyeur who liked to ogle naked young women. He knew the government could use the CCTV traffic control cameras for surveillance when they needed to.

He parked several blocks away in a department store parking lot. He wore a neatly trimmed beard, blond-haired wig, and a long overcoat when he emerged from the store's bathroom. A walk through several alleys brought him to the rear door of *Heaven*.

The odor of spilt beer on green, industrial-grade carpet greeted him when he entered. He sat on a bar stool and ordered a martini.

Each stripper took their turn circling him with feigned smiles. Leaning over, dangling their breasts beneath loose-fitting tops they each offered him a lap dance.

He always pointed at his wedding ring and politely refused. Even though they all saw him do this, they each took their shot anyway, relishing the competitive challenge to make him stray or garner his interest.

A braless waitress in a tank top leaned over the bar trying to lure a tip. "He's ready for you," she cooed.

Nikolai followed her up the stairs.

Does bedding all these women really make them more loyal he wondered? *I'll never play that game. I saw enough spiteful behavior among the women at my Semipalatinsk brothel to last a lifetime.*

The waitress entered a security code into an electronic keypad and a bulletproof door popped open.

Mikhail, the owner of the gentlemen's club, was sitting behind the manager's desk when Nikolai entered the office. The *Taste of Heaven* manager sat across from Mikhail. He acknowledged Nikolai as he left and closed the door.

"Please sit down, Major Petrovna," Mikhail said.

Nikolai glanced at the video displays mounted on the walls when he sat down: One for each of the three stripper stages, the bar, the audience tables, two from Wisconsin Boulevard, and one from the back parking lot. Two fisheye sentry cameras above the front doors provided overlapping coverage half a block in either direction down Wisconsin Avenue.

An athletic young woman was posing fully nude on stage one.

Nikolai's security team—composed of ex-FBI and ex-KGB operatives—had swept the building for bugs before Mikhail arrived. *I know we can talk without worrying about surveillance*, Nikolai assured himself.

"So why did you call me here?" Nikolai asked.

Mikhail stared with a mocking smile. "How's Yvonna… and the three rug rats?"

Nikolai glowered. "They're fine. Let's get on with it."

Mikhail handed Nikolai a stack of papers. Each had a name at the top above several neatly typed paragraphs describing the person's physical attributes, home and congressional office addresses, family members, and activities of interest—some illegal, others immoral—all embarrassing, should they ever become public.

"I want you to set up surveillance on these men and women," Mikhail said. "Make sure you aren't spotted. I need recordings of their work and personal phone calls, summaries of their business dealings, bank-account numbers and balances, financial vulnerabilities, video recordings of their clandestine meetings with lovers—you know the drill."

"What do you need this for?"

"Vladimir has identified these congressmen as people we can use for leverage. We need hard evidence to exploit their weaknesses."

Nikolai looked through the papers. He chuckled as he pointed at a name.

"This congressman who's having a homosexual relationship outside his marriage—how does he get away with that? Isn't he one of those conservative evangelical types from down south?"

"*Da*. I need video recordings of his bedroom antics—the more embarrassing the better."

"What will you use him for?"

Mikhail tightened his lips. "That's none of your business."

"Okay. I'll get you some dirt. Anything else?"

"Why hasn't your programming team hacked into Goldberg Cohen's computers? We need a copy of their code."

"My computer security experts have tried everything. Their firewalls and virus detection software is impenetrable. You'll need to find another way in. Humans are the weakest link in any computer system. Have you tried to infiltrate their IT staff?"

"We have, but Goldberg Cohen is very careful. They keep their programming team intact, and they rarely hire outsiders."

"Are we done?"

Mikhail sat back in his chair. "I don't believe you've ever met Vladimir, have you?"

"No, I haven't."

"Perhaps you will soon. He's working on a deal to sell one of the nukes to an Arab sheik, for one hundred million dollars. Your cut will be twenty-five."

Nikolai remained stoic, hiding his elation. "When will I get my money?"

"The buyer wants to inspect the weapon first," Mikhail replied. "He can't enter the US, so we're bringing it to him. I've purchased a secure storage bunker outside Munich." Mikhail chuckled. "It's one of the hideouts Hitler used with his lover, Eva Braun. I need you to bring the weapon to Havana in your yacht. My GRU contractor will smuggle it into Germany from there."

Nikolai cleared his throat. "I won't move it until I'm paid."

"We've received a ten-million dollar advance for the inspection. I'll transfer five into your account when you bring it to Cuba."

Mikhail passed him a name scribbled on a napkin. "Fyodor will meet you at the *Lanchita de Casablanca* terminal at six p.m. on Tuesday. I told him to wear a white fedora so you'd recognize him."

"I'd like to get all the nukes off my property," Nikolai said. "It makes me nervous to have them so close to Yvonna and the kids."

"Soon enough, Nikolai… be patient. Besides, you'll only have three after next week."

I don't like the arrangement, Nikolai reflected, *but the five million will cover the purchase price and fund a pilot for the 2001 Learjet 45XR I have my eye on. It'll be nice to have my own jet for my jaunts back and forth to Europe.*

Mikhail sneered. "You're dismissed, Major Petrovna."

Nikolai left the office and returned to Annapolis.

He and Yvonna ate dinner that night on the deck next to the pier they'd recently remodeled to accommodate their new seventy-five-foot luxury yacht. Splotches of pink swathed the bottoms of silver-gray clouds hovering above the horizon. A hole in a cloud shot a shaft of orange light onto a band of red oaks on the other side of the river.

Nikolai handed Yvonna his empty martini glass: A signal he wanted another.

She opened the deck refrigerator and pulled out a chilled bottle of Stoli, ice, and a jar of olives. She filled the shaker with enough vodka and ice for two drinks, shook the brew, drained the liquor into their glasses, and dropped in two olives.

He observed her round butt as she bent over to deposit the vodka bottle in the refrigerator.

This is my fifth, and she's been keeping up, he observed. *Perhaps she'll be the aggressor tonight.*

He contemplated the blood-red sun as it touched the treetops. *She's more of a mystery now than ever,* he concluded. *She rarely drank in the early days. Now she joins me every night for at least one. She still makes love whenever I ask—that's never changed—but in other ways she seems miles away. Perhaps it's an inevitable vicissitude of marriage.*

She'll become more talkative once she has drinks in her. I just need to light the match.

"Gregor told me he wants to go to Georgetown," he said. "Do you think that's the right college for him?"

"His grades are good," she replied, "and a few of his friends are going there, so he won't be lonely."

"It'll cost me a bundle," Nikolai commented.

"We can afford it, can't we?"

He chuckled. "Yes, dear, I think we can."

"He hates the name Gregor," she reminded him. "He says it sounds too Russian. Remember how the Navy brats used to make fun of him when he was in elementary school?"

"Yes, dear. It's been quite an adjustment for all of us… coming to this country."

Her gaze became wistful. "It has been quite a journey."

She took another sip. "What's Mikhail been up to lately?"

Nikolai sprang upright in his chair. "Why do you care about him?" he raged.

She bristled, gritting her teeth.

He leaned back. *She won't put up with my anger* he chided himself. *Now I'll have to apologize so she doesn't run off to her room.*

"I'm sorry I got angry," he said, "but Mikhail infuriates me. You know I've never forgiven him for killing my parents."

"How do you know he killed your parents?"

Nikolai shook his head. *I can't tell her how I know.*

"Why do you work for him if you hate him so much?" she continued.

Another good question he couldn't answer. *I'm stuck, as long as the bombs are stored here.*

"That anger you're holding toward Mikhail will eat you up inside if you don't let it go," she said.

"Is that what your therapist told you?" he retorted.

She downed the rest of her drink, grabbed the vodka from the refrigerator, and filled her glass—ignoring the ice and olives.

"Do you want some?" she said, holding the bottle over his glass.

"Sure," he answered softly.

She filled his glass and shoved the bottle back into the refrigerator. They sat in silence, watching twilight fill the sky.

"We should have a party for Gregor next spring," she said. "High school graduation is important here in America."

"That's fine with me."

He studied the river. *So many secrets below the surface, just like me.*

Mikhail had kept his word when he conveyed the horse farm to us. At least that part of the painfully coerced bargain that frigid night in Kabul had worked out.

"It's a great place to hide the bombs," Mikhail had said, the first time he'd shown Nikolai the fallout shelter. "Being next to a river and near an airport gives us many transportation options. The shelter is one of the best air-sealed containment bunkers ever built. The admiral who lived here must've been paranoid about a Soviet nuclear attack."

The horse farm is beautiful, he acknowledged. *I have no regrets about the purchase, except for the weapons. I've never thanked Mikhail for the property. How can I?*

They were halfway across the Atlantic when Mikhail had said, "I have some bad news. Your parents are dead. My men didn't know I'd made a deal with you to keep them alive."

Yeah—right! Nikolai ruminated.

I wanted to believe him at the time, but after witnessing many ruthless murders orchestrated by Mikhail to "clean up loose ends," I know it was a lie.

Yvonna looked at him. "When should we have the party, dear?"

"How about the end of May?" he suggested.

"I'll start planning it as soon as the holidays are over."

Good, he decided. *Maybe she needs a project now that she's finished college. Perhaps she won't be so sullen. She'll fret about the details for months to make everything perfect.*

He looked down at their yacht moored to the dock. *I'll take three days going down to Cuba, and four to return. That way I can do some deep sea fishing on the way back.*

"I'm taking the yacht out tomorrow," he told her. "I'll be gone about a week."

"Okay."

* * *

Yvonna was digging through her own demons as the sky darkened.

I'm angry with Mikhail too, but for completely different reasons than Nikolai, she contemplated. *He hasn't asked me to meet him in over a year.*

Simmering in the numbness bestowed by vodka, a plan began to take shape. *We'll have to invite Mikhail to Gregor's graduation party. He was at the hospital the night Gregor was born.*

Tatiana is nine now. Perhaps Mikhail will notice how much she looks like him. Maybe he won't ignore me if he knows I gave him such a beautiful child.

A shiver ran down her spine. *Nikolai can never find out. He'll kill us both if he does.*

Tel Aviv, Israel

Judith didn't tell her katsa about the backpack nuke proposal when she met him in Tel Aviv before her flight to Munich. *I want to make sure the bomb is real before I cause a stir*, she decided.

She checked into a hotel room next to Rashid in Munich the next day. Rashid had reserved the room for her when he arrived. She slipped into his room while he slept later that night and attached microdot-tracking microchips to his shoes.

Two Russians picked Rashid up in front of the hotel the next morning. She followed him at a distance in a rental car, using a GPS tracking device on her computer to monitor his movements. The Russians stopped when they reached a forest a few miles south of Munich.

She hid behind a bush taking pictures of Rashid while he talked with a tall, good-looking man who looked to be about fifty. The men disappeared into the forest. Rashid was smiling when he re-appeared a few minutes later. The Russians drove him back to the hotel.

Rashid invited Judith into his room when she knocked on his door later that night. She was wearing a traditional black Yemeni jilbab cloak with a black scarf covering her head.

He paced excitedly around the room as he spoke. "The weapon is real!" he exclaimed. "It's a Soviet-era bomb, but it's still functional. Mikhail proved it to me using radiation-measurement instruments. He said he'd include a bazooka with a launching tripod as part of the sale."

"Good," she said. "So what's the next step?"

Rashid pulled a note from his wallet. "This is Mikhail's secure phone number. He'll give us the weapon when we transfer the rest of the funds to his account. The bomb will be perfect for the upcoming summit between the Israeli prime minister and the US president in Cyprus."

Judith pulled a semi-automatic Beretta fitted with a silencer from beneath her jilbab. "Is that so?"

She pointed the barrel at his left eye for six seconds—just long enough for him to realize what he'd done—before she planted a bullet in his brain.

She picked up the shell casing, placed a voice-cloaking device over his hotel room phone, and dialed Mikhail. "This is Rashid."

The line was silent for a few seconds. "You sound odd."

"I'm using a security device. We've decided the bomb is too expensive."

"We're keeping the ten-million-dollar deposit."

"I understand," she replied. "That was our agreement. We'll contact you later if we change our minds."

She returned to her room, drilled two tiny holes into the wall, inserted pinhole cameras into the holes, and connected the wires to her computer.

Two of Mikhail's thugs showed up a few minutes later. The agents picked the lock and entered with their guns drawn when Rashid didn't answer his door.

She observed them frowning at each other when they saw Rashid's body. They took pictures and left the room quickly.

Judith returned to Yemen the next day.

She acted frightened and distraught when she met the Sheik. "Rashid was dead—shot in the head—when I went into his room."

She began to cry inconsolably. "I saw suspicious Americans... at the hotel," she said between sobs. "Perhaps they killed him. Forget about the weapon. It isn't real. It was probably a setup... by the CIA... to justify dropping more bombs on us."

The sheik rubbed her back to comfort her. "You're probably right," he said, trying to sooth her anxiety.

Judith put her new plan into motion the next day. She became a bitter, cantankerous, argumentative shrew—his worst nightmare.

When the sheik asked her what was wrong she said, "You shouldn't have sent me on such a dangerous mission."

She became irrational at every turn. She refused to have sex. She fought continuously with the other sheikas and his harem of concubines.

Then she set down the law: "You can't have sex with any of them."

When one of the other sheikas had sex with him behind her back, she broke the sheika's nose.

After having his household in total chaos for several weeks, the sheik had had enough. He initiated the Islamic process for divorce—*talaaq*.

Three months later—the standard waiting period—he placed twenty million dollars into a Swiss account to pay her off, and she was free.

She never reported the nuke discovery to her katsa. "I'm done prostituting myself," she told him when she returned to Tel Aviv.

"The hell you are," he responded angrily. "Get your ass back down there to your husband and apologize. We need you in that role."

"I'm resigning!"

She moved to Switzerland the next day to be close to her well-funded bank account.

She'd analyzed the photos she'd taken of Rashid using Mossad's facial recognition software before she left. *The tall Russian in the picture is Mikhail Volkov, brother of Vladimir Volkov.* Both brothers had extensive files in Mossad's database.

Mikhail was in the KGB for years before he resigned in 1987, so I know the nuke is real, she determined.

I'm not sure what I'll do to leverage my knowledge. Knowing about the weapon will be lucrative if I play my cards right. I'll let the aeolian winds of fate propel me to my destiny. Papa always said that's the best way to live.

14. Seduction

Annapolis, Maryland—May 2006

The weather was warm with a cloudless sky the afternoon of Gregor's graduation party. More than sixty of his friends showed up.

Nikolai gave their guests yacht rides up and down the river while Stefan, Gregor's fifteen-year-old brother and ten-year-old Tatiana played volleyball by the barn. Tatiana was tall and quite athletic for her age, so Gregor's friends readily accepted her on their teams.

Yvonna hovered near the front door to greet everyone. Her real goal was to introduce Mikhail to Tatiana when he arrived.

Nikolai assured me Mikhail would attend; she kept reminding herself as the afternoon progressed.

Most of their visitors had left when dusk descended. She joined Nikolai on the deck after the caterers pulled their truck out of the driveway. She handed him a chilled martini and made one for herself—her first of the day.

"It was a great party," Nikolai said with slurred speech. "Gregor was very happy."

She squeezed her olives, hard, over the vodka. "Yes... he was. Not that I'm surprised, but why didn't Mikhail come?"

Nikolai gulped his drink. He almost fell out of his chair when he handed her his empty glass.

"I forgot to tell you. He called me this morning to send his regrets. He's opening a new strip club in Atlantic City next week, so he's tied up giving personal interviews to his new girls."

Nikolai's glass slipped from her hand and shattered into a hundred pieces on the deck.

"Damn it!" she said rising from her chair. "I've already sent the maids home. I'll get something to clean this up."

A cloud of anger consumed her as she sauntered up the ramp to the kitchen. She returned and scooped up the shards with a portable vacuum, fixed Nikolai another drink, and said good night.

Hiding in the privacy of her bathroom, she put a wet towel over her face and cried.

Hamburg, Germany-November 2006

Beate sold her home in Virginia after she returned to DC from Colorado at the end of 2002. Although she was reluctant to move away from the neighbors who'd been so kind while she was grieving, she needed to move on.

"The house is too lonely with my family gone," she'd told them.

She then purchased a small, Victorian condominium on P Street near Logan Circle in DC, a few blocks north of the White House.

Except for an occasional visit to the cemetery, her life became all about tradecraft. One of her goals when she'd entered CIA University had been to learn Arabic. She had a passable knowledge after two years.

She moved to Hamburg, Germany, to begin her first assignment in 2004. Her senior case officer, Helmut Drach, found her a job at a vegetarian restaurant popular with the city's growing Muslim population.

"Just blend in like a fly on the wall," Helmut had told her. "Wear loose-fitting clothing and makeup that makes you look frumpy. The less conspicuous you are the better."

Helmut, originally from Potsdam, had worked as a double agent for the CIA during the latter years of the Cold War, while still employed by East Germany's ruthless Ministry for State Security—the *Stasi*. He'd sensed the winds of change blowing west before the wall fell in 1989.

After surviving several assassination attempts by former *Stasi* colleagues—all of whom he'd eliminated—the Agency promoted him to senior case officer. Now, in his early fifties, he was Beate's mentor and one of the best in the business.

Beate always pretended she didn't understand Arabic when she served her patrons at the restaurant. It took enormous concentration to act dim-witted when men made sexual comments in Arabic about her, thinking she didn't understand. She remained placid and calm as they laughed and stared.

She was convinced they discussed the same topics men everywhere did after observing them for a couple of years. "None of them seem subversive," she'd tell Helmut during their weekly briefings.

Helmut occasionally gave her other clandestine operation assignments to help her perfect her tradecraft skills. Over time, she met other CIA agents in the field as well as operatives from foreign governments.

Most of her assignments involved gathering and analyzing intelligence data. The result was usually the deportation of a suspected terrorist by a host government.

She was working at the vegetarian restaurant in November of 2006 when Helmut sent her a coded text message: <u>DEMI</u>. The code meant, *Drop Everything, Meet Immediately.*

She told her boss she was feeling ill, and took a taxi to the location designated for emergency meetings—an old Kirchdorf ferryboat used for guided tours around Hamburg's Alster Lake. The boat was smaller than modern ferries so there were fewer people.

Dark gray clouds threatening rain brooded over them as she sidled into an empty seat next to Helmut. A group of elementary school students and their teacher sat up front. The rest of the seats were empty.

The sky began to drizzle as the ferry pulled away from the dock. The cold rain kicked up a misty fog when it collided with the water.

Helmut looked around furtively. "An important mission has come up. Our friends at the National Security Agency passed us the lead."

The ferry began a slow circle around the lake.

"He's arriving from Pakistan this afternoon," Helmut continued. "He's slippery. If we don't take him out today, he'll probably disappear."

She studied Helmut's eyes. "Tell me about him."

"His name is Riza, forty-two years old, originally from Syria. He's been living in Pakistan with his three wives the past five years."

"Why does he need to be eliminated?" she asked. "Why not just pick him up and send him to Guantanamo?"

Helmut's stoic gaze didn't mask the anger in his eyes. "Riza's one of the masterminds behind the terrorist train and bus bombings here in Europe. We think he's planning another one."

"I see, and you want me to take care of him?"

"If you think you can handle it. I have a plan that won't create too much commotion. I could take him out with a bullet, but that would be messy. We need to make it look like he died of natural causes if possible. There are fewer complications that way."

The tour guide described Kennedybrücke, the bridge named in honor of the American president who'd saved Berlin during the Cold War.

A mixture of dread and excitement fought for allegiance in her soul. *I've been waiting for this day for years,* she told herself. *I'm not sure what to think now that it's here.*

Fog wafted over the water. Blurry images of Robert and Malia's charred black bodies lying cold in their coffins rose up from the mist.

"When can I do it?" she said in a voice as icy as the rain.

Helmut fastened his gaze on her blue eyes. "Are you sure?"

"Yes," she replied acerbically. "We need to do it soon, before he disappears."

He described his plan as the boat traversed the lake.

"I have an outfit for you in my van," he said when he'd finished. "We'll meet there when the tour ends. There's something else you need to know."

"What's that?"

"My NSA contact mentioned something disturbing. Using voiceprint analysis, they identified the person calling Riza from Hamburg as a man named Abdul. He popped up in some satellite calls before and after the recent train bombings."

He handed her Abdul's file. "An analyst at Langley thinks he might be the same person we trained years ago for ops in Egypt and Afghanistan. His CIA file describes him as extremely dangerous. The last entry, in 1987, said he might have switched allegiance to the Mujahideen or the Soviets. We're not sure."

She walked alone down the ramp when the tour ended. She joined Helmut a few minutes later in a white, windowless Mercedes van parked two blocks away.

Two agents from Germany's Federal Intelligence Service were waiting for them when they pulled the van into the parking lot in front of Riza's hotel. Helmut stopped next to their BMW and rolled down his window.

"Thanks for the tip," Klaus said.

The FIS agents nodded at Beate.

She nodded back. They'd worked together before.

"I'm glad you were able to track him on such short notice," Helmut said.

"We spotted him at the train station using facial recognition software," Klaus said. "I imagine you'll find out which room he's in when you hack into the hotel's guest registration system."

"I will," Helmut said. "Can you stick around to see who shows up when we're done? Most of my people are tied up with another operation right now."

"Sure. Just let us know when you're finished."

Helmut parked near the entrance.

Beate joined him in the back of the van.

He tapped a button, and a high-powered antenna rose above the roof. He broke through the hotel's Intranet security firewall with a few keystrokes on his computer.

"It looks like Riza is in room 508," he told Beate.

He tapped into the hotel's video surveillance system to intercept feeds from the entrance lobby, front desk, and fifth-floor camera. He replaced them with static, snapshot images and routed the live feeds to display screens in the back of the van.

Beate fidgeted with her hooker's outfit as he worked. "I'm not used to wearing such a short dress," she complained.

Helmut pointed at the display. "I can watch you while you're in the hallway, but you'll be on your own once you're in his room. Are you ready?"

She pulled a brush through her long, strawberry-blonde hair. She'd let it down past her shoulders for the mission. "I think so," she said.

Helmut surveyed her with a glint in his eye. "It'll be impossible for him to ignore you."

"You think so, huh? I've never done anything like this before. What should I do if he doesn't let me in?"

"Just make sure he does. It's too dangerous to kill him in the hallway."

She nodded hesitantly. "Although it's been a while, I still think I can remember how to seduce a man. It's not that hard... as I recall."

Their laughter dissolved a modicum of their anxiety.

"I'm coming in after you if you're not out of his room in five minutes," he said.

"Hey, now," she protested. "I'm not that good. How about fifteen?"

Her skirt hiked up to her hips when she stepped out of the van.

She smirked at Helmut to stop ogling her as she pulled it down. "Did you have to buy such a short dress?" she said.

His eyebrows rose lasciviously. "I think it looks great."

"Is this what your girlfriends wear?"

He laughed. "Only when I can get away with it. I'll give you ten minutes—that's it."

"Okay," she said. "So, how do I look?"

He handed her a hundred euros from his wallet.

"Very funny." She stuffed the money into her cocktail purse. "You should be careful. I might start liking this."

"You look spectacular," he assured her. "Just stay focused, and you'll do fine. Do you have everything?"

She pulled out her lipstick case and applied some. "I think so."

"Good luck."

"You mean good hunting, don't you?" she said with a wry smile.

"Yes... that, too."

Helmut hunched nervously in front of the display screen as Beate exited the fifth floor elevator. She smoothed the see-through white silk shirt over her black bra with her hand, and knocked on Riza's door.

* * *

She knocked louder when he didn't respond.

"Who is it?" Riza said from behind the door.

"Hello, Riza." She spoke in a bright voice. "I have a present for you."

She smiled in front of the view hole. *A prickly feeling on my neck tells me he's looking.* "Abdul sent me."

"Go away."

She'd studied Abdul's CIA file carefully that afternoon. One thing that stood out was Abdul's predilection for prostitutes.

She knocked again. "Abdul sent me as a gift for you, Riza."

Riza's door opened slightly with the security chain taut. "I don't want any gifts."

She gave him her best smile. "Really? He paid me five hundred euros to stay with you for an hour. I can stay longer though, if you'd like."

His stare rolled up and down her body. "I don't want any company."

"Didn't he tell you I was coming? Perhaps he wanted to surprise you."

Riza didn't answer.

She feigned concern. "Should I tell him you don't like me? Do you want a different girl?"

He looked her over again. "No... I don't think so."

"Can't I come in for a little while?" she cajoled. "We could just watch TV if you'd like. That way I won't have to return the money. I'm sure he'll want a refund if I leave now."

Riza hesitated. The door closed.

The security chain clattered and his door swung open. "Come in."

* * *

Helmut pressed the start button on his cellphone stopwatch.

* * *

Beate cupped her hands so they'd stop shaking as she walked through the door. *Relax*, she told herself. *Some women do this all the time.*

She aimed for an armchair perpendicular to the couch and sat down. Riza latched the security chain.

"So, what do you like to watch?" she said.

He picked up the remote and switched on the TV. She assessed him sideways: attractive, medium height, light-brown skin, wearing suit pants with a white-collar shirt, and black socks without shoes.

"So what did Abdul say when he hired you?" Riza said.

She smiled and crossed her legs in his direction, allowing her red leather skirt to ride up to her black panties. "He said you have three wives—is that true? You must like women."

He smiled proudly. "Yes… and six children."

"He also said you're a bit shy."

Riza chuckled. "That's what he said, huh?"

His gaze played up and down over her body.

I can tell he's interested. Now I need to hook him.

She smiled. "Abdul didn't tell me how handsome you are. I can see why so many women like you."

She rose from the armchair, moved to a mirror, and pulled her lipstick case from her cocktail purse. She noticed him staring at her ass in the reflection as she touched up her lips.

"Do you mind if I take my shirt off?" she asked.

She unbuttoned it without waiting, and placed it on the console below the mirror. She pointed at the back of her black bra. "Can you help me with this?"

* * *

Helmut's timer said nine minutes. Beads of sweat formed on his forehead as he watched the lifeless video monitor.

* * *

Riza didn't move, and neither did she. "Come on," she said. "I won't bite."

He muted the TV and walked over to her.

She watched him through the mirror as he unclasped the hooks of her bra strap. It dropped to the floor.

His jaw fell open when she turned to face him. He was staring wide-eyed at her large, upturned nipples.

* * *

Helmut shoved a Beretta into the belt beneath the back of his sports coat as the timer reached ten minutes. He jumped out of the van and hustled to the entrance.

* * *

Riza reached out with both hands to touch her breasts.

His eyeballs flashed shock when the three-inch spring-loaded syringe in her lipstick case pierced his heart beneath the sternum. A groan rattled through his throat as his lungs collapsed and his muscles froze.

She caught him beneath the armpits as he fell and guided him to the carpet. He shuddered and went still as the light twisted from his eyes; her 34C's—his last glimpse of earth.

The lethal toxin, designed to dissolve quickly, would compel even the most meticulous forensic pathologist to believe a myocardial infarction had taken him.

She pulled on the latex gloves she'd stowed in her cocktail purse and extricated the lipstick case from his chest.

She rotated the bottom, and the syringe snapped back into hiding.

She'd just unbuttoned Riza's shirt when the knock came. She dabbed the tiny entry wound on his chest with bleach.

A second knock came.

Seeing that it was Helmut, she unlatched the chain and opened the door.

Beate pulled on her bra and blouse as Helmut checked Riza's pulse.

He moved to the kitchen and rifled through documents on the table. "Riza has maps of San Francisco and the Bay Area Rapid Transit System," he said. He dumped everything into an open briefcase. "I'm taking these with us."

Beate grabbed Riza's cell phones and checked his wallet. She returned the wallet to his pocket after finding nothing of interest.

Helmut placed a pen-sized camera in a bookshelf near the TV.

They left the room and hustled down the hallway to the elevator.

He gave her the van keys. "We shouldn't be seen together. I'll meet you there in a minute."

Helmut configured the hotel's surveillance cameras to their original state from his computer in the back of the van, lowered the antenna, and drove to the edge of the parking lot.

"This is the frequency for the camera we placed in the bookshelf," Helmut said as he handed Klaus a slip of paper. "You can take it from here, right?"

"Of course. *Auf Wiedersehen.*"

"*Auf Wiedersehen.*"

They drove in silence for several minutes before Helmut spoke. "Would you like to talk about it?"

"No."

"Okay. We'll debrief tomorrow."

He dropped her off in front of her apartment.

Beate raced up the stairs, ran to her bathroom, turned on the bathtub faucets, stripped off her whore clothes, and threw them into a trashcan. She then opened a vodka bottle in the kitchen and guzzled a few mouthfuls, loaded up her music player with her favorite artists—Joni Mitchell, Billie Holiday and Mozart—and turned the stereo up loud.

The bathtub was three quarters full when she turned off the faucets. She placed candles around the edge of the tub, lit them, and turned off the light. The flames threw agitated shadows on the walls as she eased herself into the steamy brew.

Concepts like honor, courage, and loyalty—*Semper Fidelis*—crept into her mind by the time the vodka bottle was half-gone. None of these words eased her regret about the wives and kids Riza had left behind.

She admonished herself. *Sentiment is a luxury that'll get me killed.*

The soldier's dilemma—*was it revenge or duty?*—haunted her thoughts.

It had been five years since Robert and Malia's murders. *Have I balanced a ledger—or added more fuel to the enmity between our people? It didn't matter. Either way, he's dead.*

It was my duty, she decided. *The people of San Francisco and Oakland—although they'd never know—would certainly sleep more peacefully tonight. Some might question our pre-emptive strike—a de facto rule of engagement in the terror war since 9/11—but that isn't my concern.*

She scrubbed herself with soap and sucked down several more mouthfuls of vodka. Sibylline voices rang out above the *Dies Irae* sopranos in Mozart's *Requiem* blaring from the stereo.

Shadows wobbled like ghosts on the walls as the candles battled for oxygen. Fuzzy, phantasmagoric images took on human forms.

Warriors and emperors she'd studied at Quantico swirled around her. Alexander the Great—the first of many conquerors to view the world as his own—arrived on the backs of thousands of slaves marching over mountains of dead bodies. Others followed with their own God-granted manifest-destiny-zeitgeist to justify their urge to kill, rape, pillage, and subjugate—Caesar, Attila, Genghis Khan, Oliver Cromwell, Napoleon, Stalin, Hitler, Hirohito, *and others to come I don't yet recognize.*

Her hallucinations became less recognizable as her brain lost focus. Men grew bodies of horses. Heads bobbed up and down on rivers of blood.

She inspected her silhouette in the shadows. *I wasn't some procrastinating bystander waiting for someone else to do the wet work.*

She yanked out the drain plug, flopped over the side of the tub, and knocked the vodka bottle to the floor as she crawled to the toilet to throw up.

She was asleep, naked, lying on the ceramic tile in front of her toilet when her CIA cell phone rang the next morning. "Hello."

"How are you doing?" Helmut asked.

My head is pounding. The odor of vodka makes me want to vomit again. "I'm not feeling well," she said. "I'll talk with you tomorrow."

"Sure, but I want to pass along a message from the director before you go. The president is very pleased with the outcome of our operation. Langley combed through Riza's papers. A strike on the BART system in San Francisco was imminent. We probably saved hundreds of lives. The FBI picked up three al-Qaeda agents in Berkeley last night and the FIS picked up two here in Hamburg."

"Thanks for letting me know. I've got to call the restaurant."

"Okay."

Helmut paused. "Hang in there. My first time was the hardest, too. It'll get better in a couple of days."

She looked into the bathtub after she hung up. The candles had melted down, leaving long entrails on the inside of the tub. *This mess will take forever to clean up.*

She dragged herself to her bedroom, flopped onto the mattress, and pulled the covers over her head to shut out the world

15. Bring It On

New York City—November 2010

Delmonico's ornate Renaissance ceiling hovered over an eclectic mix of business executives and couples having dinner. Although the financial crisis had forced many homeowners and banks into bankruptcy the previous three years, upscale businesses like Delmonico's were still doing fine. One unforeseen benefit of the financial crisis: Good restaurants were a lot less crowded. Gone were the days of two-hour waits and hundred-dollar bribes to *maître d's* just to get a table.

Goldberg Cohen's five partners were ebullient during dinner as they discussed their quarterly results. It had been an outstanding year for the firm. The risk-mitigation controls in their trading software had protected them from the chaos that had driven many momentum-following proprietary trading firms into bankruptcy.

David Cohen's prediction that the CDO market would eventually collapse had paid off handsomely. Sean's $200 million LEAP put option investment with partner funds in 2007 had grown to two billion by the time they'd cashed out earlier that week.

The two, ten-percent-owner silent partners—Arthur Goldberg's grandchildren—departed with David Cohen after dessert, leaving Angela and Sean on their own.

Angela's lips moved to Sean's ear. "Have a drink with me," she urged.

"Sure. I don't have anything going on tonight."

The headwaiter, who'd been eying Angela appreciatively all night, came to their table instantly when she looked his direction. Sean sat back to observe. *She still looks stunning even after a day that began for her at six a.m. I know. I was in the office when she arrived.*

An odd question struck him as he watched the waiter flirt with her: *When will she tie the knot? At thirty-six, four years younger than me, she's certainly a good catch.*

She smiled at Sean when the waiter left. "I have a present for you," she murmured in a flirtatious voice.

The warmth of her breath on his neck made his heart stutter.

This was new. A present?

He'd attended many holiday parties with Angela at her parents' mansion outside Armonk, but they'd never exchanged gifts.

"That's kind of you, Angie. When?"

Her lips pursed inquisitively as she giggled. "Not *that* kind of present."

His face melted into a smile, intimating that he'd just been kidding—at least that's what he wanted her to believe. They'd been playing this flirtation game for years. Nothing serious ever came of it.

People who knew them sometimes said they'd be a good couple. Sean wasn't so sure. *She is my boss, after all, and the owner's daughter,* he reasoned. *Things will get very complicated if we cross the line.*

Eying him unflinchingly, she brushed a strand of blonde hair behind her ear. "Do you see the three men to my left on the other side of the room?"

Sean scanned the tables. "I do."

The waiter arrived with the sommelier to discuss her wine selection. Sean watched with interest as the expert described the winery in Beaune, France, where the vintage originated.

Everyone takes their opportunity to look into her dark blue eyes when they have a chance, he observed.

She raised her glass in a toast when the men left. "Santé," she said.

"Santé," he replied. He took a sip. "This is very good."

"I'm glad you like it. I think it's about time for a winery tour in France, don't you think?"

"I'd love that. So what's your present... and when are you gonna *give it to me*?"

They laughed.

Her head leaned back provocatively. "How about right here?" she said, as her hand glided over his thigh beneath the tablecloth.

He laughed and became quiet. *Be careful,* he cautioned himself. *Those deep blue eyes of hers have broken many men's hearts over the years.* He'd comforted her a few times on the other side of the equation when she needed a man's ear to justify her reasons.

Although his arm had anchored her at the symphony, the opera, Knicks basketball games, and public speaking engagements, that was as far as it had gone.

She has told me she thinks I'm handsome when she's been tipsy he recalled. He sipped his wine. "Are you still dating that assistant district attorney up in Westchester?"

"I'm not sure," she retorted. "Should I be?"

"Give me his number and I'll call him to find out."

She giggled.

Sean's heartbeat pulsed when her lips moved close to his face. He cupped his chin in his hand, enjoying the repartee, waiting to see what she'd say next. *I know she's playing with me… but I like it. Who wouldn't want one of the most beautiful women in New York to flirt with them?*

Be cautious, he reminded himself. *Your heart closed for business after Emma.*

Except for an occasional one-night diversion to quench his loneliness, he'd kept the doors to his heart closed and the windows bolted shut.

She batted her eyelashes. "Those three men are working on a merger deal."

"How do you know?"

"Isaac Bachmann, the short guy in the middle, called me earlier this week to rub it in my face."

Sean looked past her hair at Bachmann's table. A heavy-set man in his mid-thirties was talking nonstop gesticulating with his hands between two men in their late fifties. The younger man glanced at Angela every few sentences.

Maybe she's teasing him, he speculated.

"What kind of deal are they working on?" Sean asked.

Her voice became serious. "They're mining company CEOs. They'd be good partners."

She spoke as if it was a fact. *She's usually right*, he recognized.

Bachmann's eyes burned into Sean when he glanced over her ear. "So what's the deal with the younger guy?" Sean said. "He seems angry."

She giggled and swooned, enjoying the badinage. "He's a creep."

They chuckled, as if sharing a joke.

"Remember that Swiss bank that tried to crush us a few years ago?" she continued. "His company was their advisor."

"Sure, I remember. It cost us millions in lawyer fees and another million paying lobbyists down in DC. Ridiculous."

"One of the CEOs, the South American, asked me to look at the benefits of a merger with his Australian competitor last month. I told him I thought it would be a good idea after I analyzed their financials. A merger would lower their production costs and give them monopoly-like pricing power. I offered to put a deal together but he declined, saying he was just curious."

"That's too bad," Sean remarked.

"Isaac shouldn't have told me. Perhaps he couldn't help rubbing it in. His company will earn some big fees from the merger, and I'm sure he'll make a fortune with his inside trades."

Sean leaned back. "That's a dangerous game."

"Yes... and illegal, but that's the way he operates."

She touched his leg below the table. "Anyhow, this is your present. Our company doesn't have a stake in the deal, or a non-disclosure agreement, so we can make some money too, if we determine the deal's actually happening. The fact that they're having dinner here tonight means a deal may be imminent."

Sean's mind filtered through several trading strategies. "I'll take a look at their recent volume and price action tomorrow, to see if someone's been accumulating stock."

"Good. Let's compare notes later this weekend."

"Sure. I'll let you know what I find out."

Angela scribbled both stock symbols on a napkin below a smiley face with puckered lips.

He laughed. "You're incorrigible."

Bachmann was scowling. "He's staring at us again," Sean said.

"I think he looks like a rat... which fits his personality. I've known Isaac since prep school. He's been trying to get me to go out with him since his seventh-grade *bar mitzvah*. Our families belong to the same synagogue."

She is teasing him, he realized. "Perhaps you should show him some mercy," Sean suggested.

"No way. I wouldn't date him if he were the last man on earth!"

Sean laughed. "But he's a good catch. His firm's shyster financial products, like the CDOs that torpedoed the market, made them a fortune after their DC political cohorts gutted the rating agencies."

"Yeah," Angela agreed. "Bonds are a joke now, and not just here. Countries with politicians that sell entitlements as if they're a God-given right will never be able to repay their loans... yet they still have high ratings."

Sean nodded. "No one really knows what they own anymore. We're lucky we've been smart enough to figure out the rules for the casino."

She chuckled for a few seconds. Then she became serious. "We'll need to be cautious. Things will get ugly if he finds out we're piggybacking on his deal. His company has been trying to acquire us or put us out of business, since the thirties. I used to hear Grandpa and Arthur Goldberg talk about their battles when I was a kid. I'm sure they'd love to commandeer the huge accounts we've snared in the Middle East the last few years."

"I'm sure they would," he agreed.

"Father thinks they're trying to monopolize the international financial markets. He made me promise to never sell out to them if I'm running the firm one day."

"I'll always vote my shares with you, Angie."

"I appreciate that."

She squeezed his hand and sipped her drink. "I'm tired. It's been a long week. I think I'll go home and take a bath."

"Do you need some company?"

She raised her eyebrows. "I'll take a rain check. I have a date with the assistant DA tomorrow. We're going to see Faust at the Met."

"Is this a test… to see if he falls asleep?"

"He told me he likes opera. We'll see."

Sean paid the partners' dinner bill with his company credit card. The expense was a tax write-off after all—one of many loopholes created by wealthy politicians in DC to facilitate commerce among the rich.

Heads turned as Angela glided to the lobby. Her regal beauty and orchestrated poise, honed by years of ballet as a child, gave her the guise of a model when she walked.

Sean held her jacket and she slid in gracefully. They exited and walked through Delmonico's ornate Renaissance pillars to the sidewalk.

A callous wind slapped their faces when they turned left onto Beaver Street. Harold, parked halfway down the block, waved to let her know where he'd parked the limo.

Angela held Sean's bicep as they walked. "Would you like a ride?" she asked.

"I think I'll walk. I need to clear my head. Are you coming to our gig tomorrow night?"

"I wouldn't miss it. *The Quantaholics* sound better every time I hear you. Can you play that song where you change back and forth between flute and saxophone?"

"You mean Van Morrison's *'Moondance?'* Sure."

Sean nodded when they reached the limousine. "Hello, Harold."

"Hello, Mr. McGowan."

Angela ground her hips into Sean's leg when she hugged him goodbye. She kissed him on the cheek, giggled, and pulled away.

The crook yanked her purse off her shoulder and darted into the crowd.

"Crap!" she yelled. "He stole my purse."

The thief jostled pedestrians as he zigzagged down the sidewalk.

"I'll get it," Sean bellowed as he took off running.

He dodged between people, weaving his way through the herd. *This is too slow*, he realized.

He jumped into the street and ran between two columns of cars waiting for a red light. The lights turned green. Cars accelerated.

Sean pounded on the hood of a Ferrari. The driver jerked to a stop. Sean slid across the hood to the sidewalk.

The thief was looking into Angela's purse when Sean plowed into him with the force of a football linebacker.

The man jumped up from the sidewalk.

A switchblade snapped to attention.

The young Hispanic circled Sean menacingly. A blood-scraped chin signaled his introduction to the concrete hadn't gone well.

The assailant pounced.

Sean jumped sideways, evading the blade.

The thief swatted his knife at Sean's face.

Sean ducked. His right foot lunged upwards into the crook's chest, knocking him to the wall. A roundhouse kick snapped the thief's wrist as he slid to the sidewalk and the switchblade skidded away.

Sean karate-punched him three times in the face.

The thief collapsed, motionless.

Sean crouched over him with his fists ready to deliver more, but the thief was unconscious.

A crowd had gathered around them while they fought.

Sean grabbed the switchblade, folded it closed, and put the knife in his pocket. He picked up Angela's purse as she ran to him.

"Are you all right?" she asked.

He handed her the purse. "I'm fine."

She looked inside. "Everything's still here."

A camera flashed as she hugged him.

He held her close as she trembled against his chest. "It's all right, Angie," he said, trying to sooth her.

He took her up on her offer for a ride home after their statements to the police.

The *Times* published a front-page story about the encounter the next morning. There were two pictures beneath the mocking headline: *Wall Street Banker Takes Care of Homeless.*

One picture showed Sean crouching over the thief with his fists. The other showed Angela hugging him.

In addition to a play-by-play account of the confrontation, the journalist spiced things up by juxtaposing Sean's wealth with the misfortunes of the twenty-year-old illegal immigrant lying in a hospital bed with a broken rib, broken nose, broken wrist, and supposedly—a brain injury.

Sean didn't read the story before he arrived at Goldberg Cohen the next morning. He began his mining company research by delving into recent trading activity looking for unusual patterns. He discovered a stream of purchases in one of the companies from accounts in Lichtenstein and the Caymans. The buyers had accumulated more than eighteen percent of the outstanding shares the previous thirty days. *The purchased company is the likely acquisition target*, he postulated.

He also found pessimistic predications made by company officials in several industry trade journals.

Those are probably ruse—a way to depress the price of the stock—so insiders can buy it cheaper, he reasoned.

Unbeknownst to Sean, an immigration rights groups had set up camp outside GC's Broad Street headquarters early that afternoon.

"I hear we have protestors outside," Angela said when she called him.

"Really?"

He looked out his corner office window.

People far below were circling the sidewalk carrying signs.

"I guess you haven't seen the newspapers," she said. "There's an article about your confrontation with the thief last night. A homeless rights group is protesting the way you treated him."

"Are you kidding?"

"Nope. It must be a slow news day. So what did you find out about the mining companies?"

He told her about the stock purchases and trade journal articles. "So what do you think?"

"Both companies are in good financial condition, and the egos of the CEOs are reasonable. Sometimes execs won't sell regardless of the interests of their shareholders. I don't think we'll have that problem with these guys. All they care about is the money."

He chuckled. "That's good to hear… just plain, old capitalists."

"Yep. We'll need to move fast before the news leaks out. I think I'll buy ten thousand call options in my Hong Kong account tomorrow night so I get the opening price in Asia. I'll use the December option expiration date and hedge my position with a tight, downside stop-loss, in case I'm wrong. What about you?"

"The volume and price action have been rising all month, even in the face of bad news," he said. "I think someone must have inside information. I bet they'll get away with it."

"Yeah," she agreed. "It's almost impossible for the government to sniff out insider trades when they're submitted through a numbered account at a foreign bank protected by secrecy laws."

"In our case, it isn't insider trading though—right?"

"That's right. We'll report all our trades, as we always do." She chuckled. "Someone's gotta pay taxes to pay for those homeless shelters."

"Okay if I piggy-back on your trade strategy?" he asked. "Of course, I can only purchase a thousand options. I'm not quite as flush as you."

"Not yet, anyhow."

"Thank you, Angie. I'll make at least ten million if this works out."

Angela arrived at the club with several of her girlfriends later that night. They danced together while the band played.

She joined Sean on stage as he packed up his instruments. "Thanks for playing Sade's *Smooth Operator*," she said. "Your sax solo was heavenly."

"My pleasure, Angie. You *are* the smooth operator after all. I played it for you."

She laughed. "I don't know about that. My friend Charlotte is hoping *you'll* take her home tonight."

"Hmmm… How did things go with the assistant district attorney at the Met this afternoon?"

"He fell asleep. I dropped him off when the opera was over. I guess I'm single again."

"Sorry to hear that," he sympathized. "Why don't you ladies stop by my house for a nightcap, assuming we don't run into thieves again on the way to your car?"

The Sunday news channels carried a speech by the New York District Attorney saying he'd conduct a full investigation into Mr. McGowan's assault on the homeless man. The radio talk shows on Monday featured debates about the right to self-defense, or, as in Sean's case, the right to defend a friend, versus the rights of the homeless.

A television reporter confronted Sean as he entered Goldberg Cohen's headquarters building Monday morning. "Why'd you beat up a homeless man?"

"I was simply taking care of my friend when a thief stole her purse," he replied. "If the DA wants to file charges—bring it on. We still have the right to defend ourselves in this country, don't we?"

"But you have a black belt in martial arts." the reporter pointed out. "Shouldn't you have used more restraint?"

Sean smiled. "The guy shouldn't have pulled a switchblade on me. It's as simple as that."

His statements were widely publicized, along with pictures of Angela, references to her wealth, and conjecture about their relationship. A newspaper article about the thief—an illegal immigrant lying in Bellevue Hospital, his medical bills soon to be covered by the public dime—dwelled on issues of liability and fairness.

The press dropped the story when the district attorney announced he wouldn't be filing any charges later that week. The DA didn't mention the fact that the thief had snuck out of the hospital and skipped town.

The results of the confrontation were threefold. First, pretty much everyone in the city now knew who Sean McGowan was. Second, the gossip columnists began churning out stories about Sean's heroism, his good looks—and most important to the society pages—his wealth. They promoted him from villain to hero in the space of a week, anointing him to the echelons of New York's most-eligible, wealthy young bachelors.

The third and most important result of the confrontation was something much simpler in Sean's mind: *Angela got her purse back.*

The mining companies announced their merger agreement on the last Monday in November. The stock of the acquired company shot up forty percent.

Angela and Sean's call options soared tenfold, to 100 million and 10 million, respectively.

Sean's net income, after deducting US federal income tax, New York state income tax, and New York City personal income tax, was just over five million dollars.

It was, indeed, a very nice present, he told himself.

16. Mother

Langley, Virginia—December 2010

Beate enjoyed working with Germany's Federal Intelligence Service, the *Bundesnachrichtendienst*. The United States and Germany, historical enemies during two world wars in the twentieth century, were reluctant at first to share their hard-earned intelligence assets. From Germany's perspective, OSS code-breakers— predecessors to today's CIA and NSA cryptographers—had used clandestine intelligence to help bring down the Third Reich during World War II.

United by a common enemy, their hesitancy to cooperate diminished as the terror war escalated. In one operation the CIA, Germany's FIS, Britain's MI6, and France's Central Directorate of Interior Intelligence discovered a complex money-laundering network involving several banks around the globe. The money trail led them to al-Qaeda cells operating in Germany, France, and Britain: scorpions, ready to strike when activated.

Such was the nature of warfare in the twenty-first century, a world with close alliances among former adversaries and hidden enemies imbedded in the fabric of society.

Beate was a senior case officer with her own set of operatives by December of 2010. She wasn't pleased when the new CIA DS & T director called her to discuss a special assignment at Langley.

"I can't work at a desk again, sir," she protested. "I'll be bored out of my mind."

"We need to expand our threat-detection capabilities with more international data feeds," he argued. "Your connections in Europe and your IT background make you perfect for the job. You can return to the field when you're done."

"What about my agents?"

"Helmut will look after them."

"I hate politics, sir. Countries in Europe have strict personal privacy laws, and they already view the US as the Evil Empire. What if they find out what we're doing?"

"You'll need to get creative to make sure our intrusions aren't detected," he told her. "You'll be working with the PRISM team at the NSA."

"Europe's legacy applications aren't architected for integration," she pointed out. "It's not just about siphoning off data. The semantic data-mapping challenges will be dreadful."

"I'm sure you'll figure it out."

She began her new assignment at Langley in mid-December.

Perhaps I'll have time to dig into the database I designed nine years ago, she decided. *Having data from the FBI, DIA, and local law enforcement agencies was something we never had prior to 9/11.*

She came across Sean McGowan while she was analyzing an archive of reports submitted by private citizens after 9/11.

This is a fortunate unexpected twist of serendipity, she marveled.

It was the second time in a month she'd stumbled upon him. The first time was when she'd read the news article about his run-in with the purse-snatcher, which mushroomed into a national story after his confrontation prompted a homeless rights demonstration.

Her loins tingled when she pulled up an Internet recording of his interview with the television reporter. The feeling surprised her. *It's the first time since Robert I've had a visceral, amatory reaction to a man.* She laughed when she watched Sean tell the New York District Attorney to "bring it on."

The report he'd submitted on the FBI website said he'd observed a strange volume spike in his Banque Lux stock trading application a few days before 9/11. He surmised that someone with prior knowledge of the attacks might have been placing orders to capitalize on the subsequent swoon in the markets. The FBI never followed up with him.

They probably had no idea what to do with it, but I do.

Cold Spring Harbor, New York

Mikhail studied the patrons in the Harbor restaurant as he walked to the window table to meet Vladimir. His bodyguards joined Vladimir's at a table near the entrance. He shook hands with Vladimir and sat down.

The men stared out the window at Oyster Bay's idyllic scenery while they waited for their vodka martinis. The last leaves of autumn—those hardy survivors that had endured the cold nights and diminishing sunlight through mid-December— were dropping from the trees. Tall, yellow grass near the water's edge swayed gently in the breeze—a last tango before snows flattened the meadow for the winter. Several Canadian geese were making touch-and-go landings on the shoals while a flock of seagulls spun graceful circles above them in the sky.

"Khrushchev was only partly right," Vladimir remarked.

Mikhail returned his gaze to his brother. "How so?"

"We will bury them, but not with bombs. We'll use something much more lethal."

"What's that?"

"Fear."

"*Da*," Mikhail said. "So, how much do we have in our accounts?"

"Two-point-two trillion… give or take a few billion."

They pursed their lips conspiratorially, touched their glasses, and drained them. Mikhail motioned at the waitress to bring more.

Vladimir smiled as he looked out the window. "This is sure a long way from Moscow. It seems like just yesterday we were robbing tourists in the Metro so we'd have something to eat."

Mikhail pressed his lips together. "Nothing sharpens the mind like starvation. Living in that coal cave beneath the tracks gave us a priceless education—something we couldn't have gotten anywhere else. So what's our next move?"

"We need a copy of Goldberg Cohen's trading software," Vladimir said. "We lose millions every time I go head-to-head with them in trades."

Mikhail clenched his fist. "Wouldn't it just be easier to take them out?"

Vladimir bristled. "I don't want anything to happen to Angela. Besides, we need their infrastructure. They've built their IT systems in Luxembourg and Colorado deep below the surface, with redundant power sources and pulse-resistant fiber optics. Even nukes can't take them out. It would take years to build something similar."

The waitress placed their drinks on the table.

Vladimir looked out the window while he sipped his vodka. "I like coming out here from the city. It's very peaceful."

"*Da*. The town's history makes me feel right at home. Oyster Bay was a mecca for Canadian rum-runners during Prohibition," he chuckled, "and this restaurant was a brothel."

Vladimir laughed. "How appropriate."

Mikhail covered his mouth to hide a yawn.

"You look tired," Vladimir said.

"*Da*. I interviewed two new dancers at my Philadelphia *Taste of Heaven* club last night."

Vladimir shook his head. "Don't you ever get tired of all those women?"

Mikhail smirked. "No. They're all different, and once I've had them— they're mine." He gritted his teeth. "What do you expect me to do—find some stray cat like Mother to settle down with?"

A long stare connected them.

"I don't remember anything about her," Vladimir said. "I was only three when she left."

"You're lucky. She used to run off with different men for days at a time. I got a lot of scars fending off rapists and thieves in the coal cave where she left us."

Vladimir extended his hand. "Thank you for protecting me, brother."

Mikhail accepted the handshake. "*Da*. You were all I had. What else could I do?"

Vladimir nodded.

"How long until the end game?" Mikhail said.

"We need a few more catalysts. The nefarious, intertwined web of cross-border debt built up with promissory notes by capitalists who print money out of thin air will explode into a firestorm once countries default and refuse to pay their debts."

Mikhail raised his eyebrows. "Whoa—slow down, there. I didn't attend Wharton, even though I did read most of your books. What do you mean?"

Vladimir smiled. "We need to create more instability—like faults before an earthquake—so we can scoop up the pieces for pennies on the dollar. Once we control the world's commodities we can dictate policy, the way the capitalists do today."

"*Da*. So how much more do we need?"

"Another eight hundred billion should do it. The world's stock and commodity markets will collapse when China stops lending. That'll happen when they realize their loan payments from the US are nothing more than hollow promises. We'll grab controlling stakes in most of the world's resources when the market crashes. No one will be able to stop us then."

"It could take a couple of years to accumulate that much money," Mikhail pointed out. "Our Russian oil industry comrades give us good information about OPEC production plans, but we only make fifty or sixty billion with each major policy shift. We need something more dramatic, like 9/11 or Pearl Harbor, to trigger a larger rip in the markets."

"I'm working on some scenarios using the nukes," Vladimir said. "By the way, did you ever find out who burned our buyer in Munich?"

Mikhail nostrils flared. "*Nyet*. No one knows anything."

"I think they're more valuable to us now as catalysts for the apocalypse scenarios I'm working on."

Mikhail finished his drink and motioned for another. "What else is on your agenda?"

"I think we should increase our budget for lobbying and political payoffs next year," Vladimir replied.

"*Da.* I agree. Our weapons lobbyists in Congress have been very productive. More guns lead to more mass shootings, which increases weapon sales. It's a great business model, like the mutual assured destruction arms race between Russia and America."

Vladimir smiled. "The way these crazy Americans keep killing themselves off, the politicians will have no choice but to impose martial law when things really break down."

Mikhail nodded. "The neighborhood-protection product line we're developing will be huge once we kill off the Second Amendment opposition. The napalm-dispersion mortars and bazookas should be big sellers. Every neighborhood will need an arsenal."

Vladimir laughed. "I think I'll move out of the country when that happens."

Mikhail laughed along with him. "Me, too… to a country with good gun control laws so we'll be safe."

Both men laughed heartily. They finished their drinks and ordered more.

"We can meet at my mansion near Sagamore Hill next month," Mikhail said, "assuming the remodeling is complete."

"Great. I'd like to see what you've done to the place."

Mikhail eyed the brunette waitress after she delivered their drinks.

Vladimir chuckled. "I see that look in your eye. Do you still play that pick-up game—the one you made up in the Moscow Metro when you were fourteen—where you time yourself to see how quickly you can get a girl you just met to have sex with you?"

Mikhail chuckled. "*Da.* I considered it with our waitress, but I'm too tired tonight."

Vladimir sipped his drink. "How's your friend in Maryland?"

"Which one?"

Vladimir laughed. "Nikolai. Is he taking good care of our nukes?"

"*Da.* He's anxious to know when we'll sell them, though."

Mikhail ground his jaw. "I can't wait to put a bullet in his head. That bastard tried to spit on me in Kabul."

Vladimir nodded. "But he's a good operative."

"I hate to admit it, but it's true. He's always had a knack for logistics."

Mikhail's mind strayed to Yvonna. *It's good to have a woman I don't have to train when I need her,* he reminded himself.

"Are you still screwing her?" Vladimir said.

"Yvonna? Not for a while. She's changed a bit… you know, gained some weight."

"Well so have you, brother. How much?"

"Probably about three pounds… just like I have."

Vladimir guffawed. "You *are* particular." He sipped his drink. "Changing the subject, have you heard of an organization called the World Protection Council?"

"No. Why?"

"My sponsor at Wharton, John Napoleon—the guy who flew us to the Caribbean in his Learjet during my college breaks—came to see me the other day."

"*Da.* I remember those trips. Those Cuban women were very sexy."

"He wants to discuss what he calls 'a mutually beneficial business opportunity.' Can you do some background research with your KGB contacts? I want to find out what he's been up to."

"Sure," Mikhail confirmed. "By the way, the KGB was renamed FSB in 1991, after the *coup d'état* to depose Gorbachev failed."

"Ahhhh… That's right. Old habits I guess."

"Many of my colleagues disappeared after the coup." Mikhail stared off in the distance. "I was lucky I'd already resigned."

"Yeah, I remember. Anyhow, Napoleon had a woman with him named Judith. The only way I can describe her is… exquisite—dark-olive skin, beautiful green eyes—Lebanese or Israeli if I had to guess. There's something captivating and exotic about her."

Mikhail chuckled. "So you're thinking about dipping it in, huh? I thought you had your heart set on Angela. Of course, you'll never get anywhere with *her* if you don't ask her out."

"I'm not ready to meet Angela yet," Vladimir said.

Mikhail shook his head. "I know you play for keeps when it comes to women, but you're missing out. It's obvious we have different fathers."

Vladimir smirked. "Obviously."

"Women are good entertainment," Mikhail continued, "and they have their uses. Remember how much money I made from my stable of runaways I turned into prostitutes in the Moscow Metro?"

Vladimir ignored the question. "I'll set up a meeting with Napoleon and Judith in Central Park so you can take pictures."

The brothers spent the rest of the evening discussing their numerous business ventures. The restaurant was empty except for their bodyguards when they'd finished.

Mikhail raised his glass. "To being fat and rich, like the Americans we used to despise."

"Yes... but much smarter. The world will see."

They drank. Vladimir smiled. "How about another toast?"

Mikhail nodded. "*Da*... to Mother."

They kept their steel-blue eyes focused on each other while they drank; eyes they'd inherited from the mother who'd abandoned them.

It had taken fifteen years to track her down. She was living as the whore of a government official in a luxury dacha on the outskirts of Moscow when they found her.

They were polite during the reunion. After brief introductions, they took turns, one by one, emptying all eight rounds of their Makarovs into the naked couple as they lay in their bed.

17. Resurrection

New York City—February 2011

Goldberg Cohen's Chief Legal Officer, Jerome King, called Angela and Sean into his office on the first Friday in February. "I received an informal inquiry from the Securities and Exchange Commission last night," King said. "They believe you made some illegal trades prior to a merger between two mining companies last November. Is that true?"

Sean and Angela exchanged guarded glances. An SEC investigation was always serious business.

"Of course not," she said. "We did our own analysis. I'll bet Isaac Bachmann is behind this. He probably knew I'd make some trades after we saw him with the mining company executives at Delmonico's."

"You're right," King said. "My contact at the SEC told me Bachmann turned you in."

"He knows the insider trading accusations are bogus," she declared. "It's a way for his company to wound us, without any consequences for themselves."

Angela and Sean explained what they'd done.

King looked over his notes "The accusations seem baseless. I'll document your version in a response letter to the SEC, unless you want me to hold something back."

"We have nothing to hide," she said.

An SEC attorney, accompanied by FBI Special Agents Roger Hartfield and Oscar Hernandez, arrived at Goldberg Cohen's headquarters a week later for a meeting with Angela, Sean, and Counselor King. Both FBI agents were in good physical condition. Agent Hernandez was the most intimidating of the pair. His broad shoulders, compact waist, and menacing demeanor gave him the guise of a caged, welterweight boxer.

Counselor King handed the SEC attorney copies of Sean and Angela's trade transactions, tax filings and payment receipts. The FBI agents observed the meeting without saying anything.

The press lambasted Goldberg Cohen when the SEC announced the investigation a few days later.

FBI agent Hartfield stopped by Sean's West Village townhome unannounced that Saturday morning. Hartfield became incensed when Sean refused to answer his questions about Angela's private life, their relationship, Goldberg Cohen's proprietary stock trading algorithms, or their information technology systems.

"You've been very uncooperative," Hartfield said as he stood up to leave.

"Those questions aren't related to our case," Sean replied.

"We'll see about that," the agent snapped.

Angela called Sean after Hartfield visited her later that morning. They determined that he'd asked them both similar questions, which they each refused to answer.

The SEC issued a statement a month later saying they were discontinuing their investigation, pointing out that Sean and Angela hadn't tried to hide anything. They'd paid their taxes immediately after their trades—almost fifty million dollars in Angela's case.

Bachmann's firm filed a civil lawsuit against Goldberg Cohen a week later, seeking $110 million in restitution.

Sean, Angela, and David Cohen met with Counselor King to discuss their response.

"I think Isaac's company has a personal vendetta against me," Angela said.

"Why is that?" King asked.

Remember that *Journal* article a few years ago, where they quoted me saying that Isaac's firm was pressuring rating agencies to give triple-A ratings to their subprime mortgages so they could dump their crap on unsuspecting pension funds?"

"Yeah, I remember," King said. "That took a lot of courage. Many Wall Street firms viewed you as a pariah for revealing their dirty secrets."

"I was very proud of you," David Cohen told her. "It didn't take long for the judge to dismiss their case after the financial system imploded."

"Perhaps we should have sued *them*," Angela said.

"Perhaps," David Cohen said. "No offense to you, Jerome, but as I said at the time, litigation only makes lawyers rich. I just wanted to get back to business."

King nodded. "I agree. The case could've dragged on for years."

"This feels like a setup to me," Sean said. "I'm sure Bachmann knew we'd be smart enough to keep everything legal. They're trying to disparage our reputations."

"We'll still need to prepare a defense," King said.

FBI Agents Hartfield and Hernandez pulled up to the curb in front of Goldberg Cohen's Broad Street headquarters at 3:30 p.m. the following Friday. Officers in two New York City police cars pulled in behind the FBI police car and began directing traffic around the scene.

Hartfield and Hernandez arrived at Goldberg Cohen's fifty-sixth floor lobby a moment later. The soft lights and comfortable leather couches were a world away from the honking horns on the street below.

The receptionist sat behind a U-shaped partition with a white-marble countertop that matched the floor. A nametag fastened to her lapel said *Joanna Clark*. A transparent Plexiglas security wall behind her desk shielded a hallway dotted with offices.

The agents wore black trench coats with yellow FBI letters glued between the shoulder blades. Dark-blue suit jackets beneath their trench coats covered side arms in shoulder holsters.

"May I help you?" Clark said as they approached.

Hartfield displayed his badge. "We're here to pick up Sean McGowan."

She pointed at the register. "Please sign in. I'll see if he's available."

The men ignored her request as she typed.

She motioned them towards the lobby's mocha-colored couches. "Sean isn't available right now. Would you like to wait for a few minutes?"

"We need to see him *now*," Hartfield said.

Her smile melted. Neither agent moved.

"I'll be right back," she said.

She swiped her badge through the security reader in the Plexiglas wall and disappeared into an office down the hall.

Angela returned with Ms. Clark to the lobby. "Good afternoon," Angela said. "Sean isn't available right now. How may I help you?"

Hartfield smiled derisively. "We're here to arrest Sean. We need to see him *now*."

Angela's face went pale. She cleared her throat. "What are you arresting him for?"

"We'll discuss that with him," Hartfield said.

Angela turned to Ms. Clark. "Can you ask Sean to join us in the lobby?"

Clark fingered her gold necklace. "His status says *Do Not Disturb*. There's no way I can reach him."

Angela looked at the lobby clock and back to the agents. "The markets close in twenty minutes. Can't you wait until then?"

"No," Hernandez bellowed, in a thick, Bronx Puerto-Rican accent. "We need to see him *now*."

Angela punched the Down arrow at the elevator. She entered with the agents, and tapped the button marked 55. They emerged onto a floor with the same white marble as the executive suite.

They approached a security guard sitting at a desk in front of a tall set of baroque, hand-carved oak doors designed in the style of a traditional Florentine Italian rococo archway. The words *"Lasciate ogne speranza, voi ch'intrate,"* rendered in ornate, gold letters, stood like a commandment above the doorway. An English translation below the Italian said, *"Abandon hope, all ye who enter here."*

The security guard copied the agent's names and badge numbers into his visitor's log.

Angela pulled her ID card through the badge reader and the trio entered the trading floor.

The room was noisy, filled with the clamorous banter of forty men and a sprinkling of women packed around islands of desks bellowing directives through headsets in English and other assorted languages. The incessant drone of phones provided an undulating current of immediacy. The traders studied LED computer screens as they talked. A gargantuan digital lock above the doorway ticked away the hours, minutes, seconds, and milliseconds of each day's trading opportunities.

The agents followed Angela as she circumnavigated the desks to Sean's glass-walled corner office. The traders barely looked up as the agents passed. It wasn't unusual to have visitors. Wealthy clients—elderly women bedecked in jewelry, Asian and South American business executives, and Middle Eastern oil sheiks—had all made the rounds at one time or another.

The traders *did* stop what they were doing when they saw the FBI labels on the agents' coats. The hullabaloo in the room slowly subsided, like waves after high tide on a receding sea.

Sean's back faced the door when Angela entered his office. He was staring at six computer displays wearing noise-limiting headphones attached to a music player. An empty CD case on his desk revealed he was listening to Mahler's Symphony Number Two, the *"Resurrection."*

Angela knocked on the doorframe. He didn't respond.

I know he's in his zone, she recognized, *a world of deep concentration, where graphs and charts driven by complex mathematical equations beckon for his attention.*

She looked at her watch: 3:45 p.m., fifteen minutes before closing—the most important part of the trading day—actually, the month, since options were expiring. *He needs to close out his positions before the final bell,* she knew. *It's too risky to hold them overnight—or, God forbid, over the weekend!*

Brooding clouds threatened a snowstorm beyond his window. The cavernous wound where the twin towers had once stood was now under construction with a new skyscraper: The One World Trade Center.

She tapped on Sean's shoulder.

The agents entered behind her, guarding the doorway preventing escape. The guns in their shoulder holsters were now clearly visible.

Sean raised his hand without looking up. "Please don't disturb me."

Angela looked behind her through the glass walls. A sea of bewildered eyeballs stared at them. The discordant banter consuming the room a moment earlier had dissipated, displaced by an ominous hush, like a morgue before a funeral.

She turned to look at Sean's computer screens. He hummed quietly while he worked. A large sell order appeared on his pending-trades queue.

Sean adjusted the ask price of a hedged put option up a penny. The move yielded an additional $30,000 dollars. He booked his profit.

Agent Hernandez's voice punctured the silence. "Mister McGowan."

* * *

The chorus of Mahler's symphony was pulsing through Sean's headphones when the voice rudely interrupted him. *Dammit,* he decided. *I'll deal with the perpetrator after the market closes. They should know better than to disturb me now.*

Another huge sell order had just hit the pending trades queue. Markets were diving before the close, as an avalanche of panicked investors trampled each other screaming for the exits.

Sean raised his put-option ask price two cents, locking in a $70,000 profit ten seconds later. His eye jumped to the applet on the screen displaying his "trading batting average" statistic. *What a day!*

He and Pankaj had designed the program while drinking beer and discussing baseball statistics at a Yankees game. The applet now ranked every trader in the firm. The partners had even gotten into the act, establishing a $100,000 bonus each quarter for the trader with the best average. Sean's rating, eighty-nine percent, was currently the highest on the floor. *It's not about the money, though,* he reminded himself. *Bragging rights are what really matter.*

I've already made three million, nine hundred thousand dollars for the firm today. These last trades will put me over four million—not my best one-day record… but close.

He began to hum the next refrain of Mahler's fifth movement chorus when someone yanked off his headphones.

He spun around in his chair.

His anger became shock when he saw the agents. Their malevolent glares assured him this wasn't a friendly visit.

Angela's face was ashen, her voice shaky. "Sean... they're here for you."

Hernandez placed his headphones on the desk and turned off the power switch for his computers. His displays blinked and went black.

Neither man offered to shake his hand. Everyone on the trading floor was staring at him through the glass walls.

Agent Hartfield exposed his black, stainless steel 9 mm P229 Sig Sauer. "Sean McGowan, you're under arrest for obstruction of justice," he announced.

"What?"

Hartfield handed him a warrant. Sean's heart stopped as he read.

Agent Hartfield smirked. "Stand up and turn around so we can cuff you."

"I've done nothing wrong," Sean protested.

"You can discuss that with the federal prosecutor," Hartfield snapped.

"Stand up and turn around," Hernandez barked.

Sean stood and placed his hands behind his back. Hartfield latched and tightened the cuffs while Hernandez recited Miranda rights.

"... If you cannot afford an attorney, one will be appointed for you. Do you understand these rights as they have been read to you?"

Sean stared with a blank expression at Hernandez. "I think so."

Hartfield grabbed Sean above the elbow and pushed him out the door.

Beads of sweat erupted beneath his armpits as he plodded across the floor. Unanswered phones and the echo of hard-soled shoes on marble filled his ears. *My legs feel like putty, as if I'm trudging through a stream.* The handcuffs chafed his wrists with each step.

A swell of discordant voices erupted as Dante's doors closed behind them.

Angela followed the three men to the elevator. "Should I call Andrew?"

"Yes," Sean said. "Tell him what happened."

"Where are you taking him?" she asked Hartfield.

"Twenty-Six Federal Plaza."

Hernandez flashed his badge at people waiting for the elevator as they descended, telling them to "take the next one." The agents paraded Sean through the crowded foyer to the exit when they reached the lobby.

A swarm of reporters and television crews accosted him on the sidewalk. Several pointed their microphones at his mouth.

"What do you think about your arrest, Mr. McGowan?" a reporter asked.

The flashing police lights had lured a large crowd to the scene.

The snow swirled in gusts whipping Sean's brown hair across his forehead as the reporters peppered him with questions.

I feel disembodied, as if I'm part of a throng witnessing a peculiar event, instead of the main attraction.

"... Why did you do it, Mr. McGowan? Are you going to return the money? When will Angela Cohen be arrested?"

He shivered. *I don't have my coat.*

The reporters swerved their microphones like guns on a mortar battery when Hernandez began to speak. Bits and pieces crept through the haze.

"...cleaning up the city to stop white-collar crime..."

"...the ongoing investigation may lead to additional arrests..."

"...evidence will be revealed in court..."

A mob had gathered by the time they'd finished. Hartfield shoved Sean into a cordon opened by the police through the crowd to the marked FBI police car.

Angela emerged from the building as Hernandez opened the rear door. "Wait!" she yelled.

Cameras flashed as she barreled her way through the crowd to reach Sean. "You forgot your coat," she said.

Hernandez took the coat from her, checked the pockets for contraband, and placed it on the front seat next to the uniformed driver.

She stared with confusion into Sean's eyes.

"Thanks, Angie," Sean said. "Don't worry. We'll get this sorted out."

Hartfield pressed Sean's head down, pushed him into the back seat of the Ford Crown Victoria, and sat down next to him.

The metal handcuffs are biting into my wrists.

Hernandez slid into the back seat on the other side, and the FBI driver veered the police car away from the curb.

"How did those reporters know I'd be arrested?" Sean asked.

Hartfield smirked without answering.

Progress was slow through the heavy traffic even with sirens. The curious and demonizing glared at him as they passed.

I walked this same route to work this morning... and now I'm a criminal? Sean marveled. *What will my mother and sister think?*

Hartfield steered him through several neon-lighted hallways after they arrived at FBI headquarters. A guard fingerprinted and photographed him. Another guard made him pee into a cup for a drug urinalysis.

Hartfield then accompanied Sean to his new home—an eight-by-eight foot, cement-floored holding cell already tenanted by a twenty-one year old African American. The jailer removed Sean's cuffs. The hallway echoed with a definitive clunk when the iron door clanged shut.

"Have a nice night with your new girlfriend," Hartfield said, laughing derisively. "His name is Spike."

Sean sat down on a plastic cot across from Spike. A filthy metal toilet without a seat hung from the rear wall above a half-used roll of toilet paper. The cell smelled like sewer gas. A fierce light above the hallway pressed vertical shadows over them.

Sean stared at the floor for several minutes before speaking. "What are you in here for?" he finally asked.

"Selling pot." The youth's voice was defiant. "It's bullshit."

I sense fear beneath his bravado, Sean recognized. "Why are you in here for that? I thought this place was for federal offenders."

"They say one of my dealers is in Jersey, which makes it federal," the young man answered. "What about you?"

"They say obstruction of justice," Sean replied. "It's bullshit."

Sean tried to make light of their predicament. "Perhaps we should swap."

"You don't want my sentence, man," the youth replied cryptically. "This is my third strike. I'll be in prison forever if they convict me."

Sean contemplated the young entrepreneur's future. *Life in prison incarcerated with rape-hardened criminals would be hell on earth. This must be a nightmare!*

The chorus of Mahler's *Resurrection* Symphony was stilling ringing in his brain, a fitting backdrop for the thrust-and-parry derivative fencing he'd been doing, before the whirlwind vortex dropped him into the abysmal jail cell. *This can't be real,* he shouted to himself.

He knew it was real when he saw the picture of Angela handing him his coat on the front page of the *Times* the next morning. It was hard to tell if the moisture glistening on her cheeks was snow... or tears.

18. Snowbird

Andrew arrived at Twenty-Six Federal Plaza on Friday evening with plenty of cash to post bail. It didn't matter. "Administrative delays" thwarted Sean's release until Monday morning. He had to post a bail bond of $50,000—much higher than normal for his alleged crime—after the federal prosecutor convinced the judge that Sean was a flight risk because of his wealth.

"It's good to be free again," Sean exulted, as he stood with Andrew outside the courthouse hailing a cab. "My jail cell was filthy."

"Most people would make the same mistake," Andrew said. "Arresting you for talking with Angela after Hartfield's interrogation is ridiculous."

Sean fumed. "Hartfield never told me I couldn't talk with Angela about his questions when he came to my house that day. She discussed her interview questions with me, too, later that night. I'll need to be careful with what I say, so she doesn't get arrested."

"I'm sure we'll get your case dismissed," Andrew said. "Most people don't know that discussing FBI questions with another party in a case is illegal. Hartfield should've told you. Don't worry. A jury will never convict you if we go to trial."

The federal government refused to drop Sean's "obstruction of justice by tip-off" charge when Andrew met with the prosecuting attorney during the ensuing months. The Justice Department did offer Sean a plea deal the week before his trial.

"You'll spend six months in a white-collar prison if you plead guilty," Andrew said when he called Sean to discuss the offer.

"Screw them," Sean snapped. "I'll lose a lot of my rights if I plead guilty to a felony."

"That's what I thought you'd say. We have a strong case. We'll fight them in court."

"I'm sorry for getting so upset," Sean said. "I guess my lack of sleep is catching up with me. The newspapers have demonized Angela and me for months, calling us white-collar criminals."

"I know," Andrew sympathized. "I'd be angry, too. I've scoured the NYU law library and on-line legal resources seeking case precedents for obstruction of justice by tip-off. Although *technically* you might be guilty, convictions for this type of crime are almost unheard of. Agent Hartfield made a serious error. He should've told you not to discuss your interview questions with Angela. I'm confident a jury will exonerate you."

"The negative publicity will crush Goldberg Cohen if I accept the felony plea deal," Sean said, "and I'll lose my right to vote. The SEC could also bar me from ever working in the securities industry again."

Sean's face looked haggard when they met in Andrew's law office the evening before his trial.

"There's a good chance of an acquittal," Andrew said. "However, everything's a crapshoot with Judge Richter. He's unpredictable. Unfortunately, you got the most capricious judge on the bench."

"How'd we end up with him? I still don't understand how the legal system works. Why is the personality of the judge so important? Aren't truth and justice all that matter?"

"Judges wield a lot of power in their courtroom, and you can never tell what a jury might do. I wish I could give you the answer you want, but I can't."

Sean pointed at his 5'-high-by-7'-wide scroll tacked to Andrew's wall. He'd filled it with carefully drawn boxes describing every piece of evidence. Each box had arrows pointing to decision blocks with case precedents that pointed to other boxes that fed a large, rectangular box on the right side of the scroll with the word INNOCENT, typed in red letters. "What about my flow diagram?" Sean asked.

"I know you use flow diagrams when you develop software," Andrew said, "but it's dangerous to assume juries are logical. I can understand why you're exploring every angle, using every tool you know. I'd be doing that, too. Unfortunately, your diagram neglected the most important variable."

Sean frowned. "What's that?"

"Human nature. Juries are fickle. You can never predict what they'll do. You also can't control how a judge's mood might sway a jury."

"Perhaps I'm more optimistic about humans than you are, Andrew. I believe logic *will* prevail. Look at everything we've accomplished with logic… programmed into computers. We can guide rockets to the moon, land airplanes in a storm without a pilot, and weave catheters through the human body. The US and Russia could even launch a nuclear attack that would kill billions of people and make the earth uninhabitable in fewer than thirty minutes. Certainly this is simpler."

"That's my point," Andrew argued. "Do you really think our Mutually Assured Destruction doctrine with the Russians is logical? A brinkmanship grievance, a terrorist strike erroneously attributed to one of our countries, or a rogue military officer launching an attack on their own could compel both countries to launch thousands of nuclear warheads. Juries can be just as illogical as politicians."

Sean stared at his flow diagram. *Maybe I should design a program to automate court cases* he contemplated. *That would ensure justice.*

Andrew leaned back with his hands behind his head. "Perhaps the government is looking for a scapegoat," he speculated. "People are angry after all the shenanigans pulled by the banks—and why didn't they arrest Angela? She's just as guilty. You really should consider testifying. A jury won't be able to ignore the fact that Hartfield didn't tell either of you not to discuss his interviews."

"I'm not going to say anything on the witness stand that might implicate her," Sean insisted.

Andrew yawned. "We should go home. We have a big day tomorrow."

They arrived at the courthouse at 8:00 a.m. David Cohen and Pankaj sat behind them, next to Sean's mother and sister in front of several rows of reporters.

The federal prosecutor called Angela as his first witness after jury selection. "Ms. Cohen, did the defendant discuss Agent Hartfield's interview with you?"

"Agent Hartfield didn't tell him he couldn't discuss his questions with me."

The prosecutor faced the judge. "Objection, Your Honor. That's hearsay. Ms. Cohen didn't attend Mr. McGowan's meeting with Agent Hartfield. I'd like her statement stricken from the record."

"Sustained."

The judge looked at Angela. "Please answer the prosecutor's questions without offering your opinion, Ms. Cohen."

"Yes," she said. "Sean did discuss his interview questions with me."

"I have no further questions, Your Honor."

Andrew rose for his cross-examination. "Did Sean tell you the FBI warned him not to talk about his interview, Ms. Cohen?"

"No," she replied. "The FBI didn't tell him he shouldn't talk to me."

The prosecutor stood up. "Objection, Your Honor, that's hearsay again. She wasn't present during Sean's interview. There's no way she could know what they discussed."

"Sustained," Judge Richter said. "The jury must disregard the statement by Ms. Cohen." He turned to Angela. "As I've told you before, Ms. Cohen, please answer the questions *without offering your opinion*."

Her stare connected with Sean across the courtroom. "No, Sean didn't say anything about a warning from Agent Hartfield."

The prosecutor then called Agent Hartfield to the stand. "Agent Hartfield, did you instruct the defendant not to discuss your interview questions when you met with him?"

Hartfield faced the jury. "I did," he replied. "This was an ongoing investigation. I told him not to discuss my interview questions with anyone."

Sean touched Andrew's arm. "He's lying."

Andrew nodded. "I'll hit with that on my cross."

"I have no further questions, Your Honor." The prosecutor sat down.

Andrew walked briskly to the front of the witness stand. "Are you sure you told Sean not to discuss his interview with anyone?"

"Of course," Hartfield answered calmly. "I always give criminals that warning."

"Are you aware of the penalty for perjury, Agent Hartfield?" Andrew persisted.

Hartfield smirked. "Of course I am. I have no reason to lie."

Andrew's voice rose. "Are you sure you told Sean not to discuss his case?"

The prosecutor stood up. "Objection. The defendant's attorney is badgering the witness."

"Sustained," Judge Richter said testily. "Move on. He already answered your question."

Andrew glared at Hartfield. "I have no further questions."

He walked back to the defendant's table and sat down.

The attorneys presented their final arguments after lunch. Andrew repeated his assertion that Hartfield was mistaken.

Then Judge Richter gave the jury their deliberation instructions: "Not knowing the law is no defense for breaking it," Richter said, pausing for emphasis. "The legal theory known as *Ignorantia legis neminem excusat* is applicable here. That's Latin, for 'ignorance of the law excuses no one.'" The judge raised his voice. "Everyone would use their lack of knowledge of the law to escape their crimes if this principle wasn't in place. The law applies to everyone, even Wall Street billionaires."

Sean had noticed a few heavy-lidded jurors during the trial. Everyone was wide-eyed and sitting up straight now.

Judge Richter brandished the handle of his gavel at the jurors. "Ignorance of the law is no excuse. If Mr. McGowan broke the law—and he did, if he discussed his FBI interview questions with Ms. Cohen—you must come back with a guilty verdict. It's your responsibility to uphold the law!" The judge pounded his gavel for emphasis.

An elderly female juror was close to tears as the bailiff ushered them out of the courtroom for their deliberations.

Andrew scowled and turned to Sean. "The judge's jury instructions were prejudicial," he declared. "I can use that as a basis for an appeal."

The jury finished quickly. The bailiff seated them, and brought the verdict to Judge Richter. His face remained expressionless as he read.

Sean looked back at his mother and sister, who'd flown in from New Mexico for the trial. Then his heart stopped.

One of the "gray men" was sitting in the back row. The man, in his late sixties now, had the same awkward stare Sean remembered from his childhood. He hadn't seen the man in fifteen years, since he'd spotted him outside the church, the day he married Rachel in Boulder.

"Please stand, Mr. McGowan," the bailiff said.

Sean, Andrew, and the prosecutor rose to their feet.

Judge Richter glared at Sean. "Mr. McGowan, on the count of obstruction of justice by tip-off, the court finds you *guilty*."

The weight of the words plunged a dagger into Sean's heart. His mouth fell open.

"The jury is dismissed," the judge said. "Thank you for your service. The defendant will remain free on bond until his sentencing hearing."

Andrew shook his head as the courtroom emptied. "Don't worry," he said empathetically. "We'll win this on appeal."

Sean was in a daze, unable to comprehend anything.

Andrew guided him outside by the arm to a taxi. Angela said she'd take his mother and sister back to their hotel.

Sean read an article about his trial in the *Times* the next day, proclaiming that Wall Street criminals were "finally getting their due."

The harsh words jarred his soul. He put down the newspaper. *I feel like a character in a surrealistic Fellini movie, where nothing appears as it is, and nothing is what it seems.*

The press will denigrate us for another year while we wait for an appeal hearing he contemplated. *Goldberg Cohen's employees would also be targets. Some have already left because of the pressure, and we've lost several important clients. We'll lose more now.*

A wall of tears burst from his eyes as he considered his dismal fate.

He dialed Andrew when he'd emptied the till. "I can't understand what went wrong yesterday."

"I think we'll win on appeal," Andrew told him. "For one thing, there'll be a different judge."

"I'm tired of fighting. Can you discuss a plea deal with the prosecutor? Find out when I can begin my sentence. The sooner I start, the sooner I can move on with my life."

"No, Sean," Andrew pleaded. "Please be patient. We can win this."

"How long will it take for an appeal hearing?"

"I don't know. The court has a huge backlog. It could take a year—perhaps longer."

"Find out what kind of sentence you can arrange," Sean said. "It must be worth something to save the taxpayers the cost of another trial."

"The Justice Department's offer won't be very good now that they have a conviction."

"Call me when you find out." He hung up.

Sean met with Counselor King to discuss the verdict two days later.

"I'm not an expert in criminal or appellate law," King said, "but I'm pretty sure the appeals court will need a compelling reason to overturn your conviction, especially after a jury verdict. It's rare for judges to torpedo each other. They all play golf together, after all."

King's words cemented Sean's decision. *I'll take my medicine*, he decided.

Andrew tried to dissuade him, but he'd made up his mind.

Sean packed up his office six weeks later, the day before he was to report to the prison for incarceration. He carried a cardboard box filled with his belongings to his exit interview with David Cohen.

Sean looked out across the skyscrapers as he sat down. "I feel I should resign," he told David Cohen.

"Nonsense," David said. "Our business will recover once you're exonerated. Besides, I won't accept your resignation. I'm calling in favors in Washington to look into this mess. Regardless of what happens, you'll always have a job here when you return."

"Thank you, sir, but a felony conviction will probably make it impossible for me to work in the securities industry again. I think my Wall Street days are over."

"I have our attorneys in DC looking into this," David assured him. "Don't give up hope."

David came from behind his desk and hugged Sean. "I'll be down to Florida to see you soon."

Angela closed her door after Sean stepped into her office. She held him tightly as she cried. "Oh, Sean… I'm so sorry this happened." Her tears streamed down his neck.

"Don't worry, Angie. I'll be fine."

"I'm coming down… to see you… every month," she said between sobs.

"Please don't do that. I'll be all right."

He was standing on the sidewalk flagging down a taxi with a cardboard box beneath his arm ten minutes later—an inauspicious end to a fourteen-year career on the Street. He met with a realtor to put his West Village townhouse up for sale before he left for the airport.

The government wouldn't budge on his three-year sentence. However, Andrew was able to negotiate where Sean would do his time. Sean's first priority was a prison that allowed inmates to play music.

"I need something to hold on to," he told Andrew, "so I don't lose my sanity."

The Justice Department agreed to let him serve his sentence at the minimum-security Federal Prison Camp at Niceville, Florida. The fact that he owned a condominium in Palm Harbor north of Clearwater, helped secure the deal. The prison, located east of Eglin Air Force Base near Pensacola, housed white-collar criminals—an oxymoron used to describe crooks committing "victimless" crimes.

Sean dialed Pankaj, who now lived in Colorado with the rest of the engineering team while he waited to board his flight. They'd moved Goldberg Cohen's computer systems out of Manhattan to a hardened computer site deep inside the mountains west of Boulder after 9/11.

"Are you still thinking about becoming a trader?" Sean asked.

"No thanks," Pankaj replied emphatically. "Selena would never let me do that after what happened to you."

"I'll see you in three years, or perhaps a year, if they let me out early for good behavior."

Sean boarded his flight to Pensacola a few minutes later.

He tried to be optimistic as he looked out at the flat, green fields from the back of his taxi during his ride to the prison early the next morning. *I'm a snowbird now*, he told himself, *like thousands of other refugees fleeing the frigid north for the winter, and I'll have plenty of time to work on music arrangements—something I haven't done since college.*

He surrendered himself at 7:00 a.m., exchanging his tailored, $2,000 suit for a green prison uniform.

Amos, his cellblock captain, a tall, lanky African American in his early fifties, shackled Sean in handcuffs and leg irons and escorted him to his cell.

"You'll need to wear shackles when we escort you because of your black belt in martial arts," Amos said, eying Sean warily.

The manacles helped Sean assimilate the new identity now irrevocably tattooed to his resume: *Convicted felon.*

19. Indulgences

Washington, DC

Beate wasn't interested in dating for many years after she lost Robert. Things got complicated when she did start thinking about having a relationship again. She didn't want to date someone from the Agency, and all the security vetting required for someone outside was a real pain. Consequently, she remained single.

That didn't mean men didn't go after her. She was a constant target. Europe's most prolific playboy spies gave her the sobriquet *Das Eiskönigin*—the Ice Queen—after she spurned their solicitations. Her US colleagues adopted the cognomen when she returned to Langley.

Beate laughed when one of her female coworkers told her about her secret nickname. "Good," she retorted. "I hope it discourages spurious flirtations I don't have time for anyway."

She'd intended to contact Sean after discovering his FBI submission, but she had to put her plans on hold when she got too busy at work. She was stunned a year later when she saw the newspaper headline: *Wall Street Executive Sean McGowan Going to Prison*.

It gnawed at her the rest of the day: *How could a man at the top of his game have fallen so far, so quickly? Was he like Icarus, flying too close to the sun... or was something more sinister at work?*

She tossed and turned for hours that night before she dressed and drove to Langley, determined to find out what had happened to the man who'd stirred her desires.

Niceville, Florida

Sean's first night at the prison was difficult. He stared at the cement ceiling assessing his life, from the hard, thin mattress of his top bunk.

How did I end up here he wondered? *Where did I go wrong?*

It took several days to get used to all the new sounds and smells. Some of his fellow inmates had given up using deodorant, and the toilets reeked of sewer gas. Sleep was impossible at first with all the snoring, farting, belching, and noxious odors of a hundred men penned up two to a cell.

His cellmate, Albert Osterhaus, had no problem sleeping. He'd been there for two years before Sean arrived, so he'd had plenty of time to adjust.

Sean cursed his training as an engineer in his darkest moments. *My profession deluded me into believing the world is logical.* Not anymore, he fumed inwardly. *I used to believe some kind of karmic energy—what some people call God—made sure things worked out the way they should. Not anymore.*

Prison bestowed many lessons, the most important: Never show fear, and always watch your back. Bullies looking for extortion money harassed him when he first arrived, and he had to fend off an attack by a predatory homosexual in the showers his third week. He formed his Spartacus clan after the attack.

His fight with Billy Ray was a wake-up call. Realizing tribal knowledge was essential for survival; he began hosting Texas Hold 'Em poker tournaments in the exercise yard. It was a good way to assess his fellow inmates. He'd recruit the men that met his criteria into Spartacus.

He invited all types—bookies, embezzlers, shady accountants, executives convicted of insider trading, South American drug dealers tripped up by taxes, money launderers, identity and copyright thieves—everyone. Sean's winnings brought him instant respect, and a stockpile of cigarettes—a valuable form of currency at the prison.

Like Roman gladiators of old, his Spartacus clan embraced all nationalities and colors—black, brown, *and* white. The tae kwon do lessons he gave the men in the exercise yard were his most valuable currency. Giving them tools to defend themselves without weapons was especially useful in a prison.

Sean soon settled into a routine. His Spartacus clan sat together during meals, worked together, and exercised together. Every day, except when the weather was bad, he'd lift weights in the outdoor gym and run laps around the inside of the fences. He worked in the laundry every morning, and rehearsed with the jazz band three times a week. Angela and Andrew visited him once a month.

He recruited heavily among the inmates to get enough players to form a twenty-piece big band: Five trumpets, five saxes, five trombones, a rhythm section, and a singer. His jazz and rock arrangements spurred a renewed focus on practicing among the musicians. Warden Johnson began scheduling Saturday-night concerts in the cafeteria when he heard the improvement.

Not everything was going well, though.

"Your volatile moods are driving me crazy," Albert complained. "I know you're angry, but we need to live together. You need to mellow out or I'll ask the warden to transfer you. I understand why you're depressed. Most of us are. Talk with Father Sam. We all talk with him when we're troubled." He snickered. "Even I do, and I'm Jewish."

"Organized religion isn't really my thing," Sean said.

"I thought you went to Catholic schools," his cellmate pointed out. "Did something happen with the priests?"

Sean bristled. "No. The schools I attended were excellent. I just didn't buy into everything I was hearing. Look at all the massacres, inquisitions, crusades, burnings at the stake and wars we've had over the centuries because of religion."

Albert nodded reflectively. "Why do you return your friends' letters?"

Sean didn't answer.

"Perhaps you should talk to the priest about that, too."

Amos shackled Sean's wrists and ankles the next day, and they headed across the courtyard to see the priest.

"How long have you worked at the prison?" Sean asked Amos.

"I began my career with the Department of Corrections after high school," Amos responded proudly. "I've had stints at high-security prisons, too… so don't you think that just because I'm here I don't know nothin'."

Father Sam liked to hold court in the horticulture nursery. The warden donated the flowers to several nearby nursing homes.

The fragrant bouquet of roses, carnations, heliotropes, and long-stemmed irises flooded Sean's nostrils as he entered the glass-roofed building. Amos removed Sean's shackles and remained standing guard at the door.

Father Sam wore shorts, sandals, and a short-sleeved shirt below a priest's collar partially covered by an ample gray beard. He handed Sean some pruning shears. "I hope you don't mind if I put you to work."

"Not at all," Sean replied.

They faced each other across a row and began to prune the flowers.

"Why don't you tell me a little about yourself?" the priest suggested.

"Not much to say," Sean said. "I grew up in a trailer park outside Santa Fe. My father died in Vietnam when I was two. I was the only Anglo in the park, so I had to learn how to fight to survive. The other boys used me as a punching bag until my mom enrolled me in a tae kwon do class. My life got much easier once I could defend myself."

The priest touched his own crooked nose. "I used to box before I became a priest. I had to give it up. I kept getting my nose busted every time I dropped my left."

They laughed.

"My mother never remarried after the government declared my dad missing in action."

"Why not?"

"She said she still felt his presence... she's spiritual that way."

Pruning and chopping, they culled the dead and broken from the flock. The dried-up blooms and broken stems dropped to the floor.

"What was school like for you?" Father Sam asked.

"I played basketball and music in high school and college." *I don't feel like talking, so I'm not going to elaborate*, he decided.

"What brought you here?"

The priest stopped to listen while Sean launched into a diatribe about the injustice surrounding his arrest, trial, conviction, and imprisonment.

Father Sam went back to work. "What does it mean to be a prisoner to you, Sean?"

Sean frowned. "It's being in here... I guess."

"Is prison just a physical place, or a state of mind—to you, I mean?"

Father Sam's west-Florida southern drawl, gentle and comforting, had a way of instantly putting people at ease. The priest continued to work, waiting patiently for an answer.

"I guess it's both," Sean replied half-heartedly.

"Perhaps if you embrace your experience here rather than resisting it, you'll be more at peace. I hear you're returning your friends' letters. What's that all about?"

Sean stopped. He stared at Father Sam. "I don't need people's pity." He resumed his pruning.

The priest stroked his gray beard. "Do you think Christ enjoyed being on the cross?"

Sean crinkled his forehead. *I don't get it. Where's the coherence in these confusing questions.*

"Probably not. I'll bet those nails hurt like hell. Oh... sorry, Father."

Father Sam stopped. "I'm sure they did, yet he chose not to stop his own crucifixion. The Roman soldiers gave him plenty of opportunities to renounce his faith in a higher power. They taunted him, saying they'd take him down from the cross if he confessed his error, but he wanted redemption for mankind, so he stayed."

The priest returned his focus to the flowers.

"How does that relate to me?" Sean snapped.

"What do you want your legacy to be, Sean? Is your life all about building the golden calf, or do you have a deeper purpose... a more important destiny?"

Sean's gaze fell to the floor. *This was a bad idea.* He looked across the room at Amos, guarding the door. *I'll stay ten more minutes, so I don't appear rude.*

"What about all those priests, cardinals, and popes who sold indulgences to fatten their own golden calves?" Sean said sarcastically. "How could they guarantee a free pass into heaven regardless of a person's sins, and what is heaven anyway? Is it a place, or just an emotion?"

Father Sam smiled. "Is that what you came here for today... to discuss religious inequities? Or did someone tell you about our sale: one free pass into heaven in exchange for your soul?"

Sean laughed.

They reached the end of a row of daisies. Father Sam put down his shears and turned on a hose. Sean began pruning a row of bright-red roses.

Father Sam followed behind him, gently watering the roots. "May I tell you a story?" Father Sam said.

"Sure."

"I also serve at an assisted living facility here in Niceville, where most of the elderly patients spend their day's playing cards and watching soap operas. Their biggest complaint is loneliness. They miss their family, friends, and neighborhoods—even their mail carriers—people to whom they rarely spoke even when they lived at home. Essentially, they miss what was familiar."

"I could see how they'd feel lonely," Sean remarked. "I'll bet it's depressing for their friends to see them locked up. They probably don't get many visitors."

"Actually, they can leave the facility whenever they want," the priest explained. "Most of them choose to stay, though, except when they leave with a family member. But this is where things get interesting."

"How's that?"

"There's a lockup unit on the other side of the building, for people with dementia and other chronic ailments. People move from the assisted-living side of the building to the lockup side, when their disabilities require a higher level of care. Some people get very upset when they're locked up, even though it's the same building."

"I guess it must feel like a prison because they're locked in," Sean said. "Is that what you mean?"

"That's right. Some people make valiant attempts to escape. A man I know walks around in circles every evening testing every door and window. The staff calls this sundowning."

"Is that the state-of-mind thing you're talking about?"

"Yes, Sean. It's all a state of mind. Did you know that we all get dementia if a physical ailment doesn't take us first? It's inevitable, as our brains age."

"That gives me something fun to look forward to. Thanks for cheering me up, Father."

"No problem. Glad to help."

They chuckled.

Sean stopped pruning. "Are you saying we all end up in prison if we live long enough?"

"Mr. McGowan, we all end up somewhere, often in places we don't choose. Take soldiers or police officers for example. They never know when they'll have to put their lives on the line."

Sean contemplated the priest's words. *I know they're important, but I'm not sure why.* "I guess it's futile to protest when you have no control. Is that what you're saying?"

"Some things are worth fighting for even when you're not sure you can win, but that's not the point. Everyone faces challenges. How we deal with them is what matters."

"So what does that have to do with me, or the lockup unit in the old-folks' home?"

"It's interesting to listen to wealthy people with dementia in their lucid moments," the priest continued. "They brag about how they used to travel the world, living on yachts, drinking the finest wines. Funny thing is, once dementia takes hold, they don't care where they live. They start regressing into their past. Ninety-year-old women walk around carrying dolls, and grown men play with toys."

"That's weird," Sean said.

Father Sam's eyebrows furrowed. "We're all God's creatures—even people in circumstances beyond their control. We don't call people with dementia—prisoners, do we?"

"Hmmm... I guess not. Should we?"

"It's all about perception... how we look at things."

"I still don't get what you're trying to tell me, Father."

The priest smiled. "One of the advantages of being in prison is you have lots of time to think. The river of life is filled with many undulating currents—some seen, some invisible."

Sean picked up a broom when he reached the end of the row. Father Sam shut off the hose and walked beside him while he swept.

"Perhaps look at it this way—is an ant that burrows into the ground a prisoner? Are people who spend their days toiling away in an office or deep inside a coalmine to put food on the table for their family—prisoners? Once you liberate your injured ego you'll see that prison is just a state of mind—the buildings, inmates, and cells, just another transitory adventure."

Sean swept the castaways into piles.

"Why are you returning your friends' letters?" the priest asked again. "What's that all about?"

Sean leaned on his broom and looked the priest in the eye. "I feel ashamed."

Father Sam nodded. "That's understandable, but your friends wouldn't be reaching out to you if they didn't care about you. Love is a rare commodity. It shouldn't be squandered."

They worked together in silence until they'd shoveled all the scraps into a garbage can.

Sean walked to the door and turned around so Amos could latch his handcuffs. "You've given me some good words to chew on, Father. Thank you."

"Any time, Sean. I have a parting thought for you, assuming your well isn't already full."

"What's that, Father?"

"Try to find your path, Sean. It'll help you find peace." He chuckled. "And seeking solace in prayer doesn't mean you have to sign your life away to the papacy. Isn't that right, Amos?"

Amos nodded. "That's right, Father. Singing gospel music at my Baptist church is my favorite way to pray."

A severe ice storm dropped into Florida later that afternoon. As luck would dictate, the heater in their cellblock also quit working.

The humid air became frigid as night descended. Sean shivered beneath his wool blanket.

The storm kicked into high gear around midnight. Lightning flashes streaming through the window above his bed painted luminescent ghosts on the ceiling, followed by ferocious thunderclaps that shook the walls.

A large roach appeared above his mattress. It crawled in a crooked line between each lightning burst. It continued at the ceiling, unperturbed, hanging upside down until it stopped above Sean's head to scrutinize him with its huge, compound eye. It resumed its quest a moment later, foraging for sustenance in the microscopic pores of the cement.

The disconsolate rain drummed a chaotic solo on Sean's thick, wire-mesh window. He tried to digest the priest's words. *What did he mean by deeper purpose? I can live off my fat bank account the rest of my life. Why work seventy hours a week to pay half my wages in taxes to a government that throws me in prison? Why not just play music and hang out with women? Why does there have to be a purpose?*

A bright flash illuminated the cellblock, followed by a growling thunderclap. The rumble lasted for twenty seconds before it echoed away. Sean launched a prayer. *It couldn't do any harm,* he told himself.

His blankets were stiff with frost when he woke up the next morning, and the cellblock was as frigid as a meat locker.

20. Knowledge

Annapolis, Maryland

Yvonna wrote and destroyed many letters over the years as she struggled with her ambivalence about contacting Mikhail. Some were long and eloquent, describing her dreams and aspirations for Tatiana. Others were cryptic, teeming with anger about his neglect.

She'd written another one that afternoon. She placed a few pictures in the envelope before she sealed it. *Tatiana will be graduating from high school soon* she contemplated. *It's time for Mikhail to know.*

The snow was falling hard as she plodded down the long, winding driveway to their mailbox at the bottom of the hill. *Be courageous*, she urged herself as she hesitated.

She placed the letter in the chamber and trudged back through the snow to their home.

* * *

It took Nikolai's pilot three passes to wrestle the Learjet to the Lee Airport runway in the blinding snowstorm that night. Going north to Baltimore Washington International would have been safer, but he was anxious to get home. He had a special surprise he couldn't wait to share with Yvonna.

He wanted to give her something significant for their wedding anniversary. He'd signed the contract just that morning for the Napoleonic-era chateau overlooking the French Riviera. They'd often dreamed about spending more time in Europe once Tatiana was off to college. He couldn't wait to tell her.

He stopped at the bottom of the driveway to pick up the mail after a treacherous drive from the airport. The only letter he found was an *outgoing* post, from Yvonna to Mikhail. He stepped towards his car, stopped, returned, and pulled it out.

He looked to the sky for guidance as he held the letter between his hands. *Mikhail? Yvonna despises him.*

The snow whipped his face, urging him to the car.

He stared at the letter beneath the dome lights. *I shouldn't open it*, he told himself. *It's an invasion of her privacy... and what will I find?*

Curiosity hung like an anvil over his head as he sliced the side of the envelope with his Swiss Army knife. Three pictures dropped to his lap: Tatiana in her prom dress with flowers woven into her long, blonde hair; Tatiana spiking a volleyball in her Annapolis High School team uniform; and Tatiana arm-in-arm with her mother.

He unfolded the letter he found inside the envelope.

Dear Mikhail—

I know it has been quite a while since we've spoken. I believe it's time for you to know that Tatiana is your daughter. The resemblance is obvious when you look at her pictures, especially her hair and eyes.

She is very happy. Nikolai is a great father. He has no suspicions whatsoever about Tatiana, or us.

I would love to see you again. I still go to the wall looking for your correspondence every day, as we agreed to do years ago. I hope to hear from you soon.

Love, Yvonna

His heart pounded as he re-read the letter. *I can't believe it.*

He left his car at the street and slogged up the long driveway to the house. He locked the letter in his office safe, tiptoed through the hallway to their bedroom, and looked inside. Yvonna was asleep. He stared at her, bewildered. *I'm not sure what to do.*

He reset the house alarm and tramped back down to the car. Cupping his hand over his eyes, he looked up at their home from the bottom of the driveway. He became acutely aware of the sound of the snow at that moment, the way it sighed, when the flakes came to rest.

It will never be the same, he predicted.

He dialed Yvonna from a hotel in Annapolis the next morning.

"Hello," she answered groggily.

"I won't be home for a while," he said.

"When will you be home?"

"I'm not sure."

"Okay, sweetheart. Take care of yourself."

"Bye." He abruptly ended the call.

* * *

Yvonna dressed, made coffee, pulled on her coat, boots and hat, and lumbered down the ramp to the deck.

The tree branches sagged beneath the weight of the heavy snow. More than a foot had fallen overnight. Only a few wayward flurries floated around her now. A layer of ice covering the river encased the yacht.

The barren trees and pristine snow brought memories of her childhood in Ukraine. *Before my rape, before Mother followed the soldier to Kurchatov City, before the modeling agency where I met Nikolai…* she reminisced. *Our summer evenings enjoying the sunsets seem like a world away from here.*

I need to do something special for Nikolai for our anniversary. She bolted upright. *The letter!*

She launched herself up the ramp and trudged down the driveway to the mailbox, yanked the door open and looked inside. *Oh my God. The postman must've come early.*

She stared into the vacant cavity. *The missive is in motion now. I have no choice. It's time for fate to play its role.*

New York City

Vladimir pulled a prepaid burner phone from his desk and dialed Mikhail. "What did you find out about the World Protection Council?"

"Almost nothing," his brother reported. "They're good at staying out of the limelight."

"That's strange, especially considering their name."

"*Da*," Mikhail agreed. "Our mole in the State Department told me they also call themselves 'The Protectorate.' They have a vaguely defined mission to protect the world's resources from misappropriation. It sounds like bullshit."

Vladimir chuckled. "It sure does. Napoleon is certainly no save-the-world type. The steel and uranium processing mills he built in third-world countries after he scuttled his US plants are some of the heaviest polluters on the planet. What about Judith, and the guy who calls himself General Wu that was with Napoleon in Central Park? Is he really a general?"

"*Da*. Our FSB friends in Moscow ran the pictures I took through their facial-recognition software. Judith is from Israel—ex-Mossad. A note in her file said she abruptly quit after a run-in with her boss. Be careful. She could be working a deep cover assignment."

"Interesting," Vladimir said.

"Someone deposited twenty million dollars into a Swiss account for her just before she left. She may have gone rogue. These days she runs around with the jet set in the Alps, Vail, and Lake Como. That's probably where she met Napoleon. He's pretty good at staying under the radar, considering he's one of the wealthiest men in the world."

"He's always been secretive," Vladimir said.

"The Chinese guy *was* a general before he turned capitalist. His technology companies, real estate investments, and Macau casinos have made him close to eighty billion dollars. His latest venture is Internet software gaming. He owns several massive multiplayer online role-playing websites in China. He's obviously done very well under communism."

The men chuckled.

"That makes sense, based on the project he's proposing," Vladimir said.

"*Da*. We'll need to tread carefully. They could just be gathering intelligence. You know I don't like projects that rely on technology. They leave too many breadcrumbs. I'll agree to collaborate with them as long as we can pull the plug without a trace."

"Of course," Vladimir said. "We'll use numbered accounts and front-run his trades. We can learn a lot about their capabilities without showing our cards. Wu's company could be useful to us. As the great Chinese warrior, Sun Tzu once said, 'If you know your enemies and know yourself, you can win a hundred battles without a single loss.' We need to understand their strengths and weaknesses before we strike."

"*Da*."

"I'll send the trading instructions to your agents once things are in place with the general. On another subject: What's happening with the peace talks? The Secretary of State is close to brokering a deal between Israel and the Palestinians. We can't have that. We need the instability… for our defense businesses."

"I'll tell our Israeli development partner to break ground on some new housing projects in disputed Palestinian territory," Mikhail said. "That should stir things up, especially when the Palestinians respond with rocket attacks. I'll have Nikolai send Lebanon another missile shipment."

"Good. *Do svidaniya*."

"*Do svidaniya*," Mikhail hung up.

Niceville, Florida

The cellblock furnace had been out for two days. The guards passed out extra blankets before lights-out. They didn't help. Sean shivered beneath his blankets. Albert trembled in the bunk below him.

"Figures this would happen on the coldest day of the year," Albert said.

"You'd think someone could fix a heater," Sean complained.

"People who don't live in Florida assume it's always warm here. That's true most of the time, but every once in a while we get blasted by some pretty nasty ice storms."

"I missed that in the real estate brochure when I bought my condo north of Clearwater."

The same blizzard that closed airports and schools throughout the eastern half of the United States had brought freezing rain to Florida. Everyone at the prison was grouchy. The landscape work-detail prisoners were especially upset when Warden Johnson cancelled their weekly trip to the Eglin Air Force Base officers' housing unit.

It's not that the inmates liked yard work—the officers' wives were what interested them. Every week stories spread like wildfire about the women when the prisoners returned.

The women liked to sunbath wearing skimpy bikinis and drinking martinis, while the bare-chested prisoners worked their gardens. Rumors abounded about wives that bribed guards to let specific prisoners come to their homes to plow and rake. It was hard to say whether the stories about a convict getting lucky in a backyard cornfield were true.

The warden had also cancelled use of the exercise yard that day. One of the guards had yelled at the prisoners as they'd lined up after breakfast: "No exercise yard today. We don't want you fairies freezing your testicles off having swordfights out on the ice."

The guards had all chuckled.

A disguised inmate's voice had offered a retort. "I'll swordfight your ass."

The guards walked up and down the line trying to identify the culprit. No one would tell them the joker was Randy Matson.

Rumors about Randy had circled the prison instantly when he arrived in early March. He was a real crook, responsible for gunrunning, prostitution, and drug distribution in the southeast. His lawyer had supposedly finessed a vacation for Randy at FPC after a judge dismissed his $2 million drug bust because the DEA search warrant had a grammar error.

Randy, thirty-five, was medium height and powerfully built, with an assortment of tattoos emblematic of his tribe. Several of his gang members were already residents so he was right at home.

An icy squall thrashed the gray window above Sean's bunk. Lightning illuminated the fog floating above his mouth. A few of the prisoners were starting to yell about the cold.

"Do you think protesting will help?" Sean said. "It's an infraction to cause a ruckus."

Albert rose from his bunk covered with blankets. "It couldn't hurt. They can't punish all of us." Sean joined him behind the iron bars.

The entire cellblock erupted in pandemonium as the rage of a hundred freezing men echoed from every corner. They settled into a chant.

"It's cold as hell in here!"

"It's cold as hell in here!"

"It's cold as hell in here!"

The protest took on a life of its own when the warden mobilized his sentinels. They entered the cellblock in a phalanx dressed in riot gear. The noise became ear splitting as they marched up and down the hallway battering the bars with billy clubs.

The guards retreated when the prisoners ran out of toilet paper to throw. The warden turned out the lights, and the darkness served its purpose. Everyone returned to their bunks and pulled blankets over their heads.

"It was obviously a drill," Albert said. "Warden Johnson never misses an opportunity to whip his guards into shape. Now we'll have a real mess to clean up in the morning."

"I hope we have heat by then," Sean said.

Everyone knew the warden hadn't turned off the furnace as some form of medieval punishment—that's not how he operated. The heater was just old and decrepit. The heater was a mixed blessing, anyhow. The vents heaved and groaned like an elephant with constipation as the heat oozed its way to their cells.

"Good night, Sean," Albert said.

"Good night."

Albert was forty-five, 5'7" tall, heavyset, balding, and lucky. His wife had moved to Niceville from Miami with their daughter after his imprisonment. They never missed a weekly visit.

Charismatic, gregarious, and funny, Albert was the kind of person people liked right away, which was partly what got him into trouble. His conviviality convinced people to trust him with their money. A fellow Spartacus prisoner told Sean he'd read about Albert's conviction in the newspaper.

"His secure retirement income fund bilked investors—mostly the elderly—out of more than nine million dollars," the inmate said. "The FBI snared him when his solicitations crossed state lines. His bank account was empty when they brought the hammer down though. The article implied that Albert's wife was probably moving the money to the Caymans during her weekly spa visits. He'll be flush if he makes it through his six-year sentence."

"That explains why he doesn't want to talk about his case."

Albert had proclaimed his rules to Sean his first night in the cell: "We shouldn't discuss our cases. The Feds use prisoners to rat on each other, offering reduced sentences and other enticements as rewards. Loneliness can be a powerful motivator for the morally challenged—you know… for people like us, I guess."

Sean had laughed with relief, glad that his cellmate had a sense of humor. "That's okay with me. I don't trust the government, either."

"If we don't discuss our cases, we'll never have to be suspicious about each other."

"Good idea," Sean concurred.

The rumble of thunder brought Sean back to the present. The freezing rain prodded the humidity inside his window into a crude intercourse with the glass, breeding pockmarks of dew. The droplets copulated and grew until the moisture trickled down the pane, leaving ghostly colophons in their wake. Sean sensed the storm was moving south when each rumble became softer than the last.

"What're you going to do when you get out of here?" Sean asked.

"We'll probably move to the Florida Keys and spend our days in Margaritaville. How about you?"

"I think it's time to have some fun. No more seventy-hour work weeks to pay the tax man half my earnings for me."

"What's your idea of fun?" Albert asked.

"Playing music, I guess. Maybe I'll take up salsa dancing again. Tasting the pleasures of a woman will be my first priority though."

Albert laughed. "They are a gift from God, aren't they? I think even Adam would agree."

"Probably so. Eve always looks beautiful in paintings I've seen. Adam probably couldn't control himself. It's the same with paintings of Pandora. I wonder what she really had in that jar of hers."

Albert chuckled. "Maybe Eve's apple and Pandora's jar both symbolize knowledge—the double-edged sword that can be used for good, or evil."

"Yeah, or perhaps they symbolize the love that is felt when you trust someone, which makes you vulnerable to heartache."

Sean fantasized about Angela as he fell asleep. *I certainly won't pass up the opportunity to make love with her if she ever gives me the chance*, he told himself. *I was dumb not to pursue her years ago. Her loyalty, visiting me every month… must mean something.*

21. Cyclones

CLANG!

The crack of the billy club on iron jolted Sean awake.

"McGowan," Amos said. "The warden wants to see you."

Gray light creeping through the wire-mesh window signaled dawn had arrived. The warmth in the cellblock confirmed the heater was back in business.

Sean yanked on his tennis shoes and overcoat. *Wake up* he commanded himself. *A meeting with Warden Johnson is always serious business.*

He placed his hands behind his back. Amos latched his cuffs while a second guard shackled leg irons around each ankle. The sidewalk was icy as he shuffled across the grounds.

A summons was rarely good news. *I've been dreading this meeting for months,* Sean fretted, *ever since the altercation with Billy Ray Tanner. Perhaps the warden just heard about the brawl.*

With two and a half years left on my sentence—or less than a year, with good behavior—I'd wanted to maintain a low profile. That ended with the fight in the shower.

His mind spun. *Solitary confinement—I'll handle that if I have to—but a transfer to a high-security prison with additional time added for assault would be devastating.*

Amos knocked on Warden Johnson's door.

"Come in," a voice called.

The guard pushed Sean through the doorway. "Prisoner McGowan, sir."

The warden smirked. "Take those leg irons off—then shut the door and leave us."

Johnson's gaze fell to the paperwork on his desk.

Amos looked at the warden questioningly. "Are you sure?"

"Yes," he insisted. "Just stand outside. I'll buzz you when we're done."

Amos eyed Sean warily as he removed the leg irons and closed the door.

Sean sensed the warden was cranky. *He probably had a long night… dealing with the cellblock heater, the protest—and now me.*

"Please have a seat, Mr. McGowan."

Sean threaded his handcuffed wrists through the open slats in the back of the chair and sat down. The warden continued to read so he looked around.

Warden Tyrone "Cyclone" Johnson, an African American in his mid-thirties, was 6'4" tall and built like a locomotive. The walls displayed several framed newspaper articles of Johnson's football years.

Tyrone Johnson was a legend at the prison. He'd earned the nickname "Cyclone" during college as a middle linebacker for the Florida State Seminoles. His story went national when an illegal chop block his senior year ruined his knee, derailing a promising professional career. Now he ran a prison.

Johnson doesn't need guards, Sean observed. *I doubt that any of the prisoners, even the Nazis, would be foolish enough to confront him. Well... perhaps one of the crazy ones would.*

A full-page spread from the Miami Herald encased on the wall showed Johnson taking an interception across the goal line. Their opponent, FSU's cross-state archrival the University of Florida Gators, lost the game because of it.

One wall housed a floor-to-ceiling bookcase. A quick glance revealed the warden had eclectic tastes, from law books to Shakespeare. The focal point in the room was Johnson's framed diplomas: a Bachelor of Science in management from FSU, and a Master's in Business Administration from Vanderbilt.

The picture everyone talked about was on his desk: Johnson in his football uniform, holding a ravishing, golden-haired, blue-eyed cheerleader—the woman he married.

She's stunning, Sean realized.

Another picture showed the warden with his wife and three kids.

Sean smiled to himself when he imagined what the white supremacists might think when they sat where he was.

The warden scrutinized him. *He's gauging my reaction. Clever.*

"Do you know why I called you in here today?" the warden boomed.

A shiver rolled down Sean's spine as the blood drained from his brain. "No, sir."

The warden lifted an eyebrow. "It looks like you have some important friends in Washington. I got a call from an attorney at the Department of Justice yesterday—a fellow by the name of Stephen Adkins. He wants to come down for a visit tomorrow."

"Any idea what he wants?"

Johnson folded his hands. "I'm not at liberty to discuss that at the moment. He did ask me if you've been behaving yourself. I told him you've been a model citizen, except for your run-in with Billy Ray."

Crap, he groaned inwardly. *The warden knows*. "What's going to happen? Am I going to have more time added to my sentence?"

Johnson pursed his lips. "I told Adkins you handled yourself pretty well when Billy Ray jumped you in the shower."

"The guards weren't around. How'd you find out?"

"There's very little that goes on around here that I don't know about," Johnson replied. "Like Spartacus—the gang you formed to protect yourself after the fight. Why'd you choose that name?"

"Spartacus was a gladiator... pursued by a tyrannical government," Sean explained. "I thought it was appropriate, under the circumstances."

The warden leaned back in his chair. "So why don't you tell me about the fight?"

"I regret what happened, sir."

"Go on."

Sean's heart pounded. "I was taking a shower. Billy Ray grabbed me and told me to get down on my knees. Two of his gang-members were standing with him, laughing, as they watched him masturbate."

The warden smirked. "What happened next?"

"Everyone left the shower room except the three of them, so I was on my own." Sean released a sigh. "Billy tried to push me down. That's when my martial arts training kicked in. It was an automatic reaction."

Sean probed the warden's eyes. *I'll open myself up to prosecution if I confess*, he considered. "Is this off the record?"

"Yes, Mr. McGowan. I just want to hear what happened... how you meted out justice, so to speak."

Sean took a deep breath. "I side-kicked Billy in the knee, pounded him to the floor, and stomp-kicked his head a few times. It happened so fast, I didn't have time to think."

Billy's iniquitous proposition had unleashed an avalanche of fury Sean recalled. *I realized I'd done more than just defend myself, when I found out Billy Ray needed cheek-reconstruction surgery.*

Johnson leaned forward. "What happened next?"

"One of Billy's friends punched me in the back. I launched a roundhouse kick into his chest, which knocked him against the wall. They both stepped back after that. Billy was moaning when I finished my shower, so I knew he wasn't dead."

The warden nodded.

Sean looked up at a framed newspaper article of Johnson holding a trophy balanced on the shoulders of two sweat-drenched teammates.

"I know this may sound strange," Sean's voice faltered.

The warden's gaze followed Sean's to the wall. "What's that?"

"A line from Shakespeare jumped into my head when Billy grabbed me."

"Which line?"

"Cowards die many times before their deaths. The valiant never taste of death but once."

"That's from *Julius Caesar*, isn't it—when he's worried about his approaching death?"

"I believe so, sir," Sean replied.

Johnson pointed at the framed picture. "My coach at Florida State recited those lines whenever we faced an opponent that was supposed to crush us. The press predicted we'd lose by twenty points that day, but he was sure we'd win. That's when he quoted Shakespeare. It was one of the sweetest victories of our lives, probably because the odds were the greatest."

"It must have been special to play for such a sagacious coach."

"I was very lucky."

Johnson leaned back. "I could've written you up for the fight, but this wasn't Billy's first sexual assault. You don't need any more time added to your sentence either, from what I can see."

"Thank you, sir."

"Most people don't file rape complaints because they're embarrassed, or worried about retribution. Do you want to file an attempted-rape charge against him?"

"No, sir. I just want to do my time and get out of here."

"They'll send Billy to Marianna if the whole story comes out. I have plenty of witnesses that will corroborate your account. I didn't call you in here to talk about Billy Ray this morning, though. Something important is going on to bring Adkins all the way down here from DC."

"What's that?"

"I'm not sure. He did say your sentence will be reduced if you cooperate."

Sean's stomach quaked. "They're wasting their time if they're looking for a snitch."

"That's not it," Johnson said. "He's bringing another FBI agent with him from New York—Agent Hernandez. Adkins said you know him. He's also bringing a woman named Julie Stensen. I talked with her this morning. She's concerned about you. She said you shouldn't be in here."

"Hernandez is one of the agents that arrested me," Sean said.

"Adkins asked your attorney, Andrew Greenstein, to join them. He's flying down from New York later today. Your meeting is scheduled for nine a.m. tomorrow morning."

"Thanks," Sean said.

Johnson folded his hands. "Ms. Stensen faxed me a copy of your arrest report and trial transcript, so I understand your reluctance to cooperate, but you could be out of here soon if you play your cards right."

Sean sensed Johnson wasn't telling him everything. "Okay. I'll hear them out."

"There's something else I'd like to talk with you about," the warden said.

"What's that, sir?"

"The jazz band. I appreciate what you've done for the men. Some of them might be able to find work as musicians when they leave here now because of you. Having a useful skill helps prevent recidivism. It's difficult for convicted felons to find jobs."

"I lobbied the courts to do my time here because you allow inmates to play music, sir. I'd go crazy if I didn't have that in my life."

Johnson nodded. "Music and the exercise yard help me keep the peace."

Sean smiled. "There's something going on here you may not be aware of, sir."

Johnson raised his eyebrows. "What's that?"

"We've been discussing names for the band. We have one, assuming you approve."

The warden smiled. "What do you have in mind?"

"Tyrone's Cyclones."

A huge grin lit up Johnson's face. "I love it."

The warden hit a buzzer. Amos opened the door.

"I'll see you at nine a.m. tomorrow, Mr. McGowan. Amos?"

"Yes, sir?"

"No leg irons for Sean from now on. They aren't necessary."

"Yes, sir."

Sean didn't say much to Albert about his meeting with the warden when he returned to his cell. *I don't want to get myself all riled up about something that might not happen*, he cautioned himself. *A flurry of DC lawyers had stormed the halls of justice without success. Why is this any different?*

Angela was unflinching in her efforts to secure Sean's release. The press covered her exploits, writing mocking anecdotes about her struggles to get her "boyfriend" out of prison.

Her lobbying efforts with the FTC were fruitful. One of their administrators, who'd had on-going suspicions about Bachmann's firm, launched a formal, civil investigative demand.

I'm not convinced the Feds don't want me to spy on someone, Sean considered. *It's probably Randy Matson, or Albert. I won't rat out either of them.*

He didn't say anything about his meeting with the warden when he pressed metal with Randy in the outdoor gym that afternoon. They often worked out together. The fact that Sean had faced down three of his top lieutenants didn't seem to matter.

Randy liked to pick Sean's brain about computers. "My organization needs help with computers," Randy told him again that afternoon. "The Feds were still able to reconstruct my computer files, even though I erased all my data. That's why I had to plea bargain. How'd they do it?"

"The *Delete* function only erases file names and pointers... not the actual data," Sean explained. "The FBI has ways to rebuild damaged storage media, too. The best way to be safe is to make sure your enemies can't physically or electronically touch your data files."

"My boss wants you to work for us when you get out of here. You know how to hide cash, don't you—internationally, I mean?"

"I'm not sure what I'm going to do when I finish my sentence," Sean told him. "Banks in tax-haven countries are your best bet. Hiding money from the taxman has been the prerogative of the rich for centuries. Get yourself a good Swiss banker—they're experts at it."

Randy smiled. "Our business has a lot of perks."

"Like what?"

"How about all the women you want whenever you want them—at no charge!"

Sean laughed. "I've never seen that in a benefits package."

"My boss has girls from many countries. We make movies, too." Randy grinned. "We could use another actor if you're interested."

Sean snickered. *Porn star* he mused? Visions of naked women sent a jolt through his body. "Who's your boss?"

Randy looked around. "We have thousands of charge-card numbers in our database, too. We can get value from those, can't we—what you guys on Wall Street call *monetizing?*"

"Where'd you hear that term?"

"I read the business section of the newspaper," Randy boasted.

"Yeah. Monetizing is what most businesses do these days. Internet display ads are a good example. Companies use web-surfing habits to figure out what to display. It might be interesting to do an experiment with your porn customers. Do you sell hand cream?"

Randy laughed. "Not yet. That's a good idea, though."

Sean became serious. "Won't your customers be upset when they find out their identities were stolen?"

Randy scowled. "It's not my fault they give us their data."

A Spartacus guard stepped closer. Sean nodded to indicate he was okay.

"Yeah," Sean agreed. "I guess you're right. That's pretty dumb of them."

Randy's just like the sociopaths I trade against on Wall Street—people who use every morsel of information they can get, legal or otherwise, to win. Traders and analysts who spread false rumors are a typical example.

He added ten pounds to his weights after Randy left. *The extra pain will help me banish the images of naked women from my brain*, he told himself. He had to do the same thing after Angela's visits.

Sean did allow himself to fantasize about life beyond the prison walls as he lay in his bunk that night—a caprice he hadn't fallen prey to for months. *I certainly won't miss the sewer-gas odor, or the cockroaches that skitter across the floor at night.*

He smiled when he recalled his first week at the prison. Albert would sit on his lower bunk laughing at him while he went to war with the beasts.

"I did the same thing when I got here," Albert had said, "until I realized there's an inexhaustible supply. The roaches come up from the sewers and from other cells. Stomping them out just makes a mess. It's pointless."

Some aspects of prison life haven't been so bad, he decided. *I've done a lot of reading, and I'm in the best physical shape of my life. At six feet tall and a hundred and sixty pounds, I weigh less now than when I played basketball in college, and I have a lot more muscle.*

He turned over in his bunk. *Tomorrow will be important. Why do they want to see me... two FBI agents... and a woman?*

The first thing I'll do when I get out is take in the view from my top-floor Crystal Beach condominium—the reward I gave myself after making partner.

Amos escorted him to the conference room the next morning. Andrew was waiting when he arrived. The banana-yellow room had five wooden chairs, a large metal table bolted to the concrete floor, and a one-way mirror staring passively from a wall.

"Do you want him cuffed to the table?" Amos said.

"No," Andrew replied. "He shouldn't even be in here. Please take those off."

Amos removed the cuffs and closed the door. They shook hands and sat down.

"How are you doing?" Andrew said.

"Good. How was your flight?"

"A bit bumpy. Here's my latest chess move."

Sean smiled at the scribble on the napkin. "Interesting."

"I hope you'll be out of here before you come up with a counter move."

Sean picked up Andrew's pen and wrote his next move. "I have lots of time to think in here. I figured you might do that."

Andrew stared at the scrawl. "Hmmm… "

"So what did the FBI tell you?" Sean inquired.

"Not much. Adkins, the FBI attorney, told me to get down here. That's all I know."

"What do you think's going on?"

"I'm not sure. I re-read the trial notes on the plane last night. Perhaps they see their errors now. The jury had no choice but to return a guilty verdict after the harsh instructions from Judge Richter."

"That bird has flown," Sean said dismissively. "It must be something else."

Andrew pulled a bundle of papers from his briefcase and handed them to Sean. "Can you take a look at your quarterly tax returns before the Feds get here? I'll file them if they look okay."

Although Sean had given Andrew power of attorney over his business affairs, he still liked to review his tax returns. Jonas and Angela were managing his money in their hedge funds.

"It looks like Angela and Jonas are doing a great job," Sean observed.

Andrew's eyes widened. "I'll say. They made you over thirty-four million dollars the last three months. Not bad for someone on the dole, courtesy of the Federal Bureau of Prisons."

Sean's lips twisted derisively. "I'm not really on the dole. Thirty-five percent of my earnings will go to Uncle Sam for federal taxes. I am saving a lot of money now that I'm a resident of Florida, though. The State and City of New York would've taken another fifteen percent, so I saved over five million dollars in taxes this quarter. Perhaps it was worth it to come to prison."

They laughed.

Andrew pulled a check out of his briefcase. "This is from the sale of your townhome in the West Village. I'll deposit it into your account once you endorse it."

Sean signed the back of the check and passed it back to Andrew.

"The movers placed everything in storage except for the boxes marked *Rachel*. I sent those to Colorado. She's back there now."

"Yeah. Angela told me Marshall Silverman gave her the boot when he hooked up with a twenty-three year-old."

"I wasn't sure what happened."

"David Cohen came down with Angela when she visited me last week—very kind of him, considering how busy he is. He told me he's still shaking trees in Washington. Perhaps that's why Adkins is coming here."

There was a quick rap on the door. The warden entered.

Sean and Andrew stood up.

"Hello, Sean," the warden said. "Is this your attorney?"

"Yes, sir. This is Andrew Greenstein."

The warden shook hands with both men and they sat down.

"The Feds just arrived," the warden continued. "We're putting them through *our* security screening." He folded his hands. "May we talk for a moment?"

"Sure," Sean said.

"My contacts back in DC told me that the Feds need your help with a national security issue. You'll probably get a full pardon if you assist them."

Sean's eyes widened. "That's good news."

Andrew nodded. "May I ask you a question, Warden Johnson?"

"Sure, but I may not be able to answer it."

"Why do you want to help Sean? I would think a man in your position wouldn't care."

"I had an interesting talk with Ms. Stensen yesterday," he said. "Something fishy is going on. I think she'll tell you soon enough what I mean."

"Thanks for helping me, sir." Sean said.

"Let's see how things go today before we celebrate." He pointed at the mirror. "I'll be keeping an eye on the negotiations through that window."

A guard knocked and the conference door opened. An attractive woman with auburn, shoulder-length hair entered, followed by two men in dark-blue suits.

Andrew and the warden shook hands with Stephen Adkins from the Department of Justice, Oscar Hernandez from the FBI, and Julie Stensen—she didn't say which agency.

Sean watched from the corner. Adkins, in his mid-fifties, was medium height and slightly overweight. Hernandez still looked like a boxer. Sean noticed Stensen first, though. Her agile, hourglass-shaped body mesmerized him as she moved gracefully around the table.

She extended her hand. "Hello, Sean."

He felt himself blush when he looked into her eyes. "Hello, Ms. Stensen."

* * *

A jolt surged through Beate's belly when she grasped Sean's hand. *He's even cuter in person*, she realized. She sat down next to him.

* * *

"Let the guards know if you need anything," the warden said as he exited.

Silence consumed the room as everyone inspected each other.

Andrew spoke first. "So, Mr. Adkins, I understand you'd like to talk with my client."

Adkins turned to Sean. "We're prepared to offer you a reduced sentence if you help us with a case we're working on."

Sean looked at Andrew and back to Adkins.

"What kind of case?" Andrew asked.

"We can't tell you the details, until you agree to help us."

Andrew leaned forward. "Let me make sure we understand. You're saying you want Sean to help you with a case you can't talk about?"

Adkins crossed his legs. "It involves national security. Ms. Stensen can discuss it, if she'd like. The Justice Department will agree to release Sean in six months if he cooperates."

Sean stopped breathing. *It's a ruse*, he told himself.

Stensen fidgeted in her chair, crossing and re-crossing her legs.

"That doesn't sound like much of an offer," Andrew said. "He's up for parole in a few months, anyhow. I think we're done here."

Sean stood up with Andrew.

Adkins jumped out of his seat. "Hold on a minute. Let's talk about this."

"What do you want to talk about?" Andrew said. "Your offer is ridiculous."

"Okay," Adkins relented. "Three months. Is that acceptable?"

"I'm not going to snitch on anyone if that's what you're looking for," Sean said.

Adkins, Hernandez, and Stensen exchanged glances.

"Please sit down, Mr. McGowan," Adkins said.

Sean opened the door and put his wrists behind his back for the guard. Julie stood up.

Warden Johnson appeared in the hallway. "Is there anything I can help you with, Ms. Stensen?"

"I need to talk with Agents Adkins and Hernandez for a moment," she said. "Is there someplace you can take Sean so he doesn't have to go back to his cell?"

"Yes, ma'am," Johnson said. "Just notify the guard when you're ready."

Andrew and Sean followed the warden down the hallway. They took two lefts and entered the room with the one-way mirror looking into the conference room.

Sean sat down next to the warden. "This is great."

Stensen was leaning forward six inches from Adkins's nose.

Warden Johnson turned up the speakers.

Her words matched the anger reddening her face. "I want Sean out of here today! The country needs him. You know he'll be pardoned once Judge Richter's bribery arrest is made public."

Adkins remained calm. "You don't have the authority to demand anything. It could take months to gather enough evidence to bring bribery charges against the judge. The courts could overturn some of his previous cases if they convict him. It's complicated. Cases like this take time to prepare."

"That's why this happened," Andrew said. "The judge swayed the jury—for a payoff."

"Why would anyone want to do that?" Sean said.

Andrew shook his head.

"I gave you all the evidence you need to secure a conviction," Stensen continued. "You have his wire transfers to the Caymans, and the recordings of his meetings with Agent Hartfield."

"We're arranging a sting," Hernandez interjected. "It's taking a while to set up."

She turned to Hernandez. "I think you're delaying this because Hartfield's your friend. Did you look into why his gambling debts at the Atlantic City casino disappeared after Sean's conviction?"

Hernandez didn't respond.

Julie faced the mirror. "There's no reason Sean should sit in prison while you gather evidence. My director will go to the president if you don't cooperate."

Adkins rose from his chair and walked to the door. "I need to call my boss before I can make another offer. I'll see what I can do."

Adkins left with his cell phone at his ear.

Stensen faced Hernandez. "I need your help, Oscar."

"Why'd you drag me down here?" the agent whined. "McGowan's arrest was Hartfield's idea. I was just following orders. McGowan didn't appeal his conviction. That proves he's guilty. Why stir everything up?"

Julie pulled out her smartphone and showed Hernandez a video of himself: naked, entwined in the arms of a young black woman.

"I have surveillance videos of you and your stripper girlfriend in a hotel room at the casino," she said. "I'll send this to your wife if you don't cooperate. I'm sure Consuela won't be pleased."

Oscar jumped up. "You can't operate domestically. I'll have you fired for spying on me."

Julie stared without flinching. "Go ahead and try. Perhaps your bosses would like a copy of our videotapes, too."

Hernandez circled the room. "Besides, I can't help you."

"Why not?"

His gaze narrowed. "Someone upstairs is holding things up."

Sean and Andrew exchanged glances.

"Are you saying someone is running interference?" Stensen said.

"Yes," he acknowledged. "I'll let you know what I find out as soon as I can. That's the best I can do."

Hernandez sat down and clasped his hands over his head. "Please don't send those to my wife. We have four kids. She'll never forgive me."

"That's not the reason I'm here, Oscar. I need Sean's help with a national security issue. This isn't about some illicit love affair."

The door opened and Adkins entered. "The best I can offer is two months. We can't guarantee a pardon though—that's up to the president."

"This is crap," Stensen responded.

"I like her," Sean said. "She has a lot of spunk."

"She's definitely on your side," Andrew said.

Adkins shrugged his shoulders. "Suit yourself."

Stensen glared. "I've given you everything you need to bring charges against Isaac Bachmann, too. What's the holdup?"

"I'm getting directions from my boss back at FBI headquarters," Adkins said.

"I've been dealing with your bureaucrats for months," she continued, "just to get someone to look into Sean's case, and in the meantime our national security is at risk. Don't you people realize we're at war? What's wrong with you?"

"What's wrong with you?" Oscar lashed out. "You can't operate domestically."

Stensen opened the door and addressed the guard. "We're done here today. Tell the warden we'll be back soon. Now get me out of here."

"Yes, ma'am," the guard said.

Adkins and Hernandez followed her out of the room.

"That was interesting," Sean said. "At least now I know why I was arrested. The judge and agent Hartfield were taking bribes."

"Yes… very interesting," Andrew said. "I think we should ask for a full pardon before you agree to cooperate. What do you think?"

"I agree. I don't trust the government, and I want my name cleared."

"I understand why you'd say that," the warden said. "It's really none of my business, but may I give you some advice?"

"Sure," Sean replied.

"I received your release papers from the Justice Department yesterday. The only thing I needed was Adkins's signature. Something must've happened last night to hang things up. Someone wants to keep you bottled up. Perhaps they're worried you'll go to the press before they make their case."

Sean stared into the empty conference room. "This sucks."

"I'd suggest that you ask for an immediate release," the warden continued, "with a written statement from the executive branch saying you're being considered for a pardon. That way you can get out of here."

Sean nodded. "I like that idea."

"What Ms. Stensen said is right. Our country *is* at war. Something serious must be going on to bring the CIA down here."

"Why do you think she's with the CIA?" Sean inquired.

"That's the only agency I know of that could spy on the FBI and get away with it," Johnson speculated. "Otherwise, Hernandez would've arrested her."

Sean shook his head. "I don't know how I can help."

"I'll see what I can find out from my contacts in Washington. In the meantime, hang in there. I'm sure Ms. Stensen will be back soon."

Sean was just about finished with his workout that afternoon when Randy approached him. "Hey, McGowan?"

Two of Sean's Spartacus brothers moved closer.

Sean heaved his weights back into their bracket. "What's up, Randy?"

"I told my lawyer about your case when he came to see me yesterday. He said he'd look into it for you if you'd like."

Sean grabbed a towel and cleared the sweat from his face. The weather was more typical of Florida today—sunny, hot, and humid. "Thanks, but I don't think it would do any good," he said.

"My lawyer doesn't dress all that fancy, but he's sharp as a tack. He went to school at Oxford…" Randy chuckled, "…Mississippi, that is."

Sean nodded. "I'll let you know."

Randy raised his eyebrows. "Have you thought any more about your movie career… what you'll be doing when you're not working on computers? How about three women at once for your audition: a blonde, a brunette, and a redhead?"

Sean's Spartacus friends chuckled.

"I'm not sure. I've never done anything like that before."

"Sounds like you haven't lived much, McGowan." Randy laughed as he walked away.

Sean added twenty pounds to his weights and began another circuit.

22. Destiny

Annapolis, Maryland—Three Weeks Later

It took Yvonna twenty minutes to hike to the rock wall at the far edge of their estate to check for a message from Mikhail. She swung open the small decorative stone door covering the cubbyhole safe and dialed the combination.

Empty again, she fumed. It's been weeks. *I was sure Mikhail would contact me after I sent him the letter with Tatiana's pictures. Could he really be that indifferent?*

It had been easy for her to get away from the house to check for messages. *Nikolai still hasn't returned from Europe.*

It's just as well, she decided as she walked back to the house. *Nikolai's always in a foul mood when he calls now. He speaks with Tatiana for a few minutes and hangs up without saying goodbye. He even forgot our anniversary.*

Yvonna was asleep when Nikolai knocked on her bedroom door later that night. She turned on the lamp next to her bed.

"I'm surprised you're home," she said. "How was your flight?"

"Good."

He turned and walked down the hall to Tatiana's room.

Yvonna grabbed her bathrobe and followed.

Tatiana turned on her light when Nikolai knocked on her doorframe. "Daddy! I'm glad you're home!" She jumped up out of her bed.

He held her at arm's length. "It's good to be back. You look more beautiful every day."

"Thanks, Daddy."

They moved to her bed and sat down next to each other.

"How long will you be home?" she said.

Yvonna watched from the doorway. *I wish he'd been that happy to see me*, she ruminated.

"Probably just a day or two," he answered.

"Awww, Dad. I was hoping we could go riding together. It's been so long."

"I know," he admitted. "Perhaps we'll have more time this summer."

I'm envious, but I'm also glad they're close, Yvonna told herself. *The only men I knew growing up were the drunken soldiers that paraded through mother's apartment at all hours of the night.*

One of her mother's boyfriends broke into Yvonna's bedroom and raped her when she was fourteen. Her mother brought her to Nikolai's modeling agency the next day. She never saw her mother again after that.

"Do you want to see the dress Mom bought me for the prom?" Tatiana said.

"Sure."

Tatiana disappeared into her walk-in closet. She emerged an instant later displaying a small black dress against her chest. "Isn't it beautiful?"

"It seems a bit short."

"No, it isn't. That's the style. Look at the shoes Mom bought me." Tatiana held them up.

"Those are nice too, honey," Nikolai said.

Tatiana talked nonstop for the next half hour about her boyfriend, the upcoming prom, and her decision to study business in college.

"We took second place in the state high school volleyball championship," Tatiana said. "I wish you'd been there, Daddy. It was really exciting, wasn't it, Mom?"

"Yes it was, honey," Yvonna said. "You almost took first place."

Nikolai hugged her. "I'm sorry I missed it. I'm proud of you."

Tatiana asked her father to tuck her into bed when her battery finally ran down, a ritual they'd shared since she was a baby.

Nikolai said "good night" as he passed Yvonna in the hallway on his way out to the yacht.

Yvonna sat up reading in bed for a few minutes. She turned off her lamp and sobbed into her pillow a few minutes later. *How could he forget our anniversary? What's wrong with him?*

He likes sex too much to stay abstinent. He must be having an affair!

Her rage propelled her through the kitchen to the sliding door. She stopped. *I have no proof, and my radar has never sensed him having an interest in other women.*

He's had plenty of opportunities, too, she reflected, *at the Russian Embassy parties we attend. He's still a handsome man—even though he could afford to lose a few pounds—and everyone knows his import-export business is successful. I've seen plenty of young Muscovites on the prowl trying to entice him when they thought I wasn't looking. He always just smiles, excuses himself, and returns to my side.*

She crawled back into bed and pulled up the covers. *I'll dress up nice and seduce him tomorrow—whatever it takes*, she decided. *God knows I need it. He must, too. Maybe that's why he's been so cranky.*

She touched herself for relief.

Mikhail crept into her dream as she fell asleep, hovering above her like a ghost. She wanted to protest, but said nothing. He flashed a lascivious smile as he tied her to the bedposts and ravished her. She begged him to do it again when he finished.

* * *

Nikolai stood on the deck of his yacht looking up at the house. *The lights are off. Good. She's finally gone to bed.*

He slipped quietly into the kitchen and left a note on the countertop saying he had to return to Europe unexpectedly. He backed his car down the driveway with the lights off so he wouldn't wake anyone, drove to a shopping mall two miles away, parked his car, and returned on foot to the house.

He brushed away the leaves covering the security panel for the fallout shelter and punched in the entrance code: Tatiana's birthday.

A muted whine accompanied the horizontal steel doors sliding open between two large, camouflage rocks.

Nikolai entered another security code at the bottom of the stairwell, and a thick, radiation-proof cement door slid open.

He entered the fallout shelter, turned on the lights, and punched a large red button next to the door.

Both sets of doors closed, sealing him inside.

He checked the radiation detection meters on the nuclear bomb cases to ensure there were no leaks, and oiled the firing mechanisms on the bazookas he'd recently purchased. The new weapons were lighter and more accurate than the aging, Soviet-era guns they'd brought with them from Baku.

Done with the monthly maintenance, he turned on the portable computer he'd brought with him in his backpack.

The large fallout shelter had several rooms and all the amenities of a normal home, with enough food and alcohol to survive a year. It would be tight, but comfortable. Yvonna and the kids knew nothing about it. *I hope they never have to know*, he told himself.

He started the global positioning application on his computer and waited for it to link up to the electronic tracking devices he'd hidden on Yvonna's hiking boots. A red beeping dot appeared over a computer map of their property. *It's working*, he concluded.

He retired to one of the king-size beds to sleep.

The tracking software beeped at 8:45 a.m. He jumped to the computer screen. The red dot was moving in a circle around their house.

She's probably checking the flowerbeds looking for daffodils, he assumed.

The dot picked up speed when she entered the woods. It stopped twenty minutes later near a stone fence bordering a two-lane road at the far end of their estate. *That must be the mailbox.*

Nikolai typed in the precise GPS coordinates on his smart phone.

The dot meandered back to the house a moment later and the blinking stopped. *She must have taken her boots off.*

He exited the shelter and hiked to the fence using the GPS coordinates. It took him awhile, pushing against stones in the wall, to find the cleverly concealed mailbox compartment.

He removed the small safe from its chamber and placed it into his backpack. He drove to a locksmith in Annapolis familiar with that model of safe. The locksmith deciphered the combination using a codebook provided by the manufacturer.

Nikolai deposited his own letter into the safe when he returned to the wall. The letter read:

Dear Yvonna –

Please meet me at the Ritz-Carlton hotel in Washington at Foggy Bottom, room 620, at 1:00 p.m. on Friday. There will be an envelope with a room key at the front desk. I'll leave a negligee in the closet. I can't wait to see you.

Love, Mikhail

Nikolai was watching TV in the shelter the following evening when Yvonna hiked to the wall. He watched the red dot beeping on his screen as she lingered. *She's reading the letter.*

The red dot moved back towards the house.

* * *

Yvonna smiled at the moon as she hiked through the woods. Her heart was floating. *Mikhail never told me he loved me before*, she marveled. *He must really miss me.*

Her body tingled. The passion she fantasized crushed her like a wave. The fire and ache wracked her belly.

She opened her jacket and moved off the trail. She pictured Mikhail, imagining the smell of him, the length of him, churning, and filling her inside. The erotic smell of spring satiated her senses. The craving was unbearable.

She slid her hand beneath her panties.

* * *

Nikolai stared at the computer screen. The blinking dot has stopped. *She's very close to the shelter entrance.*

He checked the security cameras. *The doors are closed. She isn't visible, but she's close.*

He stared at the red dot on the screen. *Should I open the doors? Should I reveal the shelter to her? What's she doing?*

* * *

The ascending rush electrified her synapses. She grabbed a tree limb to steady herself. Staring at the moon, she quickened her fingers, luring the turgid explosion to consume her. She cried out when it came.

A hoot owl in a distant tree answered her call.

She sucked in deep, cool breaths to quench the heat in her chest as she caught her breath. She buckled her pants and returned to the trail.

Why is it always like this, she wondered as she hurried back to the house, *this toxic brew of guilt and lust? The erotic thrill of that first night in Kabul—not knowing what he'd do if I disobeyed— still consumes me.*

My therapist says I'm a submissive. I don't agree. My desire isn't submissive.

* * *

Nikolai relaxed when the red dot on his computer screen returned to the house.

The lockbox safe was empty when he checked it a few minutes later. He looked at the moon. *The thing is in motion now. The cruel weight of destiny will now play its hand.*

Zurich, Switzerland

The UN courier's message told Rahim to travel to Zurich to pick up the OTP and decode his instructions.

I'm tired of feeling quarantined from the jihad, he decided. *It's time to see who the cutout agent is that delivers my OTP cyphers. OPEC is holding a meeting in Vienna this week, so there's a one-in-four chance Abdul will use the Weinplatz Tub Man Fountain as the drop site.*

Rahim arrived in Zurich later that afternoon. He slipped into a building adjacent to the tub man fountain dressed as a janitor, and hid in an office.

A heavy-set man taped a package beneath a bench near the fountain at a quarter past ten.

Rahim watched the cutout agent with night-vision binoculars as the man scribbled a chalk signal on the side of the bench.

The man looks Russian, Rahim observed. *Why would they be involved in our jihad?*

Rahim hustled back to his hotel room to wait for his call.

New York City

Angela and Counselor King sat down in David Cohen's office. His window looked out at the Empire State Building in the distance.

"Thanks for joining me on such short notice," David said. "I just got off the phone with Vladimir Volkov."

David passed them each a copy of a proposal he'd received from Vladimir. "His Swiss bank consortium just submitted another bid for Goldberg Cohen." He looked at his daughter. "Volkov asked me if he could meet with you to discuss his offer."

She frowned. "We told him we weren't interested a few years ago. Why's he back?"

"Why not hear him out?" Counselor King said. "Besides, you have a fiduciary responsibility to bring his offer to your other partners."

"We aren't selling, regardless of the price," David Cohen said.

"That's right," Angela said. "Why waste our time?"

King nodded. "Perhaps you can dissuade Vladimir with your charm, Angela. It'll save you a lot of heartburn if you can get him to back off before he takes his offer to your other partners."

"Sean promised he'd always vote his five percent with me," Angela said. "It's hard to say what the Goldberg trust-fund heirs might do with their twenty percent though. It'll be messy if they sell out to him. Perhaps we should buy them out ourselves. I don't want to get into a bidding war."

"Why don't you meet with Volkov to see what he's up to?" David said.

Angela arrived at the Ulysses Bar on Pearl Street late the following evening. She wore a tan business suit, white silk blouse, and a pearl necklace with matching earrings that elegantly framed her high cheekbones.

An attractive man with a muscular build at a corner table stood up and grasped her outstretched fingers when she approached. "It's good to finally meet you, Comrade Angela," he said.

Vladimir's dark-blue suit and silver tie illuminated the steel-blue glint in his eyes. He ordered a vodka martini when they sat down.

Angela said, "Make it two," and the waiter left with their order.

"So what would you like to talk about?" she inquired. "We told you several years ago we weren't interested in selling. We still aren't."

"You're not much into small talk, are you?" he observed. "I was hoping we could get to know each other, or rather, I was hoping you'd get to know me. I already know *a lot* about you."

She stared passively. "I'll give you five minutes."

His smile melted away. "Okay… if that's the way you want it."

The waiter delivered their drinks. She took a sip.

Vladimir poured his down his throat and bellowed after the waiter to bring another.

He focused on her. "You've lost a lot of clients since the Sean McGowan fiasco. I hear you still have charges pending. Is that true?"

Stay composed, she warned herself. *He's trying to rile you.*

"No. That's not true," she said. "You can always contact the FBI to see how their investigation is going if you'd like."

Vladimir chuckled. "Maybe I will."

"So, you don't want to sell, huh?" he continued. "Our offer is already very generous. We may be able to improve it a bit, if money is an issue."

She folded her hands. "Why are you so interested in us? There are plenty of other banks for sale these days."

Vladimir leaned closer. "I want your derivatives trading platform… and your IT infrastructure. Your bombproof systems in Boulder and Luxembourg intrigue me. Why else would I be interested? I don't need another bank."

The waiter delivered his drink. He slurped a mouthful.

"Your software has resilient risk-mitigation models," he continued, "and you're always a few milliseconds ahead of us when momentum turns. I've spent millions on state-of-the art servers and programmers in India developing a competing platform, but we still can't beat you. You have some kind of proprietary technology we can't figure out."

She studied him over the top of her glass as she took a sip.

His jaw clenched. "I like that you've built your systems underground, too—deep enough to withstand a nuclear blast. That's very clever."

He finished his drink and licked his lips. "There's also another reason."

"What's that?"

He stared at her hungrily.

This feels uncomfortable, she realized. She drank some water.

He wrapped his hand over hers when she placed her glass on the table.

"I want *you*, Angela…" His gaze was penetrating. "In my bed."

Her mouth dropped. She squirmed in her seat.

His lips bent to a smile. "We'd be invincible as a couple, and we'd make beautiful children together."

What chutzpah, she marveled inwardly!

The primal surge that erupted in her belly surprised her. She pulled her hand away and sipped her martini, concealing her shock.

She studied him when she put her glass down: early fifties, probably 6'3", muscular, and conspicuously handsome, with a full head of gray-blond-hair.

His bold alacrity jolted her sleeping time bomb—her desire to procreate as she hurtled towards forty. Sean's face appeared in her mind.

Vladimir barked across the room for a refill. A sardonic gaze gripped his face when he looked back at her. "You must be getting pretty cold at night with your boyfriend in prison."

She slowed her breathing to conceal her rage.

"Let's get out of here," he urged. "My penthouse is across the street from Central Park."

Angela finished her drink in one swallow. She smiled and leaned forward. Using her softest, sexiest voice she said, "That will never happen—*Comrade*."

* * *

Vladimir stared at her undulating hips as she walked away.

A martini appeared. He gulped it down.

He pulled out his phone and typed a text message. He stared at it for a moment before he posted the directive to Mikhail:

Time to tame the tiger.

Annapolis, Maryland

Yvonna did her best with makeup to look cheery the next morning before she headed down US Highway 50 towards DC.

After a quick lunch with Gregor in Georgetown—he was so busy at his law firm he barely had time to eat—she strolled to the Ritz Carlton.

The desk clerk handed her an envelope with her name. It had a room key inside.

She arrived at Mikhail's room at 1:00 p.m. She inserted the plastic key and the lock disengaged.

"Mikhail," she called out softly as she entered.

The room was dark. She turned on the light, removed her high heels, and opened the closet door.

The red silk negligee hanging on the cloth hanger is perfect—just my size, and in the style I love. He remembered!

She admired the hand-embroidered flowers and small, white pearls garlanding the cleavage line. The label said Milan. *Yes!*

She pulled it on and looked at herself in the mirror. *He's in for a treat.*

She drifted across the luxurious suite to the bed and pulled down the burgundy-colored comforter. The sheets were thousand-count Egyptian cotton, the king-sized mattress comfortable, but firm—*just the way we like it.*

The room had a fully stocked bar. She fixed two vodka martinis, placed them on the nightstand next to the bed, and lit three smokeless candles she'd brought with her.

Satisfied with the mood, she turned off the light and crawled beneath the sheets.

* * *

Nikolai arrived at a quarter to two. With a quick in and out his key sprung the lock.

Shadows from the candles danced on the walls as he glided into the room. He stared at her, asleep beneath the comforter.

He lifted a chair from beneath the desk and placed it next to her facing the bed. Macabre apparitions flitted across the ceiling. *It's time to end this subterfuge*, he decided.

He reached for her shoulder.

Her eyes opened. She jumped up recoiling against the headboard.

"Do you have anything to tell me?" he yelled.

Her gaze betrayed confusion. She covered her face with her hands and began to cry. "Did he… send you?" she said between sobs. "Is that why… you're here?"

Nikolai stood up and paced around the room. "What are you doing here?" he demanded.

She cried louder.

He stopped. *Should I comfort her?* He forced himself to ignore her crying, the gambit she'd used since she was fourteen to get her way.

She burrowed herself beneath the covers in a fetal position and continued to cry.

"How long has this been going on?" Nikolai asked angrily.

The amplitude of her cries exploded. She began to shake.

He sat down next to her and stroked her back.

She settled down after a few minutes.

"Kabul... " she said faintly, remaining sequestered beneath the covers like a bat afraid of the light.

"What?"

"It happened that night... in Kabul, after you fell asleep. It's been going on... ever since."

Nikolai clenched his fists and stood up. *I'm a cuckold!* He turned on the table lamp, snuffing the shadows. *How could I be so stupid?*

Seeing the drinks, he downed one and then the other.

Yvonna darted into the bathroom as he filled a glass with ice at the bar.

He poured vodka to the top. *How could I have been so ignorant? All those times I called... when she didn't answer.*

He sat in the chair facing the bed. *When should I kill the beast,* he ruminated? *I need my payment for the nukes first, and Vladimir—whom I've never met—will be lurking in the background. I'll need to plan Mikhail's murder carefully.*

How could she have sex with that animal? I should check myself for diseases.

Yvonna returned to the bed and sat down. She faced him with her legs parted, her crotch fully exposed.

His gaze moved to her face. "Why didn't you tell me?"

"I couldn't," she replied in a frightened voice.

"Why not?"

She pivoted her long legs onto the bed and leaned against the headboard. "I was afraid of him... at first." She looked down at the comforter as she spoke. "Then I got used to it. He never calls me anymore."

Nikolai winced when he sensed her longing. He rose with clenched fists ready to pound her but stopped above her face.

I've never hit a woman before, he reminded himself, *and I'm not about to start now.*

He paced around the bed, glaring at her between gulps of vodka. "Perhaps that's why he sent me," he said derisively. "He didn't tell me you'd be here, though. He just told me to come here for a surprise."

She covered her eyes and cried. He sauntered to the door.

"I do love you, Nikolai," she called out after him.

He stopped, and returned to the foot of the bed. "How could you do this to me?" His eyes were tearing up.

She sobbed into her hands. "I don't know… I'm so sorry."

He sat down next to her. "I'm going to start doing plenty of screwing around, too. I know lots of young women in Monaco who aren't tramps."

Her slap came hard across his face. "You bastard."

She slapped him again.

He took it, feeling somehow calmer from the pain.

She cried into her hands.

He hugged her to his chest.

"I'm so sorry," she said. "I know I screwed up. I'm so, so, sorry, Nikolai. I never meant to hurt you."

He held her close. "Will you promise never to see him again?"

"Yes… I promise." She pushed the comforter away with her foot and opened herself to him.

He kissed her belly.

Her moans built up quickly to an anguished scream until she found release.

They made love then—furious, angry love. She scratched and slapped him as they wrestled on the bed.

He dressed quickly when they'd finished and left the room without a word.

He installed a surveillance camera connected to a wireless, battery-powered modem, in a tree above the wall safe that afternoon. The miniature detector switch he placed in the cubbyhole would trigger the modem and send him an email with a picture attached if someone opened the wall safe door.

The old Russian proverb, *"Trust, but verify,"* kept ringing through his mind as he worked—the same aphorism espoused by the American President, Ronald Reagan, during nuclear disarmament talks with the Soviets.

I want to believe Yvonna he considered, *but I need to be sure.*

Armonk, New York. One week later

David and Sarah Cohen were rarely late coming down from their room for breakfast. They shared the ritual every morning like clockwork. It was often the only time they'd get to see each other all day with David's busy schedule.

Emily, their household manager, had moved in with the couple when they'd hired her to be Angela's nanny. She was just out of Yale at the time, with degrees in English literature and history. After living with the Cohen's for many years she'd become part of the family.

Emily knocked twice on their bedroom door when they didn't come down. She called out to them as she approached their bed.

This can't be real, she told herself.

The dark-red mass covering their pillows didn't register at first. She screamed when she saw the hole in David's eye.

She shrieked hysterically as she ran down the stairs to the kitchen and grabbed the butler's arm. Hyperventilating, unable to talk, she pointed and screamed at the upstairs floor.

Everyone in the household was sobbing when the police arrived. Nothing looked out of place inside when the detectives investigated.

The security guards on duty in the guardhouse of the thirty-acre estate had seen nothing. The tapes in the surveillance cameras, positioned to capture every exterior angle of the house, were blank. The three Doberman pinschers guarding the property were still asleep with blow darts buried in their flanks.

No one had heard anything inside the house during the night. The police found no shell casings, and nothing was missing. It was as if the killer had entered and left like a ghost.

The Armonk police and New York Bureau of Criminal Investigation speculated the murders were a professional hit. The meticulous attention to detail was well beyond the capabilities of most criminals. They had no suspects.

Angela suggested to the police that they question Vladimir Volkov. She said he'd been aggressively coming after Goldberg Cohen's banking empire, and she'd recently snubbed his marriage proposal.

Vladimir had a strong alibi when the police contacted him. Several bankers in London confirmed that he was with them at a meeting. He'd also sent a registered letter to Goldberg Cohen—postmarked three days before the murders—saying he was dropping his bid.

Niceville, Florida

Amos roused Sean from his bunk and brought him to the prisoner's conference room at 2:00 a.m. Amos didn't know why the warden said he needed to bring Sean there. Andrew was waiting when he arrived.

"I have some bad news," Andrew said when they were alone. "Angela's parents were murdered yesterday."

Sean reared his head back. "Are you kidding?" he gasped.

"Someone shot them in their bed."

Andrew comforted Sean the best he could as he wept.

Sean tried to contact Angela several times during the next two days. They cried together when he finally did reach her. *But that's all I can do to help her from inside this God-forsaken prison*, he fumed.

Andrew accompanied Angela to the memorial service. The governor of New York, the mayor of New York City, and several senators also attended, as did all of GC's New York employees, and many of the firm's clients. Jonas flew over from Luxembourg for the funeral.

Andrew spoke with Sean afterwards. "The authorities still have no leads. The bullets that smashed their skulls were useless for forensics, and the police didn't find any shell casings or fingerprints. Even the blow darts used to tranquilize the Dobermans were clean."

23. Devil Dog

Geneva, Switzerland—Two Weeks Later

Rahim retrieved the one-time pad from the Geneva Botanical Garden drop site—a discarded newspaper folded in the shape of a triangle left on top of a trashcan. The OTP cipher was composed using letters circled in the sports section.

The source texts for the messages came from several underlined passages in an early-edition copy of Shakespeare's *Julius Caesar*. The UN courier had given him a note instructing him to check the book out from the Geneva University library earlier that day.

Men at some time are masters of their fates:
The fault, dear Brutus, is not in our stars,
But in ourselves, that we are underlings.

How many ages hence
Shall this our lofty scene be acted o'er,
In states unborn, and accents yet unknown!

The ingenious conundrum quickened Rahim's heart as he deciphered his trading instructions. *The puzzle is clever. The tradecraft: Russian rules—simple and untraceable.*

Most of Rahim's trades exploited a change in the price of crude oil. This mission was different, more complex—like the trades before the flash crash in May of 2010, when the US markets dropped ten percent and recovered in a matter of minutes.

This would be a multifaceted, two-week mission. *The algorithms for the trades will yield maximum profit after a plunge in the markets followed by a huge, one-day rally several days later,* he discerned as he studied the algorithms. *The large position in defense stocks is also unusual. Some international saber rattling must be imminent.*

He looked out from his balcony across Lake Geneva. The snow-covered peaks of Mont Blanc shimmered beneath the moonlight. *They're like Emma's breasts,* he recalled remorsefully, *the night I killed her. Please, Allah: spare me from having to kill again.*

Wednesday—One Week Later, 0600 hours.

Sean refused to display his grief to the other prisoners after David and Sarah Cohen were murdered. He remained in his cell, pretending he had a cold. He took David Cohen's murder hard. David had been like a father to him—the only father he'd ever known—as well as his mentor.

Adkins, Hernandez, Julie Stensen, Andrew, and the warden were waiting for him when Amos marched him into the conference room. Sean stared trancelike at the telephone, computer, and portable printer sitting on the metal table as he sat down.

Agent Adkins placed a document in front of Sean. "This states that you won't discuss our investigation of Judge Richter, Agent Hartfield, or Isaac Bachman with anyone, until after we get convictions," Adkins said. "You'll also agree to appear as a witness if we need you."

Sean stared at the words without moving.

"We have an extensive undercover operation underway," Hernandez added. "I want to make sure we get these guys."

"My director has gone to bat on this too," Julie said. "This is the best we can come up with for now. I know you want your name cleared, but that'll have to wait. We'll make sure the press knows what happened when the time is right."

Adkins narrowed his eyes. "Is this agreeable to you, Mr. McGowan?"

Sean looked at Andrew. Andrew nodded his assent.

Sean signed his name.

"You'll also need to provide assistance to Ms. Stensen," Adkins said.

Sean turned to her. "What kind of assistance?"

"I need your banking expertise and trading knowledge to help us track down the terrorists you stumbled upon before 9/11," she said. "That's all I can tell you now, until we finish your security clearance. I've already initiated the paperwork for that. We'll also make sure you get a pardon to erase your felony conviction, but that may take a while."

Julie looked inquiringly at the FBI agents.

Adkins and Hernandez nodded without arguing.

Sean was going to interrupt, but something about her had seized his attention. *I'm not sure why, but I know I can trust her,* he realized.

"It's settled, then," Andrew said. "When will Sean be released?"

Adkins squirmed. "Something else has come up."

"Are you trying to add more conditions to our agreement?" Andrew said.

Julie faced Sean. "Angela's in trouble. She needs your help."

His eyes lurched to attention. "What's wrong?"

"Someone has hacked into your computers," she said. "Your servers are attacking your competitor's trading systems, preventing them from executing trades."

Adkins glared. "You've also disabled the government's international payment network. Our inability to pay interest to our foreign creditors is creating quite a stir."

Sean's hands braced the table. "How can that be?"

"You tell us," Adkins said.

Julie stood and slowly circled the room. "We've traced the denial-of-service attacks to your banks around the world," she said. "The Security and Exchange Commission is drafting paperwork as we speak, to shut down your firm. My director told them to hold off until we had a chance to speak with you."

She stopped and looked at Sean. "Why would someone stage this kind of charade? Somebody must really be gunning for you."

"Is that why the markets have plunged the last few days?" Andrew said.

"This information hasn't been released to the public," Adkins said. "Can I assume that those of you without clearances can keep your mouths shut? This is a national security issue."

The warden, Sean, and Andrew nodded their agreement.

"World markets have dropped thirty percent the past two days," Julie continued. "Everyone is panicking to get out. Exchange officials expect another bloodbath when the markets open this morning. We need your help, Sean. The world financial system is collapsing."

Sean shook his head as he stared down at the table. *The negative publicity and lawsuits will put us out of business forever*, he considered. *Everything GC has built up over eight decades will disappear overnight.*

We'll be like Lehman or Bear Sterns once the government shuts us down. Bankruptcies will cascade through the world banking system when our counterparty derivatives collapse. Billions of people's financial security is at stake.

Everyone was staring at him when he looked up.

"How can I help?" he said. "I can't do anything from in here. Pankaj, our chief information officer, is the best person to help you now."

"Pankaj told me he needs your help," Julie said.

"Is this a ploy to get our attention?" Adkins erupted. "We'll shut down your business forever if we find out your people are doing this to get you released."

"Goldberg Cohen isn't behind this," Julie barked. "There's no way Sean could orchestrate this from in here. Computer and Internet access are off limits to prisoners—right, Warden Johnson?"

"That's correct, Ms. Stensen."

Hernandez stared at Adkins. "I'm convinced Goldberg Cohen's intentions aren't malevolent," he declared. "This attack is very suspicious, especially on the heels of the Cohen murders."

Sean's lips flattened. "How can I help... from inside a prison?"

"Ms. Stensen and I have made arrangements," the warden said. "The Justice Department has asked us to do whatever it takes to stop the attack. What do you need, Sean?"

The warden nodded at him, which bolstered his courage.

"I don't understand, sir," he muttered. "I can't do anything from in here."

"We've been brainstorming all night," the warden said. "I believe Ms. Stensen can explain her plan better than I can."

Julie stopped at the head of the table. "We'll need good organization and close teamwork among government agencies, technology companies, banks, and the exchanges, to make this work. This is no time for finger-pointing and recriminations."

Sean sat up straight. "How can we pull it off from in here?"

"Julie can handle it," Warden Johnson said. "Tell them why, Ms. Stensen."

She smiled. "You aren't going to make me reveal all my secrets, are you Warden Johnson?"

"No ma'am, just the important ones."

Her chin went high. "I'm a Devil Dog."

"What's a Devil Dog?" Sean asked.

Her blue eyes sparkled. "Devil Dogs never let go of their objective, no matter how difficult the odds. I commanded a company of 150 soldiers—mostly engineers—when I was a captain in the Marines. There's no way we'll lose."

Sidelong glances among the men confirmed: her confidence had united them—even Adkins.

She began to circle the room again. "All warfare is based on deception. I believe the enemy is executing an elaborate war game with the Internet. We'll need the best IT and financial experts we can requisition to hunt them down. That's why we're here, Sean. We need your help, too."

Sean nodded. "We'll need a command center—a war room—to manage this. I'll need a secure, high-speed network and powerful analysis tools to dig into our code to see if someone's inserted a virus. I can't do that from in here."

The warden flexed his muscular biceps. "Perhaps you underestimate me, Sean. We have an Air Force Base next door. We can bring in anyone you need. The Pentagon has alerted the base commander at Eglin. He's standing by, waiting for instructions, and Washington has given me an unlimited budget to do whatever it takes to squash this attack."

The warden leaned forward. "You're a student of history, aren't you, Mr. McGowan?"

"I know a few things, I guess," Sean responded.

"Have you ever heard the statement by Virgil in the 'Aeneid:' *flectere si nequeo superos, Acheronta movebo*"?

Julie chuckled. She sat down in front of her computer and began to type.

"No, sir," Sean said.

"The translation is, 'If I cannot deflect the will of heaven, I shall move hell.' Well, perhaps I can do that."

"Let's get to work, then," Julie said. "Pankaj is already on his way. An F-14 picked him up at Rocky Mountain Airport in Broomfield an hour ago. The NSA, Defense Intelligence Agency, and Federal Reserve also have people en route."

Sean's eyes lit up. "It'll be good to see Pankaj."

Julie typed as she talked. "Shall we start with the virtual private network connections to your systems? I understand they're in Boulder now. By the way, that's my old stomping grounds. I graduated from CU. We can talk about that later when we have more time."

Sean nodded. "We built a secure bunker in the mountains west of Boulder to house our computers after the 9/11 attacks in New York."

Sean turned to the warden. "Can you get us a room with enough space to set up a bunch of tables, sir? We'll need power, fiber cables, workstations, at least thirty displays, and a couple of digital projectors."

"Logistics support, too," Julie said, as she typed. "Food, bathrooms… I'll need ten phones with conferencing capabilities. We could have forty or fifty people here by the time we're done."

Johnson rose. "I'll get on it."

She printed out a list of action items and handed them to the warden. He left the room.

"I think we should organize the teams based on expertise," Sean said.

"Good idea," she said, typing fast. "We'll need networking folks, software vendors, some system analysts from the banks, and a data analytics specialist to run reports. Perhaps Eglin can send us some technicians to set up the infrastructure and keep everything running. How about you, Adkins? Can you get your FBI security expert down here—the guy that traced the denial of service attacks?"

"I'll check into it." Adkins dialed a number.

His face flushed when his call ended. "He's already on his way. My director put him on a plane a few minutes ago."

Julie and Sean had composed several pages of action items assigned by expertise by the time the warden returned.

"I've arranged a temporary transfer of the men in Cellblock C," the warden said. "Folks will have to triple up for a while, but you'll have an entire building to yourselves. Amos is in charge."

The warden smiled. "Shall I give you the keys to the cellblock, Ms. Stensen?"

She chuckled. "That won't be necessary. We'll set up a security perimeter with troops from Corry Station, in Pensacola. Come back when you're ready."

She handed the warden a list of action items. He left with Amos.

"I need to talk with Angie," Sean said.

Julie punched the conference-call button and entered a number from memory. "Hello, Angela—this is Julie. Thanks for standing by. I'm here with Sean. How're you doing?"

"Hi, Julie," Angela said through the speakerphone. "Not so well." She was on the verge of tears. "It's been hard, Sean. I wish you were here."

"I wish I was, too," Sean said.

"Warden Johnson is providing space for a command center," Julie said. "We're flying in experts from across the country. Don't worry. We'll save your company."

"Thanks, Julie. The first thing I should tell you is that we've stopped all our trading—worldwide. We aren't going to take advantage of this situation at the expense of other banks."

Julie eyed Adkins. "That's a good idea," she said.

"We'll be setting up a secure VPN connection to our source-code management system in Boulder," Sean said. "I hear Pankaj is on his way. We should get our developers up."

"The development team is already on-site at the Compound," Angela said. "They're awaiting your instructions. The Treasury Department spoke with the presidents of several banks with expertise in derivatives trading. Their experts will be joining you soon."

"Excellent," Julie said. "Sounds like things are rolling."

Angela's voice was cracking. "We need to stop this attack. This will be worse than the financial collapse after Lehman if we don't. We aren't causing this!"

"I'm sure you aren't," Julie said. "We'll get back to you as soon as we know something."

They ended the call.

Amos knocked on the door and stuck his head in. "We're ready."

Everyone followed him out, relieved to be leaving the claustrophobic room.

"Sean no longer needs handcuffs," the warden said.

Amos nodded without objecting.

24. Predators

FPC Niceville—Wednesday, 1430 hours

The markets plunged and interest rates soared when China announced they'd no longer buy US bonds because their interest payments had stopped flowing. Petroleum prices jumped when OPEC said they were discontinuing oil shipments to the US because they weren't receiving payments.

Just as the Greek Drachma, Roman Aureus, Arabian Dinar, Florentine Fiorino and British Pound had once been the premier currency for international commerce; the US Dollar was now under attack. "The Yuan should be the international currency for trade," proposed a high-ranking Chinese official. "It's much more stable than Petrodollars."

His bellicose tirade, implying that a country's failure to pay its debts was tantamount to declaring war, kept newswires humming across the globe. The US raised its military threat level to DEFCON 3.

In the meantime, technicians from Eglin Air Force Base had transformed Niceville's Cellblock C into a full-fledged military command center. Power and fiber cables ran the length of the hallway, feeding tables filled with workstations and displays. Two satellite dishes in the yard provided secure communications through the US Army Intelligence Center in Fort Huachuca, Arizona. A platoon from the Marine Corps detachment in Pensacola patrolled the perimeter with machine guns.

A cell on the periphery of the cellblock housed a coffee stand. Two cells at opposite ends—their iron bars covered with blankets—served as restrooms. Julie ran things from her command cell in the center.

Using a deep-talent database secretly maintained by the US government, Julie recruited engineers, programmers, and finance experts from companies across the country. Sean enlisted the help of several of his quantitative analyst friends from banks and hedge funds in Chicago, Los Angeles, and New York.

Almost forty men and women had arrived by midafternoon. Adkins and Hernandez made sure everyone—consultants, as well as government officials—reviewed and signed a Patriot Act Agreement when they arrived.

Julie brought her first status meeting to order. Sean and Pankaj stood next to her in the command cell. Everyone else huddled around them beyond the bars, in the hallway or in the adjacent cells.

A cigarette-box-sized digital projector attached to her computer presented a list of action items on the wall. A second projector displayed a network diagram with the names of every city where Goldberg Cohen had a bank.

"The FBI and NSA have determined the attacks are coming from Goldberg Cohen's Internet routers," she began.

Julie tapped her computer keyboard. A starburst pattern of red lines connecting GC's banks to stock exchanges and US Federal Reserve banks appeared. The complex diagram looked like a convoluted Kandinsky painting.

"Our network team mapped the routers perpetrating the distributed denial-of-service attacks to their targets," Julie said. "Goldberg Cohen's Boulder compound is attacking eighteen US banks and five branches of the US Federal Reserve."

She turned to Sean. "Can you give us an update, Mr. McGowan?"

Sean assessed the well-dressed soldiers and business professionals staring at him. *Why shouldn't they?* he reasoned, feeling embarrassed in his green prisoner shirt, light-green pants and tennis shoes. *The FBI had yanked them out of their lives and flown them to a prison in Florida because of me.*

"First of all, Warden Johnson and I would like to welcome you to our humble abode."

A few people chuckled. Most weren't amused.

"So, how about a game of Texas Hold-'Em winner takes all when this is over?" said one of his quant friends from a bank in New York.

"Sounds good to me," Sean replied.

More people smiled. Most were still in a daze. To be standing in a prison after a gut-wrenching flight in a military jet to resolve a national emergency hadn't yet percolated through their brains.

"Pankaj and I analyzed our source and object code, as well as our change logs," Sean began. "We've found nothing to indicate our systems have been compromised. The attacks must be coming from our routers. I know that doesn't sound possible based on the role routers typically play in a network, but that's all I can think of to explain it."

"I suspected that," Julie said.

Murmurs flowed around the cellblock.

Julie turned to her team of computer-industry experts. "Does anyone from the software or server team have an update?"

"I agree with Sean's assessment," a computer consultant said. "The attack is coming from somewhere outside their firewalls. Their code hasn't been compromised."

"That's a good start," Julie said. "Work the next layer of problems in your area—divide and conquer. Brainstorm amongst yourselves to share ideas. Your country is counting on you. We'll meet in a couple of hours for an update. Now let's get going."

1930 Hours

Julie asked Amos to bang his billy club on the iron bars to call the meeting to order.

"I need some status updates, folks."

She turned to Pankaj, standing next to her in her cell. "Tell us what you've found."

"The network and Internet security companies have thrown every virus tool they have against us," Pankaj said. "No one has breached our systems."

"Our tools found no malware, Trojan horse, or any other kind of virus," a network expert interjected.

The other networking experts nodded.

"What about the routers?" she asked.

"Something suspicious is going on," a networking expert said. "We've performed tier-one triage on their routers, switches, and firewalls. Dr. Boyd from the DIA can explain. He has the working hypothesis at the moment."

Dr. Edward Boyd, early sixties, a tall, hollow-cheeked, stork-thin network security expert from the US Defense Intelligence Agency stepped forward. "We think someone is using a custom-developed Darknet to route commands to Goldberg Cohen's network access points. Someone is spoofing, using Goldberg Cohen's NAPs, to send denial-of-service attacks. They're trying to make it look like the attacks are coming from Goldberg Cohen, but they're not."

A burst of chatter echoed between the walls.

Sean, Pankaj, and Angela—who'd arrived from New York an hour earlier—looked at each other with relief.

Amos banged the bars. Everyone quieted.

Angela raised her hand. "May I say something, Ms. Stensen?"

"Please do," Julie said.

Agent Hernandez had briefed everyone when they'd arrived about the tragedy that had recently befallen Angela's parents, and now… her company.

"I want to thank all of you from the bottom of my heart, for helping us save our firm," she said. "I especially want to thank you, Julie, for all you're doing. Sean and I really appreciate it."

Everyone was captivated. The grief shrouding her voice was heart wrenching. Her poise and presence were hypnotic, considering the circumstances.

"Thanks, Angela," Julie said. "We're making good progress. Don't worry. We'll get this sorted out."

Julie turned to the network team. "So Dr. Boyd, what's the next step?"

"We've placed tracers on the NAPs to spot unusual activity," he reported. "We'll need to sift through the audit logs to analyze the messages. This will be slow going, because of the many layers of encryption. Anyone with tools that can help us speed up the process should come and see me."

"Excellent," Julie said. "Brainstorm among your teams when you need to. Different perspectives are useful here. We need everyone's ideas… as long as they're good."

Her comment elicited a few chuckles.

"I forgot to mention," Dr. Boyd said. "You may have noticed that we don't have any of the foreign Internet router companies here. There's a reason for that."

He paused to make sure he had everyone's attention. "We think this may be an industrial espionage attack from a foreign government. Someone just hacked into one of our Predator drones in Pakistan and flew it towards Iran. It may be a coincidence, but I don't think so. The timing is suspicious."

His words riveted the room.

Julie nodded. "Let's get back to work. I'd like another update at midnight."

The congregation hustled back to their cells.

Julie and Sean sat down at her computer.

Angela crossed her arms and studied the pair from beyond the bars of Julie's cell.

Thursday—0000 hours

Amos pushed a large cart filled with food into the cellblock. The building instantly acquired a new ambience, as the pleasant aroma of scrambled eggs, bacon, pancakes, and coffee displaced the sulfuric sewer-gas odor radiating from the toilets.

"Grab something to eat, and let's get down to business," Julie said.

She poured herself a large cup of coffee.

Amos—who'd taken a liking to his role as Julie's assistant—banged his club against the bars to bring the meeting to order.

"I'd like to introduce you to Sonya Hemingway," Julie said, "the Assistant Secretary of the Treasury for Financial Stability."

Hemingway, a tall, attractive African American woman in her early forties stepped forward. "I'd like to thank all of you for your service to your country," she said. "I won't take up any more of your time right now. I know you have a lot to do." She stepped back.

"Thank you, Ms. Hemingway," Julie said. She turned to Dr. Boyd. "I'd like to begin with a status update from the networking team."

Dr. Boyd held a plate piled high with eggs and pancakes. He obviously had the metabolism of someone who could eat with impunity without gaining weight.

"I think they're using a routing onion, and garlic," Boyd said between chews, "to send commands to the NAPs." He swallowed. "Those commands are triggering programs in the routers that prevent banks from communicating. Only a few foreign banks are able to get their orders through to the exchanges. Goldberg Cohen's routers are also blocking the Fedwire system from transferring payments to their international counterparties."

"Could you explain what you mean by routing onions and garlic, Dr. Boyd?" Julie said.

The PhD placed his plate on the floor to free his hands. "It's actually quite interesting," he began. "A routing onion imbeds a message within itself, wrapped in several layers of encryption. It's like a Russian matryoshka nesting doll." He gesticulated to reinforce his words. "Each node in the network peels off a layer, decrypts its routing instructions, and sends the message on to the next node. The destination node decrypts the final payload—the real message. The network itself has no knowledge of intermediary nodes, which makes it difficult to trace the message to a source computer."

"How about garlic?" Julie said.

"It's similar, but different. Imagine a head of garlic that contains cloves. A given node can either decode one or more segments, or forward the message to another node. We use this architecture to send messages to kick off commands—in a sequence or concurrently—at a destination node. Unfortunately, it's almost impossible to trace these kinds of messages through a proprietary Darknet."

Julie turned to Commander Jones, an officer from the Navy SEAL detachment in Virginia. "We need to confiscate these Darknet routers," she said, pointing at locations on the network diagram, "and replace them with equipment we can trust."

"I've discussed this with Dr. Boyd," Commander Jones said. "One of the routers is in North Korea. We'll try to avoid political fallout, if we can."

"Come talk to me after the meeting," she said. "I have some contacts there that can help."

Sean raised his hand.

"Yes, Sean."

"I think the finance team should analyze the pending order queues at the exchanges," he suggested. "We need to see whose taking advantage of this situation, to locate the enemy."

"Several banks in the Caymans and Lichtenstein are still able to get their orders through," Swiss Bank-New York said. "Those banks must hold the perpetrator accounts."

"They're routing their trades through tax-haven countries," Federal Reserve-Dallas said.

"That's a good idea," Julie said. "Asian markets are open now, and Europe will be opening in a few hours. Let's find out who's doing this."

Commander Jones huddled with Julie and the network team to plan the router replacement assault. Sean, Pankaj, and Angela joined the finance team to look at the order queues at the exchanges.

Shanghai, China

The massive, sixty-foot, concave LED display screen at the front of the theatre colored General Wu's employee-soldiers blue-gray in the translucent light. The five women and thirteen men were now rich beyond their dreams. More importantly, they'd proven that the General's Massive Multiplayer Online Role-Playing gaming software was more than just an Internet gaming platform, when they'd used it to commandeer a CIA Predator drone from its secret US base in Pakistan. They flew it to China after a fake-out diversion towards Iran.

General Wu observed everything from his roost behind the semicircle array of soldiers' desks facing the screen. He'd recruited the former officers for his private company based on their MMORPG scores. Some had been only fifteen-years-old when the Chinese government originally groomed them for entry into the military based on their gaming aptitudes. They'd subsequently received computer-engineering degrees courtesy of the Chinese government before General Wu recruited them.

The employee-soldiers had just returned from a break at a nearby luxury hotel. General Wu was treating them like rock stars, with all the amenities of the best backstage rock concert venue. Each suite had a personal chef, a wide selection of libations, and a variety of international sex partners to choose from—for those needing comfort.

An important stage of the battle was about to begin. The general turned down the rock'n'roll pounding through the speakers to get their attention.

The employee-soldiers stood as one and saluted.

Wu smiled as he returned their salutation. *I have a good reason to smile*, he gloated. *The strategy Vladimir outlined has worked perfectly so far.*

General Wu's microphone fed a three-dimensional sound system integrated into the walls and ceiling of the gaming theatre.

"The most important phase of our campaign is about to begin," he said. "The markets have dropped substantially. It's time to cash in our put-option positions and purchase call options. The markets will catapult higher when we release the brakes. Then we'll sell our call-option positions to lock in the profits. Does everyone understand?"

"Yes, sir," they answered as one.

"In a moment, on my mark, we'll initiate Battle Plan Seventeen, to sell our put-option positions in the Asian markets. We'll do the same in Europe and America when their markets open. I'll flash the attack plans on the screen as the battle evolves. Things are going to move fast from this point forward. Is everyone ready?"

"Yes, sir."

"Good. Remember: Take your time with your ammunition. I know we've tested the code extensively, but this is real money. We need to liquidate our positions slowly, so we don't cause price spikes. Grind the monsters and villains until they're dead. Don't let up. Their reappearance means you have more transactions to execute. Does everyone understand?"

"Yes, sir."

General Wu turned to an employee-soldier on his right.

"Mr. Chang, I'd like you to execute Program Twenty-Eight to free up the Fedwire network. That will allow US interest payments to flow to the People's Bank of China. I'm sure the Chinese Central Committee will settle down once they get their interest payments. We don't want to start a war after all—at least not yet anyhow."

The general laughed. His troops chuckled in response.

"Remember," he continued, addressing his employees, "your remuneration will reflect your ordnance-deployment proficiency. Take your time with your munitions so you don't cause price spikes."

"Yes, sir."

"We'll erase the polymorphic routines you programmed into the routers when we've completed our trades. No one will ever know we were there. Now let's get to work."

The employee-soldiers saluted and sat down.

Wu selected a new song to juice their adrenaline—Led Zeppelin's "*Kashmir*,"—and turned it up loud.

"On my mark… three… two… one… engage!"

The theatre display at the front of the room exploded into a battlefield. Monsters and villains bobbed and weaved behind buildings until they burst into flames when the soldier's aim was true.

Each explosion confirmed a trade from an option exchange. The targeted enemy reappeared—spawning in MMORPG vernacular—until they sold all the securities in their queue.

Vladimir's blueprint directed Wu to start selling his put options when the market reached a thirty-eight-point-two-percent loss inflection point. They locked in a profit equivalent to $10 billion dollars in the Asian markets in less than an hour.

General Wu smiled. *I can't wait to see what we can do once I have an arsenal of predator drones to instigate market panic.*

FPC Niceville—Thursday, 0400 Hours

Assistant Secretary Hemingway and Angela stood with Julie in her command cell. Amos banged his billy club on the bars to bring the meeting to order.

"Things are evolving," Julie said. "The Fedwire network started working for no apparent reason a few hours ago."

"The Fedwire system is able to send payments to China now," Secretary Hemingway said. "The Chinese premier just called the president. He warned him not to fool around with their interest payments in the future."

"Angela and Sean have an idea they'd like to share," Julie said.

Angela made eye contact with everyone in the room as she talked. "I think the enemy is manipulating the markets for financial gain. The Asian markets began to stabilize when they dropped thirty-eight-point-two percent. That's a standard Fibonacci retracement level. Someone sold a massive put-option position at that point, locking in huge profits."

A chorus of agitated banter consumed the cellblock. Julie let everyone talk for a moment. She nodded, and Amos restored order.

"I'd like to summarize the multi-pronged attack plan we've developed," Julie said. "Our military colleagues are replacing the routers that have been perpetrating the denial-of-service attacks with trusted hardware across the globe. We'll launch a counterattack to block the accounts at banks that are manipulating the financial system when they're finished. Our finance team will then purchase massive call-option positions. These will crush the enemy when the markets rocket higher. We'll need to coordinate our trades to ensure maximum effectiveness."

The cellblock erupted with chatter. Julie nodded. Amos banged his club.

"It's our fiduciary responsibility to protect our companies, our clients and our citizens," Angela said. "Does everyone agree?"

Several people responded with, "Hell, yes."

Julie studied Angela. *She has great charisma, and her magnetism is alluring... and those long legs. She'll be tough to compete with if she ever sets her sights on Sean. I wonder why she hasn't already.*

Julie turned to the networking team. "Can you describe your plan for the routers, Doctor Boyd?"

He nodded. "Our network experts have developed a program that will block the accounts executing the enemy's trades once we replace the faulty routers. We'll send the commands through our own Defense Department Darknet. We've only been able to run some rudimentary unit and integration tests, so I hope it works."

"Excellent," Julie said.

Sean raised his hand.

"Yes, Sean?"

"I don't want to be a wet blanket, but unless we deal with some legal issues, you may all end up being my neighbors here in Niceville. Collusion is illegal, even if it is for a good cause."

A wave of mutters rippled through the building.

"Would you like to discuss that, Ms. Hemingway?" Julie said.

The room hushed as the stately woman addressed the group. "I have authorization from the Justice Department to pursue this strategy under the auspices of the Patriot Act," she explained. "Agent Adkins will bring you a document stating the government won't lodge criminal actions against you as long as you follow Angela's trading instructions. If anyone wants out... now's the time to leave."

Everyone chatted. Julie nodded. Amos restored order.

No one left.

"We'll make an announcement to the press when this is over stating that Internet problems caused a transitory dip in the financial markets," Hemingway continued. "Remember, you must keep this secret. Otherwise, you'll be prosecuted for violating the Patriot Act."

"Does this mean we can trade in our own accounts," a New York banker asked, "as long as we follow Angela's directives?"

"Absolutely," Hemingway answered. "That's the idea. We need you to purchase large call option positions. Anyone in the room can make this trade—today only, of course. You can consider this your compensation, for assisting us during this national emergency."

Dr. Boyd banged his shoe on the bars. Everyone hushed.

"I was getting to you, Dr. Boyd," Julie said. "Please tell everyone what we need to do before the game begins."

Boyd's eyebrows furrowed with seriousness. "We observed a continuous burst of traffic to the NAP routers in Asia just before the put-option sales… so our thesis about the Darknet is correct."

"Those routers aren't ours," a network vendor said. "They're Chinese; built by a vendor we lodged patent complaints against last year after they reverse-engineered our code. No one seems to care when we lodge unfair trade-practice protests."

"Does anyone else have something to say?" Julie said. The room was silent. "Please tell us your plan, Dr. Boyd."

"Navy SEALs are yanking out the problem routers from network centers across Europe, Asia, and the US as we speak," he said. "I'll tear them apart in my lab when this is over. We're hot plugging the new routers to avoid delays. We should be finished in a few minutes."

"That's excellent news, Dr. Boyd," Julie said. "Great job."

She turned to the finance team. "It's time to get ready to execute your trades. Follow Angela's lead. I'll let you know when Dr. Boyd is ready."

Angela raised her hand.

"Yes, Angela."

"We know the financial folks have plenty of capital to trade with, but not everyone has that luxury. We'd like to offer a one-million-dollar line of credit to anyone who wants us to execute this trade on his or her behalf. It's our way of saying thanks. We'll bring you a document to sign if you want to participate. If your account zooms to five million after our trades, you'll make four million dollars."

"That's a very generous offer," Julie said. "Is this legal, Ms. Hemingway?"

"I don't see a problem with it," Hemingway said. "I'm not going to sign up because I have a conflict of interest, but everyone else can."

"Great," Julie said. "We'll bring the paperwork around soon."

Adkins and Hernandez handed Angela a stack of signed forms thirty minutes later. Thirty-four people took Angela up on her offer, including Amos, and the warden.

Julie asked Amos to get everyone's attention. He banged his club on the bars.

"Commander Jones just informed me that the faulty routers have been replaced," she said. "The perpetrator accounts are blocked from trading."

She turned to Angela. "Let's begin the counterattack."

The computer and network teams executed programs to block the perpetrator accounts from sending messages, while the financial team typed furiously, entering orders. The European markets immediately began to rise. North and South America followed suit a couple of hours later when their stock and option exchanges opened for trading.

Shanghai, China

General Wu scowled as he watched the action on the screen. The villains and monsters on the battlefield wouldn't die. There were no blood-and-gore explosions, because the exchanges weren't confirming trades.

"What the hell is going on?" he yelled.

His soldier-programmers frantically fired their weapons.

Wu became increasingly agitated as his militia blasted away at the enemy with no kills. The expletives he screamed through the loudspeakers did nothing to accomplish his mission.

FPC Niceville—Friday, 1200 Hours

Thursday was the wildest day ever in the markets. The European and American exchanges rose forty percent. The Asian markets followed suit when they opened on Friday morning.

Everyone congregated in front of Julie's cell. She was standing with Sonya Hemingway and Angela. Someone began to clap, and soon the entire cellblock was reverberating with raucous cheers.

Hemingway raised her hands. The crowd quieted. "I'd like to take a moment to thank you before you return home," Hemingway said. "You've done a great job. Please remember—this is a national security issue. Don't discuss what happened here today with anyone."

She turned to Julie. "Would you like to say something, Ms. Stensen?"

Julie nodded. "I'd also like to thank everyone. This was the most fun I've had in a while."

The crowd chuckled, mostly because they'd be returning home with much fatter bank accounts.

"Dr. Boyd will be taking over the investigation from this point," she continued. "It's been a pleasure working with you."

The warden's timing was perfect. He entered the cellblock with several guards pushing carts filled with grilled hamburgers, French fries, and cold beer. Everyone opened a beer and dug in to the food.

The assembly gradually disappeared over the next two hours, escorted by prison guards to waiting limousines, and whisked off to Pensacola International Airport for first-class flights home.

Angela, Sean, Warden Johnson, Julie, Andrew, and Agent Hernandez were talking in a circle when Agent Adkins approached.

Adkins handed a document to the warden. "I've signed Sean's release papers," he announced.

Sean smiled as he shook Adkins's hand. "Thank you."

Everyone congratulated him.

Sean turned to the warden. "I'd like to make a request, sir."

"What's that?" Johnson said.

"I know this may sound crazy, but I'd like to play another concert for the men before I leave. I penned some new arrangements while I was grieving about Angela's parents."

Sean looked at Angela. "I had to do something to keep my sanity during those dark hours."

Tears filled her eyes. She hugged him sideways.

"I'd like to hear the new pieces before I leave," he said. "It'll be a good way to say goodbye."

"That's fine with me," the warden said.

He looked at Amos. "Please make the arrangements for Tyrone's Cyclones to play a concert after dinner tomorrow night."

Amos grinned. "Yes, sir."

"Is it okay if I come?" Julie said.

Johnson's face flashed with surprise. "I'm not sure," he answered. "It'll stir up the men to have a woman present. Perhaps... if you dress down... so you don't look so... well... you know what I mean, don't you, Ms. Stensen?"

Everyone chuckled, watching the warden squirm.

"I'll dress down, and sit with your staff. Will that work?"

"I guess that'll be okay," he replied.

Julie smiled. "Don't worry. I can take care of myself."

Amos led Sean back to his cell without handcuffs.

Sean gave Albert an oblique excuse as to why he'd been with the visitors in Cellblock C, and told him about his pending release.

He then leapt up the ladder and reclined on his bunk. He was out cold in less than five minutes—his first sleep in days.

25. Eden

FPC –Niceville, Florida

Sean's farewell concert at FPC Niceville was a resounding success. The inmates coaxed the band to new heights after every song with tumultuous hollers and applause.

The guards escorted the prisoners back to their cells when the concert was over. Warden Johnson accompanied Julie to the stage to talk with Sean.

"You sounded great," the warden said. "I really enjoyed your new arrangements."

Julie smiled. "The concert was wonderful!"

"I'm glad you came," Sean said. "You could probably tell, from the way I kept bowing in your direction."

A blush graced her cheeks. "That was nice of you."

The warden chuckled. "Slow down there, partner. You're not out of here yet."

He smiled at Julie. "What were your favorite songs, Ms. Stensen?"

The men observed her inquisitively.

"The rock songs were fun, but I liked the Miles Davis and John Coltrane arrangements the best. They were deeper, somehow... more emotional."

The men exchanged percipient glances with each other that said: *She's a keeper*.

"Your soprano sax solo in *'My Favorite Things'* was cool," she continued. "But the tenor sax solo in *'Body and Soul'*... the longing and pain... it almost made me cry."

Sean blinked. "You're probably the first woman to witness our musical soirees."

The warden snickered. "You've got that right. Sorry I have to interrupt, but it's time for you to hit the sack, Sean—last night in the castle. Lights out in ten minutes. Thanks for doing this. The singing was so loud during *'Sweet Home Alabama'* I thought the roof was going to cave in."

Sean and Julie laughed.

"That's always a hit," Sean said. "I think it must be the national anthem of the South."

The warden reached for Julie's hand. "It was nice meeting you, Ms. Stensen."

"Likewise, Warden Johnson. Thanks for all your help."

She looked into Sean's eyes. "I'll see you outside in the morning."

The squeeze of her hand jolted his loins. She smiled as they glided towards the exit.

Amos tipped his hat as she approached.

She shook his hand. "Thanks for being my assistant."

He beamed with gratitude. "My pleasure, ma'am."

Amos escorted her through two sets of iron-barred walls to the exit.

Sean addressed his Spartacus clan and his band members during breakfast the next morning. "Albert will distribute my cigarette stash to each of you this afternoon," he announced. "I wish you all the best."

Each man shook Sean's hand and bid him farewell.

Randy was waiting to talk to him when he finished.

"When will you be back?" Randy said with a laugh.

"Not for a while, I hope. I'll keep your offer in mind if I ever decide to become an actor."

Randy folded his arms. "Do you really know what's going on here, McGowan?"

Sean frowned. "What do you think's going on?"

Randy's stare spoke volumes. "Just make sure you watch your back. The people I work for don't take kindly to rejection."

"Thanks for the advice."

Father Sam was waiting with Albert in their cell when Sean returned. "Have you figured out what you're going to do?" the priest said.

"Other than walking along the beach, I'm not sure," he replied.

"You should come down to the Keys for a visit when I get out," Albert said.

"I will." Sean gave Albert a hug before he left.

Amos escorted Sean to the office, where he changed into the suit he'd worn the day he arrived. It fit looser around the waist now and tighter around the shoulders, a consequence of his rigorous workout regimen.

Warden Johnson shook Sean's hand. "Good luck, Sean."

"I hope I wasn't too much trouble, sir."

"Not at all. Thanks for the stock account. That money will send my kids to college."

"We couldn't have saved our business without you."

Amos escorted Sean through the gate to his waiting entourage.

Angela hugged him without letting go when he exited. "The Gulfstream will take us to Clearwater," she said. "We're going to stay with you for a while in Palm Harbor, if that's okay. We have a lot of catching up to do."

"That'll be great," Sean said.

She pulled Sean into the limousine after her. Andrew followed.

"Wait," Julie said. "I need to talk with you, Sean."

"Do you need a ride?" Angela asked.

A splotch of red tinged Julie's cheeks. "No. I'm fine," she replied.

She jotted her number on a card and handed it to Sean. "Please call me as soon as you can. It's very important."

"I will," he assured her. "Thanks for everything, Julie."

* * *

Beate returned to her rental car, removed the auburn-colored wig she'd been wearing, and called agent Hernandez to arrange surveillance for Sean.

I don't want Sean to catch me stalking him, she decided.

New York City—Three Days Later

Mikhail and Vladimir sat down on a park bench near the Central Park boathouse. It was early morning. They both carried cups of coffee.

"What the hell happened?" Mikhail said.

Vladimir waited for a runner to pass before he answered. "I'm still not sure," he said. "We were up ten billion before the markets turned, and then we couldn't get out. Someone blocked the networks at our banks so our orders wouldn't flow to the exchanges. By the time they freed up, the markets had recovered and our put options were worthless."

"Was General Wu behind this?" Mikhail asked angrily.

"No. He was up ten at the same time we were," Vladimir said. "He lost two billion on his European and American put options just as we did, so our net gain was only eight in the end."

"This is a disaster," Mikhail groaned.

"Not totally. We were doing fine until someone figured out Wu's routers initiated the attack. There are ways around that next time—something Wu's computer people call router hopping. It was still a worthwhile exercise."

"But you said we'd make sixty," Mikhail complained. "At least the predator theft was successful."

"I'm sure the Defense Department is shitting all over themselves trying to figure out what happened. General Wu's engineers in China are tearing the Predator apart as we speak. They'll reverse-engineer the components and build something similar. His drones could be useful in the future."

Mikhail nodded. "How soon will he have a test model?"

"A couple of years. My biggest disappointment is that we didn't get Angela to capitulate. She would've had no choice but to sell Goldberg Cohen once the SEC shut them down."

"*Da.* She keeps fouling up our plans. Perhaps it's time to take her out… like her parents. I heard she moved into their mansion in Armonk."

"I don't want you to touch her," Vladimir insisted. "I haven't given up on her. She'll come around."

Mikhail ground his jaw. "Nikolai's computer hackers can't break through their firewalls, and we can't keep McGowan on ice any longer. We need to eliminate them."

"Why weren't you able to turn McGowan? I'm sure he's bitter after what happened."

"Randy, the dealer our judge shuffled to Niceville, said McGowan was thinking about it. There's another problem we need to talk about."

"What's that?"

"Hartfield—the FBI agent we used to arrest McGowan—made a run for it after the Justice Department issued his subpoena. My agents are looking for him. We'll have to eliminate him if he isn't willing to do his time and keep his mouth shut."

Annapolis, Maryland

Yvonna was in a daze for weeks after her confrontation with Nikolai.

How could Mikhail be so cruel she wondered? *Using Nikolai as a pawn to end our relationship is beyond malicious—even for him.*

Suspecting there must be more going on, she resumed her treks to the wall safe. *It can't be over*, she decided. *There's too much fire between us for Mikhail to give me up.*

Nice, France

Nikolai dismissed his illusions about Yvonna when he received the email. The wall sentry camera didn't lie. She'd resumed her trips to the wall, looking for correspondence from Mikhail.

It isn't coercion, he realized. *She wants to be on Mikhail's leash!*

Palm Harbor, Florida

The weather was warm and sunny when Beate met agent Hernandez at a coffee shop near Sean's condominium. They were both wearing casual clothes so they wouldn't appear out of place.

"We've tapped his phones and the security cameras in his lobby," Hernandez said, "and the CCTV cameras in the traffic lights near his building. The rest of our surveillance will need to be in person," Hernandez smirked, "unless you want cameras in his bedroom."

"That won't be necessary," Beate said.

"Andrew flew back to New York yesterday," he informed her, "so it's just the two of them shacking up now. They walked along the beach holding hands this morning."

Crap! Beate gritted her teeth and stood up. "Thanks for keeping an eye on them," she said. "Call me if anything changes."

Beate was in her hotel room when Hernandez called her a few days later.

"Angela just boarded her private jet at the Clearwater airport," he said, "and Sean's checking in for a flight to Mexico at the Tampa airport. Do you want me to ask Homeland Security to pull him at the gate?"

"Hang loose for a few minutes," she said. "I want to see if he calls me. We'll yank him off the plane if he doesn't."

Sean called her a few minutes later. "I'm going to Mexico for a vacation, Julie. I'll be back in a month."

"I don't want you to leave the country," she insisted. "We need to talk."

He sighed audibly. "I don't want to get thrown back into prison based on the whim of some government official." His voice rose. "Can't you understand that?"

She paused. "You know, a vacation does sound like a good idea. You have fun down there. Don't worry—I'm not going to have you arrested."

"Thanks, Julie. I need some time to think."

"Have a good time," she said.

It didn't take long using her airline database access credentials, to discover his destination: Puerto Vallarta. It took longer to find out that he'd made a one-month reservation at the Decameron resort north of Puerto Vallarta in Bucerias.

She called a CIA operative in Guadalajara named Carlos to let him know she'd be coming. Then she went shopping.

I haven't taken a vacation in years, she realized. *I'll need a swimsuit to spend time with Sean on the beach.*

She looked at her reflection in the dressing room mirror. *The half-inch bulge above my bikini bottom wasn't there the last time I wore one.* She turned sideways, rubbing her belly. *It's okay. I'm proud of my maternal badge of honor. That's where you were, sweet baby girl.*

She was waiting to board her flight at the Tampa airport when Roberto called her the next morning. He introduced himself as one of Carlos's contacts from Mexico's *Policía Federal Ministerial*.

"Sean checked into the Decameron resort last night," he said. "He's in a ground-floor room next to one of their huge swimming pools. The manager is moving the residents out of the room next to him, so it will be available when you arrive. He'll put a sign on the door saying the room is under repair. I'm heading over there now to change the locks."

I think it's time to practice my Spanish, she told herself. "*Muy bueno. Gracias.*"

"*De nada*," Roberto replied.

Carlos and Roberto met her at the Puerto Vallarta airport that afternoon. Both men were attractive, in their mid-thirties, with ebony-black hair and deeply tanned skin.

Carlos placed her luggage in the trunk of his car and drove them to a restaurant in downtown Puerto Vallarta. The owner escorted them to a table near the beach endowed with a majestic view of the thirty-mile-wide Banderas Bay.

Several sailboats danced gracefully on the aqua-green sea to the west of them. Bands of silver flashed in the wave crests beneath the crimson horizon. The blue-gray mountains east of the city were veiled watermelon pink by the approaching sunset.

Beate pointed to a hedge bordering the deck. "What are those pink-and-purple flowers?" she asked. "I saw them everywhere along the roads."

"They're called *bougainvilleas*," Roberto answered. "They grow wild here."

The trio ordered a second round of margaritas for dessert. The sky turned blood red as dusk approached, twisting bands of orange into the whitecaps of the breaking waves.

Beate looked at the horizon. "This is beautiful."

"Yes, it is," Roberto said. "And it's a different show every night. That's why I like to call my home: *el jardín del Edén*—the Garden of Eden."

They left the restaurant and strolled along the Malecón, a long promenade bordering the beach sprinkled with larger-than-life modern art sculptures. Roberto departed in a cab when they reached the end of the walkway, and Carlos drove her to Bucerias.

She remained in his car while he checked her in. He pulled a metal valise from his trunk when he returned. She gathered up her luggage and they walked to her room.

"The valise contains the surveillance equipment and tools you ordered," he said, "as well as a laptop computer, some cell phones, and a Beretta with a silencer."

"Thanks," she told him. "I appreciate your help."

"I need to head back to Guadalajara tonight. Roberto will be your contact from now on. You can call me if you get into a bind, though."

"I'm sure I'll be fine."

They shook hands, and Carlos departed from her room.

Sean needs to be out of his room before I can install my surveillance cameras between our walls, she decided, *so I may as well go to bed.*

She heard his door close early the next morning.

She installed three miniature cameras in the wall between their rooms and an audio microphone near his patio. She connected the feed wires to a secure wireless router linked to her computer.

She watched him on her computer when he returned to his room. He was dripping with sweat. *It looks like he's been working out.*

A contraction clutched her pelvis when he dropped his shirt and pants to the floor. She studied his rippling shoulder muscles, firm butt, and deftly honed stomach. *Oh là là!* she said to herself. *What have I become now… some kind of sleazy voyeur spook?*

She called Roberto when Sean stepped into the shower. "Can you reserve another room for me on the second floor, across from the pool—somewhere I can observe Sean's patio?"

"*Sí, senora*. I'll see what I can do." he said.

Sean left his room with a towel and book beneath his arm a few minutes later.

Roberto knocked on her door. He was wearing a bellhop uniform from the resort.

She ushered him in. "Nice uniform," she teased.

He flashed a smile. "I'll move your luggage for you so you won't look suspicious. Sean is sitting down at the beach. Here's your new room key. Give me five minutes."

"*Gracias, amigo.*"

She hadn't noticed the vibrant blue, red, pink, purple, and yellow pastel colors adorning the exterior walls and covered walkways when she'd arrived the previous evening. The grass, dotted with islands of palm trees, bordered curved sidewalks edged with orange flower hedges that flowed gracefully between the pools and buildings.

The first thing she did in her second-floor room was test the wireless connection. The feeds from the surveillance cameras to her computer were working fine.

She turned out the lights and crawled into bed.

Why shouldn't I enjoy myself she reasoned? *I'm on vacation. I haven't indulged myself with a nap in years, since Malia used to suckle my breasts while we slept.*

She hardened her mind, pushing away the past. *I have to. Otherwise, I won't be able to sleep.*

Geneva, Switzerland

Abdul spread a map on the coffee table in the living room of Rahim's apartment. "You always said you wanted to do more for the *jihad*," Abdul said. "Well now's your chance. The Mossad took out one of my drivers yesterday. I have a short-term assignment for you."

He handed Rahim a picture. "This is Amir."

Abdul pointed at Damascus, Syria, on the map. "He'll be waiting for you at noon on Saturday at the Al Khawali restaurant. I need you to accompany him across the border when he delivers a truckload of rockets and mortars to Beirut."

Rahim's eyes widened. "Thank you for giving me such an important role."

Abdul walked to the front door. "Just follow his instructions. *As-salamu alaykum.*"

"*Wa 'alaykum as-salam*," Rahim replied, returning the peace-be-upon-you salutation.

Rahim looked out at Lake Geneva after Abdul left. *Thank you, Allah, for trusting me. I'll do my best to be a good soldier.*

Bucerias, Mexico

The audio alarm on Beate's computer beeped, indicating Sean had entered his room. Roused from her nap, she looked at her computer display.

Sean walked through his room accompanied by a shapely young woman with short blonde hair. They each carried drinks.

Must be drinking Mai Tai's, the way the fruit hangs off the edge of the glasses, Beate observed. *He sure didn't waste any time finding another woman.*

"Would you like to go out salsa dancing tonight, Angelique?" Sean said. "That was fun at the disco last night."

"Sure. There are a couple of nice clubs down in Vallarta. I don't have a dive scheduled tomorrow, so we can stay out late if you'd like."

Sean opened his sliding door and the couple exited to the patio. Beate's only surveillance now was an audio microphone she'd planted in the patio wall.

She turned up her computer speakers and moved to her sliding door to watch them through a crack in her curtains.

They sat down on lounge chairs facing the pool.

Sean smiled. "You're a good dancer. You have the perfect body for salsa."

"Are you saying I have a big butt?"

Sean laughed. "Not at all. It looks perfect to me."

He reached for her hand.

Angelique grinned. "Perhaps you should take a swim to cool off."

He raised his eyebrows. "I apologize if I'm being too forward."

She giggled. "I'm glad you like my butt, and you're right. We do dance well together."

I recognize Angelique from a picture I saw near the lobby, Beate realized. *She's the dive instructor. She sounds Dutch, from her accent.*

Beate adjusted her curtains so she could see more clearly between two palm trees swaying in the breeze. The high-powered microphone she'd planted in Sean's patio wall was more than adequate to hear their conversation.

I don't like what I'm hearing, though, she told herself. *I have to do something.*

Angelique faced Sean. "Would you like to get certified?" she offered. "It would be fun to go diving together."

"Sure. I'd like that."

Angelique, lithe, healthy, and darkly tanned, beamed a radiant smile.

Beate pulled binoculars from her metal valise. She focused her lens on a blue-winged angel tattoo above Angelique's butt.

The couple lay down facing west, enticing the sun to bake their bodies.

"What brought you here to Vallarta, Angelique?"

"I came here from Holland after I graduated with a degree in marine biology. You told me last night you're here on vacation. How long are you staying?"

"At least a month, but who knows? I think it's time to have some fun in my life."

Angelique's fingers stroked his bicep. "I can help you with that."

A twelve-inch, blue-and-green macaw landed on a palm tree in front of Beate's balcony. It began warbling and screeching, sounding out two-note melodies as it poked its beak into coconut flowers foraging for insects.

Its mate landed on an adjacent branch. It mimicked the first macaw with two-note counterpoint responses. The beauty of the improvisatory duet temporarily mesmerized Beate.

She returned her attention to the pool. Sean's muscular physique had attracted the attention of several giggling women. Beate focused her binoculars on Angelique's lime-green bikini. *She doesn't have an ounce of fat. Argh!* she grimaced. *Another nightmare.*

Beate picked up her cell phone and dialed. "*Hola*, Roberto. I need your help… I need you to get rid of that dive instructor—Angelique. Sean is hanging out with her on his patio. I can't have that… No. It's not okay! She's going to ruin my plans. Get rid of her… now! *Por favor?*"

Angelique leaned over and planted a kiss on Sean's lips. She then stood up, took two steps, and dived headfirst into the pool. Sean followed her into the water.

Angelique instigated a game of tag. She was a strong swimmer, so she easily eluded him when he tried to catch her.

Spectators in lounge chairs around the pool smiled with amusement at their game.

Sean eventually cornered her—or perhaps she let him—and they kissed. She wiggled beneath his arm and swam back towards his patio. He followed in her wake.

"Let's get another drink," he said as they dried themselves.

"Sounds good to me."

They walked hand in hand to the bar next to the pool. The couple bypassed their chairs and entered Sean's room when they returned.

Beate moved to her computer screen.

The couple placed their drinks on a desk and started kissing. Beate dialed Roberto as she watched Sean caress Angelique's back.

Her voice was anxious. "Roberto—you need you to get rid of that girl—now! She's in his bedroom. …No. Not *mañana*. Now!"

She clicked off her phone.

Angelique's bikini top fell to the floor. Her tramp-stamp angel tattoo was now clearly visible on Beate's computer screen.

Beate grabbed her revolver, inserted a magazine, and screwed on the silencer. *I'm not sure what I'm going to do, but I need to do something.*

THE ACHERON DECEPTION   229

She opened her sliding door and focused the barrel. Shooting out his sliding glass door will stop them, but the gunshot will freak everyone out. There has to be another way. *Think, woman! Think!*

She lowered her gun and looked at the display. Sean was sitting on the bed with his face buried in Angelique's breasts. Beate aimed the gun two-handed at a chair on the patio.

The blue macaw flitted across her view landing on a palm branch, blocking her shot. *Crap! The bird intervened. Perhaps this is a sign.*

She pulled the gun back and closed the sliding door. *I'll run to his room and knock on his door. That'll stop them. There's no way I'm going to let Miss Perfect Body have him.*

She looked at her computer. They were lying on his bed now. Angelique began to moan as his hand explored the pleasure zone beneath her bikini bottom.

Beate ran to her door and darted down the hallway. A faint telephone rang out behind her as the door closed. She unlocked her door and jumped back to her computer.

Angelique was sitting up, topless; her shapely breasts clearly visible. She seemed hesitant. The phone chimed again.

"I have to take this," she said. "It's my boss. I can tell from the ring."

She pulled her bikini bottom up over her blondish-red pubic hair and grabbed her phone from her cloth purse. "*Hola, Manuel. ...Sí. ...Ahh. Sí. ¿en serio? ...Cuándo?*"

Angelique's deep-mahogany tan provided a perfect frame for her pointy white breasts. *I see why Sean's so interested,* Beate acknowledged. *She has the physique of a Venetian goddess.*

Angelique seemed dismayed. She glanced at Sean. "*Ahorita?*"

I'll run to his room if she doesn't leave, Beate decided. *I'm not going to let this perfect young thing steal him away after everything I did to free him from prison.*

A regretful pallor melted over Angelique's face. "*Sí. ...muy bien. ...ándale, ándale.*" She clicked off her phone.

"What's up?" Sean said.

"That was my boss. He'll be here in five minutes to pick me up."

"Why?"

"I have to catch a plane for a three-week dive job in Playa Del Carmen."

Angelique grabbed her bikini top from the floor, wrapped it around her thin waist, latched it, rotated it 180 degrees, and pulled it up across her breasts. She adjusted the skinny garment to hide her plum-sized areolas.

"Some tourists want a dive instructor on their yacht. A flight's leaving for Cancun in two hours. Manuel is taking me to my apartment to pack."

"Do you really have to go?" he pleaded. "I have plenty of money."

"That's sweet of you, but I always pull my own weight. You've heard the term 'going Dutch,' haven't you?"

She grabbed a beach dress from her purse and pulled it over her head. "This is my job, Sean. I'm sorry about tonight. I was looking forward to going dancing."

"Yeah… me too," he murmured.

She pulled on her sandals and stood on her tiptoes to kiss him.

"Come by when you get back," he said. "I should still be here."

"I will." She opened the door and fled down the hallway.

Sean sat down on his bed. He stared directly at Beate through the camera lens.

Crap! He must've spotted the pinhole camera next to the mirror.

He leaned forward and rubbed the sides of his head.

Beate sighed with relief when he grabbed both drinks and exited to the patio.

Her phone rang. "Was that quick enough, *amiga?*" Roberto said.

"Yes it was, Roberto. *Gracias, amigo!* I owe you a big favor."

"*De nada. No problema.* We're not totally safe though."

"Why's that?"

"I had to pay Manuel—her boss—to say he was near the hotel. He actually won't be there for about fifteen minutes. I doubt that she'll go back to Sean's room. She needs the money." He chuckled. "Working for tips as a dive instructor doesn't pay very well."

"Thanks, Roberto," she said. "I'll keep an eye out from here."

"Carlos made the arrangements. She'll be working on a yacht that sails from Cancun. That should keep her out of your hair for a while."

"That's great. I'll be sure to thank him."

She smiled as she clicked off her phone. *Now I need a plan—fast!*

26. Communion

Beate rose early the next morning. *I barely avoided a disastrous rivalry with Miss Perfect Body yesterday*, she reminded herself. *It's time to make my move before it happens again.*

She reviewed her plan as she pulled on a sports bra, running pants and a T-shirt. *Sean began his run along the beach yesterday at seven thirty a.m., so I'll begin my run at seven, and meet him when I return. I need the exercise, anyway.*

He'll be irritated that I stalked him, she considered. *So be it. We have to talk. Goldberg Cohen's data holds the clues to the financiers behind the 9/11 attacks. It's time.*

The sun had just peaked over the mountains when she began her run. Wispy clouds streaked with orange floated haphazardly above a bank of fog on the western horizon.

A tranquil sea lapped the shoreline. Crescent-shaped imprints twenty feet from the water marked the reach of the high-tide glissades and pirouettes during the moon's nighttime lunar ballet. It was quiet except for a few seagulls squawking and the relentless undulating churn of the waves.

She stopped after a mile and removed her shoes. *I want to feel the cool, wet sand squeezing between my toes*, she decided.

She slowed to a walk after three miles. The fog to the west had evaporated. She turned around and ran back towards the resort.

Sean passed her running the opposite direction a few minutes later seemingly oblivious to her presence. She no longer wore the dark-haired wig she'd used as a disguise in Niceville.

He turned around and caught up with her at the beach in front of the resort. "Julie? Is that you?"

She slowed to a walk with her hands on her hips. "Hi, Sean."

"What are you doing here?"

"It sounded like a good idea when you told me you needed a vacation."

"Are you taking me back to jail?"

She planted her feet in the water with her back to the sea. "It's important that we talk. I'll stay out of your way until you're ready. Fair enough?"

He glared. She bounded across the beach up the steps to the sidewalk when he didn't answer.

He caught up with her at the stairway to her building.

"What do you want?" he said. His gaze fell to her sweat-drenched Marine Corps T-shirt.

"I came down here to relax, too," she said. "I needed a break after Niceville, but I also want to be near you so we don't have to waste time when you're ready to talk. It's very important."

She turned and walked up the stairs. He didn't follow.

She wiggled into her new gold bikini after breakfast and headed to the beach.

A voice nudged her awake later that afternoon. "You'll get sunburned if you aren't careful. The sun can be deceiving when the cool breeze makes everything so comfortable."

She turned onto her side.

Sean was holding a drink in her direction.

She pushed some stray hairs from her face, accepted his offering, and took a sip. "This is good. What is it?"

"Mai tai's are an excellent remedy for a hot day," he said. "May I sit with you?"

She pointed to an empty chair. "Be my guest."

They sat for several minutes without speaking watching barefoot tourists in bathing suits walk along the shoreline. Two Mexican men were casting fishing nets sixty feet from shore while their sturdy wives and children combed the beach selling trinkets to the unsuspecting.

She glanced at Sean and looked away quickly, embarrassed by the tingle in her belly. *He looks delicious without his shirt.*

Her chest heaved as she blushed.

"My name isn't Julie Stensen, by the way," she began. "That's an alias. My real name is Beate Nicholson. I work for the CIA, in case you haven't already guessed."

He reached out to shake her hand. "Glad to meet you, Beate."

"Shall I get us another round?" she said. "I need to go to *el baño* anyway."

"Sure, why not? It's an all-inclusive resort. We may as well take advantage of it."

She stood up. "I certainly plan to."

She grinned mischievously as she walked away.

She surprised herself when she returned and kissed him… just a taste. *Delicious*, she decided.

She ran quickly across the almond-white sand so she wouldn't sear her feet and stopped at the top of the stairs to see if he was watching. *I know I look good from behind—at least that's what Robert always said.*

He was looking. *Good*, she told herself. She waved, and walked down the sidewalk to the women's bathroom.

They spent the rest of the afternoon taking turns fetching drinks. She purposely avoided talking business. Their conversation became more serious as the sun dropped to the horizon.

"I saw your T-shirt this morning," he said. "How long were you in the Marines?"

"Six years. That's where I met my husband."

Sean furrowed his eyebrows. "I didn't realize you were married."

"I'm a widow."

"I'm sorry to hear that." He paused. "You're so young."

She exhaled. "Robert and Malia, our four-year-old daughter, were killed by terrorists in the plane that crashed into the Pentagon on 9/11."

He swung his feet to the sand and faced her. "That must have been awful."

She stared out at the sun looming over the water. "Yes… it was."

"My ex-wife betrayed me with another man that day, but you—losing your husband and daughter… must have been unbearable."

An errant tear trickled down her cheek. She wiped it away.

He stood up. "It's my turn for *el baño*," he announced. "I'll bring us another round."

He brought a different drink when he returned.

She drank some. "What's this? It's good."

He laughed. "It's supposed to be good. It's called sex on the beach."

"Is that so?" she retorted.

"Well, that's what Ramon, the bartender told me."

"I guess he'd know. He has quite an entourage of Canadian girls hanging around him at the bar."

A wave crashed the shore. The tides were rising as the beach emptied.

She felt his eyes scan her body. *My sixth sense tells me he's checking me out.*

"Beate… is that German?" he inquired.

"It is."

"I thought I detected a bit of an accent. Where'd you grow up?"

She told him her history, skipping the years after 9/11.

"I can't talk about Robert and Malia right now. Perhaps another time, okay?"

"I understand."

* * *

She's gorgeous, he observed. I knew she had a hot body beneath that business suit she wore at FPC Niceville.

"I can't believe we both lived in Boulder at the same time," he said. "I'd just begun my career at NCAR when you were a junior at the University of Colorado. I wonder if we ever passed each other on the hiking trails."

The clouds turned cerise-pink and crimson when the sun kissed the horizon.

She removed her sunglasses. "We may have. I was in ROTC and on the CU ski team while I was pursuing my engineering degree, so I didn't have much free time."

She's exquisite, he observed, *those firm, toned muscles of hers… That gold bikini is a delightful torture, concealing pleasures I can only imagine. Am I ready for someone like her… and what about Angela?*

"You really impressed me with the way you handled things at Niceville," he said. "Thanks for springing me from prison… and you like jazz…" He trailed off. "I don't think I've ever met anyone like you."

She laughed. "I bet you say that to all your girls."

Now what? Angela promoted me to Vice President and raised my ownership stake to fifteen percent. She wasn't pleased when I told her I needed time to figure out my life, after she asked me to move in with her.

Angelique would have been a nice diversion—perhaps more—but Beate is serious business.

He finished his drink and stood up. "I've got to go."

She looked up with surprise. "Okay, Sean. I enjoyed our afternoon together."

"I did too." He trotted across the sand without looking back.

* * *

Beate dined at the resort's exquisite Italian restaurant that evening. The maître d' sat her at a table with several other singles.

The loneliness of being with strangers makes me feel depressed, she realized. She excused herself and returned to her room after a glass of wine and a salad.

Sean was sitting up in bed, reading, when she checked the video feed. A zoom-in of her camera lens revealed a large stack of books on his desk. *He has eclectic tastes: popular fiction, stock trading strategies, philosophy—even physics.*

I feel guilty about being a voyeur, she decided as she continued to watch, *but I want to be close to him, even if it has to be like this.*

He turned off the lamp next to his bed a few minutes later. She turned up her computer speakers. *I'm curious to hear how he sounds while he sleeps.*

His breathing became heavy. Her lips curved to a smile as she fell asleep listening to him.

Her phone rang at 2:00 a.m. "Hello."

"Hi, Beate... this is Sean. I'm sorry I woke you."

"That's okay."

"May I come over? I woke up and couldn't get back to sleep. I'm ready to talk, if you're up for it. I want to know why you followed me here."

"Sure," she said. "Give me ten minutes."

She stowed her computer and brushed her teeth.

He grinned and said, "Room service," when she answered the door.

"This is a nice surprise."

He stared at her T-shirt when he entered. She wore nothing underneath.

She came to him and hugged him, raising her lips for a kiss. *Sweet... and tender... very nice,* she assessed, as she melted into him.

His lips moved to her neck. He kissed her gently, below her ear. His eyes went wide when she pulled off her shirt.

She reached for the front of his shorts, pulled them off, and pushed him backwards onto the bed. Holding him firm, she slithered down onto him. She leaned back and began to gyrate.

Her moans filled the room as their ecstasy strengthened. She swooned forward onto his chest out of breath after communion.

Her cries came softly then.

He remained quiet, holding her, gently rubbing her back.

Thank you, Sean... for not asking why, she told herself.

She rolled onto her side and turned off the lamp.

He woke her two hours later.

"I want to remember everything," he said as they began their lovemaking again. "I want to savor every inch of you."

His cell phone rang at noon. He jumped out of bed and pulled it out of the pocket of his shorts.

"Hello… Hi, Andrew. Can you hold on for a second?"

Beate pulled her T-shirt over her head.

"I need to take this," he said. He put the phone back to his ear. "What's up? …Yes, I'm with a woman."

Beate motioned frantically with both hands.

"Hold on, Andrew." Sean muted his phone.

"Please don't tell anyone about us," she said. "It may cause complications."

"We can trust him," Sean said.

"We need to wait," she smiled, "assuming you still want to see me."

"Of course I do." Sean bent to her lips for a kiss.

"I'm back, Andrew. I'll tell you about it later. So, what's up?" He listened for a moment. "…That's wonderful news. Excellent! Thanks for calling." He hung up.

Elation crept across his face. "The Justice Department just arrested Judge Richter and Isaac Bachmann, charging them with conspiracy and bribery. The attorney general wants me to come to DC to give a deposition, and the president signed my pardon."

"Congratulations!" she said. "We need to go to Washington anyhow to complete your NOC paperwork."

"What's NOC?"

"Non-Official Cover. That's what we call operatives who aren't officially with the Agency—assuming you want to work with me."

Sean frowned. "I have no interest in being a spy."

"It's for your security clearance," she explained. "NOC agents keep the jobs they have. I need your help digging through the data in your Banque Lux archives to find the terrorists you stumbled upon before 9/11."

"Terrorists?"

"Remember that report you submitted to the FBI after 9/11… about the volume-spike you were chasing in your system? Wouldn't a huge order cause a volume spike?"

Sean's eyes widened. "Is that why you've been following me?"

"One of the reasons." Her fingertip brushed his cheek.

"I reported the volume spike because I thought someone might have used the attack to make money in the stock market."

"Exactly," she affirmed. "The people who placed the orders are the financiers behind the terrorists. I need to find them before they strike again."

She stood up. "I need to take a shower. I'll brief you about the mission after lunch, assuming you're ready."

Sean pulled on his shorts and shirt and walked to the door. "I'll see you at the restaurant in thirty minutes."

Beate was drying her hair when her phone rang. "Hello."

Sean's voice was hesitant. "Can you come... to my room?"

"I thought we were meeting at the restaurant."

"I need you... to come here," he said haltingly.

"Okay. I'll be there in ten minutes."

Something in Sean's voice triggered her radar. The gnawing persisted as she dressed.

She turned on her computer and pulled up the video feed from his room.

Crap! Roger Hartfield was pointing a 9 mm P229 Sig Sauer with a silencer at Sean, who he'd shackled to a chair with his arms tied behind his back.

"You don't understand," she heard Hartfield say. "I can't allow you to testify."

"Leave her out of this," Sean implored. "I'm the one you're after."

"You sure do get around, McGowan. I though Angela was your girlfriend."

Beate attached a silencer to her Beretta and stuck it into the back of her shorts beneath her T-shirt. She picked up her beach bag and headed to Sean's room.

She tucked her T-shirt into her pants so her gun would be accessible, and knocked on Sean's door. Hartfield answered.

"Agent Hartfield," she feigned surprise. "What are you doing here?"

He backed away, motioning her inside with his gun.

She entered and shut the door.

Sean was sitting in a chair near the sliding glass door. "I'm sorry, Beate."

"Why are you doing this?" she said to Hartfield.

Hartfield stopped near Sean. "Don't come any closer or I'll shoot."

She moved to her left while still facing Hartfield, at an angle where Sean could see the gun protruding from the back of her shorts.

"Who are you working for?" she asked Hartfield.

"Put your bag down!" he commanded.

She took a step closer. "I'm sure we can work something out if you tell me who sent you."

Hartfield braced his revolver in a two-handed stance. "Put your hands up."

She dropped the beach bag at her feet. "Did you kill the Cohen's?"

"That wasn't me," he snapped. "Lie down on the bed. You and lover-boy had a spat. Unfortunately, it's going to end in a murder-suicide."

"There's a way out of this, Agent Hartfield," she went on. "We can give you a new identity."

"We both know that's bullshit," he scoffed. "They'd still find me. Besides, I don't know anything. I get my orders from the manager at the casino where you burned me. What good is that?"

Sean lunged, and fell over sideways. His wooden chair crashed when it hit the ceramic-tile floor.

Hartfield's gaze went to Sean.

Beate kicked her beach bag at Hartfield's gun. It hit his hand.

Hartfield's bullet passed over her ear as she crouched down.

She clustered two shots into his heart and one in his brain—standard three-tap protocol.

A fountain of blood spurted from his chest, slowing to a throb as his legs splayed out from under him. His eyes went dull as he slumped against the wall.

She lifted Sean so he was upright in his chair. "Are you all right?" she asked as she untied his ropes.

He rubbed his elbow where he'd hit the floor. His face paled as he stared at the blood pooling beneath Hartfield.

"What do we do now?" he asked.

Beate wiped the blood splatters from her face and arms with a wet towel in his bathroom. She pulled Hartfield's cell phone, keys, and wallet from his pockets and shoved them into her beach bag, along with his Sig Sauer.

"He may not be alone," she said.

She peered warily through the curtains of Sean's sliding door as she dialed her cell phone. "Hello, Carlos. Sorry to bother you. I need a cleanup crew at the resort. …That's right—Sean's room."

She listened for a second. "No, it's not Sean. It's Agent Hartfield, from the FBI. He tried to take us out."

"…Yeah, I know. Complicated. It's quite a mess in here. Can you arrange everything? We'll need some new passports. We need to get out of here. Be careful. He may have accomplices. I'm going to look around to see if he has a partner. How quickly can you get here? …Call me when you arrive. Thanks."

Sean stared at her. "Should we call the police?"

"No. We'll take care of it. Pack up your things. You'll be safer with me."

He gaped at her without moving.

"Let's go," she said, "before someone else shows up."

He threw everything he'd brought with him into his suitcase. They moved cautiously around the building and up the steps to her room.

She reloaded the magazine in her black Beretta, and handed Hartfield's gun to Sean.

"Do you know how to use one of these?" she asked.

"I used to shoot cans in the desert," he offered. "Does that count?"

"Good enough. I need to make sure Hartfield is alone. I'll be back in a while. If anyone breaks in—shoot them."

Sean looked at the weapon in his hand. "I want to go with you."

"It's safer if you stay here," she insisted. "I'll be back in a couple of hours."

She walked cautiously around the nearby buildings searching for an accomplice. *No one looks suspicious.*

She located Hartfield's rental car on a side street two blocks from the resort. A receipt in his luggage revealed the hotel he'd stayed at in downtown Puerto Vallarta. She found an airline ticket for a return flight to New York through Houston that afternoon.

He'll miss that, she observed.

She dumped his clothes and suitcase into trashcans as she drove his rental car to Puerto Vallarta. She parked the car near the hotel where he'd stayed the previous night, wiped down the steering wheel and trunk to remove her fingerprints, and returned to Bucerias in a taxi.

A maintenance truck abutted the door of Sean's hotel room when she arrived at the Decameron. Roberto and his colleagues had already packed Hartfield into a body bag and cleaned up the blood.

He handed her a large, manila envelope. "Looks like you had some trouble," he remarked. "Carlos told me to give you these new passports, Mrs. Kelly. He booked a room for you and your husband at a hotel in Mismaloya, a few miles south of Puerto Vallarta."

"Thanks, Roberto," she replied. "I'm sorry about the mess. I didn't expect this. Can you take care of the surveillance equipment next door? I parked his rental car near his hotel. There's a warrant for Hartfield's arrest in the states. The authorities will assume he's on the lam when he disappears."

"*No problema*," he assured her. "We'll make sure no one finds his body."

27. Mutually Assured Destruction

Beate handed Sean his new passport when she returned to her room. He looked at the name next to his picture. "Michael Kelly?"

"Yeah, and I'd like to introduce you to your new wife." She kissed him and smiled. "Megan Kelly."

He grinned. "You sure didn't waste any time."

She laughed. "I figured I needed to move fast before someone else did."

They checked out of their rooms and departed in a cab to downtown Puerto Vallarta. Beate kept her eyes peeled on the mirrors to make sure no one was following them. They walked two blocks and took a different cab south, to Mismaloya.

"Let's find a secluded beach and have a picnic," she suggested, after they'd checked into their room.

"That sounds good to me," he said. "We haven't eaten yet today."

Beate placed both revolvers into her beach bag. They purchased food and wine at a nearby convenience store and headed down to the beach.

The Banderas Bay shoreline was rockier here, with lush jungle and high cliffs that sloped steeply to the sea. They walked two miles, stepping on boulders and sloshing through foamy surf when the sand disappeared.

They stopped at an isolated patch of sand below a hundred-foot precipice. "This okay with you?" she asked. "It's a defensible position. No one can shoot at us from above and we'll be able to spot intruders coming towards us along the beach."

"Sure."

They placed their towels beneath a dilapidated straw palapa.

Several boulders jutting out of the water produced an insistent hymn as the breakers crashed over the rocks.

Sean opened the wine and filled two glasses. "Thanks for saving my life," he said.

Beate placed cheese, fruit, and crackers on a paper plate. "I know that was hard to witness," she said. "That may not have just been Hartfield trying to prevent you from testifying. Someone may have sent him."

Sean walked to the surf and stared out at the sea.

Beate remained seated. *He probably needs some space to think*, she considered.

He returned and sat down next to her a few minutes later.

"How are you feeling?" she said.

"Upset. That was very disturbing. I'm glad you're a good shot."

"Distracting him was smart thinking. Why'd you do that?"

"I figured we needed to do something, or we'd be dead. How do *you* feel?"

"It was unfortunate, but necessary," she said. Then she added, "He's not my first kill."

Sean took a bite of apple. He studied her carefully while he chewed.

"We'll be travelling as a married couple from now on," she said. "Speaking of which—what's up with you and Angela?"

He stared out at the waves. "I'm not sure. We argued when I told her I needed time to figure out what I want to do with my life. I understand her angst. She's been through a lot—but so have I. I guess I didn't like her pushing me so hard to return to New York right after I got out of prison. I need to feel confident we're compatible before I move in with her."

"Move in with her?" Beate repeated. "What about us?"

"She wants me to move into the mansion her parents had in Armonk."

Beate remained quiet for several minutes as she stared out at the sea. "You saved Angela by not testifying, didn't you?" she probed.

"There was no reason for both of us to go to prison. We discussed our interviews with each other after Hartfield questioned us that day. I didn't want to implicate her on the witness stand."

"Do you love her?"

His gaze brushed the sky. "Yes… I do love her… but I'm not sure I'm *in love* with her—if that makes sense. She's the closest friend I've ever had. Our relationship has always been confusing."

Beate's jaw hardened. "I don't think it's safe for you to return to New York right now. Angela's life could be in danger, too."

His gaze swerved to her face. "What can I do to protect her?"

"We need to find out who's behind this. The sooner we get started, the sooner your lives will get back to normal. Pulling the Banque Lux transaction data for the weeks before and after 9/11 is crucial."

"I need to ensure Angela is safe before I'll help you," he insisted.

What about me she wondered? *I guess I shouldn't have moved so fast. Now I may end up with a broken heart.*

She stared into his eyes. "I need you, too."

"Why can't the FBI deal with this? I submitted my report on their website."

"They aren't going to do anything." She paused. "I think there's a lot going on behind the scenes we aren't seeing. Your arrest, the murder of Angela's parents, the Internet attack against your company, Hartfield coming after you—these aren't coincidences."

He reached for her hand.

What's he doing? She pulled her hand away. "I think you need to figure things out with Angela before we go any further."

He nodded. "I understand."

She pulled her knees up to her chest and crossed her arms. "I'm sorry. I want to be close to you… but I don't want to end up with an arrow in my heart."

She brushed a tear from her cheek. "There's a song by Sade—*'Fear'*—running through my head now. I couldn't bear to lose you if we get more involved."

His fingertips glanced across her thigh. "Let's just take things one day at a time, okay?"

She nodded. After a moment, she leaned to him and kissed him.

"So what's next?" he said. He folded her under him in his arms.

"We need to go to DC so you can give your depositions to the Justice Department. You'll need to go through a psyche eval at the Agency in Langley to get your clearance. Then we'll go to Luxembourg to find the terrorists making trades at Banque Lux. That's why I pressed the Justice Department for your release. I want the people pulling the strings."

A huge, pterodactyl-shaped raptor with an eight-foot wingspan appeared above them. It made several orbits back and forth along the shoreline, and dived headfirst into the water, emerging three seconds later with a fish flailing in its beak. It gobbled the meal in one gulp as it flapped its long wings launching itself to the sky.

"Switzerland, Lichtenstein, Luxembourg, Singapore, and other tax-haven countries have strict privacy laws," Sean said. "I could be sent to prison again for divulging client information."

"We'll make sure that doesn't happen," she assured him. "Besides, don't you want to find the people who attacked your company? They're probably the same people that killed Angela's parents?"

Three small birds with long, skinny legs landed in the surf. They started pecking their long beaks into the foam, foraging for bugs.

Sean sat up. He grabbed a handful of sand and let it trickle through his fingers.

Beate sat upright and took a bite of her apple. "It must be difficult… all of us women trying to tell you what to do."

He chuckled. "I'm used to it. I grew up living in a tiny trailer with two women."

An armada of sailboats appeared on the horizon, compelled southward by a zephyrean breeze.

"I wonder what my life would be like if I'd stayed in Boulder doing weather modeling?" he mused.

Beate contemplated the colorful sails. "It's impossible to know where our decisions will lead. I never imagined I'd be a spook one day, but one thing led to another, and here I am."

A wave crashed the rocks, spraying them with a cool mist.

"I want to help you, but I need to be sure Angela is safe," he repeated.

"Hernandez will keep an eye on her if I ask him to. Do you see the way he looks at her?"

Sean chuckled. "Yeah. She doesn't go for the married type though."

Beate sipped her wine. "We need to keep our relationship secret for now."

"Even from Angela?"

"We won't have access to the data at Banque Lux if she fires you," she pointed out.

"She won't do that."

"Trust me. It's impossible to predict how a woman will react when someone spurns her love. You should keep up appearances with her for now."

"You understand what that means don't you?"

"I do," she said reluctantly. "I don't like it, but it's necessary, for now. I've seen worse… believe me. Besides, I need to keep my cover intact. It's safer for both of us if it appears you're with her. Some of my enemies will target you to get back at me, if they know we're together."

He shook his head side to side. "I'm not going to lie to Angela."

"Are you sure?"

"Yes," he emphasized. "I wouldn't do that to her. I'll ask her to come down to DC so I can tell her in person when we get back. I won't tell her

THE ACHERON DECEPTION 245

specifically what we'll be doing in Luxembourg though, so she has deniability."

He caressed Beate's shoulder with his fingertips. "You've been living this so long... hiding the truth. It must be stressful."

She nodded. "It is. You never really get used to it... always having to be *on*. I live in a sordid world, but it's what I must do, for now. Are you sure you really want to get involved with someone like me?"

He laughed. "Of course."

His hand glided over the mounds of her chest. "How about here, on the beach?"

She giggled and looked around. "I don't think it's safe."

She refilled their glasses. "There's something else I need to talk with you about—something that hasn't been declassified."

"What's that?"

"You grew up in Santa Fe, near Los Alamos, right?"

"I was born in Los Alamos. We moved to Santa Fe when I was two."

"I came across some information about your father while I was digging into your background. He was a mathematician at Los Alamos."

"My mom told me he worked in a mathematical field called game theory," he said.

"I found some curious notes, scribbled inside his top-secret CIA dossier."

"He was in the CIA?"

"No, but he worked on a project with the Agency. The words on the inside of his jacket said 'Operation Giant Lance.' That was a mission during the Vietnam Conflict. One of President Nixon's campaign promises in 1968 was to get America out of Vietnam. Most people thought that meant he'd bring our troops home, but he was also considering the tactical use of nuclear weapons."

"What does that have to do with my father?"

"Your father used game-theory models to develop nuclear-attack scenarios. Some of Nixon's advisors were very interested in the tactical use of nuclear weapons at the time. Perhaps he was working with them."

Sean nodded. "Game theory was a hot topic at Princeton where my father received his doctorate, before he took the job at Los Alamos. My mom told me he was working on a project called Pandora's Fire when he disappeared in Vietnam."

"I saw those words scribbled on the inside of his folder," she said. "What do you think they mean?"

"I'm not sure. I did some research on Pandora once. She was the first woman to inhabit the earth in Greek mythology. Her curiosity compelled her to open the forbidden jar of knowledge, which released evil into the world. Maybe Pandora's Fire is a metaphor. Perhaps the scientists my dad was working with thought nuclear weapons were one of the evils in Pandora's jar."

Beate's lips curved derisively. "She sounds like Eve... handing Adam the apple in the Garden of Eden." She chuckled. "Why do women always get blamed for bringing evil into the world?"

He smiled, nodding agreement. "That doesn't seem right does it, especially since men are the ones who perpetuate war?"

"Your father helped develop a game-theory military doctrine called Mutually Assured Destruction," Beate went on. "The game assumes that a full-scale use of nuclear weapons by two opposing parties will result in the annihilation of both—guaranteeing a standoff. The military-industrial complex—here, as well as in Russia—loves the doctrine. It guarantees massive defense spending every year. Even today this doctrine governs our defense posture with the Russians."

Sean nodded. "So what was Operation Giant Lance?"

"Nixon and some of his advisors orchestrated a game called the Madman Theory, in October of 1969. They sent eighteen B-52 bombers fully loaded with nukes to the Arctic Circle north of Moscow. The bombers hovered there, refueled by tankers from Alaska, probing and taunting the Soviets for two days. Our threatening posture implied that we'd blow up Moscow if they didn't force Hanoi, their ally, to surrender. The nuclear weapons in the bombers were a hundred times more powerful than the bomb we dropped on Nagasaki."

"Wow... that's crazy," Sean marveled. "We could've started a terrible nuclear war."

"That was the idea," she affirmed. "US diplomats told their Soviet counterparts that Nixon was out of control... that he had his finger on the button... that he was *mad*. We came perilously close to World War III with that gambit. Things were spinning out of control. That's where I think your father came into the picture."

"What did he do?"

"Another scribble in your father's folder said, 'Memo passed to Soviets at La Fonda Hotel, October 27, 1969.' Our B-52s were hovering over the Arctic Circle that day. The La Fonda hotel in Santa Fe is the same hotel

Oppenheimer and his colleagues frequented when they were developing the atomic bomb at Los Alamos, during the Manhattan Project."

"So, what was in the memo… assuming my father passed it to them?"

"I don't know. His file didn't say, but for some reason the Soviets decided to wait for the US to make the first strike. They didn't cave in to the pressure exerted by the bombers probing their airspace. Nixon sent our B-52s home two days later. Your father may have helped prevent World War III and saved tens of millions of lives, if the memo he passed to the Soviets told them that Nixon was bluffing, but it was treason if he did it on his own. I don't think he did, though."

"Why?"

"Some of Nixon's advisors disagreed with the dangerous madman game. One of them may have orchestrated the leak to the Soviets."

Sean looked wistfully at the sea. "My mother was pregnant with me in October of 1969. I'm sure Los Alamos would've been a prime target. Perhaps he wanted to protect us."

"Your father disappeared less than three years later, about the time of the Watergate scandal. Maybe someone wanted to shut him up. The Giant Lance fiasco would've given plenty of ammunition to the anti-nuke and anti-Nixon crusaders if he'd disclosed it to the public."

"I see."

"A third note in your father's file said 'Lubyanka, 1973.' That's a prison in Moscow."

"How is that relevant?"

"I don't know." She shook her head side to side. "Perhaps he was taken there by the Russians."

Sean stroked his chin. "Maybe that's why my mother used to think he was still alive. Some strange men used to watch us with binoculars when I was growing up. One of them came to my trial last year. Do you think he knows something?"

"That's interesting," she pondered. "Point him out to me if you see him again, and I'll find out who he is."

"It makes me sick to think of my father sitting in a Russian prison all these years," Sean lamented.

"That would be tragic… and unlikely," she said empathetically. "He probably didn't survive very long. The few prisoners lucky enough to make it out of Lubyanka describe the basement dungeons as freezing, damp, and infested with rats. Many of them had brain damage from the destructive chemicals the KGB used to extract information."

She took his hand. "Your mother must be very strong, to wait for him all these years."

"She is. She used to take in sewing jobs to support us when I was a kid. How can I find out more about Lubyanka?"

"Perhaps one of my CIA colleagues in Europe can help. Helmut Drach—my former case officer—has contacts in the GRU and FSB—Russia's spy agencies. I'll introduce you to Helmut when we go to Luxembourg."

She sat back on her elbows. "What are you going to tell Angela… about us, I mean?"

"I'm not sure things would work out with her and me anyhow," he speculated. "We come from very different backgrounds. I'll always be a trailer-trash ex-con who went to a state college in the eyes of her snobbish friends. I've been around them enough to know that."

"Has she ever said she has an issue with your background?"

Sean stared at the waves. "Actually… that's a good point. She's never been pretentious. She's told me several times that she admires how I'm a self-made man, like her grandfather."

"I saw her in action at Niceville," Beate recalled. "Her charisma and beauty are quite alluring. I can see why you like her. Perhaps she loves you more than you think."

"She's very special," Sean agreed. "I'll do anything to protect her. I hope you understand that."

Beate stared at the sailboats on the horizon. She sat up abruptly. "Do you think Emma came across something that got her killed?"

Sean's shoulders bristled. "The police said it was a robbery… and rape."

"They never found her killer, did they?"

He pressed his lips together. "No. She was a good woman. She didn't deserve to die like that."

"No one does…"

Two young Mexican boys who looked like brothers were walking towards them along the beach. They were playing tag with the waves, shrieking when the surf thwarted their evasive maneuvers.

Sean and Beate smiled as the boys approached. They sat down near the water's edge and began to build a sand castle.

"I'd like to have kids someday," Sean said.

"Aren't you worried they'd end up collateral damage in some war?" Beate said. "I think it's too dangerous to bring children into this world. I won't put myself through that again."

Sean watched the sailboats for several minutes until they disappeared. "Do you think the evils humanity perpetrates against each other are a choice, or baked into our genes?" he wondered aloud. "Take murder, for example. It's been around since Cain first took a club to Abel's head. Was that a conscious choice... or some uncontrollable emotion?"

She shook her head. "I don't know. Perhaps it's both. Maybe he thought he needed to do that to ensure his own survival."

She sidled up beneath him. "What about destiny? What place does that have in our lives... like the events that brought us together?"

They kissed for several long seconds.

She laughed. "The boys are watching."

The couple turned and waved.

The brothers smiled and went back to work—fortifying the bulwarks and ramparts surrounding their castle, so it wouldn't melt into the sea.

28. Revelations

Washington, DC

Sean checked into a hotel near Beate's Logan Circle condominium in DC using his Michael Kelly alias. Beate was with him in his hotel room when he called Angela.

"Hi, Angie. I'm in DC. ...Yeah. My vacation didn't last very long. I have to give a deposition at the Justice Department on Thursday."

His eyebrows rose. He looked at Beate. "I'm sorry we had a fight, too. Can you come down next weekend? I need to see you... and I need a favor. Do you remember those notebooks Emma had in her office, the ones I took back with me from Luxembourg after her funeral? ...That's right, with her model designs. I kept them on a bookshelf in my home office. Can you pull them out of storage and bring them when you come? ...Good. Thanks. I'll see you Friday evening."

Sean accompanied Beate to CIA Headquarters on Monday morning. He joined Beate and her team after he finished a three-hour grilling by a CIA shrink.

She was meeting with an official from the Financial Crimes Enforcement Network (FinCEN), a Treasury Department bureau responsible for tracking terrorist financial activities. The official agreed to provide Beate with a copy of a database containing twenty years' worth of stock- and option-exchange transactions.

"We'll need that data to correlate trades made by people at Banque Lux with other activities in the markets," she told Sean afterwards.

Andrew accompanied Sean to his deposition at the Justice Department on Thursday. They went to dinner at Marcel's afterwards, a restaurant specializing in Belgian cuisine.

"So how are things going with Angela?" Andrew asked Sean as the maître d' seated them.

"Good."

"And what about Julie Stensen?" he pressed. "She's cute. She seemed interested in you at the prison."

Sean looked at the wine list. "It's complicated," he replied. "Julie's real name is Beate Nicholson, by the way. You'll need to keep that to yourself. I haven't had a chance to talk with Angie about Beate yet. She's flying in tomorrow night."

Andrew shook his head. "You're a lucky man. They're both beautiful. Which one are you going to choose?" He chuckled. "Or are you going to try to juggle both of them?"

"I'm only dating Beate now," Sean said. "It sure didn't take long for my life to get complicated after I got out of prison. There's something else you'll need to keep secret."

"What's that?"

"Hartfield tried to take us out in Mexico. He's dead. Beate saved my life."

"No shit?"

"Yeah... Beate and I are travelling to Luxembourg next week. I'm helping her with a project involving Banque Lux, so I may not see you for a while."

They waddled back to their hotel seven courses later.

"I'll have a lot of calories to shed after tonight," Sean said. "It was worth it though."

"Me, too," Andrew agreed. "I've never had inch-wide fettuccini. The sauce was exquisite."

Sean slid into the passenger seat of Beate's car when she picked him the next morning. She swung around DuPont Circle, gunned the engine, and steered into New Hampshire Avenue.

"I think we have a lead," she said.

Sean held the armrest as she raced through traffic. "What did you find?"

"The data analytics program my team built with the FinCEN data uncovered a pattern of larger-than-normal option trades before and after OPEC announcements... and terrorist attacks. The orders originated from hundreds of numbered accounts in countries with bank secrecy laws."

"I'll bet that's why we were seeing volume spikes in our system at Banque Lux," he speculated.

Beate turned west onto M Street. "Is Angela flying in tonight?"

"She's arriving at seven. We have a lot of catching up to do, so I may not see you much this weekend."

Beate pursed her lips. "I'll make sure you're back in time for your date."

Sean was packing his suitcase Monday morning when Beate knocked on his hotel room door.

"I thought we were meeting downstairs," he said as she entered.

She looked at his disheveled bed. "How did things go with Angela?"

"Good. We accomplished a lot."

He pulled out several notebooks from his backpack. "She brought me Emma's notebooks."

Beate nodded.

"We decided to purchase our Broad Street headquarters building," he continued. "It came on the market at a good price, and Dr. Boyd, from the DIA, wants to collaborate with us on some new cyber-security products he's testing. I guess the government trusts us now, after what happened at Niceville."

Beate stared at him with folded arms.

"What's wrong?" he said.

"Did you sleep with her?" she demanded, looking at the bed.

He pulled her into his chest and put his arms around her. "No. She had her own room. I told her I'm with you now."

He pushed her backwards, gently, onto his bed. "I've been thirsting for you all weekend," he said as he undressed her.

* * *

They were halfway across the Atlantic in the CIA Gulfstream when he tapped Beate's shoulder. He showed her a page from one of Emma's notebooks. "Look at this."

Michel Bowen—OPEC connection? Whale trader follow-up next week.

"We should look at Bowen's account fist," she said. "We'll know he's connected if he made large trades before and after the terrorist attacks. Emma was pretty smart, wasn't she?"

"Yes... she was." He reached for Beate's hand. "Just like you."

Luxembourg City

Sean introduced Beate to Jonas when they arrived at Banque Lux. Sean looked around Jonas's office as they sat down.

"Nice office," Sean said. "How's your promotion to president of our Banque Lux subsidiary working out?"

Jonas smiled. "Thank you for trusting me to run things here."

"You're welcome," Sean replied. "You certainly cushioned my stay in prison with the trading profits you and Angela generated."

"You've been through quite an ordeal in America," Jonas said. "I'm glad we could help. So what can I do for you today?"

"We need to build a database containing all our Banque Lux's client transactions going back to 1998," Sean informed him. "Beate will be helping me analyze the data. We'll need a secure office for a couple of months."

Jonas nodded. "That's a lot of data. Transactions from previous years are stored on tapes in our vaults."

"We'll need a tape reader too, then," Sean added.

"No problem. I'll clear out an office for you here in the executive suite. Anything else?"

Sean smiled. "Would it be possible to get one of Veronica's home-cooked meals while we're here?"

Jonas chuckled. "How about this weekend?"

"May I assist her?" Beate said. "I love to cook."

"I'm sure Veronica will be pleased to have your company."

Beate and Sean developed several databases and analytic programs to correlate the FinCEN exchange transaction data with extracts from Banque Lux's client records over the next several months. Their initial focus was Michel Bowen's trades.

They discussed their findings with Helmut Drach when he visited them at Banque Lux in late September.

"Michel Bowen's been busy," Sean said. "He made huge option trades before and after several OPEC meetings and terrorist attacks—all of them profitable. That would be impossible without inside information."

"His trades only account for a portion of the volume spikes we discovered at exchanges around the world on those days," Beate added. "He must be working with others."

"I've created an alert in our system that will trigger when Bowen logs on," Sean said. "We can follow him when he shows up. Have you found out anything about my father?"

"My Russian contacts are still looking into it," Helmut said. "I'll let you know if they find anything. Records for Lubyanka are sparse. Most of the people imprisoned there disappeared without a trace."

Armonk, New York

Angela moved into her parents' mansion near Armonk after she'd augmented security and installed electric fences around the property. She converted her parents' former bedroom into a study filled with artwork and sculptures.

A brisk autumn breeze was blowing yellow and red leaves across the lawn in front of the mansion when Harold opened the rear door of the limousine. Angela stepped out onto the sidewalk.

Emily greeted her with a smile as she entered through the side door. "How did it go?" she asked.

"Great. Everything's on track."

Angela turned sideways to look at herself naked in front of her bathroom mirror a moment later. *The tests showed everything is fine*, she mused, filled with elation, *except for needing a bit more iron... and the ultrasound was amazing.*

She rubbed her belly. *It's time to meet your daddy.*

New York City

Vladimir greeted Mikhail with a handshake in the foyer of his top-floor penthouse west of Central Park. Mikhail followed his brother across a generous sprinkling of hand-woven Isfahan Persian rugs to the living room. An eclectic collection of original Impressionist paintings adorned the walls.

A map of Europe stared up at them from the coffee table as they sat down. Vladimir pulled an oversized bottle of Stoli from a silver ice bucket, filled two goblets, and handed one to Mikhail.

"To mother!" Vladimir said, raising his glass to his lips.

"*Da.* To mother!" Mikhail replied.

They looked into each other's eyes as they drank.

Vladimir stood up and moved to the large picture window that looked east over Central Park. Mikhail joined him.

Hundreds of lights coming to life in nearby skyscrapers blinked like stars in a dark sky. The beautiful fields, walkways, and ponds in the park below were melting into a gray void as night descended.

"I have something to show you," Vladimir said.

Mikhail followed his brother across the living room. They stopped in front of a medium-sized painting of a boat docked next to a river.

"It's my latest investment," Vladimir said, "a rare Renoir. I purchased it from a distressed Japanese real estate tycoon." He chuckled. "Actually, he's a former real estate tycoon. I got a good deal on it."

Mikhail chuckled. "I'm pleased by your good fortune. It's very nice."

Vladimir pressed a button behind a nearby sculpture. The painting slid sideways, revealing a hidden safe.

"I've stored all our account and asset information in here," he said. "I wanted you to know in case anything happens to me. The safe combination is Leo Tolstoy's birthday."

Vladimir touched the button and the painting slid back into place.

They returned to the couch and sat down. Vladimir refilled their glasses and they drank.

Mikhail licked his lips. "It's amazing what you can get in America these days."

Both men snickered.

"Remember how we used to attack drunks in the Moscow Metro?" Vladimir said.

"*Da*," Mikhail reminisced. "We'd keep the money and sell the watches and vodka on the black market. That changed when I tried the stuff myself when I was ten. I always kept the vodka after that."

"I remember." Vladimir chuckled. "You weren't afraid to fight anyone when you drank."

"The vodka helped keep us warm on those frigid winter nights in the coal cavern."

"Yeah... Where Mother left us."

"*Da*." Mikhail pointed at the map. "So what's your next plan?"

"Joining the Protectorate will accelerate everything."

"*Da*. I'd never heard of them until I looked into Napoleon's activities before the game experiment with General Wu. They're pretty good at staying under the radar, especially considering how powerful they are."

"John Napoleon told me I was put on a list as a child, based on a test I took in school. That's how I got my scholarship to Wharton."

"I thought your scholarship was the product of America's altruistic generosity," Mikhail remarked sarcastically.

Vladimir chuckled. "Remember those trips we took in Napoleon's Learjet to the Caribbean during my spring vacations? He paid for those, too. In any case, this will accelerate our plans... once I take over."

"*Da*. Very good. So what does this mean for us?"

Vladimir stood up. He paced around the living room machinating with his hands behind his back.

"The Protectorate already controls a major portion of the world's commodity resources and crime syndicates," he explained. "The members are all very wealthy. Judith—the Israeli—is the exception as far as wealth goes, but she's Napoleon's consigliore, part of his inner circle. Dark-green eyes...

street smart… and beautiful. I haven't figured out if she and Napoleon are involved. He's a lot older than she is, but they seem very close."

Vladimir stopped and faced Mikhail at the window. "She slept with me in Paris."

"Really? So you finally took the plunge."

"Yeah." He blushed uncomfortably. "It took me by surprise. She's an interesting woman. She told me she used to sleep with a knife under her pillow to fend off rapists when she was a teenager. Her parents used to travel around the Mediterranean like a band of gypsies when she was growing up."

"She does sound interesting."

Vladimir started to pace again. "The Protectorate loved my Four Horsemen of the Apocalypse project idea—especially the Vatican Cardinal and the two Arabs. We'll need to make sure the Protectorate doesn't have any direct links to the attacks. They're extremely secretive, with many layers of protection—even more than us."

"*Da.*"

"Napoleon's bankers in Switzerland have been watching us for years, so they know our capabilities," Vladimir continued. "He selected the dates for the first two Horseman projects when we were in Paris. He deposited one hundred million dollars into our account for the White Horseman mission. We'll receive a similar payment for each Horseman."

"Where's the first attack?" Mikhail asked.

"Germany."

"Why Germany? Does Judith want retribution for World War II? We could just as easily seek revenge. Russia lost twenty-three million on the Eastern front fighting Hitler."

Vladimir sat on the windowsill facing Mikhail. "The White Horseman project has two goals: Making money, and instilling fear. The frugal Germans are flush with cash. Their bankers are the only thing holding Europe's tenuous financial system together. The rest of Europe is in debt up to their eyeballs, just as the Americans are with the Chinese. Attacking the European financial system will trigger a collapse in the euro, which will precipitate a massive drop in stock markets around the world. The White Horseman is just accelerating the inevitable."

Mikhail raised his vodka and drank. "*Da.* Brilliant."

Vladimir pulled the vodka bottle from the ice bucket and filled their glasses. "Countries throughout Europe depend on Germany to fund their lavish spending habits and generous government benefits. The proletariat wants a bourgeoisie lifestyle, so they purchase German products on credit. The politicians created the mess; we're just taking advantage of it."

Mikhail smiled. "So what are the details of your plan?"

"We'll purchase large put-option positions before each attack, just as we did before 9-11. Our put options will skyrocket when the stock and option markets collapse. We should make three hundred billion dollars from our thirty billion dollar investment. The Protectorate is going to invest two billion along with us, so they'll make twenty. I'll send the instructions to your traders through the usual channels when we're ready."

"When does the White Horseman arrive?" Mikhail asked.

Vladimir pointed at a date on a calendar circled in red. "The explosion is scheduled for this Wednesday, in the middle of May next year. That will give the markets time to implode before options expire that week."

Mikhail scribbled a note with the date. "What time?"

"One p.m. Judith will send an e-mail to Qatar's Al Jazeera broadcast station from an Internet portal in Iran after the attack to make it look authentic."

"*Da... dezinformatsiya*," Mikhail said approvingly. "We often used disinformation to confuse and obfuscate when I was in the KGB. The nuclear-winter theory comrade Tretyakov conjured up using bogus scientific studies was our best idea. It deterred the Europeans from deploying US Pershing missiles in Eastern Europe."

Vladimir chuckled. "That was very clever. Judith's e-mail will condemn the western infidels and their ancestors—the Crusaders—for slaughtering Muslims centuries ago. A new Islamic fundamentalist group will proclaim the White Horseman attack as the first battle in their quest to save the world from decadent Imperialism. The White Horseman announces conquest in Chapter Six of the Book of Revelation in the Bible. It's the first seal of the Four Horsemen of the Apocalypse."

Mikhail sniggered. "That's brilliant."

"Judith said she'd include lots of references to the Bible to frighten the religious zealots. The television stations will be glutted with preachers saying the end of the world is at hand."

Mikhail stroked his chin. "This could ignite a global world war," he said plaintively. "Has that been considered?"

"War is more likely when the Red Horseman arrives."

"Why?"

"The Red Horseman, in the Book of Revelation, brings war. America will have to go to war when a nuclear bomb explodes over Washington DC."

Vladimir paused to gauge Mikhail's reaction. "There will be more than a half million people watching fireworks on the Washington Mall on the Fourth of July."

Mikhail nodded. "Even with the backpack nukes' limited, ground-zero kill zone, the casualties will be staggering."

"At least one hundred thousand... perhaps more."

"*Da*... I'll make sure Abdul manages these projects for Nikolai. We don't want anyone to get squeamish about the death and destruction that will ensue after the attacks."

"We need to plan both projects now," Vladimir said. "As soon as the markets recover from the German attack, we'll hit them in America."

"Tell me more about these four horsemen you keep referring to."

"I've designated a horseman for each bomb—like the Four Horsemen of the Apocalypse in the Bible. The White Horseman is the German project, and the Red Horseman is DC."

"I've never studied the Bible," Mikhail said.

Vladimir refilled their glasses. "You should. It has many clever stories, written by men with cunning words... words that still control the world, even after more than two thousand years."

"Where in Germany will the White Horseman strike?"

Vladimir put his finger on the map. "Muhlenberg."

"Why not Berlin? It has the largest population."

"We want to spare the politicians so they'll react forcefully after the attack. Berlin is where their parliament resides. Aim the bomb so it explodes over the Muhlenberg conference center. Banking leaders from across Europe will be attending a financial conference there that day. The attack should hasten the collapse of the euro. Germany may even declare war on Iran."

"How much should we pay Nikolai for each bomb? Or maybe it's time to take him out."

Vladimir moved back to the window. Mikhail joined him.

"Thirty million," Vladimir said. "I know you'd like to get rid of him, but the Protectorate respects his management skills. Tell him to pay his people out of the money, though; it's up to him how much."

"My agents in France tell me he's living outside Nice now, near Monte Carlo," Mikhail said.

"Oh, really?"

"They think he left Yvonna."

"After all these years… that's surprising. Did he ever find out about the two of you?"

Mikhail chuckled. "No. Yvonna's too careful for that."

Vladimir stared down at the dark void below them. *I'm not sure I should tell Mikhail that I met Yvonna at the Russian Embassy Christmas party two years ago*, he mused. *She looked like a queen, in her ravishing, burgundy-red evening gown.*

Her large diamond earrings and matching necklace made it obvious that Nikolai spared no expense exhibiting his beautiful wife in a crowd. Among all of Mikhail's thousands of conquests she was the only he ever talked about. Now I know why.

"Perhaps I should give her a call," Vladimir said, probing for his brother's reaction.

"I have clean girls at my clubs," Mikhail said emphatically. "You can have as many as you want."

"I think I'd prefer Yvonna from the way you describe her."

"The hell you will!"

Vladimir's head jerked sideways. They exchanged angry stares. Their gazes returned to the dark abyss below them.

The skyscraper lights glowed yellow behind the gathering fog. A few snowflakes ricocheted off the glass. Most melted like bugs drawn to a light, paying the ultimate price for their exuberance.

* * *

Mikhail encoded a message for Nikolai the next morning, ordering him to appear the following Thursday at the Hotel Negresco's outdoor café, in Nice. The directive was on its way to Geneva in a United Nations diplomatic pouch two hours later.

29. Parturition

Geneva, Switzerland

Rahim Delacroix was sitting at an outdoor café on *Place du Molard* in Geneva when the stranger approached.

"Hello, Rahim," the stranger said. "My name is Sergei. Abdul tells me you're one of his best operatives."

Rahim looked up, alarmed. "I'm not sure what you mean, *monsieur*. I don't know anyone named Abdul."

Sergei flashed a smile. "Good man. Abdul wants you to know I'll be keeping an eye on you from now on during your missions. Just ignore me if you see me—unless you have an emergency."

Rahim surveyed the man: Russian, heavyset, in his early sixties—*he's the same cutout agent who left the OTP at the Tub Man Fountain in Zurich*. A partial mustache above a burn-scarred upper lip made Sergei's smile appear as a sneer.

"*Au revoir*," Sergei said as he hustled away.

Rahim frowned. *Why would a Russian be interested in our jihad? Maybe he's from Chechnya. Muslims are struggling against imperialism there, too.*

Rahim retrieved a folded newspaper from a trashcan in the men's bathroom a few minutes later. He found two sealed envelopes taped inside. One with no address—the coded message—and one with the name Francois Moreau scribbled on the outside.

Good, he decided. *My next role will be a cutout—a deliveryman, in Nice. A simple assignment: deliver the Francois Moreau letter to a hotel, and deposit the other letter in a safe-deposit box at Banque de France.*

Nice, France

Rahim arrived in Nice by train later that afternoon. He deposited the unaddressed letter in a safe-deposit box at the bank and took a taxi to the *Promenade des Anglais*.

The walkway, angled between shops, hotels, and businesses adjacent to the beach, provided a magnificent view of the Mediterranean. Hordes of tourists paraded the route during the summer. He had it mostly to himself today.

A cool mistral was blowing down from the north—typical this time of year in southern France. He walked a mile and doubled back; stopping every hundred feet to look at his reflection in a window to make sure no one was following him.

He entered the pink-domed Hotel Negresco and handed the letter addressed to *Monsieur* Moreau to the desk clerk. The envelope's purpose was simply to notify someone that a letter was waiting for them in the Banque de France safe-deposit box.

"Could you inform *Monsieur* Moreau he has a message?" Rahim said. "I hope he can be reached today."

"Yes, sir," the clerk said. "I'll let him know he has correspondence."

"*Merci.*" Rahim handed the clerk five euros.

"*Merci beaucoup.*" The clerk's smile soured when he accepted the tip.

Rahim often experienced this when people saw his mangled hand. He laughed to himself as he walked out of the hotel. He no longer hid his disfigurement. *It's interesting to see how people react*, he mused.

* * *

Nikolai decoded the message he'd picked up from the Banque de France deposit box the next morning. *Something major must be coming for Mikhail to fly to France to meet me on Thursday*, he pondered.

He fingered the Smith and Wesson 9mm semi-automatic in his coat pocket as he approached Mikhail a few days later. The gun provided a modicum of insurance he'd survive the meeting.

Mikhail was sitting at a white table in the Hotel Negresco's outdoor restaurant. Nikolai shook hands with him to preserve a façade of decorum in case someone was watching before he sat down.

The weather was cool and breezy. The other patrons were indoors, leaving the men to themselves on the patio.

The restaurant décor complemented the adjacent beach. White tables and umbrellas mingled among large, ceramic vases replete with fragrant white lilies.

Nikolai saw that Mikhail was drinking coffee. He ordered the same.

Both men's hair, noticeably grayer now that they were in their fifties, showed no evidence of receding hairlines. Mikhail still wore the same military-style haircut he'd had when they'd met decades earlier in Kabul.

"It looks like you've lost some weight," Mikhail said.

"I have," Nikolai said. "So what brings you to France?"

"We have some projects I need to discuss with you in person. They'll take careful planning. I also have some good news to share."

The men waited while the waiter filled Nikolai's cup with coffee.

I see the resemblance to Tatiana now, Nikolai reflected. *Mikhail's eyes, the texture of his hair, and the shape of his nose, are cookie-cutter versions of hers.*

He reached into his pocket and aimed his gun at Mikhail's crotch. *It would be so easy to end it. Then I'll take out Mikhail's bodyguard, who's staring at me there through the restaurant window, and run along the beach to my car parked two blocks away.*

"Do you remember when you wanted to sell our weapons for a mere ten million dollars?" Mikhail said.

"You mean *my* weapons," Nikolai stated emphatically. "Of course I remember… and I remember that you killed my parents."

Mikhail smiled, parrying Nikolai's remarks as if they'd been a simple missed thrust of a sword.

Nikolai probed Mikhail's face for weakness, like a psychiatrist pursuing neurosis. *As usual, Mikhail reveals nothing,* he told himself.

"Relax," Mikhail said. "Your payday is at hand. You'll receive sixty million dollars for two of the bombs next year."

"Tell me more."

"Abdul will need to recruit a current or former Iranian soldier for the first mission—someone experienced with bazookas. The soldier should be fervently religious."

"What's the target?" Nikolai inquired.

A gust of wind ripped through the restaurant causing a large vase to crash to the floor. Both men instinctively reached for their guns.

A waiter rushed outside apologetically. The men remained silent while a janitor swept the lilies and pottery shards into a trash can.

Most people would've moved inside by now, Nikolai acknowledged, *but I won't bend to the weather, especially in front of Mikhail.*

Mikhail handed him a piece of paper with handwritten letters and numbers. "The details are there," he said. "You can decipher them using the one-time pad my agent placed beneath the front seat of your rental car. The first target is Muhlenberg, a town outside Frankfurt. The second target is Washington DC."

Damn it! Mikhail's men must've followed me from the rental agency.

Nikolai fingered his gun. *There's sixty million dollars at stake,* he reminded himself. He pulled his hand out of his pocket.

"The first project is called the White Horseman," Mikhail continued. "You'll see it referenced as such in our correspondence."

"Why are you calling it that?" Nikolai asked.

"Make sure the shooter creates a trail for himself from Iran to Germany. He should cross into Turkey at Bazargan so the CIA takes his picture. I'll send you the details for the second project after Muhlenberg. The Red Horseman arrives in DC on the Fourth of July."

Nikolai looked out at the tempestuous sea. *Perhaps a new project will help me forget Yvonna.*

Images from a movie he'd seen with real footage of Hiroshima clouded his mind—people burned alive... their skin melting away as firestorms cascaded across the city. *Why would God—if there is a God—allow humans to build such a cruel and destructive weapon,* he wondered?

Mikhail stood up and buttoned his coat. "How are Yvonna... and the kids?"

"Why do you want to know?" Nikolai clenched his teeth to control his rage. *Mikhail will use my emotions against me if he can.*

He reached into his pocket and fondled the trigger. *Just a quarter-inch squeeze... and it'll be over.*

Mikhail flashed a disarming smile. "I was just trying to be cordial, Major Petrovna. I'll be in touch."

He turned and walked away.

* * *

Mikhail's bodyguard walked behind him from the restaurant to the car.

Nikolai seems angrier than normal Mikhail contemplated as the limousine pulled away from the curb. *Damn! He knows about Yvonna and me. I'll have to get rid of him now, regardless of what the Protectorate says.*

He smiled as the limousine sped him towards his private jet at the Nice airport. *I'll terminate him on the Fourth of July,* he decided. *It'll be my Independence Day, as well as Yvonna's.*

Luxembourg City

Angela landed at Luxembourg's Findel Airport after a late-evening flight in the Gulfstream across the Atlantic. *I wonder what Sean will think about my surprise,* she mused, as she rode the elevator at Banque Lux.

Sean hugged her when she stepped into his office. "Hi, Angie. This is a pleasant surprise. Why didn't you tell me you'd be coming?"

Beate shook Angela's hand. "Hi, Angela. It's good to see you again."

Angela studied Beate with a frosty gaze. "It's good to see you, too. An awkward silence cloaked the room. Sean and Beate looked at each other after they noticed Angela's protruding belly.

Sean sat down next to Angela.

"I need to talk with you, Sean," Angela said.

"I'm going to get some coffee," Beate said. "Would either of you like something?"

"I'd like some orange juice," Angela replied.

"I'll be back in a couple of minutes."

Beate closed the door as she left.

Angela stared at him questioningly. "I'm pregnant, Sean... we're having a baby girl."

He gaped for a few seconds before he smiled. "Are you sure? Ah... I mean, I know you must be sure... that you're pregnant." He laughed. "This is a shock. May I feel her?"

She giggled. "Of course."

He kneeled down and placed his hand on her belly.

"She's starting to kick," Angela said.

Sean's face filled with awe. "Why didn't you tell me?"

"I wanted to surprise you. I kept expecting you to come home. What are you doing here? When is this *fling* you're having with *Julie or Beate* or whatever her name is going to be over? I need you with me."

He sat back in his chair. "I'm not supposed to talk about what we're working on," he said. "I want you to have deniability. I will say that we think we've identified a terrorist using our bank to make trades. You'll need to keep that to yourself."

She nodded. "But that's no reason not to call. I need you in New York. I'll be cutting back on my work schedule soon. How involved are you with her?"

His gaze steadied. "We're very involved."

Angela leaned into her hands and started to cry. Sean came out of his chair and hugged her. She was still crying when Beate entered.

"Shall I give you some more time?" Beate asked.

Angela wiped away her tears and stood up. "No. I'm leaving."

She glowered at Beate as she took the orange juice and walked out without saying goodbye.

Beate squeezed Sean's arm. "Follow her. You need to take care of her now. I can handle things here."

Sean caught up with Angela at the elevator.

They had a serious talk during their flight to New York.

"I want you to be a full partner with me, raising our child," Angela said. "I don't expect marriage under the circumstances, but I'd still like you to live with us. Is that selfish of me?"

"I'm thrilled you want me involved," he said. "I've always wanted children. I just didn't expect it to happen like this. I am dating Beate now, though. I hope that doesn't change your mind."

"I understand," she said, looking away. "She's a wonderful woman. I just wish you'd chosen me."

Sean spoke after a moment. "I love you too, Angie. I'm sorry it worked out this way between us. Besides, Beate doesn't want children. Perhaps this was fate... for us to have a child together."

Angela reached for his hand. "We'll be great parents don't you think?"

"Yes... we will."

Armonk, New York—March 20

Sarah Jean McGowan was born on the vernal equinox. They named her Sarah after Angela's mother.

Sean had taken over most of Angela's executive management responsibilities during the latter months of her pregnancy. He'd also taken birthing classes, so he assisted during the delivery.

Beate remained at Banque Lux, waiting patiently for Michel Bowen to show up.

Sean stepped outside the birthing room to call Beate a few minutes after Sarah was born. "Witnessing my daughter's birth was the most amazing experience of my life," he said. "Sarah's a natural. She took to breastfeeding right away."

"I wish I'd been there to share it with the two of you," she told him. "How did the labor go?"

"It took six hours. Angela is exhausted. She said quite a bit in the heat of the moment." He paused. "She's angry at me for hooking up with you. At the same time, she's happy I was there. She said she wants you in Sarah's life. She wanted me to ask you if Sarah could call you Aunt Beate. I hope you're okay with that."

Beate paused for a few seconds. "That's very loving of her."

"I'll be back in Luxembourg in a couple of weeks once everyone gets settled," he assured her.

"I understand," she replied. "This is a precious time. Babies change quickly at that age. You should savor it. They need you now."

"I know our situation is complicated. Thanks for understanding."

"It's a good thing I like Angela," she said. "Otherwise, there's no way I'd put up with this."

"She likes you, too." He chuckled. "I'll be there as soon as I can… to take care of you."

Beate released a long, slow breath. "I wish you would. I long for you. I'll be thinking about you tonight when I go to bed. I love you, sweetheart."

"I love you, too. Oh—Sarah's crying. I'll let you say hello."

Sean entered the birthing room and placed his phone near Sarah's mouth. Her crying changed to gurgles as she latched onto Angela's nipple.

He pulled the phone to his ear. "Did you hear that? She was hungry."

Beate's voice cracked. "She sounds beautiful. I can't wait to hold her."

"Angela says she'll call you when she has more strength. I love you darling."

"I love you, too."

30. Badgers

Tehran, Iran—Early May

Abdul's mind wandered as he interviewed Hafiz at the outdoor café just outside Tehran's Grand Mosalla Mosque. *The mournful wail of the Imam singing through the loudspeakers is distracting.*

I need a drink, he told himself, ignoring the Imam's exhortations to wipe their hearts clean of hatred and hostility. *Besides, thirty-two year old Hafiz is perfect. My al-Qaeda contacts vetted him well.*

He's single, so there won't be any grieving wives to worry about, and he spent six years in the Iranian army firing bazookas and surface-to-air missiles. He's also memorized the entire Qur'an, so the press will pigeonhole him as a religious zealot—appropriate, considering the apocalyptic nature of our mission.

Abdul handed Hafiz the keys to his van. "Cross the border into Turkey at Bazargan," he ordered. "I'll be waiting for you at the Minareli Cami Mosque in Erzurum. Can I help you with anything before I go? Does anyone in your family need money?"

"No," Hafiz replied. "My only family is my father and he is old. Money only brings corruption. I don't want to ruin his last days."

Abdul nodded. *He is perfect*, he confirmed.

"From Turkey, you'll drive through Bulgaria, Serbia, Hungary, and Austria to Munich. I'll give you a map with the route when we meet."

Luxembourg City

Sean returned to Luxembourg the second week in May. Beate briefed him on her efforts after he arrived.

"I'm convinced that the name 'Michel Bowen' is an alias," she said. "His lack of a digital footprint is suspicious. He's a ghost, beyond the bank. I asked the International Police Organization—Interpol—to conduct a worldwide search to identify everyone with the name 'Michel Bowen.' They located many men with that name. However, all of them could be accounted for at times when Bowen was making trades here at Banque Lux."

Jonas was sitting on the couch in Sean's office when Sean and Beate returned with coffee the next afternoon. "He's here," Jonas said. "Michel

Bowen—he's the one you're looking for, right? Is he the one who murdered Emma?"

Beate jumped to her computer. "Jonas and I had a talk while you were in New York," she told Sean as she typed. "He wants to help."

Sean nodded. "It's good to have you on board."

Beate grabbed her sweater. "Where is he?"

"He's on our private client trading floor," Jonas said. "The alert popped up while you were getting coffee."

"I'll follow him when he leaves," Sean said.

"I need to follow him by myself," Beate said. "We don't want to scare him off. He may recognize you if he saw you with Emma."

She turned to Jonas. "Can you take me to the trading floor?"

"Sure." Jonas rose from the couch.

She hugged Sean. "Why don't you gather up our things so you'll be ready when I call?"

Jonas dialed his cellphone while they waited at the elevator. "Patch me through to security... I need you to tell me when Michel Bowen comes out of his trading room. ...When? ...What does he look like? ...Thanks."

Jonas hung up. He punched the elevator up arrow button. "Bowen's heading to the lobby."

Beate stared at the floor numbers. *Hurry*, she urged the car.

"What does he look like?" she asked.

"The security guard said he's a small, olive-skinned man; probably Middle Eastern, with long black hair and a mustache."

Beate's eyes darted from face to face in the crowded lobby when they exited the elevator. "I don't see anyone that fits his description."

"I'll be right back." Jonas walked to the security guard and returned. "He hasn't left yet, or if he did, the guards didn't see him."

She turned away from Jonas. "He just got out of the elevator. He's heading to the exit."

Beate extended her hand. "Thanks for everything, Jonas. Ask Sean to look at his trades. They may indicate what's next on their agenda."

She scurried through the revolving doors and wrote down the license plate number of Bowen's taxi as he scooted away. She then hailed one for herself.

She handed her driver fifty euros. "Follow that taxi."

She dialed Langley as they peeled away from the curb. "I need you to mobilize a tracking party immediately"

The taxi driver watched her warily through his rear-view mirror.

* * *

Jonas returned to Sean's office. "We spotted Michel Bowen in the lobby. Beate's following him."

Sean rose from his keyboard and strapped on his backpack. "What does he look like?"

"He's a slight man, with light-brown skin—Lebanese or Israeli if I had to guess—with long, dark hair, a mustache, and a burn scar on his neck. Beate wants you to look at his trades."

"I just did. He made several *huge* put-option bets against the market."

Sean stared at the computer on his desk. He sat back down and began to type. "I'm going to place identical orders in my account, albeit with only one hundred million dollars, versus the one billion Bowen used. I'll place my sell limit target price so it triggers when the options increase tenfold, just as Bowen did. I'll make nine hundred million if the trade works out."

"That's pretty risky," Jonas said. "You're doing this based on a hunch?"

"Something big is coming for him to make that kind of trade. I guess we'll find out soon enough if my hunch is correct."

"I know it's none of my business, but what's up with you and Angela? Beate told me you're dating her now, but you just had a baby with Angela."

Sean nodded. "It's complicated. I'll tell you about it some other time."

* * *

Beate's taxi jerked to a stop in front of the train station. They'd lost Bowen a few blocks back at a red light.

I hope this is where he went. She paid the driver and raced inside.

Her gaze rose to the artistically painted arched ceiling and across to the ticket windows. *He's not here*, she groaned inwardly.

Her phone vibrated. "Yes."

She scanned the stairway leading to the boarding area. "…Good. Can you check to see whether Michel Bowen bought a train ticket? …Okay. Let me know as soon as possible."

She dialed Sean. "He's somewhere in the train station," she said. "His taxi dropped him off here. Look for me in the departure area, but stay hidden so he doesn't see you."

She hung up and looked at the departure display. *I can't lose him.*

Her surveillance moved around the station in a grid, to the ticket windows, down each hallway, and across to the concessionaires.

Something caught her attention. *I'm getting that prickly feeling on the back of my neck.*

She focused. A clean-shaven man dressed in a business suit had just walked out of the men's restroom. *Something about him seems familiar*, she observed.

She settled into a comfortable pace behind him. He turned down a platform and boarded a train destined for Basel, Switzerland.

It's his almost-imperceptible limp, she realized. *It makes sense. It would be easy to remove a disguise in the bathroom of a crowded train station.*

The train whistle blew, signaling an imminent departure.

Beate hopped on.

She passed Bowen in first class. He was reading a newspaper.

She proceeded to second-class, sat in an empty seat, dialed CIA headquarters, and relayed Bowen's seat number to a travel analyst. The train pulled away from the station as the analyst looked into the Swiss Federal Railway train manifest database.

"A man named 'Rahim Delacroix' owns the ticket, not Michel Bowen," the analyst said.

The train was accelerating rapidly. *Crap! It's too late to get off.*

"He's boarding a train in Basel for Geneva."

"Thanks for your help."

She hung up and called Sean. "I'm on the train to Basel... That's right. I'm sorry I couldn't wait. I had to follow my intuition. I saw a man that might be Bowen leaving the men's bathroom at the train station. He doesn't have long hair though. Can you check the trashcans for a discarded wig? ...Thanks. Talk with you soon."

Sean called her a few minutes later. "Hi, love."

"What's up?"

"I have some good news, and some bad news. Which would you like first?"

"The good news," Beate replied.

"Your intuition was correct. I found a long-haired wig in a trash can."

She exhaled with relief. "Thanks for digging through trash for me, dear. You're a real prince. How soon can you join me?"

"That's the bad news. The next train to Basel doesn't leave for three hours. I'll be behind you for a while."

"It's probably quicker for you to take a plane to Geneva," she suggested. "That's where he's going."

"How do you know?"

She laughed. "Trust me. It's my intuition."

"Ahhh... I should know better than to question that. Where in Geneva?"

"I'll tell you when I get there. Michel Bowen is an alias, by the way. His real name is Rahim Delacroix."

"How do you know?"

"I have my sources."

"Ahhh... Big Brother came to the rescue, huh. I'll see you tonight." He hung up.

Beate looked at her purse, sweater, and smartphone. *I need resources.*

She walked through several second-class compartments until she spotted two college-aged American women with backpacks stowed above them. One of them wore a red Wisconsin Badgers sweatshirt.

They're probably on their junior year abroad—a last hurrah before they finish college and join the working world. She'd practiced her American English accent on trains with college kids from America many times when she'd explored Europe with her parents as a child.

They'll probably be pleased to meet someone from their own country after travelling in strange places for a while, she assumed.

Beate saw an empty seat next to them. "May I sit with you?" she inquired.

Their faces lit up. "Sure."

Typical of their gadget-oriented generation, they had to move computers and phones to make room for her. They told Beate they were college roommates from Madison, Wisconsin.

Beate described her dilemma: "I didn't have time to pack. I need a backpack and a couple of shirts before I meet my boyfriend." She pointed at Sandra's low-cut blouse, which generously displayed her cleavage. "Like the one you're wearing."

The women frowned at Beate suspiciously. Beate pulled out her wallet.

"I'm surprising my boyfriend. I'll give you six hundred euros. I know that's a lot of money, but I'm desperate. He's only in Basel for a day."

Their faces brightened as they took the money.

Beate excused herself and went to the bathroom when she received a call from Langley.

"Rahim Delacroix lives in Geneva," the analyst said. "He has an office at the UN. He's also something of an art aficionado. He's written art reviews in the Geneva newspaper."

"Excellent. Thanks." She hung up.

She dialed Michael Chen, her Langley IT colleague, who was now the Director of the Agency's data analytics center. "I need a favor, Michael," she said. "Can you create a query for me? I need to correlate the stock transaction dates we found for Michel Bowen's trades, with the train-travel itineraries for someone named Rahim Delacroix." She spelled his name. "That's right. Search the Swiss, German, and French train manifest databases."

Chen confirmed her hypothesis a few minutes later. "Rahim was in Luxembourg on the dates Michel Bowen placed trades at Banque Lux."

"Excellent. I think we found our terrorist financier."

She dialed the travel analyst she'd spoken with earlier at Langley. "I need you to reserve a ticket for me across from Rahim Delacroix for his trip from Basel and Geneva. ...I don't care that he purchased that seat. Break into the database and create a reservation. I'll pick it up at the railway office in Basel before I board. ...Perfect. Thanks."

The train pulled to a stop in Basel a few minutes later. She said goodbye to the Wisconsin Badger girls and hustled to a bookstore near the station.

Offenbach, Germany

Abdul dropped Hafiz at a corner a few blocks from his hotel. *I don't want anyone to see me with him* he strategized. *The inevitable investigation by the Bundespolizei* will eventually lead them back to his hotel.

He retrieved Hafiz from the same corner the next morning and drove him to a small marina on the Main River, a few miles west of Muhlenberg.

He handed Hafiz a key. "I moored a dark-red speedboat for our mission at the marina last week. The boat will allow you to make a quick get-away after the explosion."

Abdul waited in the van for two hours while Hafiz made several practice runs to and from the Muhlenberg launch site.

I'm confident things will go smoothly Abdul told himself when they'd finished.

Geneva, Switzerland

Rahim's next-door neighbors were surprised when a well-dressed official from the United Nations knocked on their door and flashed his credentials. The official speaking to them was actually Helmut Drach. Helmut's information from Interpol revealed the couple was predisposed to support UN causes.

"A celebrity working with the UN needs his privacy during his stay in Geneva," Helmut said. "He'll be here for a month. The well-known entertainer, whose name we can't disclose, thinks a hotel will bring too much publicity. We think your home will be perfect. We'll give you five thousand euros for your trouble, and an all-expense-paid cruise to the Caribbean."

The couple complained when Helmut told them they'd need to evacuate immediately. They moved faster when he told them they'd be flying in a Lear jet to Aruba.

Helmut's clandestine operations team placed pinhole cameras and microphones in the walls and ceilings of Rahim's apartment after the couple left. They connected the surveillance gear to CIA computers in the couple's dining room—Helmut's operation center for the mission.

Basel, Switzerland

Sean called Beate just as she was about to board her train for Geneva. "I reserved a room for us at the Grand Hotel Kampinski on the *Quai du Mont-Blanc* in Geneva," he said. "The hotel is a few blocks from the *Gare de Cornavin* station. The hotel clerk said our room has a marvelous view of the mountains and the *Jet d'Eau*, the city's famous water-jet fountain on the lake."

"Thanks, dear," Beate said. "I'm about to meet Mr. Delacroix."

"Be careful. He may have murdered Emma. I'll bring your luggage to the hotel. The room reservation is under our married name, Mrs. Kelly."

"Excellent. Are you always this helpful?"

"I'll always be your loyal servant, my queen," he joked.

"Rahim just boarded the train. I'll call you from the hotel."

Beate made sure her cleavage was visible as she pushed her backpack into the storage rack above Rahim's seat. She extended her hand to him. "How are you?"

He returned her handshake as she sat down. She ignored his mangled fingers.

Rahim ogled her bosom. "I think there's been a mistake."

He pulled his ticket from his jacket. "I purchased both of these seats."

Beate stood up. "I'm sorry," she apologized. "I've been travelling all day. Perhaps I didn't look at my ticket correctly."

She reached overhead and fumbled through her backpack keeping her breasts near his face. *I'm sure my bosom will consume his attention*, she told herself.

She placed the two art books she'd just purchased on her seat, pulled out her ticket, and showed it to him. "The ticket says this is my seat. I'm not sure what happened."

He studied her name and seat number. His scrutiny softened when he looked at her art books.

He handed the ticket back to her.

She picked up the books and held them in her lap when she sat down.

His gaze displayed a question. "I see you like art."

"I do," she replied. "I'm not an expert, though. I'm really a math teacher. I've always wanted to learn more about art and sculpture. I plan to visit some galleries while I'm on vacation in Geneva."

"Really? I live in Geneva. I know the galleries well. I'll show you around if you'd like."

She smiled. "That would be lovely."

The pair discussed art and museums for the duration of their journey.

"Would you like to share a cab to your hotel?" he said as the train glided to a stop in Geneva.

She hesitated for a moment, and said, "Sure."

Rahim gave her his card as she stepped out of the cab in front of the Kampinski hotel. "Call me when you're ready to visit a museum."

"I will," she said, "after I explore the city for a few days."

* * *

Sergei had followed the pair in a taxi from the train station. He focused his telephoto lens and snapped several shots as she entered the hotel. *Rahim should know better than to give his phone number to a stranger*, he grumbled to himself.

He stopped at an Internet café and uploaded the photos to his GRU contact in Moscow. *I'll wait until I have something definite before I report Rahim's encounter to Abdul*, he decided. *His scathing rebukes aren't worth a mistake.*

Sergei's GRU contact called him back a few minutes later. "I came up empty on the visuals you sent," she said. "I'll send them to the FSB and let you know what I find out."

He returned to the station and boarded a train for Montreux. He'd been living there with his Swiss wife since 1991, after barely escaping the KGB purge that eliminated many of his friends after Gorbachev's failed assassination attempt.

* * *

The NSA flagged Sergei's message the instant it hit the GRU's secure Internet e-mail portal. Although they couldn't determine who'd sent the encrypted email, the photos were another matter.

Using software originally developed by the Israelis, they decompressed and decrypted the pictures in a matter of seconds. The NSA manager on duty immediately called her counterpart at the CIA, who called the European station chief.

Helmut was watching Rahim via the video feed inside his apartment when the station chief called him with the news about Beate.

This is dangerous, Helmut realized after the call. *She needs to know someone from the GRU followed her.*

* * *

The first thing Beate did, after checking into the top-floor suite Sean had reserved for them, was look out at the huge fountain spraying water over Lake Geneva. She called Helmut as she enjoyed the view.

"I just arrived," she reported. "Rahim gave me his phone number in case I need some company when I visit art galleries."

"That could be useful," he remarked. "What's your plan?"

"I don't have one, other than to follow him."

"We've set up surveillance gear in an operations center next door to his apartment." He gave her the address. "Can you come by for a few minutes? Be careful, though. Make sure no one is following you. I'll tell you why when you get here."

Beate sensed the warning in his voice. "Sure. I'll be there soon."

She doubled back several times to make sure no one was following her as she walked to Rahim's building. She wasn't surprised to see how well Helmut had organized everything when she entered the operations center. *His Germanic efficiency is admirable*, she marveled.

Seven display screens on the dining-room table delivered video and audio feeds from every corner of Rahim's apartment.

Helmut handed her a key and a gun. "Be careful," he said. "Someone's watching Rahim."

Helmut poked his keyboard. A picture of her exiting Rahim's cab came up on the screen.

"Crap," she exclaimed. "Who took that?"

"The email was sent from an Internet café in Geneva to a GRU portal."

Trepidation stirred her voice. "The Russians are involved? Should we change hotels?"

"No. That would signal we're on to them. Tell Sean to be cautious."

"I will. I'll see you back here in the morning."

31. The White Horseman

Greenwich, Connecticut—D-Day Minus One

Vladimir was sitting next to Kolnikov, the other Russian member of the Protectorate, at the large circular table in the conference room. The oak-paneled room in the sprawling Connecticut mansion of their leader, John Napoleon, displayed several Renaissance paintings on the walls.

This was Vladimir's second meeting with the secretive syndicate. His first had been at the offices of the Frenchman in the *Place de la Concorde*, in Paris.

Judith sat across from Vladimir on the other side of the round table. *Her hungry look says she has amorous intentions*, he assumed. *I'll accommodate her at my flat in New York after the meeting.*

She'd told Vladimir—after they'd made love in Paris—that she'd spent fifteen years in the Mossad. *Napoleon had taken a liking to her when they met at a party near Lake Como.*

Her forthright honesty put most of my fears about her working a deep-cover assignment to rest he ruminated. He deflected her solicitation with a smile and scanned the room, studying the rest of his new acquaintances.

Other than General Wu, Napoleon, Judith, and Kolnikov—who owned a good portion of Russia's energy and mining industries—he hadn't met any of his new associates before their meeting in Paris. Of the eight remaining members, two were from the Middle East, one was South Korean,—the only other woman at the table—one was Mexican, a Vatican Cardinal was dressed in red, one was French, one was Swiss, and one was from Malaysia.

I need to know their vulnerabilities to control them he strategized. *I'm sure they all have secrets we can exploit.*

They were probably enticed to join the Protectorate, as I was, by the shield bestowed by governments, he speculated. *The Protectorate's network of government bureaucrats on the payroll across the globe will orchestrate a carefully crafted subterfuge to guarantee our immunity if our activities are ever exposed.*

Vladimir's eye fell to Napoleon: Tall, thin, mid-seventies, with a full head of silver hair and blue, deadpan eyes. His emotionless demeanor gave him the guise of a detached aristocrat.

He's a cold fish, Vladimir reflected. *The man showed no affection whatsoever for his magnificent Renaissance art collection when we toured his mansion before the meeting. He talked about the paintings without emotion, simply as if they were investments.*

His stated nonprofit mission to protect the environment is clever, though. It gives the high profile business executives in the group a plausible excuse to meet beyond the public eye.

Napoleon banged his gavel and raised his voice above the chatter. "Let's bring this meeting to order."

Everyone settled down immediately.

"Mr. Volkov," Napoleon said. "Could you give us a summary of what you expect tomorrow? We're aware of the military operation, so you can spare us those details. We want to hear your financial projections."

Vladimir cleared his throat. "Each of our four traders is purchasing eight billion dollars' worth of put options. The value of these options will rise dramatically when the world's stock markets plummet after the White Horseman attack. Our thirty-two billion-dollar-investment should rise tenfold. Two billion of this is Protectorate funds, so your portion of the profits will be eighteen billion, after accounting for your initial investment. The algorithm is really quite simple."

He looked around the room. "Any questions?"

"I think we should buy more commodity companies with the profits," the Malaysian said. "We'll get those dirt-cheap when the markets crash."

Vladimir observed without speaking now that the focus had turned to investment strategy. *Although I have plenty of ideas of my own, I'm going to keep quiet,* he decided. *I'm curious to see how they play the game.*

"I agree," General Wu said. "However, I think we should also acquire more telecommunication companies. Information is a key resource in the economy these days. We need to gain control of the media, Internet, and world communication grids."

"Does anyone disagree?" Napoleon asked, circling the table with his gaze.

Everyone remained silent.

"Good. We'll continue our present course with commodities, and add to our media and telecom holdings. As always, our equity firms will take the public companies private once we're majority shareholders, so we can avoid government scrutiny. Controlling the media will be crucial when the planet starts choking on pollution. We'll need to disseminate our message quickly without government interference when the time comes."

Everyone nodded.

"Mr. Neruda will be hosting our next meeting in Mexico City. This meeting is adjourned." Napoleon banged his gavel.

That was quick, Vladimir noticed.

Judith planted her gaze on him. They became even better acquainted later that evening at his New York penthouse after he dazzled her with his *Impressionist* art collection.

Offenbach, Germany—D-Day

Abdul drove his windowless van to Offenbach at 2:00 a.m., retrieved Hafiz from a corner a block from his hotel, and continued to Muhlenberg. He parked near a storage pod next to the Main River. They entered the pod— Abdul had it deposited there the previous evening in a truck—closed the door, and turned on their flashlights.

Hafiz attached the fifty-one-pound, thirty-inch-long W54R nuclear missile to the bazooka on top of the tripod. Abdul adjusted the trajectory angles and altitude trigger so the bomb would explode 500 feet above the Convention Center.

The twenty-ton-dynamite-equivalent payload had a three-quarter mile blast footprint at that altitude. It would level everything within a ten-block radius, including the Convention Center where the bank officials were meeting. The pod's location next to the river would also allow Hafiz to jump into the speedboat to make a quick escape.

Abdul returned Hafiz to the same corner near his hotel when they finished. "Get some sleep," Abdul told him. "I'll pick you up at noon. The detonation will take place at thirteen hundred hours."

"See you then," Hafiz said as he exited the van.

The one p.m. attack—a couple of hours before trading opened in New York—would give the press plenty of time to frighten the markets.

It was also lunchtime, a time when many people would be walking around Muhlenberg's beautifully landscaped streets enjoying the fragrant spring flowers and melliferous tree blossoms. That would maximize fatalities.

Annapolis, Maryland. H-hour – 90 minutes

It was 5:30 a.m. on the East Coast of the United States—11:30 a.m. in Nice, France—when Nikolai called Yvonna.

"Hello," she answered sleepily.

"Do you have anything to tell me?" he asked pointedly.

"I want you to come home, Nikolai. I love you."

Their transatlantic connection buzzed with pink noise as Nikolai's enmity traversed digital-to-analog-to-digital signals relayed between satellites in one direction, and fiber-optic cables on the Atlantic floor in the other.

"Please come home," she pleaded.

"I'll see you in two weeks." He hung up.

Muhlenberg, Germany. H-hour – 55 minutes

The weather was beautiful, warm, and sunny, when Abdul retrieved Hafiz from the corner. Hafiz prayed to himself while Abdul drove him to the marina.

Show me a sign, an omen, to let me know if I should abandon this mission, he begged Allah.

Abdul pulled into a parking spot next to the Main River a block from the marina.

It must be Allah's providence, Hafiz decided.

Hafiz started the boat's engine at 12:30 p.m. He navigated the speedboat along the edge of the river east to Muhlenberg, and slowed to a crawl as he approached the launch site.

He moored the boat with quick-release hitch knots, entered the storage pod, and secured the door. He pulled on an orange radiation-protection suit, secured his goggles, inserted a propellant cartridge into the bazooka, and turned the safety switch from *Safe* to *Arm*.

His watch said 12:55 p.m.

He faced Mecca and dropped to his knees. *Thank you, Allah, for making me an instrument of your will.*

The humidity inside the radiation suit made him sweat. It was 1:00 p.m.

He looked through a crack in the doors. *I'm alone.*

He pushed the doors wide open; took a deep breath, and squeezed the bazooka trigger.

The projectile swooshed away, heading flawlessly to its target.

Hafiz jumped into the speedboat and shielded himself against the side.

The explosion was loud. The aftershock swayed the boat violently.

He pulled the slipknots, started the engine, and gunned the throttle. A gray, cauliflower-shaped mushroom cloud was forming over the city when he looked back over his shoulder.

* * *

Abdul stared east through his binoculars. A loud boom had followed the bright flash from the explosion twenty seconds later.

He placed a voice-cloaking device over his cell phone and dialed the police. "I just saw a man in an orange jumpsuit shoot a rocket over the city!"

he yelled. "The man jumped into a speedboat and headed west on the Main River."

Abdul ended the call. He broke the cell phone apart and threw the pieces into the river.

* * *

Hafiz looked back when he heard sirens. A police boat with flashing lights was following him.

He pushed the throttle to maximum as he entered some narrow locks next to a dam. *I know it's dangerous at this speed but I have no choice.*

The speedboat struck a speed barrier as he exited the locks launching the boat five feet in the air. It made a huge splash and pitched violently side-to-side when it landed.

A second police boat joined the chase on the other side of the dam.

The speedboat seems lethargic—even at full throttle he fretted! *It isn't nearly as fast as it was during my test runs yesterday.*

The police boats were closing in as he approached the marina.

* * *

Abdul watched Hafiz through his binoculars. Shouts through the police bullhorns rose above the whine of the engines: *"Achtung! Achtung! Stoppen das boot!"*

Abdul smiled to himself. *My carburetor adjustment is working perfectly.*

A crooked, black-and-gray cumulus cloud reached towards the sky behind the boats. Sirens were ringing out all across the city.

* * *

Hafiz frantically reversed gears. The boat slowed.

He steered at the loading ramp. *It will be a hard landing if I make it* he told himself. *I hope Abdul is ready for our escape.*

* * *

Abdul punched the red button on his transmitter.

The speedboat burst into a huge, yellow-and-orange fireball when the C-4 wired to the gas tanks exploded, shooting flames forty feet into the air.

The police boats veered away violently to avoid the debris.

A fifteen-foot cascade shot up from the water when the skeleton remains of the boat plunged into the river. Black smoke and fiberglass shards raining down on the surface were now the only evidence the speedboat had ever existed.

Abdul jumped into his getaway car, leaving the van for the police to find. He'd already wiped it down. He threaded his way through back roads and merged onto the Autobahn a few minutes later.

He then shifted his attention to their next project: *The Red Horseman's arrival in DC.*

Geneva, Switzerland

Beate, Helmut, and Sean were watching Rahim via the video feeds from inside his apartment when the news flash crossed their displays. They moved to the living room and turned on the television. A large mushroom cloud was rising above Muhlenberg's flaming buildings.

"Oh my God," Beate said. Helmut checked the magazine in his Glock 23 pistol. "Let's go next door and roust him," he yelled angrily. "We need to see if he's planning another attack."

Sean stared at the flames engulfing the city. "I doubt it. The markets will crash after this. They've already made their profits. Rahim wasn't even watching television when the attack occurred. He probably didn't know any of the specifics. He's just a pawn in a much larger game."

Beate braced Helmut's arm. "Sean's right. They keep everything compartmentalized. Rahim probably doesn't know anything about the actual attacks. We'll blow our cover if we question him now."

Helmut churned his jaw. "I wish we could've prevented this."

"I wish we could've, too," she agreed.

"Going after him now would be like cutting off the tail of a lizard," Sean said. "It would just grow back. They'd replace him with someone else, and we'd have to start over."

"We need to watch him to see whom he reports to," Beate said. "He'll help us smoke them out."

An e-mail from a terrorist group in Iran claiming responsibility for what they called, "the White Horseman attack," appeared on the news channels. The message caused stock markets around the world to plummet even further. The value of the euro collapsed.

The United Nations held an emergency meeting at their headquarters in New York City later that evening. Of the five permanent members on the Security Council, the Brits, the French, and the United States pledged full support for Germany's plans to retaliate against Iran. Russia abstained. China vetoed the idea.

The German chancellor called his parliament into session and mobilized his military forces.

The US Secretary of Defense ordered a DEFCON 3 alert. The National Military Command Center at the Pentagon—responsible for managing nuclear submarines, reconnaissance aircraft and battlefield commanders around the world—worked around the clock refining NATO attack scenarios. They'd be ready at a moment's notice if the president gave the order to strike Iran.

The Iranian government emphatically denied any involvement, proclaiming belligerently that the west was using the terrorist act as an excuse to attack Islam. Meanwhile, Iran's Ministry of Intelligence began a frantic search for the person who'd sent the e-mail to Al Jazeera. They traced the message to a crowded Internet café in Tehran. No one remembered the woman, dressed in a full burqa, who'd used the computer to send the message.

One of the largest worldwide medical emergency responses ever launched began immediately. The German government reluctantly accepted the world's offers to help, when it became obvious the magnitude of the catastrophe would quickly eclipse their resources. Within hours, medical teams armed with supplies, portable burn units and hospital tents arrived at the *Flughafen Frankfurt am Main* airport.

Statistics reported by the media plotted the probable death toll at sixteen thousand. One statistician speculated that four thousand—perhaps the lucky ones—were instantly vaporized. The remainder died excruciatingly painful deaths from burns, radiation poisoning, and accidents caused by collapsing buildings.

Scientists predicted that thousands of northern Europeans also received the seeds of their eventual destruction by cancer when radiation carried in the upper atmosphere fell as rain hundreds of miles away.

Sean called Jonas a few days after the attack. "I assume Delacroix's billion-dollar put option bet is now worth ten?"

"That's right," Jonas said, "and your hundred-million-dollar bet is worth a billion."

"Now we know what his friends were up to. I made that trade on the whale's coattail, but the reason it worked makes me sick. I'd like you to put the profits into an anonymous trust for the Muhlenberg victims."

"That's very generous of you," Jonas said. "Are you sure?"

"Yes, I'm sure. That's the least we can do."

Montreux, Switzerland

Sergei watched the news reports with trepidation as the Muhlenberg tragedy unfolded on his television screen. *I'll bet Rahim and Abdul were involved*, he speculated.

He was already on edge. His GRU contact in Russia had finally identified the woman in the photograph with Rahim as Beate Nicholson—a CIA manager in the DS & T. *Thank God for the dossiers Aldrich Ames gave us for every CIA employee*, he recalled, smirking sarcastically.

He'd received a copy of her current CIA dossier from their mole at the Pentagon that morning. *She's a clandestine operations agent now! Maybe I should call Abdul*, he considered.

No. The game will get a lot more lucrative with the Americans involved. I'll leverage my knowledge into a much fatter paycheck.

Berlin, Germany

Using pictures taken by the CIA at the Iranian border, CCD pictures taken at his hotel, and fingerprints found in the van near the marina, the German police identified Hafiz as the Muhlenberg bomber. They sent his fingerprints and picture through the Saudis to the Iranian government to see if they would cooperate in the investigation.

Iran immediately returned a dossier for the former soldier, along with emphatic declarations that they had nothing to do with the attack. Iran's willingness to cooperate behind the scenes convinced the German chancellor to delay a war-declaration vote in the *Bundestag*.

The war of words escalated between the countries when Germany's press revealed that Hafiz was a former Iranian soldier. Iran—using a backdoor channel through China—convinced the UN Security Council to delay a war vote.

Germany then diverted its attention to medical care for the injured and funerals for the 16,000 people who'd perished.

32. Rag Doll

Geneva, Switzerland

Beate called Rahim a few days after the Muhlenberg attack. "You said you worked at the UN when we were on the train together," she reminded him. "Is it possible to get a tour?"

"I would love to show you around," he said.

Beate placed her sweater on top of Rahim's bookshelf when she entered his office. She concealed a microdot video camera with a microphone on top of a book when she picked up her sweater after his tour.

Helmut installed a wireless receiver in a storage closet near Rahim's office. The receiver fed a modem that relayed the audio and video signals to their operations center next door to his apartment.

The CIA team was watching the feed when the visitor arrived at Rahim's UN office later that afternoon. The light-skinned Arab, a UN courier with a distinct British accent, handed Rahim a stack of papers from his diplomatic pouch.

Rahim locked them in his briefcase.

Helmut followed Rahim to the Geneva Botanical Gardens when he left his UN office that afternoon. Using binoculars, he watched Rahim remove an envelope from beneath a park bench. Rahim then returned to his penthouse apartment.

Beate, Helmut, and Sean watched the feed from the camera above Rahim's desk as he translated a set of mathematics problems into messages.

"That's a one-time-pad cipher," Helmut said. "He must have another mission."

Rahim made notes on a small piece of saliva-dissolvable paper after each translation. He placed the paper into his wallet, tore up the mathematics paper and OTP cipher, and flushed them down his toilet. He then wheeled out a portable dishwasher from his kitchen cabinet and deposited a second copy of his instructions in a safe.

"That's a good hiding place," Sean said. "I think the messages he decoded are wire-transfer instructions."

Helmut rewound the video feed they'd captured and wrote down the combination to the safe. "How do you know?"

"I recognize the number sequences," he replied. "I've done similar transfers hundreds of times." Sean paused. "I have an idea, but I'm not sure how to implement it."

"What are you thinking?" Beate said.

"We need to flush out Rahim's accomplices, right? His funds will never reach them if we change the destination accounts. I'm sure his accomplices will come looking for him when that happens."

Helmut nodded. "Then we'll follow the rats back to their caves."

"We'll need to change the account numbers on the paper in his wallet," Sean continued.

"I'll pipe some fentanyl gas into his apartment tonight," Helmut said. "We'll make copies of everything in his safe while he's asleep, and replace the instructions in his wallet with account numbers you specify."

"Do you have some accounts we can use?" Beate said.

Sean nodded. "Of course."

Helmut smiled. "You're a natural at this spy business, Mister McGowan."

Beate hugged Sean sideways. "Do you see why I like him?"

Helmut raised his eyebrows. "I thought you didn't go for spies."

She giggled. "I don't, but I do go for musicians."

Beate and Sean watched the display as Helmut, wearing a gas mask, entered Rahim's apartment. Helmut brought Rahim's wallet as well as everything in the safe back to the operations center.

Beate transcribed the wire transfer instructions Sean had specified onto a piece of saliva-dissolvable paper taken from the same notebook Rahim had used. They then started scanning the documents in the safe.

"This is a treasure trove," Beate said. "He's been making trades for years." She drew a quick breath. "Look at this!"

A cloud fell across Sean's face as he stared at the newspaper clippings of Emma's murder. An engagement ring fell out of the same manila envelope.

"It looks like you found Emma's murderer," Helmut said.

Sean picked up the ring and stared at it. "I need a gun," he said.

Helmut shook his head. "I know you're angry, but this isn't the time. We need to find out whom he's working with first. We'll take care of him later."

"That's a really nice ring," Beate said.

He handed it to her.

She pushed it onto her finger. It fit perfectly. "It's beautiful."

She handed it back. "You should save it for the girl you want to marry."

Sean dropped it into his pocket.

Helmut re-entered the apartment wearing a gas mask. He placed everything into the safe the way he'd found it—except for the ring—and deposited the modified wire-transfer instructions into Rahim's wallet.

Beate forwarded the document images they'd scanned to Langley for analysis.

Sean was napping on the couch when his cell phone rang an hour later. "Hi, Pankaj. It's good to hear from you. …Uh-huh. Contact Agent Hernandez from the FBI. He'll help us. I'll talk with you soon."

He hung up and faced Beate. "Someone is trying to hack into our computer systems in Boulder and Luxembourg again. They're using a router-hopping algorithm, and some goons in Boulder have been trying to recruit our programmers offering huge pay increases."

"Hernandez will take care of them," Beate said confidently. "I'll give him a call."

* * *

Rahim yawned when he woke up. He jumped when he looked at the clock. *That's the best sleep I've had in years, but now I have to hurry*, he told himself.

He packed quickly and hustled out of the apartment.

* * *

Helmut faced Beate. "You should stay here. I'll take Sean with me." He turned to Sean. "Assuming you're willing."

Sean stood up. "I'm more than willing."

Beate touched Helmut's wrist. "Take care of my man for me, okay?"

He smiled. "I will, although I've heard he's pretty good at taking care of himself."

Helmut and Sean sat in separate railcars behind Rahim in the train. Unbeknownst to them, Sergei sat several rows behind Rahim in the same railcar.

The train departed at 6:10 a.m. It pulled into *Bahnhof Lucerne* three hours later.

Helmut and Sean followed Rahim, separately, at a distance, while he visited two banks. Rahim boarded a train for Zurich sixty minutes later.

Helmut and Sean again sat in separate railcars behind Rahim.

* * *

Sergei recognized Helmut instantly when he spotted him following Rahim in Lucerne. Helmut had worked with Helmut decades earlier when he was a liaison agent between the KGB and the Stasi—East Germany's secret police. Helmut was a young recruit at the time.

I'll confront the arrogant bastard on the train to Zurich, he decided. *I should've killed him years ago when he sold out to the Americans. I'll take him out today after I find out what he's doing.*

He approached Helmut as the train pulled away from Lucerne. The muzzle of his gun was obvious beneath his trench coat. He stood a few feet away; close enough to be recognized, but far enough so Helmut couldn't tackle him. "Hello, old friend."

* * *

Helmut nodded. This can't be a coincidence after the pictures of Beate, he told himself.

Sergei motioned the barrel beneath his coat. "We need to talk. I'll follow you to the back of the train."

Sean ignored them as they passed.

Good job, Sean, Helmut observed. *Don't wait too long to come find me.*

* * *

A shiver ran down Sean's spine. He waited a moment and stood up. I don't have a gun. The guy following Helmut looks sinister with that scarred lip. He must be the agent that took Beate's picture.

Sean moved methodically to the back of the train, checking every bathroom along the way. The last car had an open metal platform abutting a mailroom. Sean put his ear to the door.

He heard Helmut scream. *Someone is beating him*, Sean realized.

He checked the door handle. *Locked.*

Sean braced his body against the railing for leverage, and plunged his foot into the handle.

The tae kwon do kick broke away the doorknob dislodging the door.

Bullets ricocheted on the metal around him as he fell to the platform.

"Sean. Come now!" Helmut yelled from inside.

Sean rushed in. He kicked the man in the groin and pounded him to the ground when he bent forward.

"Untie me," Helmut yelled. Blood was streaming from his forehead.

Sean started to untie the nylon ropes. He had to jump away when the man lunged for his gun. Sean's roundhouse kick dislodged the weapon.

The man crouched in a martial arts stance. He punched Sean in the chest.

Sean jumped high. His reverse-hook kick found the man's throat.

The man fell to the platform, writhing and gasping for air.

Sean shoved the gun into his pants and removed Helmut's ropes.

"Thanks," Helmut said as he stood up. He pulled a handkerchief from his pocket and wiped the blood from his forehead and eyes.

Helmut crouched over his quarry. "Now it's time for you to answer some questions, Sergei. Who sent you?"

"Screw you. I'm not telling you anything, you traitor. I should've killed you years ago, in Berlin."

Helmut pummeled Sergei's gut with his fists.

He then hog-tied Sergei's legs and arms with the nylon rope.

Sergei's coat pocket yielded a magazine for the Beretta. Helmut took the gun from Sean, loaded it, and handed it back.

"Have you ever shot anyone?" he asked Sean.

Sean shook his head. "What?"

"Shoot him in the knee!"

"Why?"

"This man has information we need. You must be willing to kill someone when you interrogate them, or they'll sense your cowardice."

Sergei smirked. "That's right. The traitor learned everything he knows from me."

"Not everything," Helmut said.

Helmut raised the gun in Sean's hand and squeezed the trigger.

Sergei's knee exploded in a tousled pulp of blood-red meat and bone. His screams were louder than the screeching rails below the platform outside.

"Your civilian training is over," Helmut yelled to Sean. "We can't waste time. We'll be in Zurich soon."

Sean helped Helmut drag Sergei out the door of the mailroom to the platform. Helmut tied a second rope around Sergei's ankles, and looped it over a baluster above the railing.

The train slowed to sixty miles an hour as it wound its way up the hilly terrain, buffeting the caboose side to side.

Helmut throttled Sergei's chest with his fists. "Who are you working for?"

"Screw you!" Sergei mouthed between screams.

Helmut yanked the rope using the baluster as a pulley. Sergei flipped upside down. Helmut pulled the rope, and shoved Sergei over the side of the railing with his foot.

Sergei thrashed like a kite in a windstorm as Helmut lowered him to the tracks.

"What are you doing?" Sean hollered.

Sergei, flopping around like a puppet, banged the side of the railcar, hard. Helmut pulled the rope.

Sean guided Sergei onto the platform and sat him upright. The hair and an ear on one side of Sergei's head were missing. His head was bleeding profusely.

Helmut leaned over him. "Who are you working for?" he screamed.

Sergei mouthed some words between his screams. "Abdul... Abdul!"

"What are you doing for him?" Helmut demanded.

Sergei flopped sideways onto the platform. Blood seeping from his knee and the side of his head streaked across the windswept platform.

"Watching... Rahim."

"Watching him for what?"

"The money... you bastard... the money."

"Tell me about Abdul. Where is he?"

"He's Egyptian," gasped Sergei. "He contacts me... I never know... where... we'll meet."

"What else?"

Sergei passed out before he could answer.

Helmut stood up. "Crap!"

"We need to get him to a hospital," Sean yelled.

Helmut shook his head. "There's no time. He's not going to make it anyhow. He's bleeding out."

Helmut removed Sergei's ropes, lifted him onto his shoulder, and dumped him over the railing.

Sergei's body bounced like a rag doll before it disappeared behind the train.

"What'd you do that for?" Sean yelled.

"The police will think it's a suicide," Helmut explained.

They cleaned themselves up in the bathroom and returned to their seats.

Rahim visited two banks in Zurich, boarded a train for Vaduz, Lichtenstein, where he visited two more banks, and reversed course to Basel for another two banks.

Sean and Helmut waited for Rahim down the street from Banque Lux while he made his last wire transfer of the day.

"I need to stay here to move the money around so the funds aren't traceable," Sean said.

"How much money are you talking about?" Helmut said.

"I'm guessing eighty billion, since he visited eight banks."

"I'm sure someone is going to be pissed when their money goes missing," Helmut remarked. "You should keep the money handy. We may need it to buy protection."

"I'll route it through several countries to one of our banks in Singapore."

Rahim exited the bank and raised his hand for a taxi.

"I'll follow Delacroix back to Geneva," Helmut said. "Thanks for helping me out back there. You did well."

"My adrenaline is still pumping. Is it always like that?"

"It's mostly a waiting game. Patience is as important as guts and tradecraft. Are you coming back to Geneva when you finish? I imagine Rahim will be getting some visitors soon."

"Yes, but then I need to get back to New York. Our systems are being attacked again."

Helmut put his hand out. A cab stopped.

He turned to Sean before he got in. "Your skills as a musician could come in handy if you decide to do some craftwork for us in the future. It's a great cover, and I'm sure Beate would appreciate your company."

"I have a business to run," Sean said. "I also have Angela and Sarah to think about."

Helmut smiled irreverently. "You only live once, McGowan. Think about it. Being a spook is a lot more exciting than banking… and you're a natural. Perhaps this is your destiny."

"Have you heard anything from your Russian friends about my father?"

"Not yet. By the way, they're not really my friends. I'll let you know if I do though."

Helmut slid into the back of the cab and disappeared.

33. Fingers

Hamburg, Germany

Abdul's emergency cell phone rang. He rose from his berth on the lower deck of his yacht and picked it up. "Hello?"

"One of your traders has gone rogue!" Nikolai yelled. "His money never showed up in our accounts."

"Are you sure?"

"Hell, yes, I'm sure!"

"Which trader?"

"Delacroix!" Nikolai fumed.

"He doesn't have the balls to do something like that. Sergei didn't check in with me last night, though. Maybe they're in it together."

"Get down to Geneva and find them! Call me when you get there."

Abdul arrived at Rahim's apartment later that evening. "Where's Sergei?" he yelled as he barged in brandishing his gun.

"There's no one here," Rahim replied recoiling fearfully. "What's wrong?"

Rahim followed Abdul as he moved cautiously room-to-room, checking under beds and in closets.

Beate captured Abdul's image on her display screen and sent it to Langley for analysis.

"We need to follow this guy when he leaves," Helmut said. "I asked Brian—from MI6—for his help earlier today. He owes me a favor. I worked with him at Thames House tracking down terrorists after the London Underground bombings. His team is positioned outside."

Good," Beate said. "I'll send him a picture, too."

Brian replied with a text message.

"Brian's MI6 team is watching the exits," she said.

Her phone beeped. She spoke with Langley and hung up.

"I think we identified the guy," she said. "His name is Abdul. He was a CIA subcontractor in the eighties. He showed up on some CCTV scans a few days before the Madrid Metro and London Underground attacks."

Helmut's jawbone pulsed. "One of ours?"

"I guess so," she replied.

Abdul pushed Rahim into the kitchen and forced him to sit down. "Where's the money?" Abdul yelled.

Rahim trembled. "I transferred it… just as the instructions said."

Abdul holstered his pistol. He retrieved his briefcase from the living room, opened it, and pulled out a hatchet.

"Where's the money," he said, swinging the hatchet menacingly, "and where's Sergei?"

"I didn't see him. I made the transfers exactly as I was instructed."

"Don't screw with me! Are you working with the CIA?"

Rahim's lips quivered. "What… what do you mean?"

Abdul pulled out his smartphone and showed Rahim a picture of Beate. "Do you recognize her?"

Rahim nodded. "She sat across from me during my trip from Basel. I gave her a tour of the UN when she called me."

"She's a CIA agent."

Rahim's jaw slackened. "What… what should I do?"

"I need you to kill her," Abdul ordered.

"Crap!" Beate stood up.

"That's a recent picture," Helmut said, "from your personnel file at Langley. I think we must have a mole. That's why I asked MI6 to help us."

Abdul grabbed Rahim's hand and placed it flat on the table. "Where's the money?" he demanded.

"I don't have it!" Rahim insisted.

Abdul wielded the ax. Thwack!

Two of Rahim's fingers jumped away from the table like acrobats from a trampoline. His screams pierced the walls. Fountains of blood spurted from his hand as he shrieked in agony.

"Stop lying!" Abdul screamed. "Do I need to chop off your other hand to get to the truth?"

Beate looked at Helmut. "Can't we do something?"

Helmut didn't flinch. "Let's see what else Abdul has to say."

Beate looked at Sean questioningly.

"Sergei told us about Abdul on the train," Sean said, staring passively at the display. "Besides... Rahim killed Emma."

"I bet this is the same guy that talked to Riza," she said to Helmut, "the train bomber we took out in Hamburg a few years ago."

Helmut nodded. "I remember."

"The instructions... are in my wallet," Rahim squealed. "Check them."

Abdul pulled out Rahim's wallet. He picked up his phone and dialed.

Beate typed. "I'll run the phone number through the system."

"I have the account numbers Rahim used for the transfers," Abdul said. He moved into the living room away from Rahim's screams. "He had a copy in his wallet."

Beate frowned. "It's a burner phone. The SIM card was purchased in France."

Abdul relayed the bank account numbers. "Uh-huh. I will."

Abdul ended the call, returned to the kitchen, and pulled a can of lighter fluid from his briefcase. "Get up."

He steered Rahim through the living room to the balcony. "Turn around."

Rahim leaned against the railing. The blood draining from his hand formed a pool beneath his feet.

Abdul sprayed lighter fluid over Rahim's clothes.

"What... are you... doing?" Rahim screamed.

Abdul lit a match. "I need you to take out the female CIA agent. Can you do that?"

"What about... our *jihad*?"

"Are you stupid?" Abdul scoffed. "Our *jihad* is about money, not politics."

Confusion flickered across Rahim's forehead. The match went out. Rahim's face twisted with pain. "I won't... kill... again."

"I think he just confessed to Emma's murder," Sean whispered.

Rahim turned around. Shaking and writhing, holding his wrist, he stared out across the lake at the Alps.

Abdul lit another match. "I'll see you in hell, then." He tossed the match.

Rahim's clothes burst into flames. A drawn-out scream punctured the air as he toppled over the railing.

* * *

Rahim's body trailed flames like a comet as he plunged to the concrete.

Brian, the black, forty-two-year-old case officer managing the four-person MI6 team looked away from the burning carcass. *I'll never forget the sickening splat of the body smacking the sidewalk* he contemplated.

Brian ran his hand over his shaved head, a hairstyle he'd adopted in the British Royal Marines before he joined Her Majesty's Secret Service. He held his nose to block the stench of burning flesh as he dialed Helmut.

"What happened?" Brian asked.

"Abdul just killed Rahim," Helmut said. "Make sure you don't lose him. He's on his way down."

"It's a real mess down here. The guy's still burning. I hear sirens. You'd better get out of there."

"I'll be down soon. Make sure Abdul doesn't spot you. He's our only lead to the financiers behind the 9/11 terrorist strikes. Don't tell anyone at Langley you're involved, okay?"

"Why?" Brian asked, alarmed. "Have you been compromised?"

"I'm not sure. We may have a mole. You okay reporting to me for now?"

"Affirmative."

"Can we use your MI6 satellites to track him?"

"Sure, but our capabilities beyond Europe are limited."

"I hope we'll get that sorted out before it's an issue." Helmut looked at Beate as he spoke. "That's one of the problems with combining databases. Everyone that contributes wants access, so it's hard to keep the rats out of the kitchen. I'll see you soon." He hung up.

"Can you get us cleared out of here while I catch up with Brian?" he said to Beate. "I don't want to lose him."

"Yes, sir."

The MI6 team followed Abdul to the airport. From there, a British satellite tracked his private jet to Hamburg, where Helmut's CIA operatives picked up his trail. They followed him to a yacht moored at the Hamburger Yacht Club and began around-the-clock surveillance.

Sean returned to New York the next morning.

Beate joined Helmut and his team in Hamburg.

Berlin, Germany

A spectroscopic chemical analysis of debris from the Muhlenberg bombsite conducted by German scientists concluded that the fissionable material in the bomb came from the Polygon—the Semipalatinsk nuclear test site in Kazakhstan that was once part of the Soviet Union. The Russian president promised he'd do everything he could to track down the thieves after he confirmed that the bomb had in fact, been there's.

Germany accepted Russia's offer to provide medical aid. The next morning three transports filled with supplies along with fifty doctors and seventy nurses landed in Frankfurt, joining hundreds of other medical professionals from around the world assisting the victims of the terrible catastrophe.

New York City—One week later

Agent Hernandez met with Sean and Angela at their Broad Street headquarters—a building they'd recently purchased. The top floor now housed an executive suite they shared between their separate living quarters, and a nursery for Sarah. They sat next to each other on a couch across from Hernandez.

"We've tracked down the recruiters chasing your people in Boulder," Hernandez said. "They were hired by Hartfield's contact at the casino in New Jersey. The manager didn't know much when we questioned him. He told us he receives a bag of cash along with his instructions anonymously. Mikhail Volkov, a former KGB officer, owns the casino. Judge Richter implicated Volkov during his plea-bargain negotiations."

"I've met Mikhail's brother," Angela said. "Vladimir. He's taken two runs at our bank in the last ten years. I haven't heard anything from him recently, though, since just before my parents were murdered."

Hernandez made a note. "They're probably working together."

"What about the hackers trying to break into our systems?" Sean asked.

"We're working on that with the NSA. The attacks are coming from across the globe. It's been difficult to pinpoint the source because they're using router hopping."

Hernandez raised his eyebrows at Sean. "Have you seen Agent Hartfield? We tracked him as far as Puerto Vallarta before he disappeared. That's where you went on vacation, wasn't it?"

Sean leaned back on the couch. "I'm not going to breach a national security oath I took at Langley to answer that. I will say that you don't need to worry about him any longer."

"That's what I thought." Hernandez rose to leave. "I'll get back to you when I have more information about the hackers."

Angela reached for his hand. "Thanks, Oscar. We appreciate your help."

"I hear congratulations are in order. May I see the baby?"

"Of course," she said.

Hernandez followed the couple into the nursery. Emily, Sarah's nanny, was sitting next to the crib reading a book. Sarah was asleep.

"She's really beautiful," Hernandez whispered as they stared at Sarah.

Angela hugged Sean. "We think so. She looks a lot like Sean, don't you think?"

Hernandez grinned. "She's a lot better looking than that."

34. Pearl

Greenwich, Connecticut—Mid-June

John Napoleon and Judith were sitting at the round table in the conference room when Vladimir arrived. Napoleon motioned for him to take a seat between them. Judith stared back aloofly when Vladimir looked at her for reassurance.

Napoleon's demeanor was placid and devoid of emotion, but his words were not. "How could you let this happen?"

"One of our traders, Rahim Delacroix, transferred the money to his own account," Vladimir explained. "He's been eliminated. We're trying to track down the funds he stole, but he left a convoluted trail through several countries. He was a lot more sophisticated than we thought. The Swiss police found Sergei—the former KGB agent we hired to watch Rahim—on the train tracks outside Zurich. Rahim must've killed him and thrown him overboard."

"This is unacceptable," Napoleon replied. "You told us we'd make eighteen billion on our two-billion-dollar investment. I've given you a month to get this resolved. I want the other four billion you owe us by the end of the week. I'm holding you personally responsible."

Vladimir sneered. "What about the sixteen billion dollars I've already given you?"

"You promised us another four, and that's what I expect. Take it out of your own profits."

Napoleon slid him a sheet of paper. "I want the deposit placed into this account by noon on Friday."

Napoleon pushed a button. His bodyguards instantly entered the room. They escorted Vladimir to the door. Judith stayed.

Vladimir gritted his teeth. *Mikhail will be furious we have to pay Napoleon from our own funds.*

Nice, France

Nikolai didn't sleep after he received an e-mail the previous evening with an attached image showing Mikhail depositing a letter into the wall-safe lockbox. He'd received another e-mail that morning when Yvonna retrieved the message.

I've given her plenty of time to call me he deliberated. *She promised to let me know if Mikhail contacted her again. I've exhausted my patience.*

He dialed her number. She didn't answer.

Annapolis, Maryland

Yvonna turned sideways to admire her rock-hard shoulders, firm butt, and slim waist in the mirror. *My personal trainer was worth every cent*, she decided, *the way he sculpted me down to 125 pounds. I look damn good for a six-foot tall woman who's brought three children into the world.*

Her heart palpitated with anticipation. *I feel like an Olympic runner in a starting block*, she reflected.

She looked over her shoulder at her exposed back in the mirror. *This titillating black strapless dress will surely make an impression.* She smirked. *He won't be getting any. If I can deflect the advances of the cute twenty-somethings at the gym, I can certainly fend off Mikhail.*

This mission is for Tatiana, she reminded herself. *Mikhail needs to put her in his will. Tatiana is his progeny after all, and the rightful heir to his fortune, not Vladimir.*

She brushed her hair, wrapped it in a pearled, silver-black Russian-style snood, and pinned it at the back.

Mikhail has never been one to talk much about family, she recalled. *When he does mention Vladimir—whom he always refers to as "the smart one"—he quickly changes the subject.*

I wonder if Vladimir ever told Mikhail about our encounter at the Russian Embassy Christmas party, she reminisced.

She'd guessed it might be Vladimir when she'd spotted him from the other side of the reception hall. His facial features were similar, yet distinctly different. He was a bit shorter, perhaps 6'3", and more muscular than Mikhail.

"My name is Vladimir," he'd said as their paths merged at the bar.

He's attractive, but not in the brazen way Mikhail is, she'd decided.

"How do you do?" she'd said, returning his handshake. "My name is Yvonna."

His face had lit up. She'd ordered Scotch on the rocks for Nikolai and a glass of champagne for herself. Vladimir asked for vodka.

"Why are you drinking Scotch?" he'd asked. "I thought vodka was our national pleasure."

She'd nodded in Nikolai's direction. "It's for my husband." Nikolai was wearing a black tuxedo, talking with the Russian ambassador.

Her gaze had instantly returned to the bartender. "I need to watch… to make sure no one spikes his drink."

"Is your husband named Nikolai?" Vladimir had asked.

"Yes. How did you know?"

"He works for my brother."

She'd turned away from his steel-blue gaze to survey the decor. The elegant reception hall housed enough early nineteenth-century Russian furniture and hand-woven Iranian carpets to make even the most gracious antiquarian blush. Several massive, crystal chandeliers dangled beneath an elegant rococo ceiling painted with scenes from the Russian Revolution.

Vladimir was staring at her when she turned towards the bar. *He has the same eyes as Mikhail.*

"I know your brother," she'd said.

"He's spoken of you."

"Can you keep a secret?"

"Of course."

He'd said it without thinking, perhaps pleased by her flirtatious tone.

"Nikolai doesn't drink vodka around other Russians anymore. It brings up bad memories for him about a night in Kabul." Her gaze hardened. "The night he met Mikhail."

Vladimir's stare told me all I needed to know, she recalled.

Their eyes had swerved to some inebriated guests standing around the grand piano singing a Mussorgsky song called "Trepak."

"I'm celebrating tonight," she'd said. *It felt right to share something with him. We are family after all, even if he doesn't know it.*

"What's the special occasion?"

"I just finished my master's degree at the University of Maryland. Pretty good wouldn't you say, for a girl whose schooling ended at the age of twelve in the old Soviet Republic?"

"That's quite an accomplishment. Congratulations!"

They'd touched glasses and sipped their drinks. Then she'd joined Nikolai and the other revelers around the piano.

Vladimir had disappeared when she looked around the room for him later that evening.

Yvonna placed pictures of Tatiana into her purse and readied herself to leave. *I wonder what Vladimir would think about being an uncle.*

Her cell phone rang. She looked at it. *Nikolai again.*

She didn't answer. *I'll have to hurry to make it to Baltimore on time. Mikhail hates it when I'm late.*

McLean, Virginia

Clara DeLuca had immediately wanted to become a ballerina after she witnessed her first Tchaikovsky Nutcracker ballet performance. The enchanting tale, colorful costumes, vibrant orchestral melodies, and perfect pirouettes were all she dreamed about for months.

Her parents finally capitulated to her pestering a few weeks later, agreeing to pay for ballet lessons if she quit gymnastics. She continued her dance classes until she was thirteen. That's when the threads of her childhood began to unravel.

Her parent's acrimonious relationship ended with divorce. Her father—who'd always affectionately called her "my little Italiana ballerina,"—moved to California to "start a new life."

The next blow came a few weeks later when her ballet instructor told her mother, "She'll never be a ballerina. The hourglass shape her body is taking now that she's sprouted breasts just won't be right for the stage. I'm sorry. It's better not to waste your money."

Her mother terminated the ballet lessons the next day.

Clara, now nineteen, spotted the advertisement for the modeling job in her Community College newspaper. Grace, the recruiter that answered when she'd called, said dance and gymnastics were important skills for a model.

She met Grace at a strip mall in McLean, Virginia, the next day. "You'll be perfect," Grace said as she walked in. "Let's get started."

Grace ushered Clara into a back room. The walls, covered with mirrors, surrounded a raised stage impaled by a floor-to-ceiling dancer's pole next to several shelves stacked with costumes and accessories: Hats, nurse uniforms, business suits, whips, flight attendant uniforms, French maid outfits, female police uniforms, a cat woman suit, and a Catholic nun cloak and habit.

Clara folded her arms. "What is this?"

Grace pointed at the stage. "Take your clothes off... up there."

Clara didn't move. Grace turned on a stereo. A bluesy rock song sprang to life.

"Take your clothes off to the music," Grace said, "facing me."

The song *"Leave Your Hat On"* by Joe Cocker pumped through the loudspeakers on each side of the stage.

Clara pursed her lips with an incredulous stare. "I thought you were looking for models."

Grace smiled amiably. "I am, but our models need to dance. That's what I told you on the phone. You'll be perfect. Men will love your luscious curves and long, dark hair. The pay's very good. You take your clothes off every day, don't you? It's not that hard. I need to see what you look like when you're dancing naked. It's part of the job."

Clara stepped slowly up onto the dance floor.

"It'll be okay," Grace said. "Just hold on to the pole and dance around."

Clara swayed slowly to the music, unbuttoning her shirt.

Grace flipped off the stereo. She stepped up on the stage.

"Don't you want to be a model?" she asked. "Do you need drugs to loosen up? I can't use you if you do. We need someone who's straight."

"I don't do that stuff," Clara told her.

"Good. Now let's try this again. Just watch me, and do what I do."

Clara's face paled. "I'm not sure I can do this."

"You'll make a lot of money... working just a few hours a week. You're a very sexy girl, so you have that going for you."

Grace restarted the song. "Sway back and forth like this." She began to unbutton her blouse. "We'll do this together. Just follow me."

Clara emulated Grace. They giggled when they dropped their blouses to the floor.

Grace unzipped her skirt. "You're doing fine."

Clara let her body flow with the music, and soon they were both naked.

"Show me some of your gymnastic and ballet moves using the pole," Grace said. "Perhaps you can teach me a thing or two."

Clara pulled herself up effortlessly to the top of the pole. Holding herself by her legs, she flipped backwards. She held the contorted position without a tremble for twenty seconds.

"Ah," Grace said. "Men will love that. You're going to make a lot of money."

Both women were on their hands and knees wearing nothing but hats when the song ended.

Grace gathered up her clothes. "That's how it's done."

Clara dressed quickly. "I'm not sure I want to do this," she protested. "Where will I be dancing? Who's in the audience? How much do you pay? Will I be working for *you*?"

Grace pulled up her panties. "You'll be working at a gentlemen's club. You'll be a dancer, but your main job will be gathering information."

Clara's eyebrows furrowed with concern. "A gentlemen's club? Is that the same thing as a strip club?"

Grace chuckled. "Yes, except the pay is better."

Clara stepped quickly to the door after she'd buttoned her blouse. "I thought you were looking for models?" she asked again.

"You will be a model; you'll just be dancing while you're modeling."

"I don't want to do that."

"You'll make three to four hundred in tips every night with those nice breasts of yours, and I'll pay you five hundred dollars every time I ask you to keep an eye on someone. I'll send a picture to your smartphone when we need your help. You'll be serving your country, too—as a subcontractor for a government agency. We'll pay your phone bill from now on, and give you two thousand a month for housing and a car."

I don't want to be a stripper, but I need the money, Clara decided. *Working six nights a week as a waitress to pay for college just isn't working. I'm about ready to give up.*

"I'll do it… but just for one night," she said. "If I don't like it, I'll quit."

Grace nodded. "Of course."

* * *

It'll be impossible for Clara to avoid the lure of easy money and men's appreciative stares, Grace envisaged. *We'll shower her with hundreds of dollars in tips her first couple of nights to make sure. Men—and the occasional adventurous woman—love the Agency-funded assignment.*

"It's an easy job," Grace continued, "we'll even teach you how to flirt with a subject to gather information. Ask him questions like where he's from, what his job is, where he's staying, how long he'll be here… that sort of thing. Men think you're interesting when you ask them about their work. Then call me with a report. Can you start tomorrow?"

Clara looked at the floor. "I think so."

"It's very important that you never tell anyone we've met," Grace told her. "Your safety will depend on it. Can you do that? Your government will be grateful for your service."

I know the "doing it for your country" pitch will close the deal, Grace reflected. *Clara's father was in the army, and military kids are inclined to be patriotic. I know. The Agency recruited me the same way twenty-five years ago.*

"You'll be working at the *Taste of Heaven* gentlemen's club on Wisconsin Avenue in northwest DC," Grace continued. "Go there tomorrow. Tell the bartender you're looking for work as a dancer. Don't worry. He'll hire you immediately when he sees you naked."

Grace pointed to the shelves. "Take some of those outfits. Just watch the other girls and do what they do. It's not rocket science."

Grace opened her purse and handed Clara a wad of crisp hundred-dollar bills. "Here's a thousand dollars. Go buy yourself some nice lingerie."

Clara stared at the money. A gnawing voice inside urged her to *"run!"* She reached for the bills and stuffed them into her purse.

"You need to listen to your mark carefully when we give you an assignment," Grace said.

"No problem. I know how to flirt, even though I'm a virgin."

Grace's eyes widened. "Your cover name will be Pearl."

"OK."

She handed Clara a business card printed with nothing but a phone number. "Call me after the audition. Here's my private line."

"I will." Clara stuffed the card into her purse and hustled away.

Baltimore, Maryland

Mikhail looked down at the harbor from the window of the Cleopatra Suite. *We'll be powerful beyond our wildest dreams after the Red Horseman project in DC*, he reflected... *and Nikolai will be dead.*

A dilemma crept into his thoughts: *What should I do with Yvonna?*

Eliminate her? That would be the logical thing to do, or perhaps she could become a madam at one of my whorehouses.

A knock on the door broke his musings.

Yvonna entered with her head held high.

He hugged her and stared into her eyes. "It's good to see you. You look more gorgeous than ever."

He stroked her ear with his thumb. Their lips found refuge.

He grabbed the back of her neck, gently but firmly, beneath her snood, and pushed her down to her knees. She looked up at him as she unbuckled his pants. Neither of them said a word as she kissed him.

* * *

Yvonna watched from beneath a sheet as Mikhail got dressed an hour later. He bent to her lips for a quick kiss. The door closed with a definitive clunk.

Maybe I should have said something about Tatiana, she considered. *I guess he would've brought it up if he wanted to talk about her.*

* * *

Mikhail made his decision as the elevator dropped from the top-floor to the lobby. *She'll be an excellent madam. Her farm outside Annapolis will be perfect for a stable, and she has a ready-made market nearby—the Naval Academy.*

Her girls can also gather military intelligence for us. I should've thought of this before.

35. Dirty Dancer

Hamburg, Germany—Late June

Helmut's surveillance team in Hamburg gathered several facts about Abdul after observing him for six weeks: He was a heavy drinker; he had a predilection for big-bosomed women; and he enjoyed rhythm and blues music.

He'd prey on females at music venues around the city. When he didn't find someone to slake his appetite, which was usually the case, he'd hire a prostitute in Hamburg's red-light district.

Abdul was also very careful. He used one-time burner phones and walked around the marina while he talked, which made it difficult to eavesdrop on his conversations. Helmut's team did capture a few words once using a long-range laser microphone that picked up vibrations off windows: Washington Mall, Red Horseman, folk festival, and Taste of Heaven.

A CIA counterespionage team at Langley discovered the mole that had siphoned Beate's file: a college student hired by the Defense Intelligence Agency as an intern. A DIA security team arrested the young man when he brought data out of the Pentagon on a miniature flash drive.

Helmut brought his CIA satellite resources back online after the arrest. It was just in time, too. Abdul boarded a flight for the Bahamas a few days later using a fake German passport. The CIA could have picked him up for questioning, but they decided instead to see where he was going.

A surveillance team at the Grand Bahama International Airport followed him through customs until he boarded a flight from Freeport to Washington Dulles. The FBI tracked him from there to a hotel in Bethesda, Maryland.

The hotel surveillance team hadn't noticed him doing anything unusual before he disappeared. The cameras they planted in his room were staring at an empty bed when the house cleaner came into his room on July 2. He'd vanished without a trace.

Greenwich, Connecticut—July 3

The Protectorate sat in a circle around the conference room table. Napoleon called the meeting to order.

Vladimir stood up to present his project update.

Napoleon interrupted before Vladimir had a chance to speak. "Are you sure you can handle the Red Horseman project? I'll relieve you if you can't."

Vladimir told himself to keep calm. "Being relieved" was tantamount to resigning, which was a death sentence.

"No one ever really resigns," Judith had told him when he brought the idea up with her. "Someone tried to once. They disappeared a few days later. Joining the Protectorate is a lifetime commitment."

Vladimir ignored the queasy feeling in his stomach. "Everything is ready," he said confidently.

"Have you fulfilled our option orders?" General Wu said.

"Yes. We'll make over three hundred and sixty billion dollars."

"Have you tracked down the money Delacroix stole?" Napoleon said.

"We're looking for the CIA agent he met on the train. Her name is Beate Nicholson. We think they were collaborating. Our mole inside the Pentagon wasn't able to locate her before his arrest. We'll extract what she knows about the money when we find her, by torture if necessary."

The members nodded their assent.

Annapolis, Maryland

Nikolai didn't say much to Yvonna when he returned from Nice. He stayed in his yacht except when he came into the house to eat.

The tenuous threads of trust I tried to weave with Yvonna are now irretrievably torn, he kept reminding himself, *but I need to get the Red Horseman project behind me before I file for divorce. I'll handle things civilly when the time comes. It'll be better for Tatiana that way.*

"Mikhail will be coming here to see me tomorrow morning," Nikolai announced to Yvonna. "He'll be here at ten o'clock."

* * *

Nikolai had to ask Yvonna twice if she'd make coffee for them. His question registered the second time like a curtain opening in a dark room.

"Oh... sure," she answered.

Nikolai turned to face her at the kitchen door as he prepared to leave. "Will Tatiana be around tomorrow? It might be interesting for her to meet one of our countrymen from the old days."

"I'll make sure she stops by to say hello," she assured him.

Nikolai studied her carefully. "Good. I'll be home late tonight."

The screen door snapped as he walked out. She didn't ask him where he was going.

Washington, DC

The FBI's Washington Field Office Joint Terrorism Task Force hosted a meeting that afternoon attended by representatives from the Department of Homeland Security, the NSA, DIA, CIA, the Secret Service, and District of Columbia Police Department. The men and women sat around a large oval table staring at an image of Abdul on the screen.

Several agencies had wanted to detain Abdul when he landed at Dulles Airport a few days earlier, but other agencies felt differently. "We need to identify his accomplices to prevent an imminent attack," several members had argued. "He's a hardened agent. He'll be hard to break, even with enhanced interrogation techniques like waterboarding."

Everyone was upset now that he'd gone missing. The recriminations were loud and vocal. The Task Force drafted a memo to the president once their anger subsided, recommending that he cancel DC's Fourth of July celebration.

"I won't be held hostage by unsubstantiated fears," the president told his national security advisor. "I need facts."

The White House did issue a directive to law-enforcement agencies across the country ordering them to increase security at their Independence Day events. The US Army, Navy SEALs, and Marine Corps subsequently transferred an additional fifty sharpshooters to Washington DC to patrol rooftops near the Mall. Each of the men and women were distinguished riflemen with expert marksmanship skills.

* * *

Beate hovered over Sean, spotting him while he bench-pressed a large barbell in the exercise room at his DC hotel. He pushed the heavy weight into its bracket and sat up. "I have an idea," he said.

Beate picked up a small dumbbell and began bicep curls. "What's that?"

"I can keep an eye out for Abdul from the stage of one of the performance venues. They have live music at the Folklife Festival on the Mall. Didn't your colleagues in Hamburg say that they followed him to several rhythm and blues music clubs?"

"That's too dangerous," she protested. "What if he sees you?"

"I doubt that he knows who I am."

Beate placed her dumbbell back on its shelf. "Perhaps I can assist one of the rooftop sharpshooter teams." *That way I can keep an eye on you,* she envisaged.

"I'll need some help getting into a band playing that kind of music on such short notice. Do you have any idea how to make that happen? I need to rehearse with them at least once."

"I'll ask my director to call the White House," she said. "It'll be hard for any band to ignore a request from the West Wing."

Beate made several calls when they returned to Sean's room.

A Marine Corps gunnery sergeant from Quantico called her back a few minutes later. "You can join my team if you re-qualify at our shooting range tomorrow," he said. "We're patrolling the rooftop of the Smithsonian Castle across from one of the performance stages."

"That's perfect," she said.

It took two hours to get an answer for Sean's request to play in a band. Charles White, the founder of *The Ebony All Stars*—DC's best-known rhythm and blues band—was disinclined to take on a new member for a number of reasons. He finally agreed to give Sean an audition after a second call from the White House chief of staff.

Charles wasn't happy when Sean called him. "Television stations across the country will be broadcasting our performance of '*The Star Spangled Banner*' before the fireworks," Charles said. "If you don't make the cut, you're out. I don't want an amateur with a bucket list fouling things up."

"I understand," Sean said. "I don't think you'll be disappointed."

The air dripped with tension when Sean entered Charles's practice room in Oxen Hill, Maryland, that afternoon. *I'd leave now if I didn't have an important mission*, Sean reminded himself. *I don't want to play music with people that don't want me.*

"You'll need to leave if you can't hack it," Charles told Sean in front of his band members.

"I understand, Charles," Sean said. "I'll leave if I can't add something to the sound. Just let me know."

The ten-member ensemble studied Sean with gelatinous skepticism as he picked up his alto saxophone. The only friendly vibes came from the three female singers, who whispered and giggled as they smiled at him.

Maybe this is a mistake, Sean realized. *I'll be the only white man in The Ebony All Stars. The band's name has an obvious ambiance. Changing it to The Ebony and Ivory All Stars just won't do.*

Charles handed Sean a chart book. He called out a song and gave the band a four count.

Sean scrambled to find his place in the music as the band began to play. *Crap*, he realized. *Charles gave me a book with parts written for a B flat tenor saxophone instead my E flat alto saxophone. Good thing I can sight-read and transpose at the same time.*

He found the tune, veered his gaze down the page, and nailed the rest of the notes for the remainder of the song. The musicians around him grew a fraction warmer when they finished. *I think they know what Charles just did*, Sean concluded. *He tried to force me out.*

The band rehearsed another twenty songs. Sean transposed everything on the fly without complaining, playing all his parts perfectly without missing a note. Everyone except Charles was grinning at him.

Charles reviewed the logistics for the performance on the Mall and concluded the practice.

"Do you guys ever play jazz?" Sean asked.

Charles raised his trumpet and answered with a blazingly fast rendition of Miles Davis's *"Four."*

Sean joined in, matching him note for note. The rest of the band began to play. After a tumultuous ten-minute jam, with everyone trading solos—including the ladies, who did some tremendous scat-singing improvisations—they ended the song with a raucous climax. Even Charles was smiling when they finished.

"We'll just call this *Affirmative Action*," Charles said as they put their instruments away.

The band members laughed.

"What do you think, folks?" Charles continued. "Did he pass the audition?"

"Yeah, sure, glad to have him," the musicians chimed in.

One of the singers—a large, beautiful woman named Maheila with a voice powerful enough to fill a stadium—came over to Sean and hugged him. "I think we should keep him, Charles. He's kind of cute."

Sean blushed as he returned her hug. She was the star. The TV cameras would focus on her while the band played the national anthem.

Charles laughed. "Be careful there, Sean. She's a lot of woman."

"He could be your token political appointment," she said, "if anyone asks why you have a white boy in the band."

Sean smiled. "Actually, I'm Irish-American. I'm not sure what the quota for that is."

Charles grinned. "Duly noted. What a great country this is, where people have so many opportunities regardless of the color of their skin."

Everyone laughed.

"Yes, it is," Sean said. "Seriously, though, although I'm going to enjoy playing music with you tomorrow, the real reason I'm here is it to look for someone from the stage... someone dangerous. It's a long shot. We know he likes rhythm and blues music."

The musicians' smiles melted as they circled around him.

"Tell us more," Charles said.

"We don't want to alarm anyone," Sean continued. "Please be discreet with what I'm about to say, but there may be a terrorist lurking in the crowd. I'll be looking for him while we play. I'll need to leave quickly if I spot him."

"How can we help?" Charles said. "We're aware of the inherent dangers of our city. We aren't going to let terrorists chase us into hiding with our tails between our legs."

The band members nodded their agreement.

"The stage is a unique vantage point," Sean explained. "Just ignore me if I have to leave in a hurry. We don't want to alarm anyone. I'll just slip off the back of the stage if I spot him."

Charles smiled. "We will. I'm glad you passed the audition on your own merits, rather than because of a mandate from the White House."

"Let's just have fun," Sean said, trying to lighten the mood. "I probably won't even see the guy. Try not to worry. This is an important night for your band. There's no need to say anything about me to the audience, either. Just do what you normally do, okay?"

Charles shook his hand. "I understand."

Sean reciprocated, using the soul handshake he'd learned from his African-American Spartacus brothers at the prison.

Charles addressed his band. "What do you say we go to the tavern down the street to anoint our newest member?"

Sean was the only white man when they entered the bar. Being with the band gave him an instant pass, negating the enmity he would have faced if he'd entered on his own.

I'm comfortable enough, he decided. *I'm used to being a minority. I was the only white kid—other than my sister—in the trailer park where we grew up in Santa Fe.*

Washington, DC

Pearl had just finished her three-song strip on stage two at the *Taste of Heaven* in DC when Grace's text came in. She gathered up her dollars, pulled on her bra and panties, and headed to the dressing room carrying her nurse's costume.

Grace sent a picture attached to her text of a heavy-set Arabic man, about sixty-years-old, with thin hair and dark-black eyes. The message was simple and to the point:

Be careful! Let me know immediately if you see him.

Pearl texted back:

He's been following me from stage to stage, licking his lips. He makes me uncomfortable.

Grace offered encouragement:

We'll put some folks outside to follow him when he leaves.

Pearl offered more details in her reply:

He propositioned me twice. His last offer was for a thousand dollars. He's given me two hundred in tips.

Walking around the stage on my hands to Aerosmith's 'Walk This Way' obviously impressed him, she speculated.

Grace responded with a warning:

Whatever you do, don't go home with him!

* * *

Nikolai entered the back door of the Taste of Heaven wearing a fake beard and a longhaired wig. *I'm not surprised to see Abdul in front of one of the stripper stages,* he reflected. *I'll finish my business with Mikhail before I talk with him.*

Mikhail dismissed the manager when Nikolai entered the office. The manager closed the door as Nikolai sat down.

"I'd like you to review tomorrow's plan," Mikhail said.

"Everything is ready. I buried the launch tripod, bazooka, and radiation-hardened case containing the bomb beneath the Venezuelan Folk Festival tent last night. The best Geiger counters in the world won't detect the nuke until Abdul removes it from its case."

"What about the Venezuelans?" Mikhail asked.

"They'll be attending a party at their embassy tomorrow night. Abdul will cut the bottom of the tent, set up the tripod and bazooka, and mount the bomb. He'll pull on a rope to open the side of the tent just before he fires. The payload will be programmed to explode a hundred feet above the Washington Monument."

"*Da.* Sounds like you're ready."

Nikolai took a deep breath. "I want to review our arrangement."

Mikhail frowned. "What arrangement?"

"The agreement we discussed last week, where you said you'd let me move on with my life in exchange for the two remaining nukes. You're still coming by to pick them up tomorrow morning, aren't you?"

"*Da*," Mikhail said irritably. "I'll need to borrow your yacht to transport the weapons. I'll return it to you on the fifth."

"And then you'll leave me and my family alone, right?" Nikolai pressed.

Mikhail stared. "That's what I said I'd do, isn't it?"

"And your brother, Vladimir—he's agreed to this too?"

"*Da*. Send Abdul up here when you leave."

Nikolai bounded down the steps and took a seat. Abdul was eyeing a beautiful young woman who'd just removed her bra.

Nikolai looked away. *She's the same age as Tatiana*, he discerned. *I would never exploit young women like this the way I did at Semipalatinsk now that I have a daughter of my own.*

Abdul leaned sideways to shake hands without taking his eyes off the girl. "Well, well, Nikolai," he chuckled. "Good disguise."

"I'm here to give you the rest of your instructions."

Abdul's stare burned into the girl's body. "Go ahead."

* * *

Pearl picked up her smartphone and pretended to text as part of her secretarial act. She forwarded the picture of the men to Grace and dropped the phone in her purse.

She crawled towards them on her hands and knees swaying her breasts in rhythm to the music. She stood up, turned, and bent over, looking backward upside-down at the men from between her legs.

The Arab seems mesmerized by me, she detected.

He pushed another twenty onto the stage.

She pulled off her panties, tossed her long, dark curls over her shoulder, and smiled.

He placed another twenty on the stage.

Weird, she observed. *The man next to him with the long hair and beard is ignoring me.*

She crawled closer to hear their conversation. She squatted and spread her legs, opening and closing them in rhythm to the throbbing beat of Beyoncé's "*Naughty Girl.*"

"Everything is set to go," the longhaired man yelled as the song ended.

The Arab handed her another twenty.

She shook his hand, picked up the rest of her earnings, and stuck them in her purse at the back of the stage.

The next song began—Enrique Iglesias's "*Dirty Dancer.*"

She bent herself into a limber gymnastics pose and looked at the Arab through her legs. *The longhaired guy is still talking to him without looking at me.*

The Arab passed another twenty from his stack onto the stage.

She stood up and thanked him with a quick grasp of his hand.

* * *

"Set things up as soon as the fireworks begin," Nikolai yelled over the music. "Run as fast as you can down Ninth to the D Street parking garage when the aftershock passes. I'll be waiting in a blue Prius near the exit. Then I'll drive you to your hotel in Maryland."

Abdul spoke without taking his gaze off the girl. "A Prius, huh? Have you gone environmental?"

"It's my daughter's car. The titanium case will prevent radiation meters from picking up the scent of the weapon," he continued. "That won't be true once it's opened. You'll need to mount and shoot the weapon quickly."

"I understand. I practiced the sequence many times before our Muhlenberg project. I'm ready."

"Mikhail is waiting for you upstairs. I'll see you tomorrow."

Nikolai left through the back door as the song ended.

A waitress tapped Abdul's shoulder. "My manager told me to take you to see the tall man that's sitting in his office."

Abdul followed the waitress to the manager's office on the second floor.

"You must be Mikhail," Abdul said as he sat down. "I was wondering if we'd ever meet."

"Do you have any questions about tomorrow's project?" Mikhail asked.

"No. Nikolai just went over the details with me."

"*Da.*"

Mikhail leaned forward. "How'd you like to earn an additional five million dollars?"

"Of course. What would you like me to do?"

"You'll make your getaway with Nikolai after you launch the weapon, right?"

"That's the plan. He's driving me to a hotel in Maryland. From there, I'll board a charter in Baltimore for the Bahamas."

Mikhail handed Abdul a Beretta. "I want you to make a detour at a secluded rest stop along the way. Hide this gun there. Tell Nikolai you need to stop to go to the bathroom. Then take him into the woods and shoot him. Can you manage that?"

Abdul flinched. "You want me to kill Nikolai?"

"That's right. I'll deposit five million dollars into your Swiss account when I have confirmation."

Abdul slowly nodded. "I imagine you have your reasons."

Mikhail lips showed a trace of a smile. "I'm pleased with you, Abdul. I'd like you to take over Nikolai's responsibilities after you eliminate him. You'll get profit sharing from now on."

"Excellent!" Abdul's eyes strayed to the video displays.

"I'm glad we understand each other. One more thing."

"What's that?"

"I want you to leave the club now," Mikhail ordered. "I don't want you to be hung over tomorrow."

Abdul's smile dissolved. "I need something else from you."

* * *

Mikhail slowed his breathing to shield his wrath. *I define the terms*, he decided indignantly. "What?"

Abdul pointed at the display. "I want that dancer—Pearl."

Mikhail smirked. *I like a good game when it presents itself... especially when I hold all the cards.* "I have plans for her myself. *She's a virgin. I'm going to break her in.*"

Abdul's eyes widened. He leaned forward licking his lips. "I want her."

Mikhail smiled disdainfully. "That'll be expensive. How much are you willing to pay?"

Abdul's face contorted. "I think you should give her to me as part of our bargain."

Mikhail laughed. "Are you kidding? She's a virgin!"

"A virgin, huh? How about ten thousand?"

"I'll deliver her to your hideaway in the Bahamas... for a million. I'll deduct it when I wire your payment."

"Are you kidding?" Abdul pressed his lips together as he stared at Pearl on the display screen. "Okay, but I'll own her after that."

Mikhail chuckled. "Of course. You need to lose your surveillance when you leave here."

Abdul straightened in his chair. "Where?"

Mikhail pointed at the external camera feed displays. "There's one team on the street out front. The other is in the back parking lot."

"Dammit."

"I've taken care of it," Mikhail assured him. "Go north on Wisconsin Avenue to the Mexican food restaurant. There's a Rastafarian dreadlock disguise and a set of cars keys in the trashcan in the men's restroom. Leave through the rear door. The car is out back. Find yourself a small hotel that takes cash. No credit card traces. Understand?"

Abdul stood up. "How soon will I get Pearl?"

"My men will bring her to your hideout in the Bahamas the day after you arrive."

Abdul left the *Taste of Heaven* through the front door.

Mikhail watched the agents jump from their cars and follow him. The wide-angle surveillance camera showed the agents talking into collar microphones outside the Mexican restaurant.

Mikhail laughed aloud. *They're probably talking to their supervisor. He'll be gone by the time they figure out what to do.*

Mikhail watched Pearl swinging naked upside down from a bar above her stage. *I'll confirm her virginity myself prior to delivery. That'll teach Abdul to make demands of me.*

* * *

Grace called Beate. "We haven't been able to identify the man with the beard. Clara, one of our dancers—her stage name is Pearl—said he spoke with a Russian accent."

"She must have a good ear," Beate remarked. "You're still tracking Abdul, right? We can't lose him."

"Yes. He entered a Mexican food restaurant down the street from the *Taste of Heaven*."

"Do you have someone inside?" she asked.

"One of our agents is waiting for him to come out of the bathroom," Grace replied.

"How long has he been in there?" Beate's voice squeaked.

"Not long," Grace said.

"Send someone in," she ordered. "Tell your agent to be careful. He's very dangerous."

"Okay. I'll get back to you."

Beate's phone rang thirty seconds later. "Bad news, Beate… we lost him. He must have slipped out through the back door wearing a disguise."

"Crap! Find him and pull him in. I'll take the heat for disobeying orders."

36. Independence Day

Annapolis, Maryland—July 4

Yvonna had already downed several cups of coffee by the time Mikhail arrived at 10:00 a.m. Mikhail shook Yvonna's hand when he entered the kitchen with Nikolai. "Hello, Yvonna."

She smiled ruefully after failing not to blush. "Hello, Mikhail."

She pulled her hand away when she noticed Nikolai's irritation.

She poured coffee into two cups and handed them to the men.

Tatiana entered the kitchen.

"I'd like to introduce you to our daughter," Nikolai said to Mikhail. "This is Tatiana."

Tatiana lifted her hand to the stranger. "How are you, sir?"

Mikhail raised her hand to his lips. "I'm pleased to meet you."

He stared deeply into her eyes without letting go of her hand. "You are absolutely stunning, my dear—as beautiful as your mother was at your age."

"Really?" Tatiana pulled her fingers away.

"We met Mikhail when your dad was in the army in Afghanistan," Yvonna said.

"That's a long time ago," Tatiana remarked. "I'm going out for a ride."

She bounced to the door in her riding breeches. "It was nice to meet you," she said as she exited to the patio deck.

"It was nice meeting you, too," Mikhail called out after her.

"Mikhail is borrowing our yacht today," Nikolai told Yvonna. "He'll return it tomorrow."

"Okay," Yvonna said. "Have fun."

Mikhail flashed a smile as he followed Nikolai out the door.

She released a long breath when the screen door closed.

That wasn't so bad, she considered.

A gnawing agitation assaulted her. *Mikhail could have at least asked Tatiana about school, or something about her life... instead of just ogling her.*

She reproached herself as she refilled her coffee cup. *What did I expect? My imbroglio with Mikhail has always been complicated... his abstruse behavior mercurial—sometimes charming, other times distant. He's like a swamp: placid on the surface, and filled with snakes below.*

The yacht's engine sprang to life a half hour later. She watched from the deck as it headed east on the South River towards Annapolis.

Nikolai walked up the ramp to the house. "I'll be home late tonight," he said. "I'm taking the Prius."

"Okay." *Perhaps I'll survive unscathed*, she hoped. "Shall I cook something special for dinner tonight? It's the Fourth of July, after all."

Nikolai stared at her for a moment before he spoke. "Yeah... let's celebrate. Can you pick up some bratwursts and beer? I'll barbecue when I get home—even if it's late. We'll make a night of it."

She smiled as he walked away. *I didn't expect him to be in such a good mood after a visit from Mikhail.*

"I'll pick some up," she called after him.

Nikolai stopped. "I know Stefan is camping," he yelled. "Tell Gregor and Tatiana I want them here tonight. I don't want either of them down at the Mall."

"But Gregor's taking his girlfriend to the fireworks," Yvonna said.

"No! I want him here. Tell him he can bring his girlfriend if he wants."

His rage triggered a chill down her spine. "Okay. I'll tell him."

Washington, DC

Sean poured ice-cold water from a decanter next to his bed into a glass and handed it to Beate. "Your reward, my queen."

She swallowed several mouthfuls. "Thanks. So you liked that, huh?"

He poured a glass for himself and drank. "Yes... I did—very much."

She giggled. "Well, there's more where that came from."

"I thought I wore you out."

She kissed him. "You shouldn't think so much."

She jumped out of the bed. "I need to take a shower. A young-buck Marine is picking me up in the lobby in a few minutes."

"Ah, that's right. You're going to Quantico for target practice."

"I want to be sure my gun sighting is accurate," she said. "I'll be keeping an eye on you from the roof of the Smithsonian Castle."

"You really don't need to do that," he protested. "I'll let you know if I spot Abdul."

"It's a good vantage point to listen to music," she said. "I haven't heard you play since Niceville."

"A lot has happened since the concert at the prison," he mused aloud.

"Are you nervous? There'll be over half a million spectators—millions, if you count the TV audience."

He nodded. "A little. I hung in there pretty well during our rehearsal yesterday."

A Marine Corps staff sergeant picked her up in front of the hotel lobby thirty minutes later. He drove her to the Quantico shooting range.

She fitted a night-vision telescopic sight to the bolt-action M40A5 rifle the staff sergeant issued her. "I prefer this to the semi-automatic," she told him. "It has fewer moving parts, so it's more reliable... although that shouldn't be an issue tonight."

Beate obliterated targets for two hours on the shooting range. She recalled the lessons her father had given her every time she pulled the trigger: *Keep your breathing smooth and steady. The shot should always come as a surprise.*

"I'm impressed," the staff sergeant said. "You're consistently nailing a three-inch target at five hundred yards."

She smiled as she cleaned her weapon. "I guess I haven't lost my touch." *More importantly*, she told herself, *I'm confident I'll take out anyone that tries to hurt Sean.*

Chesapeake Bay—North of Norfolk, Virginia

Conflicting emotions consumed Mikhail as he navigated southward on the Chesapeake. *What is it that keeps gnawing at me about Tatiana? There's something about her... something familiar... in her eyes. I have to see her again.*

He was halfway to Norfolk when he reversed course and headed back towards Annapolis. *I'll have plenty of time to take the nukes there later*, he told himself. *Nikolai will be dead tomorrow anyhow. He won't need the yacht. I need to see Tatiana now.*

Laurel, Maryland

Abdul spent the previous night at the Valencia Motel on US Route 1 in Laurel, Maryland—the same hotel used by the 9/11 terrorists before they hijacked American Airlines Flight 77 and plowed it into the Pentagon. Ironically, the hotel stood within sight of the dark-windowed National Security Agency at Fort Meade.

Abdul purchased shorts, a T-shirt, and sandals at a nearby department store. *It'll be hot walking around the Mall wearing the dreadlock wig-and-beard disguise*, he told himself. *I need something comfortable.*

He parked his rental car in the DC suburbs and took the Red Line Metrorail to Gallery Place. He spoke with a Jamaican brogue when partiers approached him around the Mall. *I'd make a fortune if I had some ganja to sell*, he reckoned. *Everyone keeps asking me for some.*

The Venezuelans vacated their tent as evening approached.

* * *

Beate was moving into position on the roof of the 145-foot Smithsonian Castle tower when Helmut called.

"No," she said. "Sean's not making any trades this time. We're either going to thwart the attack or die trying. …Uh-huh. …Lubyanka? …Yes. I'll be sure to tell him. Thanks for contacting the Russians. I know your relationship with them is strained. I'll talk with you later, assuming we make it out of here alive."

Sean won't be able to concentrate if I tell him about his father now, she decided. *I'll tell him later.*

Three of the eight Marines patrolling the rooftop of the Smithsonian Castle were women. They walked over to Beate as a group and saluted.

Beate returned their salutation. "At ease, ladies. I appreciate the respect, but my days in the Corps are long gone."

"We wanted to meet you," Master Sergeant Michelle Garcia said. "You still hold the marksmanship records at the Marine base in Twentynine Palms where we were stationed."

The three female soldiers shook Beate's hand.

Beate smiled. "Thanks for letting me know. Let's just hope I can still shoot if the need arises here tonight."

She stabilized a tripod beneath her seventeen-pound rifle, peered at Sean through her night vision scope, and activated her two-way collar microphone. "Coltrane, this is Alice. Can you hear me?"

Sean was wearing a white, short-sleeved shirt with a black hat to shield the hearing-aid-sized speaker in his ear and the microphone on his collar. He looked up and tapped his collar microphone switch. "It's nice to have a guardian angel," he replied. "How was target practice?"

She waved to indicate her position. "Wonderful. I have some bad news, though. Helmut just called. The German police just matched our photos of Abdul with an Autobahn image captured near Munich. He was in the passenger seat of the van driven by the Muhlenberg bomber."

"I'll keep my eyes open," he said. "Your surveillance team in Hamburg said he likes rock music. That's something isn't it?"

"It is," Beate replied. "Let me know if you spot him. We'll take it from there."

"Don't worry. I can take care of myself."

A Black Hawk helicopter flew over them. Several army snipers positioned inside scanned the crowd with infrared night-vision scopes attached to their rifles.

"Looks like we have lots of security," he observed.

"The Mall is surrounded by radiation-detection meters and bomb-disposal units," she replied. "No one has detected any nuclear signatures, so we're safe… for now."

"I wonder what he's up to," Sean pondered aloud.

"You and ten thousand other people out here," she remarked. "The FBI issued an all-points bulletin to pick him up. I'll let you know if they find him."

"I gotta go. Charles just stepped up to the microphone."

"Bye, Coltrane. Have fun."

"I love you."

"I love you, too."

Sean tapped his collar to deactivate his microphone.

Charles turned to his drummer. With a quick four count the band launched into a high-energy version of Spencer Davis Group's *"Gimme Some Lovin."* The song instantly lured several dozen people to the dance floor in front of the stage.

* * *

Nikolai was sitting in the parking garage inside the Prius listening to a baseball game when Yvonna called. He let it go to voice mail. *She knows she shouldn't call me when I'm on a mission*, he grumbled to himself.

He listened to her message after her call ended. "Nikolai, this is Yvonna. Gregor can't come home tonight. He and his friends are watching the fireworks on the Mall. We can still have a cookout, though. I'm going to the store now. See you tonight." She hung up.

"God damn it!"

Greenwich, Connecticut

John Napoleon insisted that everyone dress in formal attire for his lavish backyard Fourth-of-July soirée: tuxedos for the men—the Cardinal wore a scarlet red cape,—and evening dresses for the women. He'd provisioned the party with caviar, grilled seafood, a variety of expensive French wines, champagne, and chocolate soufflés for desert.

His twelve guests didn't sweat a drop beneath the large, white tent. Humidity-limiting air conditioners kept the venue as cool as a Colorado summer evening.

Napoleon strolled over to Vladimir and Judith when they'd finished dinner. "Is everything ready?"

"Yes," Vladimir said.

"My people at the storage bunker near Norfolk told me Mikhail never showed up with the weapons this afternoon."

"I'm sure he's on his way," Vladimir said.

Napoleon tapped his glass with a spoon to get everyone's attention. "Let's retire to the boardroom to watch the fireworks in Washington. It should be quite a show."

His guests meandered through a matrix of multicolored rose gardens to the mansion.

Napoleon flipped on a large digital television screen when they'd settled into their seats around the conference room table. The broadcast station was airing a pre-fireworks concert featuring a band the president had chosen called *The Ebony All-Stars*.

Napoleon turned down the volume. Everyone quieted.

"We'll meet an important milestone tonight," he began. "The funds from this operation and the profits from the wars that will follow will enable us to purchase controlling stakes in most of the world's commodity resources. Once we control the raw materials used for production, we'll shut down the factories that are ruining our planet. The ensuing famines will significantly reduce the promiscuous population responsible for this colossal planetary holocaust."

His audience nodded.

Napoleon raised his champagne glass in a toast. "It's nice to have friends committed to protecting the world."

Someone said, "Hear! Hear!" and they drank.

Annapolis, Maryland

The sun was low in the sky when Mikhail walked up the ramp to Nikolai's house after mooring the yacht. Tatiana came to the screen door when he knocked.

"My mother's out shopping," she said. "Would you like a beer while you wait? My dad won't be home until later."

Mikhail's face softened into a smile. "That would please me greatly. Why don't you join me? You're in college now, and it's the Fourth of July. It's important to know how to drink when you're in college."

She smiled mischievously. "I guess that's okay."

She grabbed two beers from the refrigerator. They adjourned to the deck as the sun merged with the trees on the other side of the river.

"What are you going to major in, Tatiana?" he asked.

"I'm taking business classes," she replied.

Mikhail sipped his beer. "Have you ever considered other occupations? There are many lucrative jobs that don't require college."

"Not really. Mom and Dad always said I should go to college."

"I have a job opening that would be perfect for a beautiful young woman like you. You can still attend college if you'd like, and you can work whenever you want."

Tatiana stared at him suspiciously. "How much does it pay?"

"You'll make a thousand dollars a day for a few hours of work in the evenings."

"That's three hundred and sixty-five thousand dollars a year," she gasped. "What kind of job is it?"

Mikhail laughed. "You did that calculation rather quickly."

"I'm good at math, and that was simple."

"*Da.* The job is easy. You dress up and hang out with people. They'll take you to dinner at fancy restaurants or to the symphony, that sort of thing."

Tatiana eyed him warily. "Is this a sex job?"

Mikhail laughed. "Only if you want it to be. The men want someone pretty to show off. Most of them are business executives from out of town. Some are politicians. Some are movie stars."

"Really?"

"Yes, and as I said, you only work when you want. No pressure. It's up to you."

Tatiana put her feet up on a stool. "Thanks for the offer, but I don't think my parents would approve."

Mikhail eyed her long legs out of the corner of his eye. *They're even prettier than Yvonna's*, he assessed.

"You're old enough to make your own decisions aren't you?" he said. "I was already running a business when I was your age. Your dad works for me. Did you know that?"

"Yeah. Mom told me."

"I made your father filthy rich, even before he went to college."

The twilight sky dimmed azure blue as dusk descended.

"You'll need to know how to fix drinks if you take the job," he said. "Can you make me a martini?"

"I think so. I've seen Mom and Dad do it often enough."

They both laughed.

Mikhail stood up. "I have some vodka, olives, and ice in the yacht. I can show you how to make a good martini if you'd like."

"Okay."

"So, how's Gregor?" he inquired as they walked down the ramp to the boat.

"You know him? He's a lawyer in DC now. He went to Georgetown."

"Yes, I know him. I was at the hospital the night he was born."

37. Fireworks

Washington, DC

Beate had a great view of the stage through her night-vision scope atop the Smithsonian Castle. She smiled when Charles pointed at Sean to do a sax solo during "*Proud Mary.*" The appreciative nods of his bandmates at the end of the song signaled his debut performance was going well.

She scanned the grounds below her. Revelers occupied every square foot of lawn space. Abe Lincoln, sitting resolute and unflinching in his memorial, reflected red-orange off the tidal basin.

Her perch gave her an appreciation of George Washington's vision when he commissioned Pierre L'Enfant to design the Mall in 1791. *Perhaps the expansive promenade represents the ideals embodied in democracy itself,* she considered, *unencumbered by the tyrannical whims of aristocratic landlords, kings, and clergy.*

She looked across the tops of the surrounding buildings. Sharpshooting teams patrolled every rooftop.

The DC police relayed a message to every soldier and law enforcement officer: "Attendance is well beyond the six hundred thousand we predicted."

The media had decided to broadcast the band's entire performance to the nation because the president liked the band. After a few more songs, they'd play the national anthem. Then the fireworks would begin.

Annapolis, Maryland

Yvonna placed the groceries she'd purchased on the kitchen countertop and turned on a small television next to the refrigerator. A band was playing a concert in DC before the fireworks.

I don't usually drink beer, but it's the Fourth of July. Gregor and his friends are down on Mall imbibing. Why shouldn't I?

She opened the refrigerator. *There were two beers in here when I left.*

"Tatiana," she called out down the hallway. "Have you been drinking?"

She must have her headphones on, she decided.

Yvonna noticed two empty beer cans on the patio table. *I hope she's not afflicted with the same predilection for alcohol her father has—both her fathers.*

Yvonna stepped out to the deck. She was about to call out to Tatiana again when she spotted the yacht. *The cabin lights are on.*

That's odd. Mikhail wasn't supposed to bring the boat back until tomorrow.

She lurched down the ramp in a run. She peered into the cabin window when she reached the gangplank.

Tatiana was lying on the bed. She had a martini glass in her hand. Mikhail was standing in front of her. His shirt was off and his pants were down to his knees!

Oh my God! Yvonna stepped lightly across the bridge to the deck. Her hand found the thin, nine-inch blade Nikolai used to gut fish.

Tatiana was facing Mikhail bending to his stomach.

Yvonna shot through the door and rammed the blade into his back between his shoulder blades.

Tatiana screamed. "What are you doing?"

Mikhail's severed spine sprayed blood as he collapsed. A dark-red pool formed beneath him. The blood smelled like iron.

His steel-blue eyes flashed anger. A drawn-out groan that sounded like "Y-von-na" spilled from his throat, and then his gaze went dull, like the eyes of a dead fish washed up on the beach.

Tatiana's screams sliced through Yvonna's shock. "Why'd you do that?"

Yvonna reached for Tatiana. "Did he hurt you?"

Tatiana jumped back. "No! He was showing me the scars from his knife fights in the Moscow Metro."

Yvonna's mind reeled. *Oh, God. What have I done?* Her mouth hollowed as she looked down at Mikhail.

She covered her eyes with her hands and began to weep. "He raped me… when I was eighteen. I didn't want that… to happen to you."

Tatiana watched her mother for a moment before she spoke. "Does Dad know?"

Yvonna began wringing her hands as she stared at Mikhail. "I told him recently. He never knew… for many years."

Tatiana hugged her mother. "That's awful, Mom."

Yvonna pulled back. "What have I done? Oh my God!"

She stepped out of the cabin. Tatiana followed.

Yvonna cried as she paced around the deck, folding and unfolding her hands. "What am I going to do?" she wailed. "Mikhail's brother… Vladimir, will kill me… or Nikolai, or both of us for doing this."

Tatiana crossed her arms. "That'll only happen if he finds out."

Yvonna stopped. "What do you mean?"

"What if Mikhail's body disappears?"

It might work. Yvonna considered. *She's clever... like her father.* "We can't say anything to Dad about this. Vladimir will torture him when Mikhail disappears. He knows about the rape."

Tatiana nodded. "I know Dad is in the mafia, Mom, even though you try to hide it from us. Gregor and Stefan know, too."

Yvonna looked at the sky. Darkness was consuming the twilight.

"Should we dump him out in the bay?" Tatiana asked.

"Yes... We'll need to clean everything, too. We can't tell anyone about this... even your father. It'll be a death sentence for him if we do."

"I saw a movie once where someone got rid of a body by dumping it in the ocean. We'll need to tie it down, so it doesn't float."

Yvonna nodded. "We'll throw the sheets and our clothes into the water to get rid of the evidence. I'll get some bleach and a change of clothes for us from the house, and leave a note for Dad, telling him we took the yacht out to watch the fireworks after Mikhail dropped it off."

"I'll gas it up so we're ready. We should hurry."

Washington, DC

Charles beamed a broad smile when someone passed him a note. He addressed the band: "The President and First Lady are dancing on the rooftop observation deck at the White House."

Charles counted off another song.

Sean's eyes veered to the music. He'd been scanning the audience between riffs. No one fitting Abdul's description had appeared in the ocean of faces in front of the stage.

The Ebony All Stars were halfway through the last song before the national anthem when something caught Sean's eye. He returned his gaze to the Rastafarian near the dance floor after a spray of fast arpeggios. *The man's build looks similar to Abdul.*

The beard and dreadlocks made Sean scan the floor again. The Rastafarian's dark eyes drew him back.

The man's lascivious grin, the way he was ogling the *Ebony All Star* singers, sent a chill down Sean's spine. *One more riff and I'll look again to make sure,* he told himself.

He played a wave of notes. His scrutiny returned to the crowd.

The man was gone. He scanned the dance floor. *Nothing.*

He placed his saxophone in its stand, stepped off the back of the stage, and ran along the side of the tent to the esplanade.

"Did you see him?" Beate bellowed through his earpiece.

Sean's head zigzagged back and forth like a bird seeking insects in a forest. He punched his microphone button. "I'm not sure. I saw someone with Abdul's features, but this guy looks like a Rastafarian."

"What's he wearing?" she asked.

"Shorts and a T-shirt. He has a dark beard and long, curly dreadlocks, but what I noticed most were his eyes."

"I'll let everyone know we have a potential sighting," Beate said.

Sean's gaze skimmed the throngs walking both directions. The song he'd been playing ended. "I'm going to look around."

Decide! Right, towards the Washington Monument, or left to the Folk Festival tents?

He jogged left.

The applause died away. Charles introduced Maheila.

She began the national anthem. Her powerful voice boomed through the loudspeakers lining the esplanade along the Mall.

Oh say, can you see, by the dawn's early light...

Everyone was facing one of the hundreds of American flags flying around the Mall. Some people had their hands over their hearts.

What so proudly we hailed, at the twilight's last gleaming?

Whose broad stripes and bright stars, through the perilous fight...

People glared at Sean as he shuffled through them, angry that he was disrespecting the national anthem.

O'er the ramparts we watch'd, were so gallantly streaming...

He ran across the street. A taxi screeched to a halt. It almost hit him.

"Be careful!" Beate yelled through his earpiece. "You almost got killed."

And the rockets' red glare, the bombs bursting in air...

He peered between the tents on both sides as he ran.

Gave proof through the night that our flag was still there...

"I'm following you with my scope," Beate said. "Let me know if you spot him."

Oh, say, does that star spangled banner yet wave...

Everyone was standing, which made it easy for him to weave his way through the crowd. Something triggered his peripheral vision. Someone else, like himself, was ignoring the song.

He stopped and turned around.

"I think I saw him, but he disappeared," Sean said. "Damn!"

O'er the land of the free...

Maheila's voice penetrated every corner of the Mall. A tremendous roar erupted as 600,000 cheering fans signaled their appreciation, anticipating the beginning of the fireworks show.

and the home... of the... brave...

Her last, triumphant note shook the crowd for twenty seconds.

A cannon blast shot a red, white, and blue firework cluster over the Tidal Basin, filling the sky with color.

Greenwich, Connecticut

Napoleon's apostles sitting around the conference table watched the fireworks on a muted TV screen. Only the occasional clink of a champagne glass interrupted their reverie.

"Vladimir," Napoleon said.

"Yes, John?"

"When is the detonation scheduled?"

"Any time now," he assured everyone.

Judith smiled at Vladimir from across the table. *She told me she wants to make love in the woods on our way back to New York tonight,* he considered. *I like her wild side... it suits me.*

She's under my spell now. We'll eliminate Napoleon after the Red Horseman project, and then I'll take control.

His heart beat faster with every breath. *Where's the explosion?*

Washington, DC

Abdul locked the bazooka into place on the tripod, and pulled on his orange radiation protection suit and goggles. He chugged the rest of his beer and dropped his cup to the floor. *I'm ready.*

Loud cannon blasts from the fireworks echoed back and forth between the Lincoln Memorial and the Capitol Building. Skeleton outlines from the pyrotechnics splashed the roof of the burlap tent with each explosion.

He lifted the lead-titanium case from the hole beneath the tent and positioned it perpendicular to the weapon.

Every second will count now when I open the case, he reminded himself. *I've optimized the sequence of steps to thirty-seven seconds.*

Abdul opened the case, lifted the nuclear payload, secured it to the bazooka's propulsion slot, inserted the propellant cartridge, and flipped the safety switch from *Safe* to *Arm*.

He yanked the drawstring on the side of the tent. The side dropped away, creating a clear path for the projectile.

* * *

Radiation detection meters spiked around the Mall. Triangulating computers tried to pinpoint the source but the diffused radiation bouncing off the buildings rendered the location ambiguous.

The Secret Service rushed the president and his family to the elevator. They reached the bunker beneath the White House in seconds.

* * *

Beate followed Sean with her scope adjusting the settings as he moved, her adrenaline pulsing through every synapse.

It would be a tough shot under the best of conditions—more difficult with the flashes from the exploding fireworks. Don't think about that!

"We've had a radiation surge," she yelled through her microphone to Sean. "There's a bomb."

She estimated he was seven hundred yards away when he took off running.

* * *

Sean plowed into the large man in the orange jumpsuit at a fast run. They toppled to the ground and jumped up, facing each other.

A six-inch blade slashed Sean's leg. He collapsed.

Abdul fell on him with a ferocious body blow, knocking the wind from his lungs. He grabbed Abdul's wrists as he gasped for air.

The thin stiletto descended towards his eye, the blade flashing with each firework explosion. Sean held on with all his might.

The tip was just above his eyelash, ready to pierce his brain.

* * *

Beate banished the fears shouting: *Your lover is about to die.* She banished her anger: *That's the Muhlenberg murderer.*

Spectators cleared away from the men like a ripple from a stone dropped in a pond. The knife above Sean's eye glinted in her scope.

Forget you love him. Forget what's at stake. Forget Robert and Malia. Breathe steady. Always a surprise... it should always be a surprise.

* * *

Sean smelled beer on Abdul's breath when the forehead ten inches from his face exploded. It burst like a watermelon hit by a sledgehammer, spraying him with a sticky, blood-bone-porridge.

A DC cop pointed his revolver at Sean. "Don't move!"

Sean slowly dragged himself out from beneath the heavy carcass. *The pain in my leg is ferocious*, he realized.

He wiped the bloody muck from his eyes so he could see. Several soldiers were pointing their guns at him.

The fireworks continued as the police cordoned off the area.

* * *

Beate bolted down the steps and sprinted across the Mall. She flashed her ID as she approached the soldiers surrounding Sean.

Two Emergency Medical Technicians were hauling him onto a gurney when she arrived. They weren't sure exactly what his injuries were with his face, chest, arms and legs covered in blood.

He attempted a smile as Beate jumped up into the back of the ambulance next to him. "Nice shot," he said.

"Nice tackle. The Washington Redskins should give you a call."

"Yeah…" It took him a few seconds to offer a retort. "But I think I'd rather play for the Denver Broncos."

No one realized the fireworks ended earlier than usual that night. The DC Mayor didn't tell the crowd there was a bomb in their midst, to prevent trampling deaths when everyone dispersed.

38. Eulogy

Chesapeake Bay, Maryland

Tatiana accelerated to twenty knots between the light buoys as she navigated southward on Chesapeake Bay. She turned on the yacht's navigation lights so she wouldn't accidentally run into someone.

Yvonna sat next to her at the helm. *I have complete confidence in her*, Yvonna told herself. *She grew up on these waters piloting the yacht for Nikolai.*

"We need to tie him down," Tatiana said from behind the wheel. "So he doesn't float."

"I'll look below to see what I can find."

Yvonna opened a storage closet in the cabin. She found six metal cases inside. Two had radiation symbols. *I've never seen these before.*

She opened one case and found a bomb. "Oh my God," she said aloud as she closed it.

Two cases contained tripods. Two had bazookas.

An image of the recent nuclear catastrophe in Muhlenberg appeared in her mind. *What wicked game are these men playing* she wondered?

She used black spray paint to cover the radiation symbols on the bomb cases. *I don't want Tatiana to see these.*

She hauled all six cases to the stern.

Tears streamed down her cheeks when she returned to the cabin. Mikhail's skin was waxy and pale. *He's already growing cold*, she realized.

She climbed the stairs to the bridge and placed his cell phones next to the steering wheel.

"I found some heavy cases to anchor him with in the closet," Yvonna said. "I'll need your help to drag him on deck when we stop."

One of the cell phones buzzed. Neither woman picked it up. The call went to voice mail.

Tatiana opened the phone and navigated to the contact list. "There are only three numbers in here." She paused. "One is for Vladimir. That's Mikhail's brother, right?"

"That's right."

"There's someone named Abdul, and Dad. That call was from Vladimir."

The phone continued to buzz every few minutes until they'd passed beyond cell tower range.

Washington, DC

Nikolai pulled on a longhaired wig and beard disguise. *I've waited long enough for Abdul to return,* he decided.

He made slow progress walking against the crowds leaving the fireworks celebration. Dozens of soldiers surrounded a cordoned-off area around the Venezuelan tent. He melted into the spectators behind the crime scene tape.

Abdul's head above an orange radiation suit was half-gone. *Gruesome. Someone shot him.*

He dialed Mikhail when he returned to the Prius. *It'll be better for him to hear the bad news from me* he contemplated. *No answer.*

He called every few minutes as he drove back to Annapolis. Mikhail never answered.

* * *

The Department of Defense Nuclear Threat Assessment team inside the tent was nervous. Disarming a nuclear bomb in the middle of DC wasn't exactly something they did every day.

Sergeant Jefferson Conner sat on a stool next to the bomb. "I've never disarmed a Soviet-era W54R," he told his team. "I've studied them enough to recognize one, though. The bomb is similar to our W54 nuke, which I know well."

"Look at this," he said a moment later.

Sergeant Conner held a large magnifying glass next to the bomb so the soldiers around him could see. "Someone cut the wire between the igniter and detonation trigger."

He sat back on his stool and looked across the Mall at the Lincoln Memorial. "The bomb has an altitude trigger, but it wouldn't have detonated. Based on the angle, payload weight and propulsion capability of the bazooka, the bomb would've sailed over the crowd and fallen into the Potomac. It doesn't make sense."

Bloody Point, Chesapeake Bay

Tatiana reversed the engine and brought the yacht to a gradual stop. "This is Bloody Point," she said. "The nautical chart says it's one hundred and seventy-four feet deep here."

Bloody Point's lighthouse to the east confirmed their location. She turned off the navigation lights and stepped down to the stern.

The women dragged Mikhail's body from the cabin to the deck. They tied the handles of the six cases to Mikhail's arms and legs with nylon rope. A gibbous moon provided light while they worked.

"Let's throw the weights over the side first," Yvonna said. "Then we'll push him overboard."

Tatiana looked down at Mikhail. "Shouldn't we say some kind of eulogy first? Isn't that what people do?"

Mikhail's shirtless torso looked pale blue beneath the moonlight.

Yvonna cried softly as she took Tatiana's hand. "God bless his soul… and forgive him his sins."

Mikhail's body faced the sky when it hit the water. He sank slowly, his pale gray face gradually disappearing as he faded into the black sea, drawn deep into the water by the nuclear anchors.

They washed the blood off the deck and cabin floor with seawater, and threw their bloodstained clothes and sheets into the bay.

Tatiana started the engine after they changed into clean clothes, and steered the yacht north towards Annapolis.

Tears stained Yvonna's cheeks as she sat next to Tatiana at the helm.

"Are you okay?" Tatiana said.

Yvonna wiped her tears away. "Yes…" The tears kept coming.

"What did Daddy do when he found out about Mikhail?"

"He couldn't do anything. That's why he's been so distant, why he's been living in Europe."

Yvonna studied Tatiana. *Her face looks a lot like her father's in the moonlight. I wish I could tell her more. Perhaps… someday.*

"I have an idea that might help protect Daddy," Tatiana said.

"What's that?"

"Text Vladimir from Mikhail's cell phone, saying he's going away," she suggested. "Then throw the phone in the water. Vladimir will think he took a boat somewhere and disappeared."

"That's good thinking, Tatiana."

"We should be within cell tower range now."

Yvonna carefully composed her message on Mikhail's phone:

<u>Vladimir, I'm leaving. Don't try to find me. I've sold the bombs. Please look after Tatiana, Yvonna's daughter. She is also my daughter, and your niece. I'm sorry it has to be this way.</u>

She punched the *Send* button. "It's done," she told Tatiana.

She heaved the phone into the water. "Now, we wait… and hope Nikolai doesn't get killed."

Greenwich, Connecticut

No one spoke. Everyone at the round table was staring at Vladimir, curious to see what would happen next.

Napoleon and Judith re-entered the conference room. They'd left a few minutes earlier, after Vladimir showed Napoleon the text message from Mikhail saying that he'd sold the bombs.

"We're done for tonight," Napoleon announced. "I need Vladimir and Judith to stay."

Judith and Napoleon took seats on opposite sides of Vladimir as the rest of the Protectorate members filed out of the room.

"Who'd your brother sell the bombs to?" Napoleon said.

"They're in the storage vault outside Norfolk," Vladimir answered testily.

Napoleon's gaze hardened. "Where's the money you promised us?"

"Screw you!"

Napoleon nodded at Judith.

She placed a stack of papers from her briefcase in front of Vladimir. "I retrieved these from the safe behind your Renoir painting last night while you slept," she said.

Vladimir scowled. "You bitch."

Her gaze was businesslike. "I believe these are the inventory records, property titles, account numbers, and passwords for all your assets."

"Did Mikhail ever tell you he had a daughter?" Napoleon said.

"He doesn't have a daughter," Vladimir snapped. "That message is a hoax."

"I think a two-hundred-billion-dollar donation to the World Protection Council is a fair exchange for your life," Napoleon continued.

"Screw you," Vladimir yelled defiantly.

"What do you think your life is worth, Vladimir? You and your brother have done well here in America. The Protectorate has been grooming the two of you since you were teenagers. Now it's time to pay the piper. Who'd Mikhail sell the bombs to?"

"He wouldn't sell them on his own," Vladimir insisted. "We're a team."

Judith showed Vladimir a picture of Yvonna plunging a knife into Mikhail's back. Vladimir's mouth dropped open.

He looked at Judith and back to the picture.

"I had a surveillance team at Nikolai's house today," she said. "They watched Mikhail and Nikolai load the bombs onto the boat. Mikhail left with the yacht, but he returned a few hours later. He didn't deliver the bombs to the storage vault outside Norfolk. Yvonna caught him trying to rape Tatiana—your niece—when she came home from the store."

Vladimir shook his head. "Is this some kind of trick? Where's Mikhail?"

"Your brother is a real piece of work," Napoleon said derisively. "…his own daughter."

Vladimir grabbed Napoleon by the throat and choked him with two hands.

Judith pulled a syringe from her briefcase and plunged the needle into Vladimir's back.

Vladimir's skin turned blue as the asphyxia caused by the hydrogen cyanide took hold. He fell to the floor jerking violently.

Froth gurgled and oozed from his mouth. His twisted expression became waxy as his skin streaked with blue stripes. He stopped convulsing and went still after thirty seconds.

Judith reached for Napoleon's arm. "Are you okay?"

Napoleon straightened his shirt and tie. He looked down at Vladimir. "I wish he would've worked out for us. He had a brilliant mind… but he wasn't loyal."

"Yeah, and the FBI was closing in after Judge Richter's plea bargain deal. The Volkov brothers would've been arrested any day."

Napoleon stood up. "I'm leaving for Switzerland tonight to move their funds into our Protectorate accounts. My lawyers are drawing up papers to transfer the rest of their assets. You can have Vladimir's New York penthouse and Impressionist collection if you'd like. I assume that'll be adequate compensation for your trouble."

She smiled. "Thank you."

She stared at the papers she'd taken from Vladimir's safe. "They have close to two-point-four trillion in assets."

"Two-point-four-five trillion," he said.

"That's what I meant."

He assessed her with a blank stare. "That was a test. I needed to be sure you weren't skimming assets off the top. I want to be able to trust you."

She hugged him and looked into his eyes. "You can trust me."

He chuckled as he pulled away. "You're very good at that seductress act. I can see why men are mesmerized by you."

He stared down at Vladimir. "My guards will get rid of the body."

He turned back to her. "I want you to meet with Nikolai tomorrow. Tell him he'll be reporting to Mr. Neruda from now on. The Volkov businesses will fit in nicely with Neruda's cartels. The eastern and western hemisphere mafias will be easier to consolidate once we have the Americas under one management chain."

She took several pictures of Vladimir with her smartphone. "I'll show these to Nikolai to prove Vladimir is dead. My agent in Annapolis told me that Tatiana and Yvonna just returned in their yacht," she continued. "Mikhail's body wasn't on board. They must've dumped him somewhere in the Chesapeake. The nukes weren't on board, either."

"Put a query out to our intelligence network to find out whom Mikhail sold them to. I'm sure they'll show up eventually."

Annapolis, Maryland—The Following Morning

Nikolai ushered Judith into his home office and closed the door. She'd called him early that morning saying she was coming to his house to give him urgent news about Mikhail Volkov.

"How may I help you, Judith?"

"Mikhail and Vladimir Volkov are dead."

Nikolai studied her warily as she pulled out pictures from her briefcase. His jaw slackened when she showed him photographs of Yvonna plunging a knife into Mikhail's back.

"Where did you get these?" he demanded.

"My agent took them last night. He was here when you and Mikhail loaded the nukes onto your yacht. Mikhail returned to your house a few hours later without delivering the nukes."

She paused. "Yvonna stopped Mikhail from raping Tatiana. You can ask her about it yourself, if you'd like. She probably didn't tell you, to protect you from being tortured by Vladimir's thugs."

A worried pallor glazed his face. "I'm sure he'll come after us."

Judith showed Nikolai a picture of Vladimir with blue froth drooling from his mouth, lying twisted on the floor. "You won't have to worry about him, either," she said. "We took him out last night. The FBI was about to arrest the Volkov brothers anyway. Yvonna did our job for us."

He continued to stare at the pictures.

"We know you were running most of Mikhail's operations," she continued. "Just do what you've been doing. You'll be reporting to a man named Neruda from Mexico City from now on. He'll be contacting you soon."

Nikolai stared at the pictures. *Could this really be true* he considered?

Judith stood up. He walked her to the front door. She shook his hand and said, "Good luck," before she exited.

Washington, DC—That Afternoon

Two armed DC police officers stood guard outside Sean's hospital room door while Beate and Angela napped on chairs inside. Sarah slept peacefully nestled under Sean's right arm on the bed. An intravenous drip pumped antibiotics and pain medication into a vein in his left arm.

The surgery to repair the knife wound in his upper quadriceps had gone well. The doctors said he'd make a full recovery, although he'd have a limp for a few months while he completed physical therapy.

A stack of newspapers filled the floor. Every newspaper in the country had published the picture that morning of Sean crawling out from beneath the terrorist.

Several witnesses told the police he'd stopped the bomber by tackling him. The press didn't know the bomb attached to the bazooka in the background was a nuke, and the government didn't tell them.

The military didn't disclose the identity of the soldier who'd shot the terrorist, so Sean was getting all the glory. Beate and the CIA wanted it that way.

Sean took several calls that morning before the nurses told him he needed to rest. He answered the next call when he saw it was from Charles.

He spoke softly so he wouldn't wake Sarah. "Hello."

Beate and Angela changed positions in their chairs.

"I'm doing fine, Charles. Thanks for calling. …Yeah. That was fun last night. We'll have to do it again sometime. I can't talk long. My doctor told me to sleep. …Sure. I'll come by for a beer when I get out."

He ended the call.

The press had mentioned that Sean was playing saxophone for *The Ebony All Stars* before he'd stumbled upon the terrorist. No one asked how he'd ended up near the Venezuelan tent a block away from the stage.

Someone knocked on his door. Beate's hand found her revolver as she stood up. She made sure the man's identification badge matched his face before she let him in the room.

The man was in his early seventies. He wore a gray suit. "I'm Agent Howard," he told Sean. "I'm with the FBI."

Sean nodded. "I've seen you before. You used to hang out around our trailer spying on us with binoculars when I was a kid."

Sean looked at Angela and Beate. "This is one of the gray men I told you about."

He turned to Howard. "My sister and I used to call you gray men because of your serious expressions," he chuckled, "and your gray suits."

Howard wasn't amused. "Can we talk… about your father?"

Sean motioned to an empty chair. "Have a seat."

Howard remained standing. "This information is classified."

"I want them to hear anything you have to say," Sean insisted.

Sean's phone buzzed. "Hold on. I have to take this."

Howard sat down.

"Hello, Mr. President." Sean smiled at Beate and Angela. "The surgery went well. Thanks for asking."

Sean listened for a moment. "I'm glad we could help, sir. The real hero is Beate Nicholson. That was a tough shot. …I will, sir. Thank you. We're looking forward to meeting you when I get out of here."

Sarah awakened with a gentle cry.

Sean chuckled. "No, sir, that wasn't me. That was Sarah, my daughter. …Yes, sir. I'll bring her with us when Angela, Beate, and I come to dinner at the White House. Thank you, sir." He hung up.

Beate lifted Sarah from the bed and sat down with her in the rocking chair. Sarah nestled her head into Beate's chest and closed her eyes.

"The president wants us to come to dinner at the White House next week," Sean said.

Angela smiled. "That'll be fun."

Howard looked at Beate. "I understand you prevented a terrible catastrophe last night."

"Thanks," she replied. "I wouldn't have gotten my shot off without Sean. So what did you want to tell us about his father?"

Howard faced Sean. "I'd like to clear some things up before I retire."

Sean glanced at Beate and back to Howard. "So what happened to him?"

"Your father was an expert in a field called game theory at Los Alamos. He developed strategies for the defense department. We believe the CIA recruited him to pass a message to the Soviets in 1969, during a military mission called Operation Giant Lance. The president didn't authorize the message. We believe your father's CIA case officer may have coerced him afterward, threatening to have him arrested for treason if he didn't follow his orders."

Sean nodded. "What happened after that?"

"We believe someone may have staged your father's death while he was working as a military advisor in Vietnam. The military classified him MIA because they never found his body. My job was to watch for him in case he returned home."

Howard turned to Beate. "The GRU passed us his father's file after they received an inquiry from your colleague in Germany—Helmut Drach."

Beate looked at Sean. "Helmut told me about this last night. I was going to tell you about it after the fireworks."

Sean nodded. "So how are the Russians involved?"

Howard frowned. "The GRU file contained notes written by a KGB agent. Your father's first meeting was at the La Fonda Hotel in Santa Fe, in 1969. They discussed a recently declassified military operation called Giant Lance. The KGB captured your father in Vietnam in 1972, and took him to Lubyanka prison, where he revealed—under chemically induced duress—the game theory doctrine we now call Mutually Assured Destruction. The Russians accelerated their nuclear weapons program after that. The Mutually Assured Destruction doctrine has governed our defense posture with the Russians ever since."

"What happened to Sean's father?" Angela asked.

"The GRU file said their KGB predecessors buried him in an unmarked grave in 1973. I'm sorry to bring you the bad news."

"What happened to his CIA case officer?" Beate said.

"He was killed in a car accident in northern Virginia in 1974."

Sean clenched his jaw. "Why didn't anyone help him?"

"I'm not sure. A disclosure from your father about Operation Giant Lance would've been disastrous for the administration as well as the nuclear weapons industry at the time. It would've bolstered calls for disarmament by the peaceniks. You're probably too young to remember, but arms-control treaties were just a dream in those days. Powerful forces behind the scenes had a lot at stake. Look what's happening now. Military strategists in many countries still believe that tactical nuclear weapons have a place in their arsenal. We still have thousands of nukes, as do the Russians, and the number of countries with nuclear weapons is *increasing* every decade, not decreasing."

Howard leaned forward. "I hope this brought you some closure about your father."

"It did," Sean replied solemnly. "Thank you."

Howard shook everyone's hand and exited the room. Sarah began to cry as the door closed.

Beate handed Sarah to Angela. "Sounds like she's hungry."

Angela smiled at Beate. "A mother never forgets that cry, does she?"

Angela pulled up her shirt and placed her breast in Sarah's mouth. "It'll be fun to have dinner at the White House," she said after Sarah latched on. "We'll have to go shopping."

Beate grinned. "I'd love to. What do you think we should wear?"

Epilogue. Ugolino

Greenwich, Connecticut—One Year Later

Napoleon pounded his gavel.

The banter in the conference room instantly trickled to a hush.

"I'd like to discuss our membership opening," he said. "Our Brazilian nominee controls most of South America's cocaine, coffee, and mining industries. I'm sure he'll appreciate the protection we can provide once he understands our global reach and the nature of our mission. We need his South American rain forests. Those lands are crucial to the world's ecosystem and economy. I'm meeting Mr. Borges in Rio de Janeiro next week. Does anyone have an objection?"

No one protested. "Good. This meeting is adjourned." Napoleon banged his gavel. "Can you stay for a moment, Judith?"

Napoleon toggled his keyboard once they were alone. The theatre screen at the front of the room presented a larger-than-life image of a man. "Are you ready for you next honeypot assignment?"

Judith touched her lip with her tongue. "He's cute. I think I've seen him before."

Napoleon toggled to the next image: The same man, accompanied by two women—one was holding a sixteen-month-old baby girl.

"His name is Sean McGowan. Seducing him may be a challenge. Angela, the woman on the left—his business partner—bore him a child, but he's dating the woman on the right—CIA agent Beate Nicholson."

Judith chuckled. "So, he has a harem. I've dealt with that before. They won't be a problem."

"We need Goldberg Cohen's trading platform to take control of the financial markets. Seduce him by stressing the importance of our mission. He developed weather models before he sold out to Wall Street, so he understands the problem. His models predicted greenhouse gases would cause the oceans to rise long before NASA confirmed his hypothesis with observation satellites. More importantly, he has good leadership abilities."

Her eyebrows furrowed. "Why is that important?"

Napoleon cleared his throat. "We need someone to lead us, when I'm no longer here. I won't live forever."

Judith assessed Napoleon. "What if he won't join us?"

"I have confidence in you, Judith. You're too beautiful to resist."

Napoleon sat back in his chair. "He'll either be our next leader... or our fiercest enemy. I've been watching Sean McGowan his entire life. I believe it's his destiny to join us."

"Why do you say that? Did the Protectorate groom him the way they groomed the Volkov brothers?"

"No. He reached our doorstep on his own, without any help from us, which is why I believe it's his destiny."

Napoleon stared at her emotionlessly. "He is my only begotten son, after all."

THE END

About the Author

Patrick F. Rooney was born and raised in Albuquerque, New Mexico. He lived in Texas and northern Virginia for several years before moving to Colorado, where he now resides with his three children.

Patrick developed defense, Internet, finance, data mining, business intelligence, and marketing software applications for many years while he pursued his creative writing hobby. He holds degrees in Electrical Engineering, Business Administration, and Music Composition. He plays music with bands in the Boulder-Denver metro area when he isn't writing.

Additional information about the author is available here:

http://www.patrickrooneyauthor.com/